THE DEVIL DRAGON PILOT

"If you like Lee Childs, or David Baldacci, you will love this new series. Can't wait for Book 3." -**Barbara Colson**

"...nicely done character development, superb technical and compelling national security detail...old-fashioned cliffhanging drama." --**Reserve Officers Association**

"I read 3-4 books/week, and this is THE BEST of the last year. It's the book I wish I had written." --**Amazon reviewer John Fillhart**

"Great combination of accurate aircraft systems detail, action packed and good human nature story. Fast paced but great description of scenes." --**Amazon reviewer Lawrence V. Larsen**

"Finished in three nights. Always love books about flying. Will look for more books by Lawrence A. Colby." --**George E. Livingston**

"A fast paced thriller involving the Chinese that will keep you on a wild ride. This is a mission like no other as consequences ride high as the stakes are high. For those who enjoy military background will find it compelling."--**Marissa, #33 Goodreads Top Reviewer on The Black Scorpion Pilot**

"What a wild ride...a top-notch aviation drama! The plot is hyper-detailed, technically relevant and fast paced. Reads like a Clancy-esque thriller with an NSA cyberwarfare edge. Really was a joy to read."--**Dennis Rosensteel, Air Force Veteran on The Black Scorpion Pilot**

THE BLACK SCORPION PILOT

"If you love Tom Clancy or Dale Brown then 'Cheese' Colby should definitely be on your radar!"--**Mark Holt, Professional Aviation Photographer, Chorley, United Kingdom**

"A fast paced thriller involving the Chinese that will keep you on a wild ride. This is a mission like no other as consequences ride high as the stakes are high. For those who enjoy military background will find it compelling."--**Marissa, #33 Goodreads Top Reviewer**

"Uber impressive. The hacking stuff was very cool...this book is going to catch fire."
--**William Walters, Corporate Pilot**

"Black Scorpion is back! Ford Stevens has to deal with a new mission and real life like PTSD issues that I can identify with as he combats his demons..." --**ilovechocolate, Amazon Reviewer**

"Awesome! Love the story! The character development is solid." --**Frank Bell, USMC Veteran**

"Technothriller author Lawrence Colby doesn't disappoint with his second novel in his Ford Stevens series. I couldn't put down this novel!"--**Heidi, Amazon Reviewer**

These titles also available in Amazon Kindle and Audible audio forms

Also by Lawrence A. Colby

The Black Scorpion Pilot

THE

DEVIL DRAGON

PILOT

A Ford Stevens Military-Aviation Thriller

Third Edition

Lawrence A. Colby

MACH278

Mach278 LLC Books

Dulles, Virginia, US

Book Formatting by Derek Murphy

Edited by: Amazon Createspace

THE DEVIL DRAGON PILOT: A FORD STEVENS MILITARY-AVIATION THRILLER

Copyright © 2017, 2019 by Lawrence A. Colby

http://www.ColbyAviationThrillers.com

Book and Cover design by Ivan Pancetta Design

Library of Congress Cataloging in Publication Data
The Devil Dragon Pilot: A Ford Stevens Military-Aviation Thriller / by Lawrence A. Colby, 3rd ed.

ISBN-13: 978-1539427643

ISBN-10: 1539427641

1. Stevens, Ford (fictitious character)—Military Thriller—fiction 2. Aviation-fiction 3. Military —United States—Fiction I. Colby, Lawrence A. II. The Devil Dragon Pilot. III. A Ford Stevens Military-Aviation Thriller

Third Edition: August 2017

For Mrs. L, who said it couldn't be done.

A portion of the proceeds from the Ford Stevens Military-Aviation Thriller Series will go to:

Team Rubicon Global

www.teamrubiconglobal.org

Team Rubicon Global provides veterans around the world with opportunities to serve others in the wake of disasters. Learn how you can support our efforts to build a global veteran community that provides assistance to disaster victims.

The Headstrong Project

http://getheadstrong.org/

Headstrong Project, a nonprofit partnered with Weill Cornell Medical Center to fund and develop comprehensive mental health care programs to treat Iraq and Afghanistan veterans free of cost, stigma, and bureaucracy.

Publisher's Note

All members and employees of the Department of Defense (DoD) are required to submit their writings for prepublication review. The prepublication review is the process to determine that information proposed for public release contains no protected information, is consistent with established Department of Defense policies, and conforms to standards as determined by the department leadership.

Author Lawrence A. Colby, whose career for DoD entailed real-world operations, abided by the policy. His manuscript was reviewed by DoD officials in Washington, DC, and returned to him after an *in-depth and extensive six-month review*. All edits that DoD determined were necessary are complete. The book is aligned with DoD for fiction publication, and all comments related to national security matters have been changed without protest from the author.

This book has been approved by formal process at the Department of Defense prepublication review.

We thank you for your understanding and look forward to your enjoyment of this book.

THE EAGLE THAT CHASES TWO RABBITS
CATCHES NEITHER.

—ANCIENT PROVERB

LIST OF CHARACTERS

John Abbott

      CEO of Corning, Incorporated, Corning, New York

Reggie Bryant

      CEO of Gulfstream Aerospace Corporation, Savannah, Georgia

Calvin Burns

      Principal Deputy Director, Defense Intelligence Agency, Washington

He Chen

      Lieutenant General, People's Liberation Army Air Force

Jason Cohen

      Executive Assistant to Deputy Director Calvin Burns, DIA

James Collins

      Special Agent, Federal Bureau of Investigation, Washington Field Office

Vic Damone

      Supervisory Special Agent, Federal Bureau of Investigation, Assistant Legal Attaché, US Embassy, Beijing, China

Robert Dooley

      Intelligence Officer, Defense Intelligence Agency, Washington

Bai Keung

      First Lieutenant, People's Liberation Army Air Force, Aide-de-Camp

Daniel B .Woods

Secretary of Defense, Pentagon, Washington, DC

Wu Lee

Pilot, Captain, People's Liberation Air Force, China

Emily Livingston

Economist, International Monetary Fund; UK

citizen

Matthew McDevitt

Admiral, US Navy, US Pacific Command, Combatant

Commander

Lance Monterey

US Consulate Officer, US State Department, China

Liu Nie

Captain, Copilot, People's Liberation Army Air Force, China

Gabe Peoples

Captain, US Navy, Commanding Officer, SEAL Team 8

Tiffany Pinkerton

Captain, US Air Force, B-1B Lancer Copilot, Ellsworth AFB

Jeff Reid

Lieutenant Colonel, US Air Force, Watch Officer, Buckley

AFB, Colorado

Chris Sans

DIA Employee, Overseas Assignment

Mark Savona

China Aircraft Analyst, Defense Intelligence Agency,

Washington

Chad Stevens

>Vice-President and Engineer, Shell Oil Corporation; father of Ford Stevens

Ford Stevens

>Captain, US Air Force, B-1B Lancer pilot, Ellsworth AFB

Chuck Waters

>Captain, US Navy, Commanding Officer, USS *Abraham Lincoln*

Prologue

Present Day
Air Force Space Command, Operations Center
Buckley Air Force Base

Air Force Reserve Chief Master Sergeant Tommy Connolly of South Boston, Massachusetts, a Southie, was on his day shift at the Buckley Air Force Base operations center in Colorado, eating a turkey on wheat. Listening to electronic dance music through his Beats earbuds hidden under his much larger headset, he had his ears on his music and his eyes on the flat-panel screens. Connolly was *supposed* to be paying attention to his array of widescreen flat-panel monitors on his console, but instead, he was waiting for his favorite song to start. He was a member of a US Air Force operations watch team that monitored the Earth for intercontinental and submarine missile launches using space satellites. As he searched inside his lunch bag for dessert, he saw out of the corner of his eye a white flash rapidly appearing on his screen. Connolly quickly ripped the earbuds out and slipped his black Bose headset back on his ears.

Connolly turned his head for a moment and took a swig from his soda can, took a long solid stare at the screen, and went back to eating his lunch. The flashes came again, lasting about two seconds in length, then disappeared. *What the hell is this? That's unusual*, he thought. No other indications were present. Not a missile warning, missile track, airspeed data, or any of the usual flight data that was frequently displayed by a somewhat routine missile launch.

A few more seconds went by, and the flashes appeared on the screen a third time. This time, they lasted about five seconds in length, then died off again. "Well, ain't dis a wicked pissah..." Connolly said aloud, questioning the billions spent on the complex heat-detection system.

He leaned forward in his seat, adjusted himself to get comfortable, and moved the drink off to the left. With his right hand, he worked the mouse, scrolling in and out of a variety of settings on the satellite software. Connolly then wiped the moisture from his palm and onto his flight suit pant leg.

Connolly again saw the robust and lengthy white flashes this time and at first thought *all* the flashes might be software errors since last night's update. Looking at an overlaid map image of central China northbound to Mongolia over a satellite feed, he leaned forward yet again toward the screens. He sat on the edge of his black-wheeled, cushioned seat, staring intently at the displays.

"Whe-rah ya, missile?" he said aloud to no one.

A few seconds more, he bit his lip and waited patiently while staring at the map. Nothing happened. He thought perhaps the light show of flashes had ended because all was calm. "Goddamn software must have corrected itself." Still no movement on the screen, so he again went back to finishing his lunch.

Before Connolly knew it, the bedazzling light display started, and it didn't stop. His screen suddenly filled with flashing warnings and rapidly filled with all sorts of indications of an airborne Chinese missile. Data such as airspeed, magnetic direction, color codes, heat temperatures, and depicted routes of flight were filling the screens. One screen even displayed weather in the vicinity, such as air and ground temperatures, dew point, cloud cover, wind direction, and atmospheric pressure. His screens were alive and signaling that something was amiss in China.

"Contact!" he yelled.

His headset and microphone, connected to the operations center floor communications, came buzzing with loud pulsed audio tones and alarms. No question now, as the first flashes he saw were most certainly not an error, and whatever he was looking at was making its presence known. At this point, the unidentified target was being automatically tracked by the sophisticated, complex, and expensive software.

"Connolly here, sir. We gotta frickin' wicked flash. We got contact," he calmly but loudly announced over the intercom. "She's already flying. Tracking target."

The massive, two-story satellite operations center facility at Buckley AFB, home of the 460th Space Wing, operated the nation's space-based infrared system, known as SBIRS, as well as its older brother, the defense support program, known as DSP. These families of satellites were America's early warning satellite systems that could detect missile, spacecraft, large Earth-based fires, and nuclear explosions, using sensors from space that could detect infrared emissions nearly anywhere on Earth. Chris Connolly was part of a much larger team of US Air Force and Air Force Reserve personnel that monitored the world, relaying the raw information to the sixteen intelligence community agencies, Missile Defense Agency, the Combatant Commands, and Pentagon, as well as the White House.

"What do you have, Sox?" asked the floor supervisor, Lt. Col. Jeff Reid, of the 2nd Space Warning Squadron, using Chief Connolly's nickname derived from his love of his Boston Red Sox baseball team. Wearing an olive-colored flight suit full of Velcro patches and zippered pockets, Jeff Reid sat in a leather chair at the center of the room elevated a bit higher than the rest of the men and women monitoring the world's launches. At a glance, it could be confused for Captain Kirk's chair on the bridge of *Star Trek's Enterprise*. The room, about the size and height of a high school gymnasium, was dimly lit and cool with air conditioning to keep all the information technology equipment from overheating. From Reid's position on the floor, he was also able to see each of the individual watch standers' monitors from a large set of wall screens in the front of the room.

"Central China, sir...ah...launch is new location that I've never seen before. Looks like now the target is over...an area...where there's no known Chinese military bases," replied Sox. With his thick, Southie accent, it took some time to develop an ear for what Sox was saying.

"All right...that's unique. How much flight data do you have?"

Sox continued to look down at the screen, moving his cursor around and scrolling in and out with his right hand, searching for more signatures from the flash. He knew time was of the essence because the floor never knew if a country was launching a strike against another country, doing a flight test, or just launching an unannounced weather satellite. Time was almost always a priority.

There was, of course, the military reason for monitoring this area of the globe. China had giant DF-5 intercontinental-range ballistic missiles that could carry three or four nuclear warheads each. Adversaries knowing when other countries were going to launch ahead of time was always a plus, but in this case, seeing it live and *already* airborne was unsettling. The crews who monitored launches usually saw a target's flash as the missile came out of the ground. The postboost vehicle, the bus, was the portion of the missile that released each warhead at its intended target, which also made a flash. Today, Sox saw none of that.

"Sir, this is way wicked. Ah...the computer doesn't recognize the frickin' launch signature," announced Sox.

Reid walked from the center of the room, stepping off his supervisor platform, and headed toward the Asia region consoles. He stood over Sox, holding his laminated checklist, pulled his headset down off his ears, and parked it around his neck. Reid was careful not to tangle the trailing black intercom wire that connected his headset to the comms system but got caught up in it anyway. Reid stumbled on his way over and was somewhat embarrassed.

"Sox, what do you mean it doesn't recognize it? What's the computer's estimate?" Reid asked.

"Sir...I just don't know."

"*Come on*, Sox. The computer has to know. We have every missile in the world in there. Right? Land-based DF-5s...DF-31As?

Type 094 JL-1s and 2s from the submarines? We got it all…"

It was just last week when Reid was involved in a situation involving a fire off the coast of the Port of Long Beach, California, and it turned out to be a deck fire at sea on the HMS *Duncan* of the Royal Navy. Also, it was only a few years ago when a commercial jet aircraft exploded in midair over Michigan and FBI agents and investigators from the Department of Homeland Security came to Reid asking if he and his team detected anything, seeking answers to the possibility the passenger jet was shot down, versus an onboard bomb or technical issue with the airframe.

The DSP database was full of rich history spanning the 1970s to the present day, primarily designed to detect missiles from the former Soviet Union. The newer SBIRS encyclopedia of detecting nearly every heat signature on or over Earth was growing rapidly every day. Every signature rocket engine that ever existed, from all twenty-four countries that flew ballistic missiles, was recorded in those databases. From over twenty-two thousand miles overhead, the satellites located high above the equator were first cues, detecting the heat signature of most manmade and natural events. The newer SBIRS constellation size consisted of four satellites in a geosynchronous orbit and two in the highly elliptical orbit. This meant that the SBIRS satellites had to be launched way higher than most so they could match up with Earth's rotation and hence essentially maintain the same spot over the ground during their useful lifespan. The mercury cadmium telluride infrared sensors could send Buckley an immediate warning and indication of a missile launch, live volcanos, and even forest fires.

The combined orbits of the newer SBIRS birds enabled the Buckley gang to retask the sensors, enabling robust scanning in both short and midwave infrared areas, enabling them to see the ground from space, while seeing a respectful revisit rate faster than DSP. This was all from a lightweight space vehicle that only weighed about one thousand pounds. These newer SBIRS, launched at the cost of near $19 billion for six satellites, were supposed to detect a launch faster than ever and precisely predict its aim point. Except for today.

"Sir, I just confirmed the target is already flying. Sensors missed the launch vehicle somehow. This baby is already passing fifty-seven thousand feet and climbing." Talking faster than usual, Sox blustered out "target speed is passing Mach 4, heading zero-two-eight degrees true."

"You gotta be freaking kidding me. All right...all right. Toward the Mongolia-Russia border area? Huh. OK, listen up everyone," said Lt. Col. Reid, headset back on his head. He wanted the rest of the room of watch standers to know what was going on in the China region. Reid transmitted the situation to the rest of the floor's team, who were monitoring others areas of earth.

Looking across the room and beyond his seat was the noncommissioned officer of the watch, Senior Master Sergeant Bill Myers, standing with his tattooed, muscular arms folded and listening in on the situation. With over twenty-four years of service, Bill Myers, sporting a smaller version of an old-school handlebar mustache, displayed a certain senior crustiness that was straight out of central casting.

"Sergeant Myers. Hey, Senior...get me the group commander down here, then the NMCC on the phone," said the colonel.

"Wait...wait...wait a minute. Hold on, sir. The target has changed direction to one-six-three degrees upon leveling off at seventy thousand feet. Now at Mach 5," said Connolly, now dripping a bead of sweat onto his keyboard in an air-conditioned room.

"Changed direction...that much? For real? What the—? OK, copy," replied Reid.

Jeff Reid was walking back to his supervisor area on the platform to speak with the National Military Command Center, the NMCC, back at the Pentagon. These were the nation's watch standers for all global situations, from terrorist attacks to troop movements to humanitarian support to earthquakes. He wanted to make sure these folks were also informed of this event.

"Whoa!" yelled Bill.

"Whoa what? I've got to call this in, Bill. You know that."

"Take a look up there...on the screen," Bill Myers pointed, displaying the skull and crossbones tattoo on his forearm and a large black digital wristwatch.

Sox pushed back in his wheeled seat. It was obvious he did it regularly due to the black skid marks on the white-tile floor. He knocked over his empty soda can in the process, and it rolled loudly across the floor.

"Sir, the target's gone. Disappeared," replied Sox, pointing at the monitors.

"Gone? What do you mean 'gone'? You can't see it

anymore?" asked Reid.

"Yeah. Yes, sir. Usually from this console, at this range setting, we see the object impact a target...or explode in the air if it's wicked busted, or...ah...see it hit the ground. I'm seeing nothing," said Sox, with a perplexed face as he pulled himself closer to the console. He moved the computer mouse around some more, changing the settings and scans.

"Stop. I've never heard of a missile disappearing," commented Reid. "Find it. *Now*." You could hear the tone of authority in his voice.

Reid stood silently for a moment, hands on his hips, focused on the six large wall-size screens in front of the room. He squinted his eyes. His intuition was telling him this was a significant event. And professional disaster in the making. Just over eighteen years of monitoring launches, and he'd never had one like this. So far, while on his watch, there was an undetected flash, an undetected launch, and a missile that was able to easily change directions more rapidly than ever seen, followed by a disappearance. Things weren't looking good.

"Well, sir. Don't know what to say," said Sox as he stood up, shrugged, and put his hands in the air. He peeked around at the other screens in the room to see if they had something in their regions. After a brief moment, he looked at the empty soda can and sat back down.

Silence filled the air, and not a soul connected to the floor's intercom said a word. In a very short amount of time, a strange and historical event that had never happened before, just took place in front of them. They went from silence to heart-attack mode to nothing, in what seemed like a few seconds. The keepers of the world's launches, the very guardians that allowed Americans to sleep peacefully at night, for the first time in history, just lost a target. An unheard of 'never' event.

The only sounds were the blowing air from the vents in the high ceiling and the electric motors in the rotating red lights that resembled the emergency lights on the roof of a fire truck. Another seven or eight long seconds went by with no tones or voice chatter on the operations center intercom. The data feeds on the monitors were blank, more like flatlined, with no live tracking numbers on the target. Other watch standers stood and looked around the room at one another in disbelief, searching for answers. Then they turned to stare at Reid.

"Sox. Come on, kid. Anything?" asked Reid.

After another few moments of awkward silence, Sox spoke up, his head down, staring at the console and floor. Quietly, with a disappointing whisper into his headset, he delivered the right-hook punch. Sox cleared his throat. "This one has disappeared, sir."

Then silence.

Sox delivered the knockout news that everyone in the room already knew, announced just as quietly. After another lengthy pause, Sox put his hands to his face, rubbed his eyes, then moved the microphone to his mouth. "Sir. It's gone."

Part 1

Link

Fourteen Years Prior
Near the Huairou District, Qingshiling Village, White River Bay,
China

Shit. I hate the water. Why did I ask to come to this? Wu thought silently. As Wu Lee sat in the back of the van, his palms were clammy, and the pit in his stomach grew as the anxiety about the river water had really started to bother him. The acidic taste in his mouth was at an eleven on a scale of one to five. His shortness of breath, racing heartbeat, and inability to focus on anything but worrying about the upcoming white-water rafting, dominated his thoughts. He wasn't sure if anyone else in the van could detect his fear, but he sure as shit had a good case of it.

Wu Lee, a skinny fifteen-year-old Chinese boy who towered over most of his Beijing neighbors at five foot, ten inches tall, sat in the American family's van and leaned his head on the window, emotionless and lost in thought about the water. He tried to think about his goal of flying airplanes one day, but he was obsessing about this trip on the water. *Why did I say yes to attend this?* He wore a white T-shirt and black pants, and he was eating some Chinese almond cookies that smelled delicious and was driving to the White River with his best friend, Ford Stevens, and his family. Although not feeling well, he was infatuated with the larger and warm Stevens family, along with their generous sharing of American culture.

"Mr. Stevens, ah, what is it like to white-water raft? How do you...steer?" asked Wu, with continued curiosity.

Wu was a single child raised by his mother, residing in a small, two-bedroom apartment in a high-rise on the same floor as the Stevens family. He excelled at running, math, chess, and American movie trivia, and like any teenage boy, liked talking to girls. Wu's father, a deceased pharmacist who died when Wu was young, never had the opportunity to bond with his son. Over the past seven years, Wu had grown close to the Stevens family in Beijing and looked upon Chad Stevens, the patriarch, as the father figure he never really had in his life.

"Wu, it'll be a great day. I promise. Beautiful weather, water, wildlife, and some fantastic scenery. Fresh air out of the smog and pollution. We'll take care of you...show you how to hit the water and have some fun," replied Chad Stevens as he drove the family van from the city into the countryside. "Ford will show you, Wu."

Ford Stevens, the teenage boy of the American Stevens family, was in the back of the white van, too. Ford was also fifteen years old. He wore blue jeans and a forest-green sweatshirt, and he had tightly shorn brown hair and an athletic build. He was one of three kids in the Stevens family, and at six feet, he was also the up and coming varsity defensive end football player at Saint Paul American School in Beijing; he had exceptional athletic talent and strength. He, too, had dreamed of flying at a young age. Ford had grown up from age seven to the present day with Wu as his close friend, and although they attended different schools, they were able to spend much of their free time outside of school together.

Ford's father, Chad, a Vice-President and petroleum engineer at Shell Oil, accepted this China promotion years ago to help expand Shell's presence in the country. The Stevens family, resilient and flexible enough to accept moving regularly; they had previously moved with Shell Oil from Calgary, to London, to Washington, DC, three different times, then Cairo, and, of course, Shell's North American office in Houston, Texas. Shell was due to rotate Chad this summer back to Washington yet again.

Piped in to the van's radio using a smartphone was Armed Forces Radio Network, airing an American football game from back in the states.

"The Dallas Cowboys will be kicking off here in a second. Playing the Lions!" said Ford from the far side of the van, excited to hear his favorite team playing again on a time-zone delay.

Wu gave Ford a slap handshake. "Listen to all the fans in that stadium, watching the game in person. And the music, and cheering, and the singing. So much opportunity for everyone in United States," Wu said as he listened to the game. Sitting in front of him were Ford's younger sister, Samantha, and younger brother, Charlie.

"We got a game, Dad. Kickoff!" said Ford as he shook his fist up and down like many quarterbacks do after completing a forward pass. Ford knew it was going to be an exciting game because of the recent team-owner drama, but more important, he was happy Wu was there to experience the day. Chad Stevens listened in closely, too.

"Chad, can you slow down please? You're speeding along

this road like you're an Indy race-car driver. Slow it down, Tonto," said Marion Stevens, Ford's mom. Wearing black pants and a pink fleece, her long brown hair up in a ponytail, forty-five-year-old Marion was attractive and in great physical shape. She turned around in the front seat of the van to see Wu making a funny face.

"Wu, what's with the face?" asked Mrs. Stevens.

"What does *Tonto* mean, Mrs. Stevens?" replied Wu, wondering what the American term meant.

The Stevenses looked at one another then broke out in laughter. Little Sam looked at Wu and told him it was a character from an old television show in America.

"Thank you, Sam. Sometimes in English...the translation...it takes me a while," said Wu, laughing at his own gap between Mandarin and English.

"Wu, what is Wu short for? Wulson? Or, Wilson?" asked Charlie, chuckling to himself.

"Umm, what is Lee short for? Lee-o-nardo? Is your real name Wilson Leonardo?" Sam said, laughing hysterically, due to a lack of understanding of Chinese names. Both little kids broke out laughing.

"That's his real name, kids. People all around the world have different names, and Wu's parents named him Wu. Like you're Sam, and your brother is Charlie," explained Marion. "Lee is his last name, after his father."

"Maybe one day, my new American name can be Wilson Leonardo!" Wu announced, making everyone laugh.

Mr. Stevens beamed with great pride that the rafting trip was all planned out, coordinated, and researched. The detailed and comprehensive engineer in him also extended to his personal life. Maps, weather, travel directions, and food, Chad Stevens had it covered and was always up for a teaching moment for his kids. The message was to always be prepared.

"Well, we're about ten minutes out from the Qingshiling Village. It's just outside the White River Bay. Almost there," announced Mr. Stevens.

The White River Bay area had a resort and was a great destination for taking the family outdoors for the remainder of the weekend. It was well known as one of China's best rafting destinations and loved by Westerners visiting Beijing. It was only about ninety-five kilometers, or sixty miles, from their house and an easy van drive away.

"Tremendous. We're out of the pollution for once!" Marion commented, fed up with the city's rising population and industry smog levels. Recently, Beijing officials ordered hundreds of corporate factories to shut and allowed school children to skip school as unbelievable choking smog overcame the city. The US Embassy in Beijing recorded over twenty-five times the safe levels, which was extremely unsafe for breathing, both short- and long-term.

Wu translated the distance announcement pretty easily and understood what was going on. He wasn't celebrating in his mind, though. *Oh, shit. Water already?* he said silently to himself.

The White River had beautiful mountains on both sides of the river, a variety of plants in the forests and hillsides, and best of all, clear water to paddle in. With two people in a raft at a time, it was gearing up to be a fantastic weekend.

"Ah...I don't know how to swim," said Wu, finally admitting it aloud and hoping it was not going to be an issue. "I have never been on a river."

"It's OK, Wu, we can get you a life jacket to wear," said Ford, thinking of his last time white-water rafting on the Snake River in Wyoming two years ago. "We will all wear one. You wear it around your neck. I'll show you."

While everyone enjoyed the ride and listened to the football game on the radio, Wu was still quietly thinking of the river. The trip came down to one major concern of Wu's: he was very afraid of the water. Wu was excited for the trip today, but since his mother never took him to a pool or gave him swim lessons, he always had a strong fear of the water and being stuck under, not able to breathe. Last year, his mother took him to his father's grave near the YongDing River, and he was able to stick his feet in the water for the first time ever. Other than that visit, he'd had no other exposure to water.

Ford could tell his friend was somewhat excited at the idea of attending today, but something was amiss. Ford didn't let on he knew but could feel Wu's apprehension. As for Wu, butterflies grew in his stomach.

"Cowboys just scored!" yelled Charlie, listening intensely. A cheer of applause was heard around the van.

Wu half smiled at the events of the football game but knew once they got on to the water, he was going to feel even worse. His clammy palms were near wet, he had a full case of cottonmouth, and he was sweating, and they weren't even at the bay yet. *Don't they know what it's like for me? This is crazy. What*

I am doing? I'm not going. No way. Wu's anxiety about rafting was at a peak, and he was downright petrified.

Shores of the White River Bay

The rafting company was well established and had the rental of rafts and oars down to a science. There was an area for customers to wait in line and pay fees, another area that resembled a gift shop to purchase sunblock, T-shirts, and hats, and another area to obtain photographs of a customer's day-trip on the river.

On a far wall inside the office was a large combined topographical and picture map of the White River. It displayed the rafting route with a distance scale, from start to end, with appropriate nature areas and recommended stops to take photographs. There were sample photos from guests through the months and years on display, like something out of a marketing campaign. Happy customers all around, it seemed.

Wu and Ford walked behind Mr. Stevens inside the office while he arranged for the boat rental and guide information. The boys walked over to the map.

"Check this out." Ford gestured with his hand. "Our route today."

One item that the boys noticed on the map was the waterfall, about seventy-five minutes into the river trip. Both boys pointed at it on the map and took note and interest in stopping there to take a photograph.

Something else on the wall caught Wu's eye, though. On

the bottom right side of the wall map was a warning notice in large red letters. It announced the rapid speed of the water and the natural whirlpools, which would be an issue for all rafters if they were not paying attention. The whirlpools, rotating water due to the curvature of the river, speed of the water, and unpredictable currents, could easily overturn a raft if not navigated correctly. The warning notice went on to advise all rafters to wear life jackets and to take precautions for a safe ride by following the marked signs.

"Boys, let's get going. We're all paid up and ready. Our river guide is ready to brief us on the day," said Mr. Stevens.

Wu was looking at some of the gifts on display and glancing at the pretty teenage girls across the office. "LA Woman" by the Doors was playing in the lobby of the rental company, an iconic rock band and song, and seventies rock music was yet another thing that Wu loved about America. It was also his favorite song.

"Let's go, Prince Charming," Ford said to Wu, and they walked out the back door of the shop to the river front where the rest of the group was forming.

Marion took Charlie into her raft, which was partly out of the water and sitting on the gravel, and Mr. Stevens took care of Sam. They brought with them a waterproof bag with some sweatshirts, along with some bottles of water, snacks, first aid kit, and a disposable film camera. Of course, Sam had to go to the bathroom at the last minute, but it didn't delay their start.

Their guide, Xi Wong, addressed the crowd in English because the raft guests for the day were from Germany and the

United States, and everyone found that to be a common language. Between the Stevens's rafts and the other three from Berlin, there were six rafts in their party.

Xi Wong, a graduate student from Peking University, explained the operation of the orange-and-blue rubber rafts, plastic-and-wooden oars, raft safety, and their itinerary for the day. He spoke of the wildlife they might see, the water currents, helmet, to wear and use life jackets properly, and the timeline if they wanted to take photos along the way. It only took about fifteen minutes for the brief.

Wu and Ford listened but were horsing around in looking at the blond-haired girl from earlier in the gift shop. Smacking oars and laughing, they paid more attention to the unique German accent of the pretty fifteen-year-old, as she and her family were in their raft party.

"Ford. *Ford!* Hey, you paying attention?" asked Mr. Stevens, fully knowing what was going on with the goofing around. He was adjusting the life jacket and helmet for Sam, while he buckled his own. He carried with them the near identical waterproof bag and the larger oar to steer from the rear of the raft.

Ford knew the tone of voice and what his dad was getting at. "Yes, Dad. Sorry."

Wu was just as guilty but didn't say anything. He glanced over at his raft, seeing the location in the front where to sit, and held his oar as Xi demonstrated. "Like this, Ford?" whispered Wu, kidding, holding the oar like a sword. He quickly then held it properly.

They got ready to launch on the river, as the water was smooth, the wind calm, and the sun was bright and keeping them warm. Wu was easing into the idea of the water, checking out the river from the shore more often now. It did look stunning, and the scenery was indeed breathtaking. The view of the far shoreline, along with the greenery of the tall trees and snowcapped mountains in the distance, was gorgeous.

There were still butterflies in Wu's stomach, especially after seeing the rapids photos in the gift shop, but he did not demonstrate any real anxiety in front of Ford and especially in front of their new friend, Gretchen, the German beauty.

"Pull the front of your raft into the water using the rope, and have the first passenger get in. Then, the second passenger can get in once you are farther along in the water," shared Xi, guiding his flock.

The Stevens family had all entered the water, followed by the Germans. Xi was offshore now, and all of the orange rafts were waterborne and following. The Germans had a four-person raft, with Xi riding in the rear, acting as the sternman, steering the vessel.

"This is really tremendous, Wu. Take a look around. Awesome," said Ford, looking around at the landscape.

"It is. Look over there at that cliff. I can see those hawks flying in and out of their nest. Over on the left. That cliff over there comes right up to the river, then goes straight up toward the tree line," said Wu, nodding in agreement. "Maybe the locals jump off there for swimming?"

Peaceful and quiet, each raft was developing a rhythm

with their paddling. They were able to coast down the river at times with the ease of the current, while other times they had to paddle pretty hard to get some speed. Of course, Ford took the opportunity to splash both his siblings with water, and Marion was able to get everyone wet.

All was not well with Wu, though, as he continued to think about being so far out on the water and away from the shoreline. He felt alone and afraid, and he was in a dark place. It was not a good feeling for him, and he felt like something life changing was about to happen. His sixth sense was talking to him.

White River Bay

They were only about half an hour into the trip when they heard a thunderous motorboat engine behind them, getting louder as each second passed. The sound of the engines made it seem like the boaters were traveling at high speed, and it was getting loud enough to make Mr. Stevens turn around. Ford and Wu also turned their heads, as Ford wondered how a boat with a motor could make it through the shallow water and rocks in the low parts of the river.

The entire raft party was able to stop paddling and turn themselves to face upstream. The noise was becoming louder than any boat they had heard before because of the echoes off the steep canyon walls. The sounds were amplified due to the terrain they were currently in.

"Look at that! Awesome!" shrieked Ford, pointing his finger to where the water met the sky behind them. Flying just above the water and inside the canyon walls were multiple Chenjang J-11 fighter jets, the Chinese version of the Russian Su-27.

"Look at their speed!" Wu yelled as the roar was thundering and loud and getting louder as the lead fighter passed over them.

"This is very impressive!" yelled someone from the German raft.

"Ford, take a look at the rest of the formation. There are a bunch of them in a line. The ones following in the back!" Wu pointed out.

The fourth-generation J-11 fighter jet, known in NATO counties as a Flanker B+, was a single-seat, twin-engine jet. Powerful, fast, and deadly, it most definitely caught the eye of the rafting party. It reminded Ford of the US Navy Blue Angels F/A-18 Hornet plastic model that he and his dad built when Ford was a kid.

"You can see the pilots inside!" yelled Mr. Stevens from his raft to the others.

Wu and Ford looked at each other and didn't say anything but nodded with smirks on their faces. It was as if each boy was transmitting a silent message that they were in love with the idea of flying. To be in the cockpit, flying on a beautiful day like this, was not a job but a calling.

"This is cooler than shit, dude," Ford said to Wu.

The first gray jet screamed overhead no higher than a hundred feet above the water, with such thunder that the younger Stevens kids were startled. The twin tail of the jet was all that was seen now, as the pilot was able to maneuver the aircraft to follow along the natural curves of the river. Ahead of the rafting party upstream, the river curved to the left, to the northwest. So did the jet, rolling on its side to make the tight turn.

"I am in love with these jets. This is the coolest freaking thing I've ever seen. The roar of those engines is making my body vibrate. Goose bumps," Wu replied.

Ford shook his head with full confidence and conviction. "This is it, dude. I still feel the same way. This is what I want to do with my life, Wu. When I grow up, I'm going to be a military pilot. And so are you. This is the coolest. We're going to fly."

The second Chinese fighter jet was already on the trail of the first one. Just about the same low altitude but offset to the right from the first, it flew closer to the shore and was still visible. He, too, came screaming over at about eighty feet, banking his wings from side to side.

"Hey, he's waving at us. That's what jets do when they say hello," Mr. Stevens yelled over to Ford and Wu from his raft nearby.

The second jet followed the first one, making the turn in the river.

From the time they spotted the jets, it could not have been more than a minute, but since the stronger current had them traveling downstream at a pretty good pace, the rafts traveled a considerable distance. Ford glanced over at Xi to make sure he was paying attention to the river, and he was.

The third jet, and what looked to be the last, was directly aiming at them in the rafts. Or, at least it appeared to be.

"Wonder what this guy is going to do?" said Wu.

As the last jet came over the rafts, the pilot pulled back the aircraft in a sharp upward maneuver that the boys had only seen in movies. The pilot moved his left hand forward on the throttle, pushing it to afterburner while pulling back his stick with his right hand to increase the pitch to near eighty-five degrees nose up. Both of the engine exhaust nozzles tightened and glowed orange, and a white mist started aggressively flowing off each of the aircraft wings. The mist was almost dancing, as the pilot was going straight up.

The boys laughed with delight, and Ford nearly had a tear in his eye. "Oh my God! Look at him go! Wu, that's us, buddy!"

All three jets had departed the river area, and the raft party started to settle down. As they glowed after the impromptu air show and looked ahead on the river, they could see two enormous, white billboard-like signs posted on the riverbank. They were painted with red lettering and looked like the warning signs they saw at the raft office. They were written in Chinese characters, in addition to English.

Another minute or so of heading down river allowed them to read the first of the two signs. The first one read: ATTENTION—ATTENTION. CLASS III AND IV RAPIDS AHEAD. LAST CHANCE TO EXIT RIVER BEFORE RAPIDS.

The second sign was just as large, and that read: WARNING—WARNING. NO ROWBOATS OR SWIMMING. DIRECTLY AHEAD ARE DANGEROUS RIVER RAPIDS THAT MUST BE NAVIGATED SMARTLY OR INJURY OR DEATH MAY OCCUR.

Wu read the signs and looked down into the raft. *No,*

no...no rapids, Wu said quietly to himself. Nothing was said too loudly, as he was becoming frozen with fear. The dark and plummeting feeling Wu had earlier quickly returned.

The rafts entered a narrower portion of the canyon as the speed of the water picked up pace. More gray rocks and larger boulders were visible beneath the water line, and a superfluity of rocks could be seen above. The water was increasing in pace every second, and the white water was much more visible now.

"Ford, I don't like this. I don't like this speed at all. The water...can we pull over to the shore?" said Wu more loudly, as the raft was nearly uncontrollable and sliding downward in and out of the water.

"What?" Ford yelled back, barely hearing him over the roar of the splashing water on their raft now, in addition to the downward water flow due to the elevation change.

"*I have to get out! I don't like this, Ford,*" Wu yelled, clearly terrified and was moving the oar in the water, trying to push the raft away from the rocks and toward the shore. It was not working. His efforts were fruitless, especially when the raft turned sideways. "*I have to get out.*"

From the look of Ford's face, he was enjoying the rapids. Moving the oar with the water and not fighting the rapids, it was a terrific ride. As Ford turned his head sideways to see what Wu was doing in the rear, he gasped.

"Wu. *Wu!* Get your leg back in the raft! What the hell are you doing? Wu!"

"I have to get out. I don't like the water!"

"No, you have to stay in the boat. Shut up. The whirlpool is just up ahead!"

"The water...the water. No, I can't do it!" wailed Wu.

"Stop it, Wu. Yes, you can. Cut it out. The whirlpool is just up there. Just up ahead."

Just as Ford was telling Wu to stay in the raft, a blur of disastrous events began. Ford could not only see how terrified Wu was but noticed something very troubling. Wu never fully snapped his life-jacket buckles together, so it was only resting on and around his neck. The white buckled straps were dangling down on his sides. The longer strap should have been around his waist and snapped in, but it was now dragging in and out of the water.

Wu was having what seemed like a panic attack and could not think clearly inside the raft. The raft movement of side to side was throwing him around, and by putting his leg over the side, he made his center of gravity even more unstable.

Ford gestured to Wu to buckle his vest then yelled "Buckle! Your! Vest!" Wu did not hear him. *Shit! It was no use to get him to do it*, Ford thought. He quickly turned his head to see the distance from his raft to his dad, or even Xi and the Germans, but the distance was way too far to yell over the roar of the rapids.

Plop! Plop!

Wu slid into the turbulent water. In class IV rapids, the last place you wanted to be was in the water, especially without a life jacket, but that was where Wu was.

Ford turned around again to look at Wu, and the back of the raft was empty. He looked beyond the raft, and all he saw was an orange life jacket floating behind them but no Wu. "Wu! Wu! Where are you?" he screamed. *Holy friggin' shit, he's out of his life jacket!*

The rapids were finishing just upstream, but another tremendous obstacle was sitting in their path. The whirlpool, a large and natural rotation of the river water that had tremendous currents and fast-moving water in a circular motion, lay waiting. If one was in a raft, the whirlpool was perfectly navigable. To swim it without a life jacket meant almost certain death by drowning.

"Wu! Wu!"

Xi and the Stevens' rafts were already ahead in the quieter portion of the river. The speed was faster and swirly, but much less noisy, and they could easily hear Ford's commotion.

"Ford! FORD! Where is Wu?" yelled Mr. Stevens.

"Dad! He fell out! He's not wearing his life jacket!"

Wu was underwater and twisting with the current. His body was being held under water with immense pressure, tumbling him, continuously rolling him around on the river bottom like a small pebble. He was able to pop up for air for a brief moment, only to have the cold, swift water pull him down again with the violent undertow.

"Help," was heard from behind Ford's raft, along with coughing. "Help!"

"Wu!" Ford yelled again, seeing his white T-shirt on top of the water, then descending as rapidly as he saw it. Ford looked ahead to see the length of the Whirlpool portion of the river. He determined that it was way too long to stay underwater and instinctively knew that Wu would not make it unless he made a rapid decision. "Dad!" Ford yelled ahead, pointing down twice with his hand. He jumped into the cold river water to search for his best friend.

Marion Stevens and Xi both gasped, and the Germans looked on with silence but intense concern, as was the German way. "Oh, Ford..." exclaimed Marion.

Ford was completely in the water, his hair wet and moving his arms and legs in an attempt to feel for Wu. *This water is freaking cold*, Ford thought. He could not help but wonder how Wu missed snapping his life jacket as the river's momentum floated him backward. Ford thought about the *how*, and then the answer hit him. The horseplay with the oars and checking out Gretchen, the pretty German blonde, was a distraction to both of them. Ford was able to snap his own jacket easily out of habit, but since Wu never wore one before, he didn't complete the buckle snap.

Wu was still underwater, being thrashed around. His lungs were filling up with water, and they burned without air. He saw flashes of light when he was facing upward toward the surface of the water, then blackness. His knees, palms, and elbows scraped the riverbed.

Ford put his arms out in front of him to protect his face from the oncoming rocks and felt a piece of material with his right hand. It was Wu's pants. They must have ripped off him in the current and undertow. *His freaking pants?*

"Ford! Hang on, son! It's not too much longer! Calm water ahead!" yelled Mr. Stevens.

It *was* too long, though. Ford was still floating along and now out of the rapids, but the rotation of the water was as strong as Ford ever felt. He was now caught in a gigantic, rotating, circular motion and could not move upstream or downstream. Ford was stuck, rotating in an enormous circle.

Wu surfaced again, and just as Mother Nature was turning his body in the water, he slammed his forehead on a large boulder, just below where the helmet was providing protection. Ford heard a thump, like a watermelon being dropped on the ground during a warm summer day. The clear water rolled right off Wu's forehead, so the new wound was visible and clean. He looked to be conscious, but there was no question, the blow to the head was serious.

"Wu, Wu, I see you! Hold on man!" Ford shouted, as he was close to Wu. He was floating face down on top of the water now. There was no movement. Ford rolled him over. The gash above his right eye, about three inches in length, was bleeding profusely. The life jacket Ford was wearing was able to hold both boys above the water safely. Floating out of the whirlpool now, Ford's incredible strength was a true asset, and he was able to pull Wu to the eastern shore where there was a small beach clearing. One arm stroked, with the other pulling Wu. Ford was able to pull him out of the water and onto the pebbles and sand.

"Dad! I'm down here," Ford called. He crouched down next to Wu. Ford moved his hand to clean his face. He lightly slapped Wu's face to get him to revive. "Wu. Wu, I'm here, buddy. Come back." There was no response.

The raft party was down the river, at least two minutes ahead, and there was no way they could paddle back to meet them. This meant Ford had to administer CPR to Wu alone.

"Come on, Wu, come back to me," Ford told him. Ford cleared his mouth of any debris with his fingers. Nothing was there. He tilted Wu's head back and pinched his nose. It was just like the instructor from his old Boy Scout days taught him to do it. One breath. And another. Ford looked at his chest to rise. Another two breaths. Again, Ford checked his chest. No sign of breathing. Ford sighed and wanted Wu to breathe with every ounce of his being.

Just as Ford was getting ready to start chest compressions, Wu began breathing normally. He spit up a few ounces of river water, and Ford helped him turn to his side to cough some more. "Come on, Wu," Ford encouraged him. "Come on!"

Ford looked up river and could see the others getting out of the rafts on the shore. Mr. Stevens was running down the shoreline and through river wood, tall grass and large stones.

"Ohhh. What happened, Ford? My head." Wu moaned. The blood was still coming out from just above his eye. Ford was able to put his hand on it to help stop the bleeding, but it was running out of his fingers.

"Ford, I'm here," Mr. Stevens said, opening up a first aid kit from the raft company.

"Wu, you fell out. Or jumped out...out of the raft. Back there in the rapids. You were underwater for a while, then dinged your head on a river rock, I guess," explained Ford.

"Let me see him, Ford," Mr. Stevens said, moving Ford's hand out of the way so that he could place a clean bandage on Wu's head. He grabbed a gauze wrapper, which had *Colored*

Surgical Sponge written on it, and quickly placed it on Wu's wound.

Xi and the rest of the Stevens family ran up to them and looked at Wu on the ground. Marion bent down to hug Ford then knelt down to help attend to Wu. She peeled the medical tape to help fasten the colored gauze to Wu's head.

"He's all bloody!" Sam pointed. She was quickly shushed by Marion.

"I just called for help on the phone. There is a river access road just through those trees there. We can get him help in about ten minutes," said Xi, nodding toward the tree line.

Ford switched knees to rest on and moved his hands back down next to Wu, holding his head. Ford was troubled at the situation but relieved that he was able to help his friend. Ford knew they averted a tragedy.

"I am so sorry, Stevens family. So sorry. I just have never been in the water," said Wu.

"Wu, we are just happy you are here and alive. Don't be sorry," Ford told him.

Wu just looked up at the sky and blinked slowly. He stared off into the abyss, thinking about what just happened. In his heart, he was forever indebted to Ford. "Jojo rising," Wu said, barely, with a slight smile, referring to their favorite band the Doors and their "LA Woman" song from the 1971 album. The original lyrics sung by lead singer Jim Morrison were "mojo rising," but when Wu first heard the song, he could not make out the words. So he started singing "jojo rising" instead, and it stuck.

"Jojo rising, Wu," Ford replied.

"Jojo rising, their private saying, meant to them a greater spirit and internal flame that enabled them to do things together and tackle life. It was their special sauce that gave them the determination to accomplish goals. Wu loved the American music video of the lead singer, Jim Morrison, just cruising and driving around Los Angeles, California, in his Mustang, and to Wu, it was classic America. Just driving around, taking in the palm trees and ocean and warm weather, doing what you wanted to do, when you wanted to do it. It was very noncommunist, non-China, which was why Wu loved it. Some critics argued Jim Morrison put a sexual connotation to the phrase, but that's not how Ford and Wu took it at all. It meant boundless, no limits, land of opportunity. Go out in the world and make something happen. It was, to them, simply, jojo rising.

Mr. Stevens removed the surgical sponge since it was full of blood, noticing it was completely red in the center. The outer edges of the sponge had a unique florescent blue and green liquid-proof material attached to it that repelled blood. These outer colors helped health-care teams with seeing the sponge. Mr. Stevens looked at the used one more closely, never seeing it before, and thought how innovative the idea was.

"Marion, this sponge company is from the United States? Woulda saved Sheila's life if her surgeon used it," Chad said, referring to Marion's sister. Years ago, Marion's sister died of infection after a routine hysterectomy procedure when her surgical team left inside her a camouflaged, saturated surgical sponge. He tossed it on the ground, opened another new package, and taped it to Wu's head.

"Ford," Wu said softly, turning from looking up to facing Ford. "Ford, I will never forget what you have done for me. You saved...my life," He cough a bit more. "I could have died back there in the water, and...I owe you."

Ford gave him a small smile and just nodded his head. He then grabbed Wu's hand with both of his.

"Ford," Wu said again quietly, squeezing his hand. "Ford, I am grateful, and...and I will never forget your actions. Ever. I owe you. Thank you."

Part 2

Smoke and Fire

Present Day
Ellsworth AFB, Rapid City, South Dakota

US Air Force Reserve Captain Ford Stevens, thirty years old, was walking out to the flight line wearing his pilot flight gear and carrying his helmet bag full of supplies for his flight in the B-1B Lancer. His olive-colored flight bag consisted of kneeboards, flight manuals, checklists, oxygen mask, snacks, and gloves, among a spread of other survival gear. He and three other crew members, all of the US Air Force's 28th Bomb Wing, just briefed up a simulated mission that included instrument flying, a low-level navigational route, a close-air-support mission, and air-to-air refueling.

Ford was a unique military officer and pilot, flying as a full-time Air Force Reservist, embedded in an active-duty squadron. President Harry S. Truman signed into law the US Air Force Reserve formation back in 1948, and since then, they have been a key piece of the US Air Force team. The Air Force Reserve performed about 20 percent of the missions, which composed of everything from cyber and space, to cargo and fighter aircraft. Ford began his career in the active component Air Force and transferred his global flight experience to the Air Force Reserve team a few years later.

"You double check the TOLD?" Ford asked his copilot, Captain Tiffany "Pinky" Pinkerton.

TOLD was the *takeoff and landing data* which, when calculated, informed the aircrew of the expected performance of the jet based on its weight, the runway length, and atmospheric conditions. If the runway was short, and it was hot and humid outside, it would fly sluggishly and differently than a longer runway in a colder environment. In their cooler South Dakota environment, especially since it was November, their aircraft performance would be above-average.

"Yup, we're good, Ford," replied Pinky, holding the white kneeboard-size card that was full of penciled-in numbers and computations. The card was full of lead and erasure marks, and wasn't pretty, but it showed that she computed the numbers.

"Good. Thanks. I just talked to the weather briefer about the storm we talked about earlier down in Colorado, and I'd like to head to the southeast around it. Down toward New Mexico. From there, we can head over to southern Nevada," said Ford, making a quick change to their planned route. "Just filed the flight plan, too."

"Got it. I'll talk to the rest of the crew here in a minute," said Pinky.

Ford approached the aircraft with awe, as he did for every flight. Both Ford and Wu had dreams as teenagers long ago to fly for the military, and after years of careful planning and pursuit, they did it. It was not easy for Ford, though. After playing second-string football and studying in Air Force ROTC at the University of Notre Dame, his dream was accomplished, and he was commissioned as a second lieutenant. Summers at US Army Airborne School learning to parachute; undergoing survival, evasion, resistance, and escape training; and later toward graduation being embedded in a fighter squadron, all contributed to Ford being where he was today. He was able to compete successfully for a coveted pilot slot with the other Fly Irish! Detachment 225 of ROTC cadets, gaining a shot at earning his wings. Ford continued to Vance AFB to Joint Undergraduate Pilot Training and learned to fly the T-37 Tweet, then the T-38 Talon, and eventually the B-1B Lancer. He was living his dream.

The path to success was not easy for Ford, though. He nearly failed English 101 and Accounting 102 at Notre Dame as a freshman for skipping too many classes, and he got into trouble during his junior year with the university's administration for a toilet paper prank outside the student center. Later, in flight school, he failed a written exam on meteorology and another time failed to accurately perform the landing checklist in a simulator flight. He also spent a lot of time volunteering with the Knights of Columbus but soon realized that if he spread himself too thin, he couldn't focus on his studies. There were no guarantees of getting a Notre Dame degree or pilot wings.

His biggest personal hurdle came during the formal psychological exam and interview by the Air Force Flight Surgeons, checking to see if he had the mental "right stuff" to become a pilot. It was a personal hurdle because it was something you couldn't prepare for. No studying. Either you had it, or you didn't. It was also a hurdle to Ford because although he was smart, he wasn't a rocket scientist with outstanding academic scores. While athletic, he wasn't an Olympic competitor. While he earned OK grades, he wasn't tearing up the report cards. What he did have, though, was leadership, the special ability to get others to join him in accomplishing goals. Whether it was related to ROTC, or toilet papering college buildings at two in the morning, he could get groups of others to make things happen. Young Ford had no idea what to expect, and since there was no way to prepare, he just acted himself and listened in awe at the psychologist's results.

The psychologists told Ford he had somewhat of a unique pilot personality, meaning he had certain characteristics that made him physically and mentally different than your average bear in America. Of course, upon hearing that, Ford sat up straighter in his chair. Personality-wise, they told him, he was reality based and independent, and because of the skills required in aviation, it would be convenient. His parents raised him to be independent, which he was, and because Ford wanted a task to get done, they said he probably had some difficulty trusting anyone to do the job as well as he could. *Yup, that's me,* he said to himself silently. Occasionally, Ford was apprehensive and even distrustful, but the doctors said in small doses, this characteristic would serve him well and would be helpful in his upcoming high-speed environment. *So far, so good*, he thought.

They continued with their assessment. Ford's competitive, be-on-time obsession, like setting two morning alarm clocks and his smartphone so he could get up earlier than anyone else, was to beat competitors to the punch in the morning. *Those guys at the unit aren't going to beat me!* Ford was rated as intelligent but was not ranked as intellectually gifted, which was fine for the Air Force and for Ford. He wasn't about getting on the honor roll but to perform successfully in flight school. The doctors also told him he was solid and practical in his thinking, and was extremely goal oriented. *True, true.* One of the two doctors also told him that he most likely craved parties and exhilaration, and a typical nine-to-five job like his college buddies had would drive him crazy. *Yes! That's me!*

Ford listened intently and wanted to know the bottom line, seeking if it was a yes, or no. *Come on, Docs, can I attend flight training or not?* They continued, telling Ford that he was occasionally modest, an achiever, and handled failure mostly well, with which he agreed. He was a risk taker, someone who would also put his life on the line for others when given the chance. They observed that he had a low tolerance for mistakes, circumvented self-analysis, and sometimes found it challenging to reveal and express his own feelings. *Ouch, but OK, true.* He could be unemotional from time to time, which would aid him in the future as a pilot in dealing with emergencies in the cockpit, as he was told, but they also remarked to him that it could also affect his relationships with women. *Uh-oh.*

At the end of the day, he was approved. The doctors finally gave him the news he wanted to hear, and Ford Stevens was approved for flight training years ago. He continued to be satisfied that he selected the right occupation, and Ford loved being a pilot.

Later in flight training, Ford took an elective titled Human Factors in Aviation and laughed at the list of personality traits of pilots because he saw himself in the data. *These all fit me like a glove!* The laundry list of traits mentioned things like being physically healthy, lacking signs of neurosis, seeking responsibility and novelty, and exhibiting anxiety when feeling too close to women. The list also mentioned that pilots might be cautious about close relationships, and they avoided revealing true feelings. His studies at the time, which included academic work by the NASA Astronaut Office, validated his own thoughts on becoming a military pilot.

"Great day to fly, Sergeant McCoy!" Ford announced as he approached the maintenance airman, standing near the nose of the jet. McCoy shook his hand but did not say anything in the cold morning air.

Ford stood in front of the B-1 and gave it a long glance. A once-over. Ford continued to be impressed at not only the large size of the aircraft but at its high-speed performance for being so *large*. To Ford, it performed like a sports car. More important to him, he was getting paid to do something that he loved so much. To strap on something like this and wear it on his back and perform with a group of aircrew was something he would have done for free.

To think that he and best friend Wu Lee both had a dream as teenagers to become military pilots and that his dream came true, was extraordinary. From application to medical physicals, written exams, psychology screening, and the constant scrutiny of every single training flight being criticized and graded, the graduation rates were staggeringly low. At best, it might be that only 10 percent make it through all the way from applicant to earning their wings.

As Ford was climbing the ladder behind the nose landing gear to get inside the cockpit, Sergeant McCoy climbed up in back of him.

"Hey, fellas," Ford greeted the other two aircrew members who were already inside the jet.

"Hi, sir," replied the two navigators, settling into their work positions in the rear of the cockpit.

Their responsibilities included always knowing the position of the aircraft, maintaining the safety of their payload (nuclear or conventional weapons), and handling radio calls and onboard systems. The navigators were an important part of the crew, especially in a complicated aircraft like this one.

The Boeing B-1 Lancer was a four-engine, supersonic, variable-sweep wing bomber and was used by the US Air Force as a low-level penetrator for nuclear and conventional bomb delivery. It was designed during the Cold War as a supersonic bomber to fly at two times the speed of sound, or Mach 2, to replace the aging Boeing B-52 Stratofortress. Both jets, along with the B-2 Spirit, make up the US Air Force's three bombers, and a fourth one is being designed today. The B-1, weighing in empty at 192,000 pounds and a top height of thirty-four feet, make her a big girl.

Ford could hear them punching in the aircraft position into the self-contained navigational systems before the GPS satellites could be grabbed. "Forty-four degrees, eight minutes, forty-seven seconds north...then ah...one-zero-three degrees, four minutes, and twenty-nine seconds west," he heard them converse.

Ford met up with Pinky, who was already seated in the copilot seat on the right side of the cockpit. He placed his bag on the left side, the pilot seat. Sergeant McCoy was there with the three of them now.

"Sir, just got scoop on the two-way radio that we got us a delay. 'Bout an hour delay due to snow plows on the taxiways and runway. Will take them a while to plow runway thirteen/thirty-one," Sergeant McCoy reported to Ford.

Runway 13/31, the longest runway at Ellsworth AFB at nearly 13,500 feet and made of concrete, could handle any large aircraft the US military had. Because of the size of the B-1, this runway was needed to both take off and land safely. Having a slippery pavement was the last thing you wanted when you flew something of any size.

"OK, Sergeant McCoy. Thanks for coming up here and letting us know. Why don't you just close the hatch and stay warm up here with us? Get you out of the elements," Ford offered.

"Yeah, great idea. Thank you, sir. I will," Sergeant McCoy said, taking off his fur-lined parka hood and large gloves. "Captain Stevens, a few of the boys and I were wondering if you could tell us about your last tour...the carrier...with the navy. We never heard of any pilots doing that joint tour thing...since we have some time to kill and all."

Ford was thankful the flight was delayed a bit because he wasn't feeling that great this morning. He had an upset stomach and some lower-back pain, which was very unusual for him. It wasn't anything to take himself off the flight schedule, but he knew something wasn't right. He was happy to have the flight delayed a bit and just talk with the crew.

"Yup. Of course. Yeah...it was a terrific experience." Ford was selected three years ago by a formal board at Headquarters Air Force to participate in a unique joint cross-training program with the US Navy. Ford was able to be embedded in a navy F-18 Hornet squadron as an Air Force pilot. After finishing a six-month training program in Florida, he reported to squadron VFA-105, the "Gunslingers," at Naval Air Station Oceana. Flying under the squadron call sign "CANYON," he was a full-up pilot trained by the navy.

"So, bottom line, it was a blast," Ford started explaining. "Carrier ops, single-seat jet time, close air support, dropping bombs...life on the ship. Excessive fun."

Life on the aircraft carrier was like no other place on earth. By any slice of measurement, it was a distinctive place to live and work for a variety of reasons. Besides living on a floating houseboat without windows with over three thousand of your closest friends, you also worked there, flew from there, and shared a bedroom with complete strangers with no windows.

There were all sorts of culture items for Ford to get used to that did not exist at Air Force bases. For example, the ship offered midnight food, nicknamed midrats, short for its official name: midnight rations. At all times of the day or night, steel chains were dragged along the flight deck for aircraft tie downs, which were important in rough seas so aircraft didn't roll overboard. It was also important for people who thought they were going to sleep, because the dragging chains sounded like rolling thunder to those under the flight deck in their beds. Then there were the ship announcements over the loudspeaker system, constant cleaning, paint chipping, high-speed flowing steam, twenty-four-hour cooking, and the loud slamming of aircraft upon landing.

The ship was also famous for pilot shenanigans and practical jokes, which Ford enjoyed, where aircrew earned their call signs appropriately. If some young pilot went to the showers without any footwear on, he would be named "Shower Shoes," of course. Another pilot might notice something completely obvious in the Ready Room, point it out to the other pilots publicly, and she would be called "Moto" for "master of the obvious." Other call signs had to do with human physical imperfections, such as a maybe a shorter finger (Badfinger), a large and strange birthmark on your neck (Spot), or a less than ramrod posture (Hunchback). Other call signs were related to last names, which usually corresponded to a famous person. You could imagine what a pilot's call sign would be if their last name was Clinton, Kardashian, Pitt, Brady, Trump, Bieber, or Clooney. The joy in naming those rookie pilots! Besides the camaraderie of these nicknames, the tactical reason for using them was because you could not use real names on the aircraft radios. At least there was some military reason behind the military buffoonery and side-show comedy.

The navigators, or navs, heard that it was story time up front in the B-1, so they moved from the rear of the aircraft and came up to listen in. From outside the aircraft at Ellsworth, the scrapes of the plow blades were heard on the runways and their rotating yellow lights reflected off the snow and into the cockpit.

The sun had not come up yet on their early morning scheduled flight, so the bright yellow lights traveled far.

"Squid!" one the navs yelled as he was coming forward into the pilot seats area. "Squid" was a humorous term called by army, marine and Air Force members to their navy brothers. It was usually followed by "rust picker" or other humorous term, with some innocent ribbing and laughing.

"Very funny, Torchman. You'd never make it with these guys on the ship," Ford told him. "Too hard a lifestyle for a Ritz-Carlton, Merlot-drinking rich kid from Orange County like you." The rest of the crew laughed. "They would have killed ya and thrown ya overboard."

Chengdu University of Traditional Medicine, Qingyang, Chengdu, Sichuan, China

Chengdu University of Traditional Medicine had a portion of the building devoted to the crossbreed treatment of patients, focusing on both traditional and integrative medicines. The traditional Chinese medicine, or TCM, consisted of more than two thousand years of practice, included various forms of herbal medicine, acupuncture, massage, exercise, and dietary therapy. The integrative medicine approach used some of the TCM, along with other treatments known in the West.

The nurse stood in the hallway looking at the patient's records one more time, double checking his vitals and history, the traditional science data, before reentering the room. The waiting room was jammed with patients, but she flipped the folder to look at the interior pages, wondering about his TCM info. TCM's opinion of the human body placed little importance on anatomical arrangements and was engrossed in the functional things. The interior section of this patient's record had plenty of data on this subject about digestion, breathing, and age. TCM also believed that overall health is connected to the outside world and that disease is understood as a conflict in collaboration. The science of medicine, and TCM, combined when she looked again at the patient's pulse, tongue, skin, and eyes, in addition to looking at his eating and sleeping habits.

The nurse knocked on the door, then entered the exam room. He sat on the edge of the table in the exam room with his feet dangling off the floor and above the small stepping stool. Dressed in a white undershirt and dark pants, the man, in his late twenties or early thirties, who perhaps at a time not too long ago was in top physical fitness shape, looked up at the nurse.

"The doctor will be in to see you in a brief moment. I'm not sure what to make of your stomachaches. You don't have any other indications of being sick from what we can tell. Your blood pressure is fine. You are breathing fine. Eating seems OK. Perhaps it is work related?" she told him.

The patient was finishing a text on his smartphone, hit send, then put it away and looked up. "Yes, I understand what you're saying, but I just do not feel well. Between my abdominal pains, some vomiting, and sometimes some back pain, I feel like I am sick. I am just not myself," he told her.

Just then, the doctor entered the room, did a quick exam

by asking plenty of questions, and reviewed the charts. He must have felt his stomach, chest, and neck three or four times.

"Sir, you are not from *here*. You are not one of our regular patents. We do not see you regularly. It is tough to understand your medical history if you do not share with us your past records," the doctor told him, reviewing the sheets of paper in the thin manila folder, writing down some of his findings.

There was some yelling from outside the doorway, most likely from Chinese patients getting mad at a doctor, a common occurrence in China. Patients were routinely growing in anger at doctors because of both prices and outcomes not being favorable. The noise settled down quickly.

"I am private about my health and...ah...didn't want my employer's doctors taking a look at me. That is why I pay in yuan and will take my records with me," replied the patient.

"That's OK, that's OK." The doctor waved his pen around. "All I can recommend is that you come back and see us, or visit another provider in the future. I'm thinking of a massage for the moment. But you should come back. If you have more problems, visit a traditional emergency room as needed. Other than meditation and a massage, I recommend nothing else. There is nothing wrong with you."

Disappointed that the doctor could not give him a firm answer, he left the hospital and returned to work discouraged. Despite the doctor's lack of findings, he knew something was wrong.

Shandan, Zhangye, Gansu Airstrip, China

The Chinese army Air Force general officers, some not fitting so well these days in their official uniforms, were lined up along the tarmac in the reviewing stands along with some of the political leadership. They were all in VIP seating, complete with escorts for protocol, a small sound-system for announcements, and porta-johns behind the stands. A number of finger food and alcoholic drinks was readily available, especially the drinks, as they flowed steadily across the crowd.

The flight crew was the only show in the air that morning, so there was no need to converse on the aviation radio frequencies and ask for permission to do anything like land. The pilots just did it. No other aircraft were within one hundred miles or more of them, so there was no requirement to coordinate their safe movements in the air. They were their own air show.

Wu Lee, now thirty years old, a People's Liberation Army Air Force captain and pilot, pushed the throttles for all four engines forward a wee bit more, although there was little forward thrust felt in the cockpit. The temperatures and pressures all moved on the engine indicators in the green, as well as the altitude and airspeed indicators, but they felt no firm jolt. Instead of flying directly over the runway like most aircraft demonstrations, Wu had a trick up his sleeve, designed partly to entertain himself and partly to scare the generals he was not so fond of. Wu was already south of the airfield at a thousand feet in altitude above ground level, and instead of maneuvering to the east, to the right, to line up on the east-west runway, he started a descent.

"Descending. Set altitude bug at one hundred feet, Liu," Wu instructed his copilot, Captain Liu Nie.

Liu raised his left hand up to a round black dial that twisted like a radio volume dial in a car. He moved the dial counterclockwise, and some digital numbers appeared in a window and counted down. By doing this, the jet would descend in altitude and level off at the new altitude. About a hundred feet prior to the new altitude, the jet's avionics notified the crew with a tone in their flight helmets.

Down on the ground, the alcohol was rolling, the fake smiles flourishing, and the Chinese political scene was strong. Over the VIP sound system, a voice was heard addressing the crowd.

"Distinguished guests, ladies and gentlemen, if you look down the runway on your right, just above it, our latest, most *spectacular* aircraft will soon make its debut..." announced Lieutenant General He Chen, the father of the program, spoken with much pride.

Wu kept in the descent, leveled off at the altitude he wanted, and kept up the airspeed. Wearing a gray helmet, black flight gloves, and a dark visor, Wu smirked at what he was about to do.

"Six hundred ten knots, one hundred twenty feet," Wu, the aircraft commander and test pilot, said over the two-way intercom.

Liu adjusted his harness again, ensuring it was locked.

Wu was bringing up the jet from behind the crowd,

knowing that they would never see him, nor hear him coming. The sound of the engines was usually heard the loudest from behind the aircraft, so if the aircraft was coming at you as you stood on the ground, it would be a low murmur until the aircraft passed overhead. He was near silent when creeping up from behind, especially at that speed, and the crowd would never know he was there until it was too late. Plus, Lieutenant General Chen focused the crowd to the right, expecting this new jet to appear over the runway.

Vrrrrrr...whoooo-shhh!

All the VIP people in the stands ducked out of habit, nerves, and terror. A buzz was heard from the crowd, then euphoric yelling and clapping.

Wu brought the jet over the heads of the crowd at an alarming airspeed, grinning as he zoomed over the stands. They both smiled inside the cockpit, and Wu brought the jet up into a climb by pulling back on the stick between his legs and moving the throttles that sat on the console between them.

"Liu, I'll bring her up to about fifteen hundred feet, come right into the pattern, then fly over the runway. We'll let the crowd see her from all the angles," Wu told him.

Wu pulled back on the stick ever so slightly, and the jet popped up in altitude. The crowd was able to see the rear of the mysterious black jet and then the top of her. The pilots could also feel her, with her four powerful engines purring loudly, producing the enormous thrust unlike any jet in history. They brought her around at slow speeds, fast speeds, inverted, steep climbs, and even did a roll. At one point, Wu did slow flight with the gear down, just above the runway, but never touched his wheels on the surface.

Lieutenant General Chen, standing on the pavement alone, grabbed the sound system microphone again. "Ladies and gentlemen, our pride. Our future. Our newest military bomber! Our first Chinese long-range stealth bomber, The... Devil...Dragon!"

Loud cheering and applause was heard as the Devil Dragon completed its private demonstration flight. The crowd of proud, pleased Chinese political and military officials was ecstatic to see what was in the planning, building, and test phase for so long. At last, a grander weapon that many Chinese military strategists thought would command respect from other Asian nations as well as the United States. It didn't matter to them *how* they obtained this stealth technology, only that *they had it now*.

Over the last ten to twelve years, the People's Liberation Army Air Force increased their duration, range, and number of routine military aircraft flights offshore, away from the mainland and into places like the waterways and seas of Asia. China wanted to maintain a permanent and constant presence in locations like the East China Sea and the Pacific and Indian Oceans, and routinely conducted military exercises with the aggressive backing of senior military and political leadership. The constant expeditionary war games and assessments of potential island bases in the South China Sea was just the very beginning in their strategic plan.

The location of the island chains in the South China Sea, combined with China's extensive and lengthy history in the world and long-term strategic plans on expansion, were all part of their combined army, navy, and Air Force strategy. The strategy Lieutenant General He Chen was attempting to execute incorporated exercises and operations beyond their first island chain. The South China Sea was the perfect area to build up a manmade island and construct an airstrip. Ever since 1933, when China sent a warship to the region to signal a protest against a French annexation, the minuscule islands were first described as tiny coral reefs. Without skipping a beat, China would continue their aggressive stance on the tiny coral reefs, announcing it was China's to claim. And geography-wise, it was excellent reach and capability for all their ships and aircraft. Combat capabilities into these waters allowed China to reach out and touch someone.

Lieutenant General He Chen wanted more, though, and considered the words and guidance of his former leader, Chairman Mao Tse Tung. Chen never forgot reading about Mao's 1949 island campaign guidance to the Chinese Communist Party on the future of China. Mao told them to first have the party stay in power. Second, they should expand the country's economy and trade. Last, have a strong defense and military. For the last fifty-plus years, this was exactly what the party worked on.

Due to geography, China had rare earth elements in her possession, and because of the rise in high technology such as smartphones and electric cars, the world demand was high. And with all the rare-earth elements and metals that China had embedded in her rich soil and rock, it only solidified China into a dominant powerhouse on all three areas of Mao's guidance. *Ha!* Chen thought, *even the Americans were caught off guard! They were consumed with terrorism and humanitarian assistance and the Iraq War, and we came in through the front door.* Chen was referring to the demand that China served, while the United States paid no attention over time. Chen even quoted in his graduate paper at the People's Liberation Army National Defense University in Beijing: "The Middle East has oil, China has rare earth elements!" *How foolish are the Americans that we, as China, continue to trade and make enormous yuan off our sales...we use their prized ideas and concepts for our military! They even pay us for half a ton of rare earth elements for each copy of their expensive F-35s!*

Chen, ever a future planner, had his own strategy to support the party and the military, though. A personal strategy within a strategy. *What good was it to have an airstrip on an island, if you didn't have something to fly from it?* This was what led him to pursue the stealth bomber plans from the United States, using a great tool in his toolbox: cyber. As soon as he got his hands on those stealth plans, he was lathered up into a frenzy of activity. His science and technology team revised the plans, worked on the revisions day and night, and modified the original intent of the American's technology. Chen and his team designed and made something unusual, as well as distinct.

He Chen established the goals and training requirements for the new aircraft to reach out beyond their borders. Chen's newly hatched stealth jet was the service's secret quarterback. Other countries could see the airstrip being built and the frenzy of activity around it, and the diversion of the island would take the United States' eye off the ball. Their intelligence and military machines would focus on the airstrip, all while China built one of the best flying machines in history. The deception plan was perfect.

Lieutenant General Chen worked with the senior military leadership, in addition to the political leadership, for funding to expand this reach with the new stealth bomber, built in near-complete secrecy. There were certainly a few senior members both in uniform and in the political arena that knew she was being built, but most had no idea the Devil Dragon even existed. A few admirals were getting their credit for increased patrols, building *Neptune*, and perceived standoffs with the United States in the South China Sea, and the fighter generals were getting their J-31 spotlight...but now Chen wanted his turn. Chen wanted *his* accolades for *his* work. Chen thought it was *his* turn to shine.

Chen planned aggressive testing with a flight schedule that was hard for the aviation-support team to keep up with. The demanding general, like many generals and flag officers, was a force to be reckoned with. Chen wanted it *his* way, so that his Air Force was ready when the call came in. He wanted the jet to be able to provide the intelligence that was required for the rest of their military team, in addition to delivering precision weapons without anyone knowing they were coming. Chen wanted the aircraft project completed successfully as soon as possible...thinking, dreaming, planning that this aircraft was his golden ticket—the golden ticket to either a fourth general star or a powerful senior political position. He *chased* both relentlessly, and Chen's impatience was a sight to see in-person.

Either way, the uniformed and political leadership wanted

to bring the powerhouse of China back to her original strong and global historical roots. They wanted to deter potential adversaries and, at the right moment, let them know that the Chinese dragon was awake. Power, glory, empire. The Devil Dragon was their answer.

Defense Intelligence Agency, Bolling AFB, Washington, DC

Jimmy Buffet's "Son of a Son of a Sailor" was blaring out of the speakers of Mark Savona's 1957 red Chevrolet Bel Air sport sedan as he sat in the light traffic flow on Highway 295 in the early morning. Driving from his one-bedroom apartment in National Harbor, Maryland, above the Granite City Brewery to his job just up the road, made the commute pretty easy when compared to other Washingtonians. He liked to get up about 4:00 a.m. and beat the heavy traffic on his way to DIA, achieving his goal of getting a good parking spot.

The Defense Intelligence Agency, known as the DIA, specialized in defense and military intelligence and was located on Bolling Air Force Base in Washington, DC. The pre–World War II runways no longer held propeller-driven naval aviation and Air Force aircraft on the intersection of the Potomac and Anacostia Rivers in DC but now buildings. Located in a large, seven-story, blue-gray building, the DIA Headquarters building stuck out from the other worn, red-brick buildings of the base. If you were to pass Bolling AFB from a boat on one of the DC rivers, you would wonder what modern and innovative company owned and operated it from there.

Like any large intelligence agency, it has a robust section of operations directorates, clandestine teams, analyst teams, and even a science and technology section, all focused on national defense and military topics. Unlike their brothers and sisters at the Central Intelligence Agency, CIA, whose mission was focused on more general national security topics, DIA was focused on foreign militaries.

DIA analyst Mark Savona was an expert on Chinese aircraft and enjoyed working for DIA since joining the team some six years ago. Mark, a cum laude graduate of Johns Hopkins University in Baltimore, not only earned an undergraduate degree in aeronautical engineering but a master's degree in international relations. He brought with him nearly five years of experience from Pixar Animation Studios in San Francisco, California, before answering an ad he saw in *Foreign Affairs*. An avid poker player, fantasy football fan, and devout follower of the Washington Nationals, Mark lived the single life that many men under thirty-five years old only dreamed about.

Mark Savona was also an outlier. If you were ever to judge a book by its cover, one could easily question how Mark was able to obtain a top secret security clearance. He wore shoulder-length hair in a building full of short-cropped, conservative veterans or military members. Sometimes he wore Hawaiian shirts with clashing pants. Some months he was able to wrap his hair back into a ponytail or man bun, and once he even returned from summer leave with a goatee. He was also a human resources director's nightmare, sometimes cursing or openly speaking his mind as needed.

One day last week, he surprised his supervisor by wearing different-colored socks with sandals, plaid pants, and a flannel shirt without a tie. He kept the same blue blazer on his cubicle seat just in case some big wigs from upstairs came to his directorate area for a meeting. While others wore the Washington, DC, uniform of a starched white shirt and dark suit, Mark was just being himself. Being himself also landed him extra training classes. Last year, he loudly argued passionately with a supervisor about the performance characteristics of the Chinese J-31 fighter jet, which landed him in a human resources training class on sensitivity. Two years ago, while on probation, he argued with a senior executive, an SES, about working his ten hours a day by starting at twelve noon because that was when he was most productive. *Why start at seven thirty in the morning if you can max your hours out at another time?* It was useless government rules like this that drove Mark crazy.

These actions painted only half of his unique personality. This critical thinking and outside the box emotional intelligence was what DIA Deputy Director Calvin Burns saw in him and was the reason he was hired. Calvin Burns was the oil in the DIA machine, and he made the organization hum. His knack for acquiring talent in special places was the Deputy's unique flair, and locating eccentric Mark was one of the greatest finds ever. For example, when many bureaucrats were clocking out for the day in the late afternoon to head home, Mark would escape work to think and then return to the office in the evening to tackle a difficult problem.

Not too long ago, it was baseball season in Washington. Mark was studying a China aircraft-related problem at the office and then left early in the day to attend a 4:05 Washington Nationals baseball game across the Anacostia River. It helped him to think, to do something different. Mark called it "white space," something he learned from his creative time on the West Coast. Psychologists and time efficiency experts would refer to this as allowing the subconscious mind to do its job, but Mark knew the stuffy bureaucrats would never understand the concept. Ever.

"Well, well, well. What have we here?" Mark announced aloud from his cubicle, in a farm of hundreds of cubicles on a large and open office floor. Mark was assigned to the China desk as the resident aircraft expert, and he was reading the morning reports on his computer screen.

"What do you have, Mark?" asked Robert Dooley, a cubicle mate on the China team. Robert was an expert from the DIA clandestine office, the team that focused on the human collection of information from another country. Ever a stoic, Robert Dooley was a man who was all about business, and that was how he acted at home. It was worse at work. Raised in North Padre Island, Texas, and a graduate of the University of Texas, Robert joined DIA straight out of the US Army Signal Corps. He was an expert in human intelligence, being ever so persuasive in gathering information from people, or convincing them to take care of hands-on operations-related business. Operations business meant getting out of the office cubicles that he was currently stuck in. Robert rarely smiled, but he was a trusted teammate and a hard worker, respected by Mark and the China team.

"Looks like the bozo missile guys are tackling a meeting this morning to discuss a Buckley incident from last night," Mark replied, after reading the morning report. "Very. Interesting," Mark said under his breath, but Robert heard him.

"What is?" asked Robert.

"We weren't invited to the meeting." Mark was so eccentric that sometimes his sister offices did not invite him to certain meetings because they didn't want to put up with his crap. This one was an invitation-only meeting down on the third floor, in the auditorium.

"I know what you're thinking. You pulled this stunt years ago after the North Korean rocket incident," Robert said.

"Whatever...maybe I'll stop in. On a different subject, I received a text in the parking lot earlier that Emily was running late on the GW. Could you pencil her a note and have her meet us in the cheap seats of the auditorium? I'm going to run downstairs," Mark said.

The George Washington Parkway, the GW, was a main, two-lane highway that ran alongside the Potomac River. It was a commuter nightmare because of the volume of cars and often was jammed up due to accidents or passing motorcades. It was both loved and hated by locals. Loved because it was fast to get around on outside of commuter hours but hated because if you got caught speeding, you had to attend federal court since you were breaking the law on federal land.

"Oh, boy...yup. Absolutely. Doing it now," Robert replied.

Emily Livingston, running late due to traffic, was another

member of their China desk team. She was a liaison intelligence officer from the United Kingdom. Specifically, she was a member of the British intelligence agency, the Secret Intelligence Service, known as MI6. Military Intelligence, Section 6, supplies the British government with foreign intelligence. Similarly, MI5 supplies the British government with internal British intelligence. Petite, athletic, with blond-brown hair and an attraction to fashion and acting, she came to the United States complete with her stunning accent. Emily was an expert in operations and human intelligence, especially in China, but you would never know it from her outward appearance.

"Hang on a sec. Just want to check two more things before we go," Mark said. He started flipping through some papers on his desk then turned back to his computer. At one point, he started going through the paper newspapers, an odd sight to see in these modern times of digital technology.

Mark was keenly interested in this report from Buckley AFB and was puzzled by the incident details. He checked the other source reporting from the National Security Agency, the NSA. Found nothing. He checked the military's joint staff intelligence reports, the J-2, and that, too, turned up nothing. Mark was bothered. Perturbed was more like it. Perturbed because it was unusual that Buckley detected a missile without any other communications or indicators, and the reports reflected no opinions from analysts. *No secondary? No other indications?*

Mark ran down a mental list of possible secondary indications that might indicate employees were working at the launch site. *Did the Chinese have their kids in the day care late?*

Was fast food delivered to the missile control room at strange hours of the night? Not one piece of ground or air radio communications from the launch pad? Complete silence? Mark thought about it, and it was particularly curious to him. Then, to Mark, the icing on the cake was that it disappeared in flight. *What! Disappeared in flight? Never saw that before.*

"Let's go. We're attending this little get-together," Mark told Robert. Thinking about the situation, he could not recall if a condition like this had ever happened before. He was no missile expert, so he wasn't sure of the tracking specifics, but as a critical thinker, he sure had a lot of questions. *Did they really lose it? Perhaps it reached its target on a local range without an explosive warhead?* He would find out for sure after attending the meeting.

"C'mon. Meeting is eleven minutes out, and the Deputy is invited. Need to do a pit stop, too," Mark invited Robert again.

"Are you kidding? Not sure what is more entertaining. You and your quirky personality in a large group of introverts, or a Chinese missile that apparently disappeared in midflight."

Ellsworth AFB, South Dakota, Flight Line

The navigators in the back of the B-1 jet rode as a crucial part of the crew. They were smart and talented, and Ford Stevens could not imagine flying without them. He also enjoyed busting their chops. Sometimes Ford and the other pilots would call them passengers since they had no flight controls in the rear. Other ribbing came from the fact that they wore eyeglasses. Nearly all navigators wore them, though, and because of it took a lot of heat from pilots. The usual ribbing surrounded the perception that navigators could not pass the vision test to be a pilot. Based on part fact and part legend, navigators selected or were thrown in to their second-choice aircrew position of navigator. Ford wasn't shy about busting navigator chops, as all the pilots did in the squadron.

One of the snowplows was on their B-1 parking ramp now, and the scrapes of the blade were louder, pushing the snow off to the side and making room for the aircraft to maneuver. The yellow strobe light continued to flash and beam through the windscreen and into the rear of the cockpit, only because the snowplows in South Dakota were gargantuan. These weren't the small landscaping dump trucks with a plow bolted to the front; these were of professional magnitude. Powerful, tall, and tough, these industrial plows meant business.

The B-1 crew, delayed because of the plows, was still asking Ford about his time on the navy carriers. "Look, all of us can land...or fight in the aircraft. They just do it in and around the ship. Sure, it's a challenge to land on the carrier, especially at night, but any trained aviator can do it," Ford said humbly, but he knew that only a small percentage make the grade.

"Aim point, airspeed. Aim point, airspeed. Same cockpit scan. We flew an AOA, the angle of attack on the heads-up display, and looked at a landing lens light to come down on the ship," Ford said, moving his hands in a downward motion to the top of the copilot's seat.

"The Hornet heads-up display, the HUD, has all the

instruments projected onto a glass screen that you can see through, and it aids in the landing. We had the same checklists, for the most part, as the B-1. Except we had a tailhook in the Hornet to catch a cable on landing. Drop the hook and bring her in."

"What happens if you missed the landing area, or...had to go around...when you're out at sea?" McCoy asked. The rest of the crew laughed.

"Well, we had the opportunity to catch one of four wire cables across the flight deck, our moving runway. Ship moved along at fifteen or twenty knots away from you...into the wind. The number-three wire was the goal...ah but you could catch any of them. If you missed it, called a 'bolter,' you just went around in the pattern and did it over," Ford said. "You also gave the Hornet full power on wheels on the deck, which was different from Air Force flying. We are usually at idle on the runway in the Air Force, but in naval aviation you have to be prepared to go around again and make another attempt."

As Ford was telling flying stories, they all felt a hard jolt of the B-1 on the ground as if it was moving. Something hit and jarred the aircraft. Looks flew around the cockpit, and it was evident they were all startled.

"*What the hell was that*? You guys feel that?" McCoy asked.

Everyone in the cockpit leaned over to the windows to see outside to the ground and groaned. Sergeant McCoy left the cockpit immediately without looking and slid down the ladder to the ground as fast as he could.

Pinky had the best viewpoint from the copilot seat on the right side of the jet and was able to turn around to see the right side of the aircraft. "Aw, man! No, no...that snowplow...it just drove under our right wing and hit us! It's stuck!"

Ford raised his eyebrows and had everyone evacuate the aircraft immediately. "Out. Out. Everyone outta here, right now!" Ford was last, and by the time he got outside, fuel was coming out of the right-wing tanks and cascading onto the plow like rain. There was a small fire brewing on the top of the plow, but one look at the proximity to the rest of the wing tanks, and you knew the plow and aircraft would soon be engulfed in flames. The B-1, when fully fueled, could hold ten thousand gallons of jet fuel, so it was only matter of time before there would be an explosion.

"Where is the driver of the plow?" Ford yelled over to Sergeant McCoy, attempting to be heard over the wind.

McCoy shook his head and turned his free hand palm up. He was on his two-way radio, telling the operations desk inside to notify the crash, fire, and rescue unit and have them roll out immediately. Within moments, everyone on the flight line could see the red flashing lights at the far end of the tarmac, but it would still take at least two minutes or so to reach them.

Ford, not seeing the driver standing on the ramp with the rest of the aircrew members, ran around the large plow truck to have visibility into the cab. With each passing moment, the fire grew larger. The three things needed for a fire to start were fuel, air, and an ignition source, and this morning was the perfect trifecta. The heat was intense and worsening, and it could be felt around the right B-1 wing and plow truck. The heat started to melt the snow. Thick, black, petroleum-based smoke was pouring into the dark sky with a purpose and became more visible as the sun started to peek on the horizon.

Ford was able to see in the snowplow cab pretty clearly now and saw that the driver was still inside. He hopped up on the driver's running board, grabbed the door handle, and yanked it. It didn't open. He tugged on it again, but it still didn't budge. The door had been jammed on impact of cab. Ford ran around to the passenger door to check, and that, too, was jammed. It was impossible to open the doors without tools from the fire department. The rapid build-up of heat and flames meant there wasn't time to wait.

"HEY, HEY, we have to get you out of there!" Ford yelled at the driver. He pointed. "You are on fire back there!"

The driver's window was the only available option, but it was up and closed. Ford pounded on it with the side of his fist, but it wouldn't shatter. The driver turned sideways in his seat and attempted to kick it out, but nothing happened.

Ford jumped down off the truck and looked around. Pinky was standing close by and off to the side, and Ford waved her over. "Pinky, hey, grab this portable fire extinguisher with me. I'm going to climb up on the hood of the truck, and I need you to hand it to me." Pinky was in a daze from the chaos of the fire. "Pinky! Hey, pay attention! You understand?" Ford yelled.

Pinky was overwhelmed with the intensity of the fire but understood enough to lend a hand. The fuel was now gushing with force out of the wing of the aircraft, most likely aided by gravity. Pouring out, it flowed generously down the side of the truck where the sand was stored and was now pooling on the ground. The top of the aircraft wing was on fire, burning aircraft electrical wires, truck paint, and insulation, and the crash, fire, and rescue crews were still not there yet.

"After you give this to me, get everyone away. Got it? Take everyone away over there, and wait for CFR trucks to arrive," Ford told her, pointing to the area closer to the flight line buildings. "Do it quickly."

As Ford climbed up on the front hood of the snowplow, on top of the large Caterpillar Diesel engine, Pinky raised the fire extinguisher above her head and handed it to him. Ford lifted it up. Then with every ounce of the muscle and strength he'd developed at Notre Dame, he smashed it into the laminated safety windshield of the truck. It bounced off the strengthened glass. Again, Ford hit it hard, as hard as he would hit when he was with Fighting Irish. Nothing.

"Come on. Come on. Get me out! Get me out of here!" the driver was screaming. He was in full panic mode.

Ford smashed it again and again with full vigor and intensity. His face was scrunched up, windburned, and cold, but Ford was determined. Again and again, he hit the windshield. And again. On the sixth or seventh try, the windshield cracked but did not shatter. Ford worked it and worked it, until he was able to peel it back like a banana peel from the upper right corner and outward.

Auto windshields were not panes of glass like a bay window at your house, which breaks into shards. On the snow plow truck, as in all automotive glass, the manufacturing process requires the front windshield to be what is called "laminated glass" for safety reasons. Ford was experiencing the safety glass, with a flexible, clear plastic film called polyvinyl butyral, layered between two pieces of glass in the windshield. This plastic film was holding the snowplow windshield glass in place while Ford was breaking it, helping to lessen injuries from flying glass. Designed to be difficult to penetrate, as Ford was facing, was not helping in this time sensitive situation.

"Let me have your hand! Let me have your hand!" Ford yelled to the driver.

The flames were larger than a two-story building now and busting out heat on exposed skin like a summer day in Florida. The ramp area was full of thick smoke, which made it hard to both see and breathe. The fuel vapors were wafting up their sinuses, as dangerous as anything any of them had ever experienced. Ford knew enough from flight-school-staged accident demonstrations that this was a recipe for disaster.

Ford was able to grab ahold of the driver's hand and arm. Ford laughed silently when he saw that the driver was a bit of a large man and clearly overweight. "Aw, come on. A fat guy. Figures," he said under his breath. With Ford pulling, the driver was able to finally squeeze through the windshield and had half his upper body through now. The driver had to step on the steering wheel and dashboard while Ford pulled, and he would be through.

"Kick those legs off the dash. Come on, keep pushing," Ford told him.

"I am. I am. My feet are pushing off the wheel."

What wasn't helping them was the wind, making it loud and harder to communicate. Great for takeoff, not so great for talking or the fire. The whipping wind was not only interfering with their hearing, but it was fanning the fire. Ford was also concerned about the fuel flash point. Aviation fuel is different than auto fuel in that it ignites at a much higher temperature, but in these weather conditions, there were enough vapors building in the atmosphere that it could ignite. The flash point for aviation fuel was about 38 degrees Celsius, and 210 degrees Celsius for autoignition temperature, which meant that at the proper temperature, it could still cause a catastrophe.

Ford and the driver were now both sitting and kneeling on all fours on the hood of the truck, respectively. Both men turned around on their stomachs and began sliding off the hood feetfirst as fast as they could. The drop from the top of the hood was at least eight feet, and they would be free shortly.

As Ford and the driver both rounded the turn of the hood near the grille to hit the ground, an explosion hit. The JP-8's yellow kerosene-based fuel that was being used that day had just enough warmth to ignite the vapors. The fire science triangle at that moment became one.

Whoosh...boooom! The fuel vapor cloud had ignited into a mammoth vertical fireball of flame, heat, and smoke. Ford and the driver slid off the hood and were shoved to the snowy pavement by the force, both men facedown on the icy ground.

Defense Intelligence Agency, Bolling AFB, Washington, DC

Mark and Robert trotted down the staircase, stopped in the bathroom, and then walked over to the entrance of the DIA auditorium. Mark looked at his watch and saw he was at least a full five minutes early before their brief started, so he stopped to wait in line at the Starbucks kiosk. Robert rolled his eyes again, as he always did when Mark wanted a Starbucks.

"You keep this place in business. The owners would be broke if it weren't for you," Robert commented. Mark nodded.

"Good morning, Judi," Mark greeted the barista, "the usual, please."

Robert turned to stare at Mark. "What's the usual this month?"

"Venti, nonfat, extra hot, cinnamon dulce latte, two shots, and one extra pump."

"Oh, for heaven's sake. Are you freaking for real? I'm sorry I asked."

Mark used Starbucks for walking the halls at DIA in between meetings or projects for three reasons. First, the caffeine kept him going, giving him the fuel for his job. Second, he used it to collect information from other teammates in the organization. Sometimes it was gossip, sometimes networking, but either way, it always helped in contributing to a hot project. The third and most important reason was the collection of information about adversarial militaries. *The 9/11 Commission Report*, formally named *Final Report of the National Commission on Terrorist Attacks Upon the United States*, is the official report of the events leading up to the September 11, 2001, attacks, and a large criticism in the report was that the intelligence community was too private, too closely held, meaning that agencies did not talk to one another enough. The interagency did not network as effectively as they could, and if they only worked together as a team a bit more, they could help solve complex, volatile, and ambiguous problems. Mark knew it took a team of experts to tackle these problems, something he learned while working in the movie industry at Pixar and especially on the movie *Toy Story*. Cartoon movies prior to *Toy Story* were made by hand; *Toy Story* was the first one made by totally by computer. Mark learned that while technology was a welcome tool, it also prevented people from interacting and communicating.

Judi made him his special drink and handed it to him. Mark dug out his loyalty card from a pocket full of receipts, notes, scrunched up cash, and old sticks of gum, and asked Robert again if he wanted his trademark black coffee.

"Stop. No coffee. Let's get going," Robert grumbled. All paid for, and the green stirrer pulled out, they made for the rear doors for the brief.

Mark turned around after a few paces. "Thanks, Judi! See you later today," Mark yelled.

"OK, Mark. Thank you," Judi replied.

They entered, opening the wooden doors quietly at the rear of the large room with the cathedral ceiling. Down in the front of the auditorium, which sloped like a traditional movie theater, was a crowd of people talking quietly, along with a screen that displayed PowerPoint slides. The first few rows were pretty filled, and the VIP seats closest to the end were still empty. That told Mark and Robert that the Deputy director was not present yet.

On the title slide already on the screen was a logo for the Missile and Space Intelligence Center, Redstone Arsenal, Huntsville, Alabama. These were the bozos that Mark had referred to earlier. His loyalty was with the National Air and Space Intelligence folks from Wright-Patterson AFB in Ohio. *More bureaucracy and infighting*, Mark thought. *Wonder who would get the lead on whatever headache the Chinese had today?*

The briefer, Michael Klubb, an obese, balding, and disheveled civilian government supervisor with a rank status known as a GS-15, stumbled through the start of his morning brief by introducing the missile event that took place at Buckley AFB yesterday. Mike Klubb, wearing thick eyeglasses with dark rims, sporting a wrinkled white shirt, short gray pants, white socks, and scuffed brown shoes, was the spitting image of a government bureaucrat. Mike was well compensated, being a Virginia Tech grad; held a high security clearance; and was part of the older, original pension system at near sixty years old. But he would never make it in corporate America. His job started at 6:00 a.m., and he took thirty minutes for lunch, the exact amount of time per the human resources manual, and was done at 2:30 p.m. Not 2:31 p.m., and certainly not later, despite whatever hot project he was assigned or when it was due. He was paid for forty hours a week, and that's what he worked. Stay out of the doorway after 2:30 p.m. because most likely you'd get run over by Mike and others like him.

A few years ago Mike was reprimanded by his supervisor

when his directorate was assigned a time-sensitive operational issue with foreign military missiles on a submarine. During this incident, the US Navy had been tracking a Chinese submarine off the coast of West Africa. A request by the navy, specifically a rear admiral, had come in at 2:03 p.m. EST. The admiral needed Mike to do an in-depth analysis of unique signals emitted from the sub's missile silos. Because Mike always had an eye on the clock, he worked on it for exactly twenty-seven minutes then departed for the day. His argument was that he had worked his eight hours that day.

This morning, though, Mike was ready for his brief. He was sweating profusely and dabbing his forehead with a handkerchief, and he was not more than ten seconds into the first slide when the principal Deputy director of DIA, Mr. Calvin Burns, walked in.

Principal Deputy Director Calvin Coolidge Burns, a career Defense Intelligence Agency senior executive, spent his entire life in either the Navy or at DIA. A well-respected senior leader, Calvin, a native of Richmond, Virginia, was an intelligence officer's officer. First educated at a famous historically black college, Savannah State, he earned an MBA from the Naval Postgraduate School, followed by some doctoral work at the George Washington University. Calvin Burns worked his way up the ladder for thirty-one years. If you included his time at the Power Lab up on Cape Cod, Massachusetts, his Federal Executive Institute experience in Charlottesville, Virginia, and time in the navy, he had over thirty-six years of experience. Last year when he was ready to retire, his wife encouraged him to stay, knowing how much he enjoyed the work and people. So, after sleeping on it for a bit, Calvin stayed but planned on only giving one more year.

Nearly all of the DIA team loved him because he knew so many by name over the years, and if he didn't know someone yet, he always showed a sincere effort to get to know that person. Calvin Burns knew the military services, the Office of the Secretary of Defense (OSD) and the Pentagon, and the political ways of Washington. As an example of reaching out to the workforce, just last year he put into effect a new policy that made either himself or the director of DIA, personally attend each new-employee orientation session. The workforce team responded favorably when he walked down the hall, and he greeted many employees by name.

"Umm, good—good morning, sir," said briefer Mike Klubb.

"Hi, Mike, sorry I'm late. Please continue," replied the Deputy.

"Yes, sir." Mike Klubb went on to describe the detection from SBIRS, the internal detection timelines, the actions of the watch standers, and any updates to Chinese intelligence, which was zero. He talked for about twenty minutes or so, and so far, no one asked any questions.

Whispering to Robert, Mark leaned over. "Something isn't right on this one."

"I knew you'd have something to say about this. What are you thinking?"

"Huh. Well...I'm going to call out there to Buckley. My old college roommate is stationed there, and I'm gonna find out who was working that day...see if we can get some more info. I already have a hunch. Based on what I've read and a gut feeling, there is something we're all missing. Something just isn't right."

"What's your hunch?" Robert asked but didn't get a reply.

Klubb finished his short brief and opened it up for questions. Strangely, no one asked anything. Perhaps it was because the Deputy was present, but in a room of folks who should have been communicating, no one said a word. Status quo for a room full of government employees.

"That's it. I'm asking questions," Mark said.

"No, no. Sit down," Robert said to him, whispering. "What is it? What are you thinking?"

Too late. Mark stood up in the rear of the auditorium, nearly hidden in the shadows because the lighting was up front.

"Holy shit," Robert whispered under his breath.

"Hey, Mike," Mark yelled from the back. "Hey, what does the rest of the interagency have to say?"

The audience murmured, and nearly everyone turned around to see who was asking from the back of the room, when everyone was sitting up front.

"Who is that back there?"

"What did NSA say? Why aren't they pulled into this?" asked Mark, walking down the aisle of the room, holding his trademark Starbucks.

The room full of quiet analysts suddenly turned one notch louder and followed Mark with their heads as he walked.

"Oh, Mark, it's you. Hi, yeah, um, I'm sure you're interested, but this isn't in your lane. It's missiles' lane. Not yours. And by the way, this is a closed brief," Mike Klubb told him, apparently thinking this would put Mark in his place.

Mark held his Starbucks in his right hand and waved his left hand around the room, pointing to the screen every so often.

"All the intellectual firepower in this room, and no one is asking pertinent questions about what might have happened in China yesterday? Where's your critical thinking?"

The Deputy director turned, smirked warmly at Mark, but remained silent. He knew Mark well because he'd hired him years ago out of the San Francisco area and helped bring him to DIA. Calvin Burns was well aware Mark was against the Washington establishment of short hair, conservative thinking, white shirts and neckties, and being a yes-man. It was a very rare concept in any DC organization to be an independent thinker like Mark because most organizations tended to be filled with like-minded yes-men. Calvin treasured the diversity and let Mark go on with his theater.

"I bet NSA has some tape of transmissions. Air Force may have been flying and picked up signals. State Department may have some diplomatic traffic. Even open-source analysts may have some stuff right out of the *China Daily*. Yet, in five or ten minutes or so of yapping up there, you mentioned none of that," Mark said, questioning the audience.

"Look, Mark, this is just, ah…just the initial brief about the facts of last night and—"

"Negative, bro. This audience is as quiet as church mice and would park this event on the shelf if you let them. What's your plan? What. Is. The. Plan?" Mark said with emotion.

"Well. The teams in here will go back to their offices and do some research, and we can meet again tomorrow morning. We have our liaison folks in here with reach-back capability to both Alabama and Ohio," Klubb told him.

Klubb and his team of folks were treating this event like it was an everyday event. *Average day at DIA* was what Mark was thinking of the Mike Klubb team, when it was really anything but an everyday event.

"Zzzz. Boring, Klubb. Come on, man. This is a major, significant event. Come on, dude. Elevate this puppy and get some real horsemeat...some critical and creative thinking about what happened. For Christ's sake, you don't even have the IT contractor in here to validate the equipment was working. Did you even *call* out there to Colorado?"

"Well...no."

The Deputy smiled and agreed with that comment by nodding, looking around the room a bit more now to actually see who was in there. Calvin Burns focused on the reaction of the crowd then turned back to Mark.

"It's just day one, Mark," Klubb said, attempting to defend himself.

British teammate Emily Livingston now entered the rear of the auditorium quietly and sat next to Robert. She was wearing fashionable business casual from Nordstrom consisting of a Vince Camuto turtleneck and leggings, no one down below in the front seats heard her enter. She normally turned men's heads because she was certainly a beauty.

Mark was in the far front of the room now, stealing the show, but not at the podium mic. He didn't need to be on the stage, nor did he need a microphone. He *was* the room at that point, dominating the spotlight and influencing others right under Klubb's nose.

"Hello, Mark," said the Deputy, finally nodding his head and acknowledging Mark's presence. "Thank you for joining us this morning."

"Hey, sir," replied Mark.

Calvin knew that if Mark was already in this much of a frenzy, he was already thinking of something that others had not thought of yet. Calvin was only half present in the auditorium, though. Following this meeting, he had his upcoming US Senate Intelligence Committee brief, plus a budget brief with the Under Secretary of Defense for Intelligence at the Pentagon. His mind was already full.

"Sir, I know you are busy...but I think something isn't right with this event," Mark explained.

"I can see that. Great to see your passion. What are you thinking, Mark?" asked the Deputy.

The Deputy's assistant, Jason Cohen, stood up, giving the sign that it was time for Calvin to roll to the next event on his schedule. Calvin pulled out his pocket schedule from his suit jacket and saw the next event was a cake-cutting ceremony for the US Marine Corps birthday celebration.

"Well, sir," Mark said, clearing his throat.

The murmur was still active in the large auditorium, most likely gossip about Mark Savona, who wasn't even invited to this event.

"Come on, Mark. Sit down already," Mike Klubb told him, looking at the wall clock and huffing harshly.

"No, let him finish," said the Deputy director. "Go on, Mark. Please."

The room, looking at the Deputy, moved the focus to Mark.

Mark bit his lip then let his thoughts fly. "What if it wasn't a missile?"

The gossipy whispering about Mark came to a halt.

"What if it wasn't some missile from the Chinese? What if...what if it was an aircraft?"

Silence filled the room, and the Deputy's head turned slightly in thought.

"Please, Mark. We would already know it was an aircraft from other intelligence sources and from satellite images. We'd have some electronic signatures or something," Klubb replied.

"Really, Mike? What makes you so sure it was a missile? Is that because you're a missile guy? You poorly assumed it was a missile because you were looking for a missile. You haven't even checked other sources, so why don't you..." Mark sipped his drink and made a face, almost enjoying the theater. "Look, Mikey Klubb, and everyone in here. Question your assumptions, already."

Some analysts in the auditorium started to look at one another.

"What I am saying, sir, what I am saying is..." Mark said, then hesitated.

"Go ahead, Mark. It's OK. Say it," Calvin told him.

"What if it was a new, special aircraft that couldn't be seen or detected from a satellite."

The murmur started again.

"Aw, shit," Robert said under his breath from the second to last row in the auditorium.

"*What?*" Emily said to Robert, grabbing his arm and leaning in to him.

"You still have my attention, Mark. Continue," the Deputy told him.

Mark usually lined up his theory with data and analysis in his thoughts a bit more, but today it was all becoming clearer to him. His years of study of Chinese aircraft, their historical love of theft, and their historical roots of deception, all helped Mark come up with his obscure theory. It all made sense to him now. From the time he read the report, to standing in line at Starbucks, to a career studying the country of China, it clicked. *No way could we lose a missile*. He hesitated.

"Mark?" Calvin asked.

He took in a deep breath. Then another one. "Stealth," blurted Mark. "A stealth aircraft. Stealth technology. *OK*? A fully tested stealth aircraft that can fly undetected by conventional means. One that has such a low radar cross signature...an, an, an RCS...it would show up on our radar as a goddamn seagull's eyeball."

The room was disconcertingly quiet. The room full of PhDs, analysts, and smart pocket-protector experts didn't say a word.

A brief moment of silence went by inside the auditorium. Then Klubb spoke. "The Chinese don't have stealth aircraft, Mark. Why don't you—" said Mike Klubb, who was a missile expert.

"Really, Mike. How do you know? How the *frig* do you

know? Are you a Chinese Air Force pilot?" replied Mark. The room laughed. "You know, Mike. If you worked at a for-profit company, you'd have been fired a frigging long time ago. I've been in competitive profit-and-loss environments before DIA, and they'd eat you for breakfast. Put some effort into this already. I was bothered by your effort during the last Spratly Island incident, or *lack* of effort. For Christ's sake, work this one, would you? Don't be concerned about your smoke breaks. And your timecard. And getting the appropriate amount of sick time. And getting out of work at exactly the right time every day. Just do your goddamn job." Mark's emotion against the establishment and bureaucracy was really coming out. "Yeah, *stealth*, OK?"

The radar cross signature, or RCS, was a measure of how an aircraft could be seen on radar. The larger the RCS, the easier it is to detect an object; the smaller the RCS, the more difficulty to detect it. An aircraft reflects, like a mirror, a certain amount of radar energy. There are a few reasons that determine how much electromagnetic energy is returned to the radar source, such as the size of the aircraft or missile, the material the flying object is made of, the incident and reflected angles, and the orientation of the aircraft.

A commercial airliner, such as an Airbus, will have a high RCS due to the bare metal, the curved surfaces of the fuselage and wings, and the antennas and engines that return a reflection back to the source. A stealth aircraft, designed to have a low RCS, is designed with absorbent paint and aircraft surfaces that are specifically angled to reflect the signal somewhere else other than the source. Since the early 1940s, when radar was first used, countries have been working on avoiding it and playing hide-and-seek from radar.

The Deputy director turned to his assistant and yelled over, "Jason, tell them I'm going to be ten minutes late." Calvin put his schedule back in his pocket.

"I'm intrigued, Mark. Tell me more," said the Deputy.

Mark paused to gather his thoughts. He had been successful before on hunches related to this, like the Chinese Shenyang J-31 Gyrfalcon. It was starting to hit him that this was much bigger because it involved multiple DIA directorates, but Mark considered it a potential moment to shine. He continued with his same sassy and aggressive attitude, switching hands to hold his fancy drink.

"Well, sir, the Buckley report stated that the China watch stander observed the target already in the air. No flame detection out of the silo on launch, nor a flight motor," explained Mark.

The DF-5 Chinese missile did, in fact, have a launch motor to get it out of the ground, then another engine to help it get to its destination, which should have been detected. It wasn't. Based upon history, so far, his thinking was valid.

"The SBIRS and the old-school DSP detected an initial flash, then nothing. That went on a few times. What if that flash was an aircraft's pilot, moving the throttles in and out of military power and afterburner? That would show for sure." Mark considered the technology some more. "Look. It could be all about scramjets. Those engines mix together air and liquid fuel at supersonic speeds, and could propel aircraft at hypersonic speeds—at unbelievable Mach speeds."

Mike Klubb huffed. "The Chinese don't have scramjets, Mark. Please just—"

"Hold your horses, kid. If I remember correctly, last fall, a Chinese university professor received an award from the Chinese Society for Aeronautics and Astronautics. He was able to design China's first scramjet engine. He took the top billing at the annual China Aeronautical Science and Technology Conference. The ah...the Feng Ru Aviation Science and Technology Elite Awards, if I remember correctly." A pause, then, "So, Klubber, with that, what if they were already doing it?"

Afterburner was an engine throttle setting on military aircraft. That setting on the throttle, controlled by the pilot, poured raw fuel right into the exhaust of the engines. It not only accelerated the engines and therefore the entire aircraft to incredible speeds but caused a large flame out of each engine nozzle in the rear of the aircraft, sometimes to the tune of 3,000 degrees Fahrenheit. Again, Mark's thoughts were effective in gaining looks from the audience, and a few heads were nodding.

"The Buckley team then saw it change direction, possibly because the pilot was maneuvering the aircraft," said Mark. "Maybe airspace. Perhaps deconfliction of another aircraft...or even birds. Even the flight test itself might have called for a turn or turns." Mark thought some more. "Then...the target disappeared? Yes? Disappeared? Something that has never happened before," Mark said, waving his hand around.

Mike was looking at the podium, making a note with his pen, avoiding direct eye contact with Mark. "In aviation, we call that a landing. The Buckley team thought they lost it because it didn't impact its target. Perhaps, all the pilot did was reduce the throttles out of afterburner, out of full military power, to calmly reduce speed, drop his gear, and land."

Mike looked up. He did not look at Mark but at the Deputy.

"Mark, what about those excessive speeds? Too fast for an aircraft?" asked the Deputy.

"Well, sir. No. No, sir," Mark shook his head. "Our teammates over at the ranch...Area fifty-one...already have new hybrid engines on test beds that are forecasted to easily fly into those Mach speeds," referring to the dry lake bed in Nevada, known as Groom Lake. "We are already flying some things in restricted airspace R-5808 that we can't talk about in here, but we both know the boys over at Lockheed and Air Force are working on some technology."

Groom Lake, also known as Area 51, in addition to Tonopah, was located north of Las Vegas, Nevada. The flying activities there were legendary both inside and outside the military and intelligence community, and clearance to know what went on there was always on a "need to know" basis. As it turns out, Mark never had the need to know. To his surprise, as well as the rest of the world's surprise, in late October 2013, the National Security Archive declassified much of the existence of the secret base. Stories of test-flying Soviet MiGs under the Red Eagles Program, U-2, A-12 Oxcart, and later the SR-71 Blackbird, were declassified and open to analysts and fans alike. They were absolutely fascinating reads to all. Mark enjoyed the pilot stories, the aircraft capabilities, and the work that they produced, impressed with the accomplishments from so many years ago.

Mike Klubb stood there, considering Mark's approach, and bit his lip while thinking. Then Mark delivered the final nail in the coffin. He knew this was pushing it, but he figured what the heck, he was already in the deep end of the pool.

"Sir, what if...what if the Chinese are already doing it?"

"Mark, for real? What are you talking about? We would have known already," Mike commented.

"Mike. Please," Mark told him, putting his hand up and gesturing him to be quiet.

"What if they already figured out how to design, build, and now test fly, a Chinese stealth aircraft?" announced Mark. "How do we know they didn't get the test data from Area 51...or get their engineers together and start flying something? It wouldn't be the first time, now would it?"

The Deputy stood up in the front row, and Mark slowly walked toward him. His blue-and-white checkerboard shirt contrasted terribly with the maroon carpet and seats of the auditorium. Mark said his last words loudly so everyone in the room could hear him.

"He's wearing red-and-white wrestling shoes today? Oh, brother," Emily quietly said to Robert from the back of the auditorium.

"Sir, what if they, the Chinese, already built a stealth *bomber*, right underneath our noses?"

All eyes in the room were on Mark. A number of analysts sat in silence while others were whispering again to colleagues. "Sir, let's consider that for a moment. Since the days of Sun Tzu, twenty-five hundred years ago, the Chinese have prided themselves on deception. He wrote, 'Be extremely subtle, even to the point of formlessness. Be extremely mysterious, even to the point of soundlessness. Thereby you can be the director of the opponent's fate,'" Mark said, clearing his throat quietly. "What if...what if they already are flying it? It could literally fly anywhere the Chinese wanted, worldwide, to include the United States."

Mark paused for moment then turned his head toward the wall on the left, realizing the magnitude of his theory on US national security. He shook his head gently, raised his eyebrows, and pursed his lips. "Sir. We'd never see them coming. And if we did...it'd be too late to do anything about it."

The room was silent as Mark quietly made his way over to where Klubb was standing. Klubb stood behind the podium, holding his Sharpie and wasn't sure why Mark was coming so close to him. Mark leaned over close enough so that only Mike Klubb could hear what he had to say. Klubb pulled back and scrunched his face.

"Mikey. For Christ's sake...your zipper is down," Mark whispered to him. Then he walked away.

Ellsworth AFB, Flight Line

Ford and the snowplow driver slid off the hood of the truck and fell down in-between the front bumper and the tall and wide yellow blade of the plow. The drop down to the icy pavement was actually a blessing in disguise. This small area was just enough space to fit both men safely and acted as a natural barrier to protect them from the hot gases and flames of the explosion. The blade of the plow was enormous, wider than the truck itself, and had terrific height to push thick, dense snow. This abnormal height and width may have saved both men from severe burns or worse.

Their heads were down, eyes closed, but they both felt the wave of heat pass over them. Ford was first to make a move. "Let's go! Let's go! This way!" He tugged the driver by his arm, and they crawled out on their hands and knees from their hiding space.

The driver slowly followed Ford, and they were able to crawl and then slowly jog away, toward the approaching fire trucks. The driver, dazed, stumbled and then fell. Ford couldn't tell if he slipped on the ice, or if the event just overtook him with emotion. Between the cold temperature, the high winds, the accident, and the explosion, it was a lot for anyone to take in. Ford turned back and helped pick him up off the tarmac.

"Thanks...thanks," the driver said to Ford. "What's your name?"

"Stevens. Ford Stevens. I'm the pilot on that B-1."

One ambulance stopped at their position while another few stopped at the aircrew area off near the buildings. The medical teams immediately tended to the driver and Ford, helping them into the rear of the vehicle. Ford stayed only to ensure the driver was taken care of. Then he jumped out to reach his aircrew.

The airport fire engine apparatuses approached the burning B-1, spraying dry chemical material from powerful high-capacity pumps with their water and foam cannons. The $700,000 Oshkosh Stryker high-speed fire engine, unique in look and size, was built to negotiate rough terrain inside and outside the airport area and carried large capacities of water and foam. The four-ton six-wheeler was designed to be able to accelerate from zero to fifty mph in less than thirty-five seconds. The Ellsworth Air Force Base crash, fire, and rescue team aimed the bumper and roof-mounted foam and water turrets using joysticks, and sprayed the jet from 150 feet away at twenty-six hundred gallons a minute. The twin agent nozzle/injection systems inserted a stream of Purple-K dry chemical into the foam stream to knock down the fire faster.

The second Oshkosh apparatus, looking near identical to the other, was more elevated and extended its extinguishing roof-mounted boom arm sixty feet in the air to spray foam. The third truck was Ellsworth's newest. It had a reinforced nozzle, called a "snozzle," that pierced the side of the B-1 fuselage, dispersing the form agent inside to fight the fire from the inside. The snozzle was also able to provide cover to any escaping aircrew, generating a raining "water umbrella" over the B-1s airframe at 250 gallons per minute.

As Ford stepped out and toward his aircrew mates, the driver hollered over, "Hey, thanks, Ford."

Ford gave a wave to the driver and arrived to the rear of the second ambulance, glancing over at the B-1 and watching the sun come up for the day. It would be a long day, explaining who did what, in addition to establishing a timeline to the Air Force mishap investigators. Ford was pleased no one was seriously hurt and looked down the flight line to see crowds gathering.

"How is everyone?" Ford asked his crew, seeing them all in the back of the ambulance. They gave smiles in return, and Ford was reassured they were all going to be fine.

Ford, though, may not have been fine himself. He had one hell of a headache and he was nauseated. He was in terrific physical shape, yet today, he did not feel himself at all. Something wasn't right, and Ford just could not put his finger on what was bothering him. He didn't let on to anyone of his recent condition and wanted to confide in the flight surgeon who just arrived.

"Hi, Ford, how are you feeling?" asked the flight surgeon in the back of the ambulance.

"Well, Doc, my adrenaline is pumping. Got myself a stomachache, and I'm a bit nauseated. Just don't feel myself."

"Completely normal. Let's go over to the clinic so we can do the blood and urine work. Don't worry about it. Normal procedure after a mishap. You OK with providing that?"

Quietly, Ford answered the flight surgeon. "Absolutely, Doc. Yup. Will ride over with you guys."

Before departing, he wanted to give one last zinger to the crew. "Hey, Pinky, we still have the spare aircraft. Who wants to fly this morning?" Ford asked with a smile. The aircrew all turned their heads, even McCoy, and stared at Ford with straight faces. If looks could kill, Ford would be dead.

Although Ford was joking about taking up another jet, most aircraft maintenance departments did assign aircrews a spare aircraft in the event there was a maintenance issue with the primary aircraft on start-up. Sometimes after starting a jet, a new problem could develop, and the crew would have to switch over to the spare.

Ford took his ride to the medical clinic with the doc, took out his phone and opened the text app. He saw he had a few texts but replied to only one of them. He typed to Wu.

Wu: You are never going to believe what happened today. Let's talk soon.

Defense Intelligence Agency, Bolling AFB, Washington, DC

"Well, Mark, you certainly know how to spice up the morning," commented the Deputy. The Deputy stood in front of his seat, rubbing his chin. He looked down at the ground for a brief second and then looked up. "You have your work cut out for you. Let's see the data on your concept. I like it. When should we meet again? Tomorrow?"

"Yes, sir. Totally. I'll get the team on it right away."

"For everyone in here." The Deputy director stepped forward then turned facing the audience. "I embrace diversity of thought, as you're aware, which is why I listened to this closely this morning. If Mark is wrong, so be it. He took the chance. We had nothing to lose by listening. If he is right, well, then...it changes the national security ball game, doesn't it?"

Most of the analysts quietly answered with a yes.

"Mark, if you and the crew get any hard data today, I'll need it soonest. I'm heading to the Hill later, and the director is meeting with USD (I), and he'll want to know."

The Under Secretary of Defense for Intelligence, the USD (I), is one of five Undersecretaries who report to the Secretary of Defense. A Senate-confirmed position, he is the lead intelligence officer in the Department of Defense and sits in the prestigious outer ring at the Pentagon, called the E Ring, a few doors down from the Secretary of Defense. Like a bull's-eye, the Pentagon's outer ring is the E Ring, while the innermost ring is called the A Ring. Other agencies that report to the USD (I) at the Pentagon are the National Security Agency (NSA), the National Geospatial-Intelligence Agency (NGA), and Defense Intelligence Agency, in addition to the military services, all of which have their own intelligence agency.

What complicated the intelligence community in Washington was the newly formed Director of National Intelligence position, established by Congress in 2004. The director, known as the DNI, served as the head of the intelligence community, overseeing and directing the implementation of the National Intelligence Program and acting as the principal advisor to the President, the National Security Council, and the Homeland Security Council for intelligence matters related to national security. This complicated arrangement meant that many agencies had two bosses, the Secretary of Defense and the DNI, which provided a sporty atmosphere for everything from briefs to the President to funding turf wars.

Emily stood in the rear of the auditorium with Robert, stretching her arms above her head. "That was entertaining. What team is Mark referring to?" she asked, full knowing well it was her and Robert.

Robert turned around in front of his seat to ensure he didn't leave anything. He turned back around, and Mark was there, sipping his fancy Starbucks.

"We are taking some leave...vacation and will be back in two weeks," Emily told Mark, smiling and pulling his leg.

"Very funny. Let's get back to our spaces. I've got to call out to Buckley...phone a friend," Mark said. "Well. You can't make this stuff up."

Shandan, Zhangye, Gansu Airstrip, China

Wu and Liu had completed the demo flight for the generals, admirals, and Communist Party leadership, and took the Devil Dragon outside the airport's airspace to the north to perform some repositioning maneuvers for a lineup and then checklists before landing. Wu made some tight turns to the left and right and rolled inverted and upright. Today's flight test card was VIP centric, but it also included aerodynamics and aerobatics, measuring stability, and timing of specific flight performance maneuvers. Complete with the VIP demo and test card, they slowed the aircraft down to flap speed. If they were too fast, the flaps would rip off the aircraft, causing a catastrophic failure. The pilots always checked the airspeed and shared that fact out loud with the other pilot for good aircrew coordination and communication.

"Good speed, flaps fifty," Wu ordered. *God damn, I don't feel good.* He kept the thought private as he went through the procedures.

Liu moved the flap lever, located between the two seats, and the flaps located on the wings moved down to the 50 percent position. The Devil Dragon slowed down considerably, attempted to pitch nose down due to the center of the pressure of the wing moving rearward, but she still wanted to fly due to the extreme aerodynamic shape of the machine. She was tough to slow, as Wu realized in early test flights, so he always gave himself extra space to get the speed burned off. *Perhaps spoilers should be installed on the flaps to create more drag.*

"Gear down," Wu announced.

"Roger, gear down," Liu repeated, but by accident, he transmitted his voice out over the UHF radio frequency, externally. That meant his audio transmission, his words, left the aircraft and went over the radio waves and outside the aircraft. Most likely, no one heard it because it wasn't on the airport control tower frequency. "Sorry, Wu. The intercom button and transmit button are too close to each other in here."

It was a big deal, though. For a secret and stealth aircraft to transmit, by mistake, a radio call, meant they may have disclosed not only their position but the fact that they even existed. Wu kept his concern quiet, but it was significant.

Liu moved the gear handle on the right side of the cockpit to the down position.

Wu made sure his seat harness was locked and the brakes were pumped, and then...he saw it. The right, main landing gear safety light wasn't illuminated. There should be three green lights, and they only had two illuminated, which meant they could not confirm all three wheels were down to land. One of them may be stuck in the up position. "Liu, take a look at that. The gear lights. The indicator light isn't lit." He pointed with his index finger while keeping his hand on the throttle.

"All right, let me take a peek," Liu said, eyeing the light. Liu considered cycling the gear up and then down again, thinking it would trigger the down and locked position. If the light did not say it was down, they had a real problem on their hands.

"I'll do a few circles out here before we come back inbound to the runway," said Wu. "Radar is clear, so let's troubleshoot."

One of the newest avionics screens was their onboard radar that could detect other aircraft flying near them. The Devil Dragon actually had multiple radar systems that worked in tandem. One could detect threats using a low-frequency, long-range radar. The other was a higher-frequency radar that was used to track threats and target data to intercept airborne and adversarial aircraft. Finally, there was a ground-tracking radar for vehicles and another for terrain avoidance for low-level missions.

Wu glanced over at the instruments and could see another aircraft about eighty miles to their southeast and heading in their direction. The screen displayed the Hainan Airlines Boeing 737–84P, flight number HU7840. Wu thought it was impressive, as he could see their altitude at thirty-two thousand, with ground speed of 419 knots, ground radar station F-ZLJQ1 tracking them, and the squawk code 7073. Wu smiled that he didn't have a squawk code, because they were invisible to radar.

Wu considered his landing gear options as he did left hand

turns at 160 knots at about eighteen hundred feet, which took up a few miles of airspace. He did some hard thinking about the aircraft's systems while keeping the bomber in the turn and struggling with some constant pain in his lower back. Here he was, flight testing the capabilities of the new Devil Dragon stealth bomber for the very highest of Chinese party and military leadership, including Lieutenant General He Chen, but there was no one to call on the ground in this case to ask for help because the aircraft was so new. Wu was calm, but he certainly did not like the situation.

"My head is down, checking the manual," Liu announced, but it was over the frequency again. Wu was concentrating on the flying and how it would look to the VIPs over at the airport, so he wasn't as concerned at the moment.

Wu considered a low pass again, but then Chen might see that his right main gear was not down, spinning up an already emotional man for no reason. Wu was also unsettled because Lieutenant General Chen was, for lack of a better term, a complex leader, and that was putting it lightly. *Any pilot in the People's Liberation Army Air Force would be thrilled to achieve Chen's level of military access, but should they aspire to lead like him?* Chen was a leader in rank only, and everyone knew that his success relied heavily on the backs of others. *Yeah, my back,* Wu often thought.

"With your permission, I am going to cycle the gear, then go into the back and see if I can visually check that the gear is down, through, ah...through the cockpit floor," Liu said to Wu.

"OK, do it," Wu replied. "Make it as fast as you can though, because General Chen is most likely wondering what the hell we are doing out here."

Liu cycled the gear up, then down again. The light still did not come on. Liu then unbuckled his seat belt, left the cockpit, and crawled slowly behind some of the hot electrical circuit breaker panels to peek around. He looked through the lightweight composite carbon fiber on the inside of the airframe, through the new microlattice open-cellular polymer structure of the sidewalls and floor panels, and through the miles of electrical wires. Liu stretched his head down in to the cavern and finally saw that the gear was not in the gear well, meaning it was in the down position where it should be.

Wu flew the aircraft alone for a few minutes, having the rare opportunity to just fly without being told what to do. He was just about in the Gobi Desert, on the border where the green vegetation blended with the brown sand down below. Wu had the chance to just enjoy the flight, the clear blue sky, and look down at the terrain below. He glanced out his window on the left and saw a peculiar tree in the middle of an open field. *Huh...that tree is all by itself, losing its leaves. Dying. Alone.*

Liu pursed his lips while in the far rear of the cockpit and looked away for a moment. He ran through the gear system in his head and was pleased that it was down. *Was the gear down and in the locked position? Could they land and have it collapse?* He came back and strapped in, getting his helmet back on. Moving the mic close to his lips, Liu explained the situation and what he saw.

Wu thought for a second then spoke. "Thanks, Liu. So, gear

is down. Potential issue. We may lose the gear on landing and skid down the runway. Or the light bulb might be burned out, and we have no in-flight emergency. It'd be a lot easier if we could just test the damn bulb from here on in the cockpit, versus maintenance getting it from behind the cockpit panel," Wu said aloud, not really looking for an answer. *Will make a note for maintenance.*

Wu considered what he would do if he were just flying a regular mission, but this was no regular mission. He was the aircraft commander of a secret jet that had not been unveiled to the world. It could fly anywhere China wanted without a soul seeing them. Worse yet, he had a grandstand full of the nation's leaders, including a three-star general boss whom he despised.

"OK, final decision. We are bringing her in," announced Wu, "we're landing." This time, Wu transmitted outside the cockpit by accident.

"Roger, landing checklists complete. Landing speed 142 knots. Runway is three thousand meters, er, 9,843 feet. Clear." Liu looked through the cockpit window, straight ahead. Again, the transmission was outside the cockpit on the UHF radio frequency.

Both Wu and Liu knew that this simple mistake of keying the mic the incorrect way could have huge consequences. This was at least the third time. Strict procedures in the testing phase of this aircraft prevented any transmissions for reasons of security, and here in one flight they broke the procedure three times. The magnitude of the emergency negated this small fact, but it nagged at the back of Wu's conscience during this ordeal because of its potential consequences. But there were bigger fish to fry at the moment, like landing the airplane safely in front of the Chinese brass.

Off the runway centerline, the stands were visible because of their size. This airport, chosen for its distance from most things in Asia, sat on the Gobi Desert border. To Wu and Liu, the stands were a beacon, a way point of sorts from the air. They could see one parked passenger jet sitting on a far-off taxiway from Tianjin Airlines, a white Embraer 190 with its red tail and yellow logo, but it was not a flight issue for them today.

Wu slowed the aircraft down so his airspeed indicator was in the green zone for gear speeds. He looked at the runway numbers painted on the beginning of the pavement and distance markings, then scanned the horizon. He checked his landing speeds then outside again. Wu repeated the pattern, as Liu read off the altitude from the radar altimeter.

"Looking good. Keep her coming down, Wu."

Their jet passed the altitude marker previously set for five hundred feet from inside the cockpit. A tone was heard in their helmets, notifying them of the descent.

"Runway in sight. Land," announced Liu, as he called out the altitudes. The weather was clear and visibility unlimited.

"Seventy-five feet."

They continued the approach.

"Fifty-feet."

Devil Dragon seemed to coast forever at fifty feet down the runway, but Wu was holding the nose up a bit to bleed off just a few excess knots of airspeed.

"Twenty-five feet."

This was the moment of truth. In seconds, the pride of China would either land safely, roll down the runway, and park to applause, or, burn up in a fiery ball of titanium in the middle of China.

"Flaring!" announced Wu.

"Ten feet!"

Defense Intelligence Agency, Bolling AFB, Washington, DC

One of the younger female analysts in the auditorium sat in silence in the front row, her body language displaying that she was downright aggravated about something. Both of her arms were folded across her chest and her legs were crossed. She shifted her body in the seat. Crossing and uncrossing her legs a few times, she scowled. At a glance, it seemed like she was fuming with anger and annoyance.

Her name was Ms. Michelle Boyd, a foreign-missile analyst with brown hair and a marathon runner's body. Michelle had been moving around the world for DIA for the last eight years and enjoyed the job and most of the people she worked with. She was thinking this special Buckley case would be a solid stepping-stone for her to get the GS-11 promotion she was shooting for. Educated by an information technology scholarship at the University of Scranton and born and raised in Lewisburg, Pennsylvania, her combined college education and current government job had been her ticket out of the economically depressed area of Central Pennsylvania, hoping to never return.

Her high school friends were still living there and would never understand the "secret" career path she'd taken, or the ways of the big city. They were happy marrying their local sweethearts and working in places like the Susquehanna Valley Mall in nearby Selinsgrove, Pennsylvania. Michelle was always known at home as "the friend who left us" and "she's the one with the big secret job in Washington." Comments like these bothered her a tremendous amount, because all she wanted to accomplish in life was to do better than her unemployed boozed-up mom, angry alcoholic father, and part-time power plant employee brother.

Michelle had a chip on her shoulder, though, coming from a backwoods Victorian home built in the early 1900s on Pennsylvania's Route 15, complete with chipped dirty white paint, a potholed loose-gravel driveway, her brother's abandoned cars on blocks, all located near miles of empty retail stores. Her somewhat negative attitude and short temper was derived from the so-called rich kids who attended nearby Bucknell University, where the students coming from the wealthy areas of Philadelphia, Northern New Jersey, and Long Island made fun of the locals, or "townies," as she grew up.

Sometimes the poking of fun at the locals was through the drunken fighting in the downtown bars and restaurants, where liquored-up students full of beer muscles thought they were better than the townies. It was also easily overheard on the sidewalks, or when she walked through the mall on a Saturday afternoon. Other times it was the straight-out rude laughing and pointing of the rich kids at her local friends because of their clothes, their 1980s makeup, or their outdated hairstyles.

Michelle was indeed a townie at heart and by blood, only differentiating herself by education to get out of the area. When she detected that someone with a pedigree was pompous and flaunted their money, or if some stuck-up bitch with a European automobile showed off, thinking that she was better than her, Michelle took it to heart. Deep inside, she was self-conscious, always thinking it was personal because she was from the middle of nowhere: Lewisburg, Pennsylvania. So when someone like Mark Savona came into her life and Michelle felt like she was being talked down to, it drove her crazy with fury. There was no way she was going to accept anything from this city slicker.

Putting her head down and working hard on weekends, holidays, and late nights to monitor North Korea's missile launches over the years, staying well past her eight hours a day and taking remote assignments, including two Middle East tours, Michelle thought she was pleasing her bosses and appearing on their radar. Her beef today was that Mark Savona came in and stole her show, her stepping-stone to promotion. *Who the hell is this guy? Where did he go to school? Villanova? Georgetown? Bucknell?* Michelle had worked with Mike Klubb all night on putting together the "private" brief, and then to receive no credit from the Deputy was heartbreaking. For the assignment to get moved to another directorate within DIA irked Michelle and fueled her resentment.

Michelle left the auditorium fuming, went back to her cubicle, and was relieved her coworkers weren't back yet. She put her wallet down on top of her desk calendar, glanced over at all her kitten photos, tabby calendars, cat posters, and took a deep breath. She put down her leather-bound notebook next to her wallet. *That son of a bitch!* Another deep breath. Michelle casually looked around and verified no one was present.

In the drawer on the left side of her desk were her printed Microsoft Outlook contacts from each of the jobs she had been assigned to during her career. The list was thick, bound at the top with a black alligator clip. Michelle paged through the list alphabetically, passing D and I and stopping on the S.

Moving her index finder down the page, she searched. Next page. Michelle was on the hunt for a very specific contact. She stopped at S for Senate, a job she'd held for two years just a few years ago. Her contacts there were still hot, and lucky for her, Michelle's cousin was assigned there. Michelle's former position was as the DIA liaison to the Senate Select Committee on Intelligence, located in the Hart Building on Capitol Hill.

Michelle was about to call family for a favor.

Shandan, Zhangye, Gansu Airstrip, China

"Touchdown!" Wu said loudly over the intercom to Liu, who was ecstatic at the safe landing. The red-and-white drag parachute was out, helping with the slowing of the fifteen-thousand-pound beast.

"There's our green light on the right main gear...was down the whole time," Liu said, as they landed and rolled down the runway to the end, cooling the wheels, brakes, and skin of the sleek black jet. "Damn it."

Even the tires on the Devil Dragon were special, hiding in

her airframe body landing gear wells, ensuring they wouldn't melt at such high airspeeds. Chen and his engineers mixed in aluminum with the latex during manufacturing and filled them with nitrogen at over 400 psi, knowing how much heat they would generate. As a comparison, car tires were usually filled with air at about 35 psi.

"Make a note, will you, Liu," asked Wu, "to have the ground crew take a look at that gear switch."

Wu sighed, now that this little aviation challenge had ended. They taxied up the sharp-looking jet to the front of the stands so she could be presented to the leadership of China, the ground crew hurriedly disconnecting the drag chute. Wu was proud of the jet and his flying career but not proud to be part of the Lieutenant General Chen flying team. Wu continued to have a tremendous amount of personal and professional issues with Chen, as well as the country of China, but today was the unveiling of this fantastic flying machine.

Liu unstrapped, took off his helmet, and dropped through the floor of the cockpit near the nose gear. He wanted to do a postflight exam of the jet and be outside before Wu so they could meet and greet the crowd. Chen had mentioned during preflight that he wanted both of them to meet some of the party members upon landing.

Wu sat in his commander seat on the left as his stomach acid did gymnastics. He dry heaved and coughed, then quickly took a brown paper bag out of his helmet, looked inside, and threw up in it. He figured it must have been nerves from the gear situation, so he wiped his mouth, took a drink of his water, and kept going with postflight items. No one could see him, for which he was thankful, but his medical condition was influencing his energy level. Wu grabbed a mint and hid the paper bag in his helmet.

This Chinese stealth bomber, never seen by most of the senior political leadership prior to today, was receiving her first look in front of the VIP stands. The observers looked on in awe, only imagining the insane heat and speed a jet aircraft of this kind was capable of. The attractive titanium-and-alloy construction was the first of its kind in China, and Chen took great personal pride as he saw the VIPs walk to inspect the jet. The speeds that this machine could reach were something only the United States had previously achieved, and Chen was most proud of his accomplishment.

Chen, a pilot himself, was personally involved in the design and construction of the Devil Dragon. The extremely low radar cross section and swooping angles were a complete chaotic mess for radar detection, which was what Chen desired. He also added things like the special black color to assist in the baffle of radar detection. He grabbed these ideas after visiting the Smithsonian Institution's Air and Space Museum at Dulles Airport in Virginia and receiving photos from the Air Force Museum in Dayton, Ohio. *On display for us to see!* Chen often laughed at the Americans when explaining the details to the other engineers.

The afterburner performed magnificently, and J-16 and J-20 chase aircraft in early test stages could not keep up with Devil Dragon. Her beautiful supersonic afterburner produced a diamond pattern of purple and yellow-orange in the engine exhaust. This diamond pattern was formed by the extra thrust delivered by the afterburner throttle set by the pilot, which was supersonic, making continual shock waves. Her four engines could achieve an unfathomable airspeed of Mach 5, which was five times the speed of sound. Two of the four engines were built with a special bleed valve from the compressor to the afterburner, which gave Devil Dragon increased thrust at high speeds. Sixteen feet in length and five feet in diameter, these two custom engines had an eight-stage axial flow and single-spool compressor, with a six-can annular combustor and two-stage axial flow turbine. These two Devil Dragon engines were closely held secrets and never discussed, while the other two engines were standard, high-performing turbofan engines. Her entire engine package would push the external skin temperatures to such high heat that it would melt measly conventional aluminum airplanes. Test flights early on scared the crap out of ground crews, primarily because they had never experienced the thunderous vibrations of such enormous power. During a speed-test run at altitude about seven weeks ago, the Devil Dragon created such chaotic sonic booms that a portion of the Great Wall in Jiayuguan was permanently damaged.

Chen also demanded a double-reinforced pressurized cockpit so that the pilots did not have to always wear fully pressurized space suits while flying in the stratosphere's low air pressure. At sixty thousand feet of altitude, blood can boil, and so every time Wu and Liu had a flight planned for high altitudes, they had to breathe oxygen thirty minutes prior. This was to reduce the amount of nitrogen in their bloodstream and make their bodies react to the high-altitude environment much better.

Depending on their flight test, the partial-pressure suits that they wore provided mechanical counterpressure to assist their breathing at altitude.

The airports that they were flying out of lately were already at five thousand feet above sea level. Between sea level and ten thousand feet was the physiological-efficient zone, which meant that the oxygen levels were usually high enough for Wu and Liu to fly without supplemental oxygen. The physiological-deficient zone went from about thirteen thousand feet to about fifty thousand feet, and there was always a chance of trapping gas in the body as it expanded, called dysbarism. Evolved-gas dysbarism, known to pilots and flight surgeons as decompression sickness, was when gases such as nitrogen could form in the body. This was considered an exceptional incident, but it did happen.

Above thirty-five thousand feet, an oxygen-rich breathing mixture was required for Wu and Liu to simulate the oxygen levels closer to earth, and flying Devil Dragon above forty thousand feet was almost always under positive pressure. When Devil Dragon flew above sixty thousand feet, known as the Armstrong limit, liquids in the lungs and throat could boil away. The special pressurized cockpit that Chen designed bypassed most of these limitations, and if they were scheduled for these high-altitude rides, the ground crew could suit them up in the pressurized suits as a precaution.

Devil Dragon, designed to photograph thousands of miles of terrain for analysis, collect electronic emissions, or deliver a nuclear or conventional payload, was the world's fastest jet at home and abroad. She was an aviator's dream to fly and a potential nightmare to an adversary strategist, Prime Minister, or President.

No one knew she existed.

Defense Intelligence Agency, Bolling AFB, Washington, DC

"Hi, Roger. This is Michelle Boyd from DIA. I'm looking for Jessica. Is she around?" asked Michelle.

Michelle was on hold, her foot kicked out to the side and waiting, when two of her cubicle mates came by to drop off their things at their desks. Michelle closed her eyes, hoping Jessica would be just a few seconds longer, and turned away.

"Hey, Michelle, this is Jessica. How are you, cuz?"

"Great, girl. How are you doing? What's new?"

Michelle's cubicle mates left the area and went to the bathroom. She knew they would be a few minutes, so the opportunity to talk was now or never.

"Really good. Since I saw you last, Joey and I have been talking about getting married! Ah, work is going OK, but, ummm...I'm excited! Ohh, and the chair talked to me about coming with him to work on his reelection campaign and—"

"That's so great, Jessica. I'm happy for you," said Michelle. "I don't have more than two minutes, girl, but I need a favor."

"Oh. OK. What is it?"

"The Deputy is coming over then for a Hart hearing this afternoon, right?"

"Let me check. Ah...yeah, an open hearing. Starts at two

fifteen."

"Good. Can you...pass to the chairman that he should ask the Deputy about the auditorium brief this morning?"

Silence. "Oh...kay. That's a bit weird. Why? What subject?"

"You know I can't talk about it over an open phone. Just have him ask."

"Michelle, it's an open hearing. Plus, you know he's going to ask me why and what subject."

"I know he'll ask. Don't tell him it's from me, just have him ask what the latest update is on the topic covered in this morning's DIA auditorium brief."

"I don't know about doing that, Michelle. This doesn't sound right. Are you sure because—"

Michelle was growing impatient and interrupted her. "Jessica, it will apply pressure where pressure is needed. I need, and you need, to weed out some turds who are being good-idea fairies in public and unfortunately have the Deputy's ear. We have yahoos over here shooting from the hip without any factual data, so...put it that way."

"Are you sure, Michelle? This seems like—"

"Yes, Jess. It's big."

A long silence and a huff of breath. "OK. I'll do it."

Inside Aircraft Hangar, Gansu Airstrip, China

Drinking vodka again and this time stumbling a bit, Lieutenant General Chen saw Wu and headed directly from the political and general officer reception right over to him. Wu was not fond of the lieutenant general and rarely let someone know of his emotions. Chen knew Wu was the best pilot he had in their Air Force, which was why he was selected to test fly the Devil Dragon.

"Wu Lee! Lee! I see you. Get over here!" he screamed, but the hangar was so vast and loud, not that many onlookers heard what was going on.

Wu walked over, wearing his flight gear and carrying his helmet, in addition to his helmet bag and flight notes. He had a stack of notes on his kneeboard after every flight and, whether things worked great or not during a test flight, usually typed the performance data afterward for maintenance and engineering review.

"Lee. Get out of that dirty flight suit and get over to meet with the party officials some more. They want to talk with you," Chen told him. Then squinting his eyes a bit, he eyed Lee. "You are losing some weight, Lee. You look unhealthy. Sick. Why are you losing so much weight?" Chen asked aggressively. Then without waiting for an answer, returned to the reception.

"Just exercising, sir. Running. OK, OK, I'll be right over," Wu answered to the general's back, dreading having to go over and glad-hand the politicals in the party. Wu thought about all the leaders he had in his Air Force, and there were many good ones. Unfortunately, Chen was not one of them.

Eagle Ranch Road, Elder, South Dakota, outside Ellsworth AFB

Ford Stevens was complete with his medical physical and made it home, officially exhausted. Still feeling sick to his stomach with an aching that wouldn't stop, he took some of the Tylenol and Tums the flight surgeon prescribed and plopped down on the dirty cream-white sofa in the house that he and his three roommates rented. It was midafternoon, and he would now be known as the aircraft commander of a ground mishap until he could clear his name.

Complete with full statements to the flight surgeon, wing mishap investigator and chief of the crash, fire, and rescue team, he sat in silence for a moment at the house, wondering if they were going to pin this mistake on him. Someone was always responsible in the Air Force, and after all, he did sign for the aircraft, so at that moment, he had responsibility for the jet. At this point, it was a waiting game for the Ellsworth AFB leadership to formally establish the mishap investigation board and have the pilot member of the board call him for additional statements and information. Ford was obviously concerned, because if he was found responsible, it would be the end of his flying days and his career.

Ford stood up, unzipped his flight suit, pulled it down around his waist, and tied the sleeves around himself. He bent down to get his smartphone from his lower-left side pocket on his leg. He looked at the phone, scrolled through, and saw his texts. Ford looked out the back window at the vast open space on the Dakota prairie, then back at the phone to the text app.

Wu and Ford had kept in close contact though the years.

Although from two different countries, they remained the best of friends and accomplished their mutual goals of becoming military pilots. Ever since the aviation bug bit them while white water rafting, they were both obsessed with flying.

Over the past ten years or so, Wu made it a point to visit the Stevens family just about every year, seeing them in the summers wherever they lived. Mr. and Mrs. Chad Stevens retired to Hilton Head Island, South Carolina, and Wu and the adult Stevens kids had all vacationed as a family on the beach island.

While Ford did his joint tour with the navy, flying F-18 Hornets, Wu was busy as a Class 1 test pilot student with the Test Flying Academy of South Africa. Wu was able to either fly or fly profiles in simulators for the Rafale, Mirage 2000 D/N, Typhoon, PAK FA T-50, Socata TB 30 Epsilon, Puma, Airbus A340, Tiger, Mi-24, DHC-6 Twin Otter, and Denel Rooivalk, and also the AS532 Cougar helicopter. He was also able to do a three-month fellowship after graduation with the Civil Aviation Administration of China, then three months with the China Flight Test Establishment, finishing up his training at the Nanjing University of Aeronautics and Astronautics.

Chen stacked the deck for Wu with education, assigning him and another two Chinese pilots at Nanjing to perform high-risk flight test activities, such as spin-and-stall tests for fixed wing aircraft, and engine-off autorotation and hover-diagram testing for helicopters. These fellowships led him to be an expert for Devil Dragon, focusing on his extensive flight test experience in loads, flutter, stability and control, certification, and systems development test programs. Two other pilots were qualified for

Devil Dragon stealth flight testing, but Chen had selected Wu over the others.

Working with the Devil Dragon engineers before the flight test, Wu weighed in with his research to develop efficient computational methods for large-scale fluid-structure interaction-optimization problems. His class 1 academic load also gave him enough experience in functional analysis, aeroelasticity, finite element and structural analysis, optimization, and computational fluid dynamics, all to ensure Devil Dragon was the best. Ford used to laugh at Wu's smarts, because all Ford used to say he did as a pilot was point the aircraft's nose in the proper direction, and it went kind of where he wanted. Wu never told Ford about Devil Dragon, though.

He let out a long breath and glanced out the back window facing the prairie and, further on the horizon, the mountains. Ford then went to his Google News app and checked out if the B-1 fire story at Ellsworth was on there, and it was. The Air Force had already, via their public affairs machine, released some of the details, but no aircrew names were released. That was good, he thought, because Ford had not called anyone to let them know he was OK. It would not be long before the story did release names of people involved, though.

Ford quickly considered the order of phone calls to make. First, he'd call his parents, then his girlfriend, and then his brother and sister. He scrolled through the recent calls on his smartphone and found his girlfriend first, so he changed his mind. With his thumb, he hit her name, and the phone dialed her work number.

Part 3

Diseased

Xi'an Jiakang Hospital, China

"THANK YOU FOR COMING IN TODAY," the medical doctor told the patient. "I see you have been having these symptoms for a while. And you have already sought medical care?" The doctor flipped the paperwork around, reading the reports while talking. "You are young and seem to be in good physical shape. Hmm...a few months, you say?"

"Yes, Doctor, thank you for seeing me. I have a job that allows me travel around China. I don't always get the opportunity to see a doctor, but I feel strange. I don't look myself. My stomach hurts. My lower back hurts," replied the patient. "Saw a TCM doctor recently, too."

The patient took out his phone, looked at the incoming text, and put it away. He smiled slightly at what he read but did not answer.

The medical team at Xi'an Jiakang Hospital was more Westernized and less TCM and saw all sorts of patients, from the elderly to newborns. Citizens sometimes traveled for hours from the villages in the countryside to see the doctors, while others in the city stopped in from just down the street. Some of the best Western-educated doctors were employed at Xi'an Hospital.

"You are not from around here in Xi'an. Why not see your doctor at home?" asked the nurse, standing in back of the doctor.

"Travel. I travel with my job, and it is tough to see him," replied the patient, which was not entirely true.

The doctor placed his hands on the patient's neck, just like the last one did. He felt around, pressing on his neck from below his jaw and moving his hands down to his collarbone. The doctor went back up, feeling every inch of his neck. He then stopped at a specific area and felt around some more.

"Hmm. You have enlarged lymph nodes. Quite large actually," the doctor said out loud, telling both the patient and the nurse. She took a note on her clipboard and looked up with her eyes, without moving her head. Her facial expression changed, as if she knew what all the signs were leading to. The doctor went on the check his lungs.

"Let me go check on your scans and your blood work. I'll be back in a few minutes." The doctor and the nurse left the room.

"I am very private person, Doctor. I've already put in a yuan deposit with the hospital and would like the scans and reports to only to be shared with me. Do not keep them in your database...I will take them with me when I head home. That's if I *should* take them with me, for some reason," the patient replied.

"Yes, yes. I understand, I see your payment on the charts. Back soon. Please wait here," the doctor answered.

In China, a patient had to pay the finance department before treatment began. Scans, blood work, or physical, the requirement was to have a positive balance in your account first. Money first, treatment second.

The doctor and nurse met in the hallway before going to

the nurse's station to verify some of the results on the computer screen. The doctor wanted to see the results of the blood work and CAT scan to see what they had. His gut was telling him the diagnosis, nearly screaming what it was, but he needed to verify and line up the facts first.

"Let me see his blood work," the doctor told the nurse. She handed him the report, and he read the complete blood count, CBC, for the patient. A CBC measures the amount of three types of cells in the blood: white blood cell count, red blood cell count, and white blood cell differential. "I know you're new from nursing school, so let me explain what's going on with this patient. His white blood cell count, the leukocyte count, gives us a measure of the total number of white blood cells in his sample. You know these cells protect us from infection by attacking invading bacteria and viruses, right? So some white cells also attack cancer cells. And this guy's...this patient...white count is off the chart."

"I remember, Doctor, yes..." the nurse answered.

"Yeah, and...you remember the white blood cell differential? Measures the five major types of white blood cells. You remember them from school?"

"Yes. They are neutrophils, lymphocytes, monocytes, eosinophils, and basophils."

"You are good. Very good. All right...tell me about the red blood cell count."

"Red blood cells carry oxygen. The count, called a...erythrocyte count? Gives us an indication of the amount in his sample. We measure platelet count and hematocrit. That's the percentage of blood that is made up of red blood cells, and I think I remember...hemoglobin. That's the amount...ah, the amount of the protein in red blood cells that carries oxygen."

"Well done. So, this presented case has out-of-whack numbers on that, too. He's got a real problem here. Your first complicated case."

The doctor continued reading the reports, attempting to build a picture for a diagnosis. Blood work, combined with the physical, told a partial story, but not the whole story. To be sure, the scans would have to be reviewed, and the physician would have to consult with medical experts, to see where the patient stood.

"What other tests can we do at this facility?" the nurse asked.

"Plenty, but I think between the scans and the blood work, combined with what I think is going on, we can paint a picture. We can always do immunophenotyping, to identify cells based on the types of antigens present. We can do a culture...ah, a sputum cytology, to check his lungs. You know, abnormal cells in his mucus brought up from coughing."

"Oh, my. He is...coughing a lot."

"Yes. Oh, and tumor marker tests. We could do those, too."

"What are you thinking, Doctor?" the nurse asked.

"Cancer."

Cancer is when cells develop out of control and attack other human tissues. The cancerous cells become that way due to the accumulation of defects, or alterations, in their DNA cell structure. There are specific alterations in the genetic code that are inherited from biological parents that can increase the risk of cancer, as well as some environmental factors like pollution and heavy metals in drinking water. These certain environmental factors, such as air pollution, excessive sunlight, and certain chemicals, in addition to poor lifestyle choices of tobacco and alcohol, can all lead to cancer.

They walked over to the computer station that displayed the scans on large screens. It took a brief moment for the scans to come up, and the doctor called over the radiologist and endocrinologist from the station next to them. Everyone looked on as they paged through the main scan screens, and then the medical doctors began talking through each of them.

"Your patient has a mass from here to here," said the radiologist, reading the scan and putting his finger on the touch-type screen, measuring the tumor. "It's pretty large. Pretty solid. Pancreatic. Been there for a while. You can see it has metastasized to his stomach, lungs, perhaps some other organs, and tissue. Went undetected until now."

"What's your breakdown for TNM categories?" asked the attending doctor.

The TNM categories are used worldwide for the cancer staging system. Doctors describe cancer using this system for cancer reporting, especially when diagnosing for a pathology report. T refers to the size and extent of the tumor, the main tumor being referred to as the primary. N is the number of nearby lymph nodes that are embedded with cancer. M is whether the cancer has metastasized, or spread from the primary tumor to other tissue and parts of the body. There are also numbers associated with each letter that indicate more details about the cancer.

"Ah...let's see. I give him a T3, as the cancer has grown outside the pancreas into nearby surrounding tissues but not into major blood vessels or nerves that I can see just yet. But pretty close. The mass is at five centimeters. Category N1, as the cancer has spread to nearby lymph nodes. And an M1 because the cancer has spread to distant lymph nodes and most likely distant organs. Overall? Case is a stage 3–4, worsening. Terminal," replied the endocrinologist.

"Thank you. Yeah, I agree. I performed a physical on the patient a few minutes ago, and he has pretty good lumps in his neck," added the doctor.

"Hmm...mmm. I've verified it with his blood work," added the endocrinologist. "Concur. He's definitely stage 3.5."

"We just reviewed his blood work, too. Read the CBC report. Ah, what's this here? Here," asked the physician attending to the patient, pointing to the screen with his black Sharpie marker.

"That's his pancreas. Taken completely over by the cancer. That's why you don't recognize it. That's the five-centimeter mass I measured earlier but on a different image level than the others," replied the radiologist.

"OK. OK. Thank you, Doctor. And ah...how long do you give him?"

"At best, three months. *Maybe* four months. But it could be as little as two months, as these are large right here. Here. And here. We can't see how embedded it is above his neck. We should also CT his upper body again and his brain," answered the endocrinologist.

A CT, also known as a CAT scan, are distinct X-ray scans that generate cross-sectional images of the human body using X-rays and a computer. The scans are also known in the medical community as computerized axial tomography, or CAT.

"Can we do anything else to help?" asked the patient's doctor.

The endocrinologist shook his head, "Nah, not this far along. I'm surprised he can function this well. If he was maybe a bit earlier, we could have performed the Whipple procedure—ah, you know, surgery—but not when it's caught on like this and spread." He pointed to the scans. "It's everywhere. We all know that by the time the patient knows something isn't right on pancreatic, it's too late. Soon, he'll need painkillers. And then a morphine drip. Bedridden. Only a matter of time, maybe four to six weeks, before he'll need that level of care."

The doctors looked over the additional scans, scrolling over the screens. They chatted some more looking at the tissue, the slices of the cancer, and where it attacked his body. The initial CT scan only did a short scan, to see if there was anything present, which there was. The patient would definitely need to be rescanned to establish a new baseline, but there was sufficient data presenting itself to be a definite concern.

The doctors shut the screens down before they could see the patient's name again. It would take about a minute to restart the screens and have them warm up, so the attending physician turned to the nurse standing just behind them.

"Nurse, let's cut him a prescription for a few bottles of capsules of Tramacet for the pain and give him a few Zamadol bottles to take with him. Can't believe he's not on morphine yet. And, the...ah...the patient—what is this patient's name and age again?" asked the doctor.

"Let me see. Name. Name..." She picked up her clipboard and turned it sideways to see what was written on the side of the folder and paperwork. "I have it right here."

Defense Intelligence Agency, Bolling AFB, Washington, DC

"Hello, Ford, how are you, love?" Emily answered at her desk. With her thick British accent, it sounded like "Hah-low, Fooord, ha ah yeh, luv?"

Ford and Emily met when she was working at Harrods on Brompton Road in London, five years ago this September. Ford was working on the US European Command staff and visiting the US embassy in London for a briefing with the defense air attaché, when he visited the world-famous department store.

Walking through the ground floor of the legendary store, he passed the jewelry department on the main aisle, and that was when he spotted a young blond bombshell standing behind the glass counter in the diamond section. Emily was working part-time at Harrods for some spending money during her college days, and she enjoyed working at the mythical and well-known store. Ford walked right over to her, struck up a conversation about nothing, and was smitten with her petite size, long blond hair, and attractive British accent.

Little did Ford know that while she was an undergraduate taking finance at the University of Westminster, one of her college professors from Global Financial Markets 401 class recruited her for MI6. Emily had the right mix of emotional intelligence required for the job. Her special ability to read other people's emotions, handle herself with confidence, and her ability to persuade, made her a great fit for Her Majesty's Intelligence Service. Sprinkle her physical-fitness lifestyle into the mix, and Emily was a perfect member of the clandestine team.

Ford was busy with United States European Command business and then transitioned back to flying when she went through the application process, so he continued to have no idea of her true occupation. Ford thought she was employed at the International Monetary Fund, the IMF, on Pennsylvania Avenue in Washington, DC. *Or was it the World Bank?* This position explained her frequent moves throughout the globe.

"Good, good, Emily. How are you?" Ford replied, not wanting to lay into the accident details just yet.

"Very good. We are just getting ready for a meeting with my team. May I please call you back?" Emily asked, looking at the cubicles and seeing Mark and Robert giving her the hang up the phone signal with their hands and laughing.

"Well, uh, I just wanted to let you know there was something at work today. You may see it on the news," Ford said. "A fire. One of the air base snowplows was plowing the runways on the tarmac where the jets were, and it hit us in the right wing before we started it up for our flight this morning."

"My goodness. Are you OK? Was there any damage?"

"Actually, yes. Wait, no, I am fine. And so is the crew. But, yeah, it started a fire, and a jet was lost. An explosion. No one hurt, though."

"Wow. Wow. I'm so sorry this happened. But happy to hear that everyone is OK. How were you involved?"

"I'm OK. Look, maybe we talk later about it?"

"Of course. Gotta run. I'm so happy you're all right. Talk later. I love you."

"OK, talk later. See you Friday night." Ford pressed the red button on his smartphone to hang up the phone.

It was not lost on Emily that he didn't reply, "I love you, too." She sat in her seat while her team was walking off toward a small meeting room they had in their office section. Emily glanced over at a framed photo of the two of them on the beach from earlier in the year, sitting on a blanket and smiling. She didn't think much of his reply, considering the fire he was just in, but she did find it peculiar.

Senate Select Committee on Intelligence, Hart Building, Room 219, Capitol Hill, Washington, DC

Two black Chevy Suburbans were already parked in front of the DIA headquarters entrance and waiting for Deputy Calvin

Burns to come down stairs for his trip to Hill. Outfitted with up-armored plates, antiflat tires, tinted bulletproof windows, and a roof rack of antennas for complex communications gear, the mini motorcade was ready for nearly anything. At a minimum, the low-profile vehicles presented a high-visibility image because of the way the drivers followed one another so closely. In a city that prided itself on titles and status, arriving to a committee hearing on Capitol Hill with a personal protective detail was the only way to do DC business.

The Deputy entered the second vehicle via the backseat, and others were seated and waiting for him. Up front were two men in suits, armed with Sig Sauer P228 pistols and M-4 rifles, and in the rear was his executive assistant, Jason Cohen. Jason was armed with a thin three-ring binder and a Blackberry.

"Good afternoon, sir. In the binder you'll see tabs of the topics expected to be covered later today. In the front is your opening statement, followed by the first tab. That's the DIA budget with regards to MIPR...and the second tab is NIPR," Jason said.

The US intelligence budget consisted of all the funding for the sixteen agencies of the US intelligence community, including DIA. The DIA fit into one of the intelligence budget's two components, the National Intelligence Program (NIPR) and the Military Intelligence Program (MIPR). Before the DIA could spend any money on intelligence, the cash had to be authorized and appropriated by committees in both the Senate and the House of Representatives.

"OK, thank you, Jason. Any questions from the PSMs that

have come up since we talked the other day? How about the committee members?"

"No, sir. I called over there to the professional staff members earlier this morning and nothing was mentioned. Good to go, sir. Should be a no-brainer. Ah, just as a courtesy reminder, this is an open session today."

The PSMs, or professional staff members, were powerful and influential staff officers who worked directly for the chairmen of committees. When they spoke, people listened, and it was often assumed that they always had the ear of the committee members. It was an indication of where the power was, as the Deputy was asking about the staff and not the members themselves.

Jason led the Deputy to the holding room off the floor of the committee room, where there were seats and couches, in addition to bathrooms, tiny meeting rooms, and light refreshments. Sometimes the committee members would come in and stop to discuss private matters or even rehearse questions and answers for the public record. It was a delicate dance while in the committee room and very much a theater show, where the public might think the answers were off the cuff. When the cameras were on, it was show time. No members visited Calvin Burns this morning.

A young, pretty college girl, most likely from the George Washington University Capitol Hill Internship Program just a few blocks away, entered the holding room and opened the door slightly. "OK, sir, we're ready," she said with a Midwestern accent, opening her arm and palm, showing the Deputy where the witness tables were located.

The Deputy walked in the large room with cathedral ceilings, shook hands with the few members present, and sat down at his long witness table. Jason put his prepared opening statement in front of his seat. Jason then sat down directly behind him and was fully ready to pass up answers to questions via handwritten note as he had for so many of these proceedings. His backup to get instant answers to unknown questions during a proceeding was to send a note using his Blackberry to a DIA member back at headquarters.

Behind the large desk that dominated the room from wall to wall was where the senators sat, facing the witness table with briefing books, notebooks, handwritten notes, and an on/off button for their personal microphone. Sometimes each senator would stop briefly with a member of their staff to chat about an upcoming vote, a recent phone call, or even an update on a world event. This morning, though, it was different for Senator Tim Ricks, the committee chairman.

Senator Ricks thrived on stirring the hornet's nest because he knew any publicity was good publicity. And if Senator Ricks's staff got a hold of potential or controversial information, he wanted to know about it. After all, this was politics, and he wanted to know so he could use that information to his advantage. So when his staffer, Jessica, reported in to him as she had been trained in the ways of Washington with a potential DIA auditorium issue, the senator was most pleased. "Thank you, Jessica. I'll bring it up for sure," he told her, smiling deviously, giving her a little wink.

The chairman opened the hearing up with the usual protocol of the Senate and this committee. Nearly all of the members of the committee were present halfway through the opening statement, but that was not always the case. Usually, the members came in late and left early, only coming to ask their one or two questions to the witness on camera and then depart.

"Ah, Mr. Burns, go ahead with your opening statement," the chairman directed.

"Good afternoon, Mr. Chairman, and ladies and gentlemen of the committee. It is with great honor that I appear before you this afternoon to represent the great men and women of our civilian workforce, in addition to our thousands of professionals in our armed forces. I am here this morning to discuss the upcoming Defense Intelligence Agency fiscal year budget request. The Department of Defense released today the MIP appropriated top line budget for the fiscal year. The total MIP budget, which included both the base budget and overseas contingency operations appropriations, was $16.8 billion. The department determined that releasing this top line figure does not jeopardize any classified activities within the MIPN or other MIP budget figures or program details will be released, as they remain classified for national security reasons..." the Deputy spoke into the microphone, continuing on for a few more minutes.

"Thank you for your opening statement, Deputy Burns." The senator leaned forward in his seat and turned his head to the left. "We'll, ah, we'll ensure your opening statement makes it into the record."

The television cameras were all on in the room, and the

murmuring in the rear of the room was heard as political junkies, reporters, and tourists looked on, but it was not disturbing. Nearly anyone with an Internet connection could watch the hearings live, too, or look up the schedule in the *Washington Times* to attend in person. There was no question that this was live theatrics, and if you were sitting at the witness table, you had to be ready for anything. You had to be ready to perform, and Calvin Burns knew the game.

"Ah, Mr. Burns, I'll open up today's questions for the committee," as he covered the microphone with his hand and spoke to another young, college-aged girl on his staff, for one last clarification on a separate, upcoming vote.

The Deputy took a drink of water and then looked at the Senator from Vermont, Tim Ricks.

"Thank you, again, Mr. Burns. I usually would open up a session today with something related to the great state of Vermont. As you know, our Air National Guard has contributed to these wars for many years and made great strides fighting terrorism with our proud 158th Fighter Wing. I sure do love visiting home, meeting our brave men and women working and flying the F-16s from Burlington. But something has come to my attention this afternoon that I would like to ask you about. Something *very* interesting."

Never miss a moment to praise constituents from the home state.

"Yes, Senator. I am familiar with the 158th and their mission," replied Deputy Burns as Jason shifted the weight in his seat, curious where the senator was going.

"It has been presented to me that you had a significant meeting this morning in your auditorium. You met with your folks?"

All eyes in the room were upon him, and the red light on the two cameras were illuminated and pointing in his direction. Out of the corner of his eye, he saw another two senators sat down with their assistants.

Shit. Shit. Shit. Calvin Burns immediately wondered two things. *Why is he talking about the auditorium meeting for, and why would he be bringing it up here and now?*

Xi'an Jiakang Hospital, China

The nurse fumbled around for a bit more, then read the patient's name out loud. "Lee, Wu. Age twenty-nine."

"OK, thank you. Mr. Wu...Lee."

The doctor came back into the room, along with the nurse, and sat down with Wu. He pulled up the screens, and Wu was eager to see to see what the diagnosis was, if anything.

"Hello, Doctor. How did the results look?" asked Wu.

About five seconds of silence passed, and only electric fans embedded in the ceiling could be heard.

"Mr. Lee, I'm sorry. What I am going to tell you will come as a shock. You have cancer," the doctor told him. He hesitated before saying anything else so that it could be comprehended. "The cancer most likely began in your pancreas, and it has, unfortunately, spread throughout your body. It is very hard to detect the cancer there, and it grows undetected in the human body until it is too late to do much, if anything, about it. It seems that is the case with your cancer. Pancreatic cancer...is very difficult to detect."

"Cancer? Me? *I* have cancer? *Me*?"

"Mr. Lee, yes, I'm sorry to share with you this news. Cancer. It will only be a few weeks more before the pain from your stomach area where your pancreas is located will really begin to be intense. You will feel nauseated most of the time and throw up often. Holding down food will be an issue, and you'll drop more weight than you said you have lost already," the doctor said.

"Cancer. Cancer? *Cancer*? Wow," Wu said stoically, but the emotionless man began tearing up as the reality of the situation set in.

"You may have two or three months remaining with your terminal cancer, Mr. Lee. We can make you feel comfortable and make sure you have dignity."

The doctor and nurse had an excellent bedside manner and talked with Wu for over an hour. It was important to them to give him the best care they could, considering the situation. The nurse wrote most of the information down on some documents, intended to be scanned and sent to Wu as attachments for reference.

Wu was in tears now, crying, but not sobbing uncontrollably. "I wanted to get married. I wanted to have children." He wiped his nose with a tissue. "Are you sure? Me? *Me*?"

"Yes, we understand, Mr. Lee. I know this comes as a true

shock. There were two other doctors besides myself that reviewed the scans and blood work. No mistakes about it as the evidence is pretty clear. Again, I am sorry," replied the doctor.

"Is there anyone we can call for you?" asked the nurse.

Wu thought about it, and there really wasn't. He was an only child, and his mother had passed away three years ago. Wu's father died when he was a small boy, and he lived alone. Wu lived the pilot's lifestyle and had plenty of girlfriends over the years, but he just never settled down with anyone. He always thought he had plenty of time for that.

"No, no, there is no one here. Local, that is. I do have some very close friends that I consider family members, but they do not live close," Wu answered, thinking of Ford Stevens and the Stevens family in America. "I...I will ask them to take care of me. Thank you."

Wu walked outside the hospital with his paperwork in hand, discharged, and never felt lonelier than this very moment. It was the loneliest he ever felt in his life. More tears rolled down his cheeks, and he stood on the busy sidewalk with his arms folded, just looking at the people, all going about their business.

He took out his phone, saw the text from Ford and replied.

Ford, Let's talk soon.

Earlier, above the East China Sea, forty-two miles southwest of South Korea

The US Air Force RC-135 Rivet Joint surveillance aircraft out of Kadena, Okinawa, Japan, was flying in a holding pattern at forty-one thousand feet in left hand turns along a 010 and 190 degree path. Using the call sign "ROCK 23," her technicians and operators in the rear, all wearing flight suits, were working electronic warfare gear to listen and collect adversary radar signatures, pinpoint exact locations of transmissions, aircraft frequency use, GPS communications, and computer transmissions, and they were enormously busy. The array of antennas attached to the fuselage and wings was overwhelming to the untrained eye, as they popped out wherever you looked. If something was transmitting in the electromagnetic spectrum, they could find it.

"Center, ROCK 23, request," the pilot asked on the VHF frequency that controlled the airspace between North Korea and China.

"Go ahead with your request, ROCK," replied the center controller.

"Any chance we can extend our legs today. Looking for another ten miles or so to the north on A-326, just past intersection MUDAL."

A pause of white space on the frequency, most likely while he looked up on the radar scope.

"Approved, ROCK 23. Continue to hold as requested. You're cleared up to DONVO intersection on G-597. Come back to me on this freq when you are complete."

All aviation intersections, usually the crossing of two invisible roads in the sky, or airways, were labeled with a five-letter identifier nickname. MUDAL and DONVO were intersections in the airspace off Korea and China on airways A-326 and G-597.

The specialists in the back, monitoring all sorts of things from a whole host of countries, intercepted some unique transmissions through the years. Sometimes it could be a phone call, or a training mission, or a local radio station broadcasting unique news stories. Using their direction-finding equipment, they could sometimes get an exact location of where someone was transmitting and listen in, no matter what the device or language.

Sergeant Rae Davis, a three-year member of the Eighty-Second Reconnaissance Squadron and a linguist in Mandarin, was monitoring a variety of frequencies, scanning the UHF bands to see what she could detect. *Whoa, what's this?* she said to herself, listening in. "Hey, listen to these Chinese pilots on button three in Section A5...ah...correction, A6. A6," said Davis to another one of the operators flying a console in the rear of the Rivet Joint.

She turned to her supervisor in the rear of the aircraft, Technical Sergeant Frank Franklin. "His stuff is encrypted. Pretty good technology...new? I filtered it...out twice, ran it through the box, and retuned. Radical avionics gear, but we can hear him." Davis ran her fingers through the walled equipment. "Interesting. Huh. If I use the radar scanner to see what he's flying, I come up with nothing. No returns."

"You can hear him but not paint him?" asked Franklin, the supervisor, listening in the back on his headset. "For real?"

They would not be able to see the aircraft from this distance but could send an electronic signal out and usually receive it back, and the computers would tell them if he was flying a crop duster, a helicopter, or a modern fighter.

"Yes, Sergeant. Pick him up to monitor on button three," replied Davis.

Franklin did as Davis asked but couldn't get anything. "Nothing there. Play it back for me," he asked.

"All right, here it is: 'Roger, gear down,' and then a few minutes later, 'Roger…landing checklists complete. Landing speed 142 knots. Runway is 3,000 meters or 9,843 feet. Clear.'"

"Odd, er, abnormal. No landing clearance from tower? And no radar signature?" asked Franklin.

"No. Just the transmissions," Davis replied. "Wait…wait. He's got a data downlink system for the engine performance. Can't see the full readout, but he…has…let's see here. He has four engines. Looks like two of one type, and…two of *another*? Ah, he's also using an encrypted GPS for his navigation, off…ha! Three of *our* satellites. Shit, the Chinese are using our satellites for navigation! No kidding?"

The engines were able to transmit performance to an onboard smartphone to capture data because the Devil Dragon was not fully operational yet. Most business and commercial jets transmitted their performance via satellite for maintenance reasons, as do test aircraft, but tactical aircraft do not. Especially this one.

"He's using GPS satellite birds USA-248, USA-258, and USA-260," said Davis.

"Nice. Got to love it. The Chinese are using *our* GPS satellites. Well…we got him. Tab it on the tapes so we can bring it home. Good work, gang," said Franklin.

P-3 Orion over northern Myanmar (Burma)

US Navy Lieutenant Commander Earl Brooks was essentially out for a joy ride, taking the P-3 Orion aircraft out with his crew to get his monthly flight time boosted up before he applied for a position at United Airlines. He despised the office life back in the navy squadrons and was thrilled to do some joint training in Rangoon, Burma, when the mission came down from US Pacific Command. "Train and fly with the Myanmar Armed Forces" was how the message traffic read, and he and the crew didn't skip a beat in volunteering. The only requirement was that the P-3 had to fly "hot;" that is, the aircraft had to have all its special mission equipment "on and scanning" when flying. The crew loved the nightlife, so they flew eagerly so they could enjoy the liberty call. Translation for Earl Brooks and crew in Burma: beer and women.

The Lockheed P-3 Orion, on loan from the joint 455th Air Expeditionary Wing at Bagram Airfield, Afghanistan, was not your father's standard turboprop airplane. This gray airframe offered the US Navy and joint intelligence community military more endurance, allowing greater time in the air. This standard P-3 fuselage looked like it was on steroids. It performed overland surveillance on moving targets, had a synthetic aperture radar—an electro-optical and infrared system, known as EO and FLIR—and a streaming video data link. It also had a distinguished magnetic detection boom, used for submarine hunting, pointing out the back. It was a high-performance turboprop with a pressured cabin with crew of eleven, and it was nothing close to a small business jet in both speed and luxury. In fact, navy P-3s were being replaced by the Boeing P-8, which was why Earl Brooks was massaging his apps for United Airlines.

Its latest piece of gear was not only eyes in the sky but also ears. The DroneShield detector, bolted to the fuselage of the Orion just under the right wing, could listen, rather than look, for potentially dangerous airborne threats. The usual threat detected by DroneShield was drones, but the system could cross-reference the audio it picked up to determine sonic signatures and find a match. Routinely found on office building roofs, prisons, airports, and other sensitive government facilities, the military found a way to use this system wisely. They also had a StingRay system that could scan phones and ground towers.

Navy Lieutenant Commander Earl Brooks did as instructed by flying hot and always landed on time. The naval flight officers (NFO) in the rear retrieved the blue box from the rear of the P-3 by unlocking a compartment door upon landing, pulling the box that made recordings, and locked it back up again with the aircraft keys. As long as Brooks and the crew were flying regularly at Yangon Airport and not chained to the cubicle life, they didn't care what the antennas were doing.

He then had the aircraft towed inside the hangar that the navy rented for them. Once inside the hangar, the ground crew chocked the wheels, thanked the aircraft tow driver, and departed for the hotel on Merchant Road in Rangoon.

The forty-six-minute trip was without traffic, and the P-3

crews in their vans found it to be a nice drive this time of day. Earl's van had *Voice of America* on the FM radio and was closely following the news back in the States. Upon arrival to the hotel, Earl and one of the rear NFOs hit the business center in the lobby and made a secure, encrypted connection over the hotel Wi-Fi via a laptop. They needed to transmit the secure data from the flight to the Joint Intelligence Center in Hawaii, and this was the safest method to do it while traveling. Blue box to laptop, data to Hawaii, and they'd soon be downing cold brews.

Navy Chief Petty Officer and Intelligence Analyst Stan Michaels was on duty in the Hawaii Joint Intelligence Center and received the downlink from Burma. Stan Michaels, forty-four years old, smart and as sharp as a tack, was a technical analyst on his third deployment tour to support the US Pacific Command mission. He usually provided advice on foreign and adversarial militaries to the combatant command leadership and staff, but today he was just scanning the technical information from Earl's P-3 flight. Stan was a mechanical engineer from Lehigh University, but he started learning the technical intelligence information after obtaining a defense contracting job about sixteen years ago. After becoming bored with his engineering bench-testing position at Northrup Grumman in Amherst, New York, after a few years, he researched the navy option and enlisted.

Stan saw the data come in from Burma, and he scrolled through it on his computer screen. The usual data collection ranged from business calls to television shows to firefighting and police radios transmissions. He checked out the radar feeds, but nothing caught his eye. Stan went page by page on the displayed data, checking out the maps, commercial traffic, and cell towers. Then, something made him stop and stare.

He wrinkled his face. "Weird. What the heck are these signatures?" he said aloud to himself. "Never saw these before."

Stan, and the advanced software program that sifted through large amounts of data, had discovered a few unique items. The acoustical signature discovered by DroneShield was not in the database, which was rare. The second item the software program found was a unique phone number, which by itself was not unusual but, when combined with the data Stan found, was peculiar. The special Orion that Earl Brooks and his eleven-person crew was flying had the ability to pretend to be a cell tower, thereby rerouting all the calls in the vicinity through the aircraft. This well-known technology, called StingRay, was how the DEA and FBI were catching bad guys back in the States. The DIA could do it, too, and was able to grab actual phone numbers, their phone and text lists, and the phone's geographic locations.

Stan also checked out the EO and FLIR images and was fascinated by something. He was able to capture what he thought was the signature of an aircraft with unusual skin and engine exhaust temperatures, but he could not make it out due to the distance. *How could this be? The skin was six hundred degrees? Not too shabby*, he thought, but the combination of all these strange things had him perplexed.

Stan pulled up a digital map of China that overlaid the thousands of phones that were intercepted. He could see nearly everything about the phone but, more important, which towers were transmitting the signals. What caught Stan's eye was that one phone was jumping around from cell tower to cell tower at alarming speed. At one point, the time/date stamp had a specific phone signal at a location in the Shandan and Zhangye area of China, and minutes later the phone was connected to the tower in Dehong, way, way in the south. Hundreds of miles to the south. Then again, just minutes later, the same phone was detected in Kunming, then Chongqing, Hebi, then along the Mongolia border, and remained in Shandan again. *Impossible distances.* The distances between the towers were obscene, ranging into the hundreds—and at one point, over a thousand—miles from one another. In each city, the cell towers would ping the cell phone and register the time.

This is absolutely bizarre. How could a cell phone travel to all those places, thousands of miles apart, so fast? He thought about it, downloaded the contents of the phone and its numbers, and wrote up a report for the joint intelligence, known as the J2, database. *This is for someone at headquarters to sweat over,* Stan thought.

Defense Intelligence Agency, Bolling AFB, Washington, DC

"Yo, we need to do some work, kids," Mark told the team. In the small meeting room with no windows was a rectangular table that sat six, along with a whiteboard with some dry erase markers.

Mark stood to write down tasks for the team, only to find no ink in two of the markers. He dumped the black and green markers in the small trash can and walked over to the phone.

"Where is Emily, already?" Robert asked aloud, knowing she was still back in the cubicle area.

Emily was hanging up the office phone when she decided to take a peek at some of the intelligence reports on her computer before heading to the team meeting. She looked at the agenda of the chairman of the Joint Chiefs of Staff, status of US and UK forces, the recent open contracts signed by the different countries, US Congress and political news, and some cyberreports. Last, she scrolled down to US aircraft reporting by date, searching by geographic location at reports filed by aircrews from around the world.

Her eyes opened as wide as saucers. "Oh boy."

Emily had spotted and read a Rivet Joint report, taken about fourteen hours ago. She read the script about the Chinese pilot's dialogue, and the analysis from the collectors about how they usually had a radar signature from what type of aircraft it was. This report mentioned specifically that no aircraft was identified because it had no radar signature.

"No signature?" Emily blurted. "What—it has to have one. Unless. *Unless...*"

She hit print and took the job off the printer. Emily ran down the hall to the meeting room, only to find Robert sitting there and Mark on the speakerphone.

"Yup...yup...OK. Yeah. What about the flashes your guys saw in the beginning?" Mark was asking the person on the other end of the phone.

Emily was jumping up and down. "Hang up, hang up, hurry

up," she kept whispering to both Robert and Mark.

"Understand, Jeff. Just wanted to understand those initial flashes. Thank your guy, Sox, for me, too," Mark said. "Right. Got it and take care."

Emily figured he was on the phone with Buckley AFB from when they originally detected the flashes from the SBIRS satellite.

"OK, man. Thanks again. Rock on," Mark told him, and he hung up.

"What, are you in the sixties? Rock on?" Robert said.

"Look! Everyone shut it!" Emily commanded.

The men looked at her, and they immediately obeyed and quieted down.

"Hush. I just read a report from the Eighty-Second Reconnaissance Squadron from Kadena. A Rivet Joint crew who were doing collection on China a few hours ago, flying off North Korea over the water. They intercepted a Chinese flight crew putting down their gear."

"So what?" exclaimed Robert.

"Shut up and listen. When they scanned the area with radar to get a signature, nothing was there," Emily said excitedly.

"No radar signature?" Robert asked.

"*No radar signature*? NO RADAR SIGNATURE!" Mark repeated loudly.

"Woo-hoo. That's our girl!" Mark yelled out, ecstatic with joy.

Emily looked quickly at her watch to see what time it was and saw it was getting late.

"Oh, brother. Look at the time! I've got to run home and

then to the airport. Are you guys OK without me? Wait, why am I asking? Don't call me. You two *can* handle this without me."

"We promise we won't call you. Really. Unless we do another report scrub and find something blazing hot," Mark told her.

"Yup. Blistering hot," Robert added.

"No. No. No way. Don't call me. Please don't call. I'm picking up someone at the airport and have a big weekend planned," Emily said and then departed DIA headquarters for home and then Ronald Reagan National Airport in Arlington.

Bollocks...I know they are going to call me, she said under her breath.

Senate Select Committee on Intelligence, Hart Building, Room 219, Capitol Hill, Washington, DC

"Ah...yes, ah, Senator, I meet with my staff all the time," replied the Deputy.

"Well, if I understand correctly, it was quite a meeting. Please elaborate on the nature of your discussion," asked Senator Ricks.

Calvin Burns's facial expression said it all, and it was not a positive appearance. Burns knew that the senator knew, and

Burns was caught unprepared. Nor was he ready to discuss something this early in the process.

"Not at this time, sir. Once I can get further information, I would be happy to discuss it further."

"Mr. Burns, this committee has oversight of DIA. Yes? And when we ask a question related to military intelligence, we expect it to be answered."

Jason was panicked, wondering what was going on. He immediately texted his point of contact, Jessica, to ask.

"Yes, Senator, I understand your responsibility and the responsibility of the committee," replied the Deputy, "but I am not at liberty to discuss the nature of the meeting at the moment."

"Mr. Burns, what was the nature of the discussion?"

Calvin Burns did not expect this line of questioning and knew that the PSMs had ample opportunity to call him ahead of time, meet with him privately, or ask just moments before the hearing began. This interrogation was for the cameras.

"Senator, I appreciate your question. I would be happy to take your question for the record and get on your schedule soonest."

"No, Mr. Burns. It is this committee's understanding that your meeting was about a significant national security issue, and we feel that as oversight of DIA and the other Defense Department intelligence agencies, we have a right to know what you know. Now, what went on?"

Calvin paused. "Senator, that's classified, and this is an open hearing. We can either go closed, or it will have to wait. I'm sorry. Do you want me to stop?" replied the Deputy.

The senator and Calvin Burns had an old-fashioned staring contest.

"Well, Mr. Burns, no, we do not need to stop this hearing. But this committee wants to know. You've piqued my interest, Mr. Burns."

Calvin Burns thought for a moment about how the news of a possible Chinese stealth bomber could have gotten over to the Hill that fast. It didn't surprise him though, but it was going to make things tough for Mark Savona for his team with the latest Hill interest. More like pressure.

"Yes, sir. I assure you that myself, or the director, will come over and give you a full brief," replied the Deputy.

"I yield the remainder of my time back to Senator Wilson, the distinguished gentleman from New York," said Senator Ricks.

Jason thought this was very unusual, and from the look on the Deputy's face as he turned around in his seat to give Jason a look, so did he. The remainder of the hearing was uneventful, and Jason continued to monitor his e-mail for a reply from Jessica.

The men departed Hart Building's room 219 down the large and wide staircase near the elevators that led to the open atrium, walked past the uniformed Capitol police, and headed for the vehicles parked on C Street, Northeast.

"Well, that was interesting, Jason. Did you have any knowledge of what he was getting at?"

"No, sir. *No knowledge.*"

Deputy Burns smiled and said, "Shit. We can't talk about it here...the senator was fired up, though."

The Deputy and Jason got into the Suburbans and got on Second Street south toward the Navy Yard. They stopped off at Second and M Streets to get a late lunch at Five Guys Burgers and double-parked out front. To the locals, it was completely normal to see a mini motorcade like this in town. To the visitors from out of town, though, the sight of two black trucks with dark windows, complete with guys wearing earpieces, was a treat.

Jason's Blackberry vibrated with an inbound text. He read off the e-mail silently, then to the Deputy aloud. "Sir, our liaison, Jessica, said she was not aware of the topic Senator Ricks was interested in, and it's not in her portfolio."

Being a former liaison himself, Calvin Burns nodded, understanding the game. He smirked and nodded slowly. "OK, got it." Calvin remained silent for a moment, then turned to Jason. "It's in her fucking portfolio, believe me. Please. Make sure Mark Savona and his team are on my schedule Monday." The Deputy knew he was being played.

Washington, DC

Ford Stevens took American Airlines flight 5379 via Detroit and landed at Ronald Reagan National Airport a bit later than planned. He took out his phone on landing rollout and texted Emily to say he landed, mentioning that he was sincerely excited to see her again.

"I'm here! Can't wait to see you! I love you."

Ford thought maybe the B-1 fire came at just the right time for him personally, as a week off from the squadron commander was great timing. Ford was also still bothered by the pending investigation and dreaded the future interviews that came with it. He wasn't overly concerned as there was nothing he or his crew could do about a snowplow hitting his aircraft (other than make sure everyone got out safely), but there was always that chance. In typical US Air Force fashion, he would not be flying again until the mountains of paperwork were complete and appropriate regulations were pored over, which was what truly irked Ford. For the time being, he was very happy to see Emily again, and he plowed through the TSA exit gate with his wheeled carry-on to find Emily.

"Hello again, girl," he said, giving her a big hug. They kissed.

"Hello, love, I've missed you. Thank you for making the trip again. I know you are busy," Emily told him, as they walked through the airport terminal to the Metro station.

They stood outside on the platform, looking at the city in the distance to the north, then looking at each other. From an observer's point of view, they looked like a happy couple in love. And they were. The Blue Line Metro train arrived so they could head to Emily's apartment in Rosslyn, Virginia.

They sat on the orange plastic seats. Ford turned to Emily. He smelled her perfume and hair. He loved it. Then he whispered, "I've missed you so much. Between the fire, my flight schedule, and all the travel, I'm so happy to see you." Ford reached for both her hands.

"I've missed you, too, love. Thank you for coming."

They arrived in Rosslyn, dropped off his luggage at her

apartment quickly, and walked over the Potomac River on the Key Bridge into Georgetown. Their favorite restaurant and bar was Clyde's on M Street NW near Wisconsin Avenue, and the fifteen-minute walk in the cold evening air would be nice.

"This is striking, Ford. Look down there at the river. All the city lights reflecting off...it's beautiful," Emily noted.

"It is stunning, although I'm glad to see you don't have any snow yet here," Ford replied, enjoying the pause in their conversation. "Look, Emily. Let's stop for a second. I'm sorry I did not reply earlier to you on the phone when you said 'I love you.' I was under some stress from the mishap at work, not feeling well with a stomach thing, and just arriving back to the house. You know that sometimes I am not a man of words. Please know that I love you," Ford said, ensuring that he relayed his feelings to her. The bridge and breathtaking view felt like a great spot to do it.

"Thank you, Ford. It did bother me, but it's OK now. I understand," Emily said, kissing him again and holding his hand. "My work has been both stressful and stimulating, too. Some new things have popped up, and it's keeping us busy overseas. The IMF is very demanding as of late, especially with the rising interest rates by the US Fed. More than a few countries are concerned, and that's square in my lane. I love you, too."

"We can still do our hot air balloon dream in New Mexico, wineries in California, and a marathon in New York City?" asked Ford.

"That's for starters, there, you bomber pilot."

They held hands and talked about their future together. Their dreams of travel, experiences, kids, and where they wanted to live when they got married. The list of things they wanted to do together was endless. No limits to their adventures. They were in love and full of warm emotions toward each other.

Still holding hands, they got to M Street off the bridge, made a right turn to head eastbound, and walked to Clyde's Restaurant. The big glass window that faced the sidewalk was exceptional for people watching, and the foot and car traffic was just starting to pick up for a Friday evening. With the sun already set and the night kicking in, the city was ready to start humming with excitement. Their table was always the first one in on the right, in the bar section, and tonight was no exception.

The waitress came over and greeted them. Ford ordered an Old Ox Black Ox draught, and Emily ordered a house white wine. They looked at menus for a few seconds before Emily excused herself to the ladies' room. Ford enjoyed the people watching outside on the street, looking through the glass windows, and realized how different South Dakota really was. This, to him, was a *city* that never slept.

While sitting in the stall in the bathroom, Emily's phone rang on vibrate. She looked at the screen and saw it was Mark Savona.

"Bollocks. No way, Mark. Not answering," Emily said quietly. She finished her business in the bathroom, then walked through the bar, glancing at the college basketball games being aired. Emily then felt her phone vibrating again. Ignoring it, she made her way through the Friday night crowd of happy young DC people.

"Sorry, there was a line. Ladies' room," nodding to the rear of the restaurant.

"Yeah, I understand. Just enjoying the view here," Ford said, smiling to Emily. "I missed you. Sit down!"

"I will, I will!" she said, laughing, and sat. Glancing at the menu, she looked up. "I forgot to ask you earlier, Ford, are you still doing your volunteering next week with Team Rubicon Global?"

Emily placed her phone on the table next to Ford's, and they looked at the menu together. Not three seconds went by before the phone rang again, vibrating on the table. Emily pretended to ignore it.

"Yeah, I am. Team Rubicon Headquarters out of El Segundo, ah, in Los Angeles. But Emily. Emily...you-hoo. Emily, you have a call," Ford said, looking down at the phone.

"Oh, sorry. That's OK, I'll get it later. What does Team Rubicon Global do again? Tell me about them," she said.

"Well, it's for anyone who wants to help others in need. Some guys I know, William, Jake, and Clay, started it for veterans to provide disaster relief to those affected by natural disasters, either domestic or international. Team Rubicon links up skills and experiences of military veterans with some first responders, a few medical professionals, and modern technology."

"Oh, I love it. Maybe I can volunteer with you?" Emily asked.

"Sure. Absolutely. They also have Team Rubicon United Kingdom to help those in need back at your home." Ford looked down closer at the phone and turned it sideways so he could read it.

"Hey, *who* is Mark S?" he asked, looking down at the smartphone screen.

"Oh, he is someone from work. It's OK," she said, not looking up off the menu. "He's just a coworker."

The vibrations stopped, and Ford could see that Mark S called four times.

"You have four missed calls from Mark S, Emily," Ford told her, "sounds like an *emergency* at the IMF," Ford said, putting his hands up in quotes when he said *emergency* with full sarcasm.

Emily didn't know if Ford was being serious, because banks don't have the same emergencies that he did in a high-performance fighter and bomber aircraft. Especially yesterday after the fire he was involved with.

She sighed with disgust. "Would you mind, Ford, if I returned his call? I am so sorry," she asked.

"No. No, of course not. What would you like me to order for you?"

"Thank you. Let's get the crab tower, and I'll have the grilled chicken salad," Emily replied.

The waitress came over, and Ford ordered for both of them and added another round of drinks. Clyde's was standing room only now, and the noise was picking up. Plus, the music was up a bit, too, and the atmosphere was electric for a good time.

Ford looked through the window and then at the doorway. He immediately recognized two guys entering, both with short hair, the dead giveaway for fellow military members.

"Wait, I know these guys coming in," Ford said, giving a wave as they came in the door.

"Dude! Whoa! What's up, man? We just heard about the fire in Ellsworth. You all right?" said Brian George, a fellow B-1 pilot from Dyess AFB in Texas. Brian gave him a high-five, and his buddy with him shook his hand.

"Yeah, yeah. I'm fine. Wow, news travels fast. In town for the Andrews AFB conference?" replied Ford.

"Yup, just ended today. Boring as usual. General So-and-so, another General So-and-so...boring. Hey, look, you saved that guy's life! That's the word on the street," said Brian.

"It was nothing," said Ford, putting his head down for moment, being humble. "Hey, this is my girlfriend, Emily Liv—"

Before Ford could do the full introduction to his pilot buddies, Emily had already placed the call. She smiled, waved, then turned toward the wall and covered up the phone a bit with her hand.

"She's on a call from work. Anyway, fellas, great to see you. Thanks again. Don't want to keep you from a drink. I'll come over later for a beer," Mark said to the two fellow pilots, and they went inside.

"Hello, Mark, this is Emily," she said, talking into her phone, returning his call.

"What's up, sister. Hey, we've had a few new developments here at the office. Robert is here with me. Ah, the...new developments are significant. We need you to come in," Mark said.

"*What*? No, not now," Emily replied. "I told you only if it was an emergency."

"Yes, now. It's hot. Big news," Mark said.

"I'm out to dinner. I'm not coming in," Emily told him.

"Yes."

"*No, I'm not,*" Emily replied.

"Yes, we need you."

"Nope, not happening."

Ford looked at her and wondered what was so important on a Friday night.

"Come on, Emily!" Robert yelled in the background, "We *neeeed* you!"

Emily closed her eyes, opened them, and looked at Ford. Ford nodded, held her hand, and gripped it warmly.

"It's OK," he said quietly.

"Look, Mark, I'll come back to the office, but it's not going to be all night. Yes?" Emily told Mark.

"You got it, lady. I'll get you at the Metro and bring you in," Mark said.

Emily disconnected and ended the call, looking down at the table, then up at Ford.

"I'm sorry, Ford. Something has turned up at work, and I need to return for a bit."

"OK, I understand, Emily. I do. Just catch up with me at the Caps game. I'll send you your ticket as an attachment, and just meet me there," Ford reassured her.

Emily did feel badly but knew it would not be that long. It also would not take long for her to get from her Metro line over to the Verizon Center, home of the Washington Capitals, the Washington-based NHL hockey team.

"Thank you, Ford." She looked at her smartphone. "Just

got it. Oh, section 101? Is that good?"

"Yes. Fantastic seats. It will be a great game. Against the Flames," moving his hand to shoo her to the doorway "OK, get going...so you can hurry back."

"Again, I'm sorry, Ford. I'll make it up to you. I love you."

"I love you, too, Emily. See you in a bit." He got up to give her a kiss.

Just as Emily departed Clyde's, a text arrived to Ford's phone from Wu. He thought about opening it but decided to hold off and left it unread for the moment.

Defense Intelligence Agency, Bolling AFB, Washington, DC

Emily walked off the Metro platform and down the stairs. "You and Robert owe me big time," Emily scolded Mark, pointing at him, as she walked down the stairs from the Green Line Metro stop.

They scanned their IDs into the extensive security system and scanned their retinas into a display. Then they entered the nearly empty headquarters building on a quiet Friday evening. Most of the employees were gone, and the only people besides them were the cleaning crew and watch standers. As they got into the Sensitive Compartmented Information Facility, or SCIF (pronounced "skiff"), Emily was hot under the collar.

"What the hell is so important that you guys had to drag me in here on a Friday night?" she demanded. "I told you two!"

Robert entered the office cubicle area holding a memo

pad and waved them both over to the meeting room just outside their office spaces. He entered the meeting room, lowered the large wall-size white projector screen, and waited for the projector to warm up. "Hello, Emily, welcome. We do have a few updates for you and need your help," Robert said.

"Screw you."

"Thank you for coming back, Emily," Robert said, attempting to calm her down. It wasn't working.

The computer and projector were powered up, and the PowerPoint slide show was in view. Robert and Mark had just finished four hours or so of deep dive into raw data, and they provided analysis on a whole host of information. From checking reports and making calls to other DIA offices, to applying critical thinking steps, they both felt all the bases were properly covered. They also felt their findings were significant and on the tip of something big.

"*Yes, hello, Robert. Lovely evening. Whatever.* Please, tell me what is so damn important already!" Emily fired back.

"This is..." Mark hit the space bar on the computer, and the first slide came up on the screen.

Just as their eyes were comprehending what was on the screen, Calvin Burns, the Deputy director of DIA walked in on them. He was most likely the only other senior leader in the building, and it showed his dedicated work ethic to the job. Working late on a Friday night was the norm, not the exception. "Hello, everyone, looks like you're burning the midnight oil. How are things going?"

"Oh...ah, good evening, sir...come on in. We were...just

157

going over some of the findings from when we last saw you. We hit the mother lode," Mark said, showing the Deputy a seat.

The small conference room they were in was certainly not for executives. The table was full of crumbs, the trash was overflowing, and chairs were far from leather. Emily was a bit embarrassed they were talking to the Deputy in there, but he'd come to *them*.

"Thank you for inviting me in. I had a feeling you were all here. What have you found out so far?" the Deputy asked. After a brief pause, he turned to Mark. "Not sure if you heard about my time on the Hill earlier today, but there was a call placed to the committee about our time in the auditorium this morning. They are asking what the deal is," explained Calvin.

"Huh. No, sir, we didn't hear. Been face down in reports, doing some analysis of the data. We've found some remarkable information," Mark said.

"Oh? Like a good team. I wouldn't expect you guys to be involved with the politics, but the Hill sure was breathing down my neck. I was really hoping you had something. So, what do you have?"

"Plenty. Take a look at these gems." Mark nodded up at the screen. "Robert, you start. Take it away."

Washington, DC

Clyde's was still humming with a Friday night vibe, with the smell of burgers, music jamming, and people feeling their alcohol. Although Emily ran off to work after only one glass of wine, Ford grabbed her food to go so she could eat it at the hockey game.

Ford knew how to get to the Verizon Center from here pretty easily, so he figured he'd stay for another round and enjoy the scene. It was way different than the Rapid City, South Dakota, nightlife, which was the largest city closest to Ellsworth AFB. Rapid City was fun, but this was a different type of fun because it was a college town inside a city—so many young, energetic go-getters, all in one spot.

He took out his smartphone while he sat at the table and reviewed Wu's texts. There were a number of them on the phone:

Wu: dOing som flying today. Good wx. Saw in news a Dalls Cowboys game ison this weekend.

Ford chuckled to himself at the misspellings on the text. That was unlike him, and it was either a reflection of typing while wearing flight gloves, or, Wu had been drinking. Second one was there, too:

Wu: how are you doing, Ford Would likke to see you and fam soon. Miss everyone. A lot. Can you talk soon

Being an only child his whole life was something Wu had talked about when they were all kids, and the topic even arose later when they were adults. Ford had consistently heard Wu wish that he had siblings to celebrate birthdays with, holidays, and have another family around. Wu also shared with Ford regularly that he wanted a large family himself, and when he found the right girl, they were going to have a houseful of little ones running around.

Ford took a drink from Emily's wine since it was going to waste, pulled out his credit card for the bill, and waited for the waitress. Ford decided to reply to the texts:

Ford: hey bro, awesome to see you're making things happen over there. We got up for an early hop, only to have a ground mishap. All OK.

Ford: Had a snowplow hit our jet while on the ground. Big fire on aircraft. Burned up good. We all got out and no injuries. Earned a week off!

Ford: In DC now, visiting Emily. Off to a Caps game in a few minutes. Section 101, row M, seat 1 just off the ice!

The waitress returned with the check, and Ford signed it. He noticed that the drinks were not on there, so he double checked and asked her on her trip back to the table.

"Your buddies from earlier, Brian and Pat, picked up the tab. Said you were a hero. Saved someone's life recently," the waitress told Ford. Ford shook his head in amazement and was grateful. He nodded at her and said thank you.

He continued texting Wu:

Ford: I am heading to hockey! Caps game! When can you talk?

To Ford's surprise, Wu was typing something back already, as the bubbles appeared in his smartphone, notifying Ford he was replying.

Wu: Enjoy hockey. Yes, need to talk. Something serious has come up. Busy right now. Thanks for text. Talk soon.

Gansu, China

Chen and the Chinese military leadership rarely parked the Devil Dragon at the same airport or airbase for more than one night. They constantly moved it around the country, parking it in different areas so that its visibility to others was held to a minimum. This rotation of locations was not just for military members working on the project but for curious locals, too, in addition to adversaries who might be looking for something. The flight schedule was closely held by Chen and not established that far in advance. This meant planning was difficult for home and social lives, and created a somewhat expeditionary force who lived out of suitcases.

The Chinese military dedicated a Shaanxi Y-9 transport aircraft to ferry ground crews around the country ahead of Wu and Liu's arrival on every flight so that when the Devil Dragon landed, the mechanics and technicians were prepared to receive the jet. About the size of a C-130, the Y-9 was good for lifting lots of people and supplies but slow going on airspeed, especially when compared to the Xi'an Aircraft Industrial Corporation Y-20 Chubby Girl jet.

After landing, Wu and Liu would do their normal postflight debrief, write up issues with the aircraft for maintenance via pencil and computer, type out a separate report if they were testing a new piece of electronic warfare gear or avionics, and then head to their hotel or room on an air base. Wu did not know Liu that well but was forced to fly with him because of his connection to Lieutenant General Chen. Although they flew together fine, Wu was used to squadron mates who also bonded outside the cockpit, which helped the socialization in the squadron offices at the hangar.

Lieutenant General Chen always dictated which airports or airbases they were going to use, which Wu was against. Most pilots wanted the decision where to go and when, which was part of the freedom of being a pilot. One could escape the confines of earth, leave the bureaucracy behind, and be among the clouds. Chen, on the other hand, was a hammer about freethinking pilots and ran the Devil Dragon flight program with a sledgehammer. He was hypersensitive about citizens taking photos, US spy satellites passing overhead, and gossip of members working on the jet. By moving the jet around daily, he was comfortable with his mitigation strategy.

Last month, Wu and Liu had an unscheduled hydraulics emergency onboard the Devil Dragon that affected the primary flight controls and braking system, and at one point they were going to land at an airport that was not part of the plan. Originally, it could not be helped—when an emergency pops up and you have to land, you go ahead and land. It would have taken the ground crew about seven hours to fly to the area of China they were considering landing in, then taking up time to set up their ground maintenance equipment. It would have definitely overexposed the jet to everyone and everything. Wu decided to land the jet at the designated airport as scheduled, and luckily they did. After Chen got wind of the postflight report and their considerations for landing, he called them in and gave them an ass chewing, loud enough for the entire maintenance department to hear. His yelling was nothing more than hot air, scolding them for even thinking of landing at another airport, but was still unnecessary. Chen told them they were to land at the airport he selected, and that was final.

Wu got a ride to the Sunshine Hotel on Donggang West

Road in Gansu. After checking in at the front desk, he put his helmet bag on the desk in the hotel room, took off his flight suit, disposed of his brown paper bag from earlier, and lay down on the bed. Wu was way more tired than usual, bordering on exhaustion. Not being able to sleep well due to the side effects of the meds, he decided to text Ford back. He took out his smartphone, thumbed through it, and let out a long breath.

His idea was to text Ford about his medical condition, keeping it private from wandering ears of the Chinese government. He wanted to keep his cancer out of the hands of the Chinese military and depart this life on his own terms. It was to be when *he* was ready. The last thing Wu wanted was the bureaucracy and red tape of the leading test pilot leaving the Chen program for cancer. He'd have more physicals, more paperwork, and more Chen conversations, all of which he hated. Wu was kind of private like that and did not want to draw attention to himself within the flying world. What he did want was the love of family, and in China, he did not have that.

Wu lay in his bed on top of the hotel bed covers with his head on his pillow. He was alone, not only physically, but socially and emotionally. Wu was dying of stage-whatever cancer, worked for someone he despised, and had no one to spend his remaining days with. He thirsted for someone to hold him, someone to hug him and hold his hand when he was scared. Wu began to cry. He longed to have someone help him through the struggle of the pain and suffering. *Why me? Why me! This happens to other people.* With his mom gone and no brothers or sisters, his only family was the Stevens family. Wu was reflecting on his life, and one of his greatest personal regrets was that time ran out on getting married and having children. He had none of the desired love around him that he once had years ago, and Wu was realizing he was doing nothing of significance with his remaining days left on earth. Here he was, lying in a strange hotel bed, in what Wu perceived was the middle of nowhere, rotting. Wu stared at the ceiling, tears streaming down his cheeks, as the reality of his disease sank in. He bawled his eyes out, terrified of what was to come. Wu was more scared than he'd ever been in his life. He looked over at where the ceiling and wall met, where the circular chrome fire sprinklers stuck out, and let out another long breath. He reached over to the bed stand, grabbed a tissue, and blew his nose.

Wu continued to think about his life, just staring off into the air. His thoughts drifted to his fond days of regularly visiting the United States, always comparing China and the United States, and constantly thought of the United States as the land of opportunity. Wu figured the United States was a country where you could do what you wanted, when you wanted it. He always had a problem with China's lack of freedom, its economic stability...even the restriction on how many children a couple could have. He really disliked China's political system to boot and knew they were not capable of responding constructively to the instability. The United States had its stuff together.

Wu also considered the long-term fiscal headache China was in and compared it to the visit he had three years ago to Wall Street in Manhattan. *The markets! Based on truth!* He always thought he'd be back, to visit the land of the free markets...much more honest! Wu also compared the unhealthy dynamic between Chinese society, production, the political system he hated, and Chinese state capitalism. All these things that turned him off to China.

Wu glanced down at the floor, thinking of an article in last week's *New York Times* on the future of China...massive land seizures, their caste system, and forced relocations, combined with slave wages that were paid to the masses, just depressed Wu further.

In the Sunshine Hotel, room 232, Wu was coming to grips with his terminal condition. His anger at cancer was in full stride, and he was full of emotion at the diagnosis. The dream about one day moving to the United States was not going to become a reality. His mother, before passing, would argue with him regularly about staying in China versus the United States, but Wu had made his mind up as a teenager. Wu always attempted to sway his mother's opinion, using demographics for his argument. "Mom, how can you believe our government? All they do is lie. We have a shrinking labor force...relentless aging...extreme gender disparity, and a falling population," he would say to win his argument. It was a smart choice on both their parts to bring up these taboo subjects, as many Chinese teenagers did not have a clue in these areas. Wu did, and it only fueled his dislike for the country he was a citizen of.

It was just then that the idea hit him that he could still do something about his future. *Hold everything*, he thought. He sprang up in his bed and stared at the mirror facing him. *Wait a minute*, he said to himself. *Could it be possible?* Wu asked himself.

Could we really pull it off? We...Ford and I...could we make it possible? Yes! No one would know at first, yet everyone would know. Best of all, Chen deserved it, that son of a bitch. The real satisfaction in this new idea would demonstrate his true loyalty and love for the USA, the country he had loved so much, for so many years.

Wu rapidly got dressed and nearly skipped down the stairs to the hotel business center, leaving behind the depressing reality of his cancer, feeling a renewed energy and recharged mind. At this time of night, the hotel lobby was empty; not even the doormen were present. He scanned his room key into the business center and sat down at one of the three computers available. He was glad he did not have to enter his name or room number.

The main home page of the computer was of the Sunshine Hotel, but he quickly went to Yahoo.com. He first logged into his personal e-mail, searching for the medical records the nurse had sent. Wu opened up the e-mail and then the attachments. For the first time since being diagnosed, he was able to read the reports from the doctors, review the blood work, and see the images from the CT scan. He saw the tumors on the images, felt that he saw enough, and quickly closed out of the e-mail to focus on his new idea. This electrifying notion of his had merit, and to him the plan was as clear as any idea he had ever generated. Wu decided that after sending this e-mail he was about to write, it would be the beginning of the end.

Scrolling around the page, he saw the Yahoo purple envelope icon and clicked it. That brought him to a sign-in page, with the option to "Sign up for a new account." Wu filled in all the boxes and drop down menus for an account, making up all of data required, from name and address, to phone number. Not a lick of the data was accurate as he quietly typed in the spaces, but it was exactly how Wu wanted it. The e-mail account was free, established quickly, and the plan about to be hatched would get the point across to Ford.

The new Yahoo e-mail account, registration to a fake sister, Ang Lee, of Beijing, China, was established. Wu opened up the new e-mail icon and began typing his e-mail in English.

To: Ford.Stevens267111@yahoo.com
From: Ang.Lee369369369@yahoo.com
Subject: Visit to United States via US consulate, Chengdu, China
Dear Ford,
My brother Wu recommended I contact you regarding an
upcoming visit to the United States. I was wondering if you could
help me arrange a visit to the US consulate in Chengdu. My visit is
scheduled for tomorrow where I will make arrangements for a visa
for tourism to the United States.
Please reply back soonest.
Thank you.
Ang Lee

Wu read it to ensure it was basic enough for Ford to understand. He hit send. The decision was made, whether Ford received it or not, that tomorrow he was going to make a special visit. Tomorrow, he would ferry the Devil Dragon to Jinniu Qu,

Chengdu Shi, Sichuan Sheng Air Base per the flight schedule, then get over to the US consulate as fast as he could for *the* special visit.

Next day, US consulate, Linshiguan Road, Wuhou, Chengdu, China

Wu and Liu got the jet safely over to Jinniu Qu, Chengdu Shi, Sichuan Sheng Air Base for a dawn landing and were mission complete for the day already. Wu hurriedly changed out of his flight suit and put on his civilian street clothes to go over to the Chengdu Garden City Hotel. He was able to get a ride from the base to the hotel, check in at the desk along with Liu, then head back out quickly and quietly. Before departing his hotel room, he popped some more of the painkillers the doctor gave him.

In front of the hotel, he took out his smartphone and opened his Ulmon Maps app. The directions told him it was a forty-two-minute walk for a 3.2-kilometer distance. He looked at the digital map, saw the turn off Zhihui Street to Renmin Street, then cross the Jinjiang River, and the consulate was down on the left. *Great...crossing a river...water.* Wu was dragging energy-wise, but he bought a tea and started his trek.

He worked up a sweat walking down to the consulate and arrived outside at the guard shack. A smaller, bullet-proof shack that was separate from the consulate, was where he would obtain entry to the building. The consulate looked like any other building in the city but was surrounded by cement and plastic barriers, a large black iron fence, cameras, and armed guards from the US Marine Corps and the Chengdu city police. Wu was confident there were also plainclothes Chinese government and intelligence officials around, but it did not bother him, as he was hell-bent on his mission. Plus, he'd been to plenty of consulates before to arrange visits.

Wu was familiar with the Chengdu Police Department because of their recent active recruiting campaign. Their department had posters made, inspired from recent Hong Kong action movies, seeking former military officers familiar with tactics, kung fu, crossbows, and guns, and sought people who had "toughness" and "bravery." The posters made the pilots in Wu's former squadron laugh.

Wu entered the guard shack after showing his picture ID and passed through the metal detector. There were a number of cameras around the room, video screens, some sort of tactical gear in tall metal cabinets, and an array of landline phones behind the counters. Higher up the wall was a set of framed set of color photos, consisting of the President of the United States, the secretary of state, the American ambassador to China, and the consul general of Chengdu.

"Hello. I would like to fill out the paper request to obtain a visa to visit the United States," Wu announced to the guard.

"Yes, sir. Please go through the door and inside to the right. You will see the window where you can pick a number for a foreign service officer. The line looks pretty good, sir...not long in waiting time," the guard told him.

"Yes. Thank you."

Wu walked in, confident that he would once again fill out paperwork for another trip to America, a place he had visited so many times in his life. There was the trip to New York City, the visit to Los Angeles and Las Vegas, and the trip to stunning Yellowstone National Park, always attending with the Stevens family. To Wu, coming into a consulate yet again, would not raise any alarming red flags for the Chinese government. Even if they checked the citizen database for historical records, what Wu was doing was completely normal modus operandi.

While waiting for his number to be called, Wu sat watching *Titanic*, one of the highest-grossing films of all time in China, on the TV. It continued to be a favorite of the Chinese people.

Bing-bing...now serving...window number five.

Wu heard the announcement over the loudspeaker and walked over to bay number five. Sitting behind the window at a counter was a member of the US State Department, a Foreign Service Officer, a young man about twenty-five years old, Lance Monterey, already bald, with black Oakley eyeglasses and wearing a navy-blue suit. Wu could tell he was very attentive to the customer base in China. Wu sat down in the seat in front of him; the bay was designed to provide privacy from the waiting room as well as the bays on either side.

"Hello, sir. I am Lance Monterey, a Vice Consul. How may I help you?" asked Lance, speaking in Mandarin.

Wu had already taken out of his jacket pocket a handwritten note, generated when he was in the hotel room. It was written on the hotel stationery in black ink and folded two times over into a square. Wu had his hand on it, rubbing, for so long that it was warm and clammy to the touch.

"I speak English. Hello. I am a frequent visitor to the United States as a tourist, and I wish to return. I am here to complete visa paperwork," Wu told him.

"I would be happy to help. What is your name, sir?"

"Wu Lee. Spelling is L-E-E," he replied quietly, nearly whispering.

Just as Wu said his name, he took the folded piece of paper, did not open it, and slipped it to the Vice Consul across the counter. "This is at least my fifteenth visit to the United States. I enjoy the visits very much," Wu said, just in case there were Chinese intelligence officers listening. Wu suddenly became excessively nervous, knowing that this was the moment that had no return. It was impossible to turn around now, and the pain in his stomach turned to queasiness.

Lance Monterey, not skipping a beat, continued to type with one hand, and grabbed the note smoothly. He picked up some of the papers for Wu to fill out and opened the note hidden behind the forms. The handwritten note said:

"I wish to talk to a US intelligence officer. Captain Wu Lee, People's Liberation Army Air Force, pilot."

As if this event happed regularly, Vice Consul Lance Monterey still continued to type on his computer. He had pulled up the Wu Lee file and saw that he had indeed traveled to the United States quite often. Lance looked up at Wu and nodded. "I think I can help with your request. Let's see, Mr. Lee. I am in your account now and...can see that your...photo for the file is somewhat outdated. Can you wait a moment?" Monterey said, purposefully nodding to Wu, knowing the photo was indeed current.

Lance Monterey scrolled through a few screens on his computer and found the icon he was looking for. He pulled up a chat icon on his computer and messaged his supervisor, the regional security officer (RSO). From his seat at the bay 5 customer service window, he began typing:

"I have a walk-in at B5. Captain Wu Lee, Chinese AF pilot. Link below for his account. Taking him for updated pic to mtg rm. Get the Three Horsemen warmed up."

The Three Horsemen, as they were well known at both the US embassy in Beijing and all the US consulates, were the CIA station chief of mission, the senior FBI agent/legal attaché, and if the walk-in was military, the DIA intelligence officer. Certainly, the RSO would be involved in Wu Lee's arrival and details, but the Three Horsemen would be the leads.

"Mr. Lee, please walk down to the end beyond bay one on your left and meet me there. I will come around and open the door for you," Lance Monterey told him.

Wu was far from calm now and was absolutely freaking the hell out on the inside. His heart was in his throat, his knees weak. He was trying to keep a calm demeanor but was thinking, *This is it, man. This is my last play. Arrested right here and now, while waiting for this dumb door to open? Shit on a shingle.*

Wu did as instructed and waited by the Walt Disney World cardboard cutout advertisement of the *Cinderella* castle, in addition to a cutout of the *Frozen* ice princess, *Star Wars* characters, and *Toy Story*'s Buzz Lightyear, all in the front of the waiting room. Walt Disney had a formal marketing agreement with the US State Department and had marketing items throughout their facilities. This was all in coordination for the Shanghai Disneyland Park, which just opened.

He stood there in a near-empty room, just looking around and feeling silly. *Titanic* was still playing. Ironic that the scene playing was when the ship was going down and sinking. He smirked at the timing and humor, turned away, and walked toward the water fountain. On arrival in this waiting area, Wu put another two pills in his mouth, hoping the uncomfortable feeling he had in his stomach would feel better. It was piercing pain now, not nervousness, and felt like an ice pick piercing his inner organs. What made it worse was that he knew it was the cancer eating away at his healthy body tissue. *Just so much intense pain. And why isn't this fucking door opening?*

"Sir, the photo room is available now." The door was opened for him to enter. As it opened, a whole host of local Chinese employees who worked at the consulate were getting out of their shift work, and the doorway was jammed with folks. Wu was always fascinated about this portion of Chinese culture where citizens rarely waited in line in any type of organized fashion. They pushed and shoved rather than waiting their turn. In fact, when the Chinese hosted the Olympics in 2008, there were signs all over the city, explaining to local citizens that the rest of the world stood in lines and that it was considered rude to rush for a door or a bus. Wu squeezed in the chaos and was thankful that the small confusion of folks coming and going helped hide his arrival in the event someone was watching him. *Oh, crap...my legs are suddenly so stiff...can barely walk.*

Wu followed the Vice Consul to a room that was labeled "Photos, Room 143." But there was no photo equipment, lighting, or backdrop. *This is no photo booth.* Present in the room were a few chairs, a meeting table, what appeared to be a standard two-way mirror, bottled water, and carpeting. Wu smirked, thinking the setup in the room was just like the movies.

Upstairs, the state department supervisor whom Lance Monterey had notified by message earlier walked down the hall to check if any of the other consulate Three Horsemen were around. Not one was in the office. *Where the hell are these guys?* the supervisor thought. He continued down to the senior defense official's temporary office, and the general was also out. *They must all be in the same meeting.* Finally, the supervisor arrived at an office suite and found the DoD office with Christopher Sans sitting at this desk. Chris, a career DIA officer for the last twenty-four years, handled military-related walk-ins.

"Chris, you just had a walk-in, a Chinese pilot named Captain Wu Lee. Got him in 143," the supervisor announced.

"Oh, for fuck's sake. Another one? Is this guy legit?" Chris sighed. "All right. I got it. Listen. Do me a favor, see who is around and have them meet me in 143A?" he asked.

"Will do, Chris. I'll call the CG and let him know. He's on travel. RSO already notified via message." The consul general went by the nickname "CG" at every US consulate, worldwide.

Chris reviewed the electronic file for Captain Wu Lee and was pleasantly surprised to see Lee was a legit guy, but he did not know him from being in the business, the tradecraft of espionage. Chris was thinking that it was someone he had not worked with before, someone who had not previously shared information with the United States. He wasn't sure what this Lee guy wanted, but he hit Print on what he had in the system and walked down a few flights of stairs to the small meeting room.

Chris had been through plenty of sticky situations in his career, from strange walk-ins of mentally ill people wearing tinfoil antennas to communicate with aliens, to selling weapons to rebel groups, to Southeast Asian military coups d'état. He fondly remembered the street battles from his early career days in the US Marine Corps infantry, too. Chris was tired today and was hoping that this guy, Lee, would be a quick visit. Most of his job these days was dealing with the endless and mundane budgetary and sequestration paperwork that plagued most of those in government jobs, especially since the astounding inaction of the US Congress.

Chris entered room 143A, the small and dark meeting room that held the viewing portion of the two-way window.

"Hey, Vic," said Chris.

"What's up? What do you got, Chris?" asked FBI Supervisory Special Agent Vic Damone, the second senior FBI agent and assistant legal attaché to China.

Vic had his main office at the US embassy in Beijing, but he regularly visited each of the consulates across China. Today was Vic's scheduled visit to Chengdu. Vic was also a native New Yorker, born and raised in Douglaston, Queens, and he had the mannerisms and accent to boot. After finishing Manhattan

College, Vic became a certified public accountant and worked in Manhattan for eight years. While living the city life of Yankees baseball, Rangers hockey, Southampton summers, and New York City bars, he still wanted more out of life. By luck, he spotted a poster ad in his office lunchroom looking for CPAs to take the FBI special agent phase I written exam, a three-hour test consisting of cognitive, behavioral, and logical reasoning skills. The ad was looking for CPAs, lawyers, linguists, and former military members. Before Vic knew it, he not only passed the written exam, physical fitness test, extensive oral panel-interview process, and polygraph, but soon reported to the massive 547-acre training facility at the FBI Academy at Marine Corps Base, Quantico, Virginia. Months later, he rolled to the Cleveland field office, working Medicaid fraud cases as a rookie special agent.

"We got us a classic walk-in, Vic. This guy is named...ah...Captain Wu Lee, a pilot. Solo. As you can see, he is pretty well dressed, speaks Mandarin. His English is better than half of Brooklyn, and he has requested to speak with a US intelligence officer. Made the request in writing on his hotel stationery."

"Hmm. Anyone know this guy?" asked Vic. After a brief pause, he said, "Huh...he looks kinda...kinda jaundiced. Yellowish. This guy sick?" Complete with a pinky ring, Vic talked while waving his hand around with his pinky out, as well as his index finger and thumb, a classic New York mannerism.

"OK, I'll do the talking and interview him. As usual, I'll ask you to stay in here and take your notes, and we'll compare in a bit. Good?" asked Chris. He got a clean sheet out on his spiral-bound notepad. Vic nodded.

Chris left the small meeting room and entered the hallway. He took off his jacket, hung it on the hallway hook, and took off his tie. If the person being interviewed was street dressed, he did not want to walk in like he was an investment banker from Wall Street. Chris knocked on the door and entered.

"Good morning, Captain Lee. My name is Chris," Chris said in Mandarin.

"Yes, good morning. I appreciate you speaking our Mandarin, but we both know I speak English very well."

Chris stared at him and didn't say anything. It was the silent treatment to see who would blink first.

"I also appreciate you meeting with me this morning," Wu said. His mouth was dry, eyes dilated, and he was still scared shitless.

Chris thought for a moment and agreed. *This guy did speak better English than most New Yorkers.*

"Let me get right to it. Why I am here today. I would like to talk with a specific United States citizen, a close friend of mine, over one of your secure video teleconference systems. He is one of your US Air Force pilots."

Chris did not say anything nor write his name down. The two stared at each other without any expression.

"His name is Captain Ford Stevens."

The staring continued for what seemed like forever but was more like thirty or forty-five seconds, and without a soul flinching. Chris then spoke first, putting on his act as he had been trained.

"Captain Wu Lee," Chris tapped his pen on the table a few times. "You did all this to talk to a friend? If he is your friend, why don't you just contact him yourself? Why would you come in here and ask to speak with one of us?"

"After I speak directly with him, there will be no misunderstanding about why I've come today."

"I still do not understand, Captain Lee. You came today to us for a reason. What would you have to talk to him about that requires our involvement? Please elaborate. Because from where I sit, you're wasting our time. We don't know you. We don't have a relationship with you. And you come in and ask to speak with a personal friend of yours in the States."

"Mr. Chris, I have something that I need help with...this something, once you hear what it is, will require your help as well. It will be a tremendous benefit to your government, your leaders, the country, and your military forces."

"OK, what is it you're talking about?"

"I wish to speak with Ford directly, so that he may hear it from me first," Wu said adamantly and confidently.

"Come on, Captain Lee. How I can I help you if you can't help me?" They sat looking at each other. "Look, this little interview, this little fireside chat we're having," as Chris waved his hand around, "isn't going to go anywhere unless you share *way* more information. You are...an Air Force pilot, yes?"

"Mr. Chris, I'm in the military. I am a military pilot. Furthermore, I am a test pilot. I am aware of your two hundred U-2 pilots flying your thirty-three U-2s through history. Your SR-71s and your B-2s. Your 10,500-foot reel of wet film and cloud-piercing radar in the U-2 nose. I am also aware of such unique things as your high-altitude pilots having triple the number of brain lesions as nonpilots. I know of places like Beale, Kadena, and Whiteman. Black Cat squadrons. Technical speak on aerodynamics and fluids that would make your head spin. Listen to me. Yes, I am a pilot, and I know my stuff," Wu replied. *Don't screw with me.*

"I see. And your interest today...your interest today is related to something in aviation? Flying? What is—?"

Wu cut him off. "I will share with him first, then I would be happy to share with you. I will tell you my background, which you can verify. Again, I am a test pilot. I am on a special project and work directly for Lieutenant General He Chen, of our People's Liberation Army Air Force. You and your intelligence apparatus are aware of Lieutenant General He Chen. He is my direct boss," as Wu turned his glance away from Chris, and for the first time, acknowledging the two-way mirror with a long stare and a nod, as if telling people behind it that he was the real deal. Wu's confidence was growing, and his patience was thinning.

"OK, Captain Lee. We'll need to verify your relationship and status, and your request, of course. It will take some time to locate this Captain Ford Stevens, and if he is willing, bring him in to a video teleconference location."

"I understand. But Ford is expecting you to contact him."

"*Ford Stevens*. He is *expecting* us to contact him?" Chris said, his eyebrows raised.

"Yes. I have e-mailed him."

Chris's mind was racing. This was a unique case. A Chinese pilot who knows an American pilot, and maybe the right-hand man to one of the most powerful Chinese lieutenant generals in their country. He thought this was most interesting.

"Either way, Captain, it may take a while for us to find him."

"That is perfectly OK, Mr. Chris. I have all day, and I will wait here," Wu said, persistent in his words and actions to prove he wasn't fooling around.

"Why don't you write down your name and contact information here—and your request—as well as all the contact info you have for Captain Ford Stevens, US Air Force, and we can go from there?"

Chris glanced up at the red digital world clocks across the wall that showed the time zones across the world. It would be early evening in the United States, depending on what time zone the Stevens guy was located in.

"Here you go," Wu slid the pad back to Chris.

"We'll see, Captain Lee," Chris said as he looked over the page of names, phone numbers, and e-mail addresses, "I'll talk with my managers and see if this is even possible. I'm not promising a thing."

"I want to talk to him, not fly him here for dinner," Wu replied, acting like a smart-ass.

Defense Intelligence Agency, Washington, DC.

Robert sat at the meeting table, along with Emily, Mark,

and Calvin Burns, looking at the slide on the screen. Robert was fully prepared to share the facts as they knew them and monitor the situation as best they could. With time, and as history has shown, they would fill up databases with reports, and the story, if it developed, would make it over to CIA, the chairman's office, then eventually *Jane's* and *Aviation Week*. In due course, photos would be taken, and a terrific story would mature. But for today, they were at the very beginning of tracking something immense. Something special. Something they hadn't ever seen or experienced before.

"Sir, the premise of our brief tonight is to share with you some of the facts, via reporting and analysis, about a potential Chinese stealth jet," Robert opened up the brief. "We feel the Chinese must have obtained some of our stealth technology through cybermeans, without our knowledge, from a US corporation or the Air Force. We also feel they modified the design for a fighter, reconnaissance, or bomber aircraft that can fly at alarming speeds. Speeds that we have never seen before in the history of aviation."

"*Really*? How the heck did they do that without us knowing?" the Deputy asked, shaking his head. "Impressive...how the hell did they do that? Never mind, please don't answer, as I am sure it is just speculative. Please continue," Deputy Burns said, sighing.

"Yes, sir. So the question we were trying to answer was if the original flashes caught in the SBIRS at Buckley was a missile or an aircraft. The facts led us to certain information in reports, obtained from our sensors and aircraft. The following chart provides the information."

Robert displayed a chart with a timeline that showed when certain readings from SIGNIT and MASINT were captured, using what platform, and why it was significant. Mark shifted in his seat because he knew Calvin Burns would be surprised.

The intelligence community had a large number of avenues for collection of information. In fact, there were seven major intelligence disciplines, with a few subordinate ones to help analysts build a picture, or report, of what was going on with an adversary. While SIGINT was intelligence, and MASINT was measurement and signature intelligence, there were more to choose from. Other disciplines included were: IMINT (imagery intelligence), HUMINT (human intelligence), OSINT (open-source intelligence), TECHINT (technical intelligence), and CI (counterintelligence). A synchronized collection plan using some of these disciplines, along with an operations plan, allowed senior leadership to make adjustments on a foreign target. Famous cases in history that combined many of these were Winston Churchill and the Enigma and General Dwight Eisenhower and the Operation Overlord D-Day invasion. In this current case, *looking* for a target was a combination of some of the disciplines.

"Sir, block one on the chart...the top line, displays that our SBIRS have, for weeks or longer, been detecting flashes, but the length of the flash was usually short. The computer database does not have a signature for the target and therefore doesn't assign the captured reading to anything. If we programmed it and said, for example, it was a new DF-20 missile, then the computer knows what to look for and saves it for record. Buckley captured eighty-four flashes over an eight-week period."

"Whoa. My gosh, eighty-four? How can we check on that?" asked the Deputy.

"Already did, sir. I called out there," Mark weighed in. "Called out to Buckley and spoke with the watch officer who was on duty during the last flash. He followed up our call with an e-mail and attachment of the time/date stamps. It checks out," answered Mark.

"Why the hell didn't we know about the other eighty-three?" Calvin asked. "Sorry, just keep going."

Mark was hoping that was good enough for Calvin Burns and would not require him to fly out there, as in the past. Deputy Burns was a stickler for details. Mark was hoping that along with the other evidence, they could build a solid storyline.

"Sir, the next line on the slide is the report from an RC-135 Rivet Joint out of Okinawa, flying up north, feet wet, and west of Korea. Using call sign ROCK, they recorded Chinese pilots discussing checklist items in the cockpit, but it seemed like they may have transmitted in error."

"Feet wet" was an aviator term, meaning the aircraft was flying out over the water. "Feet dry" meant the opposite, in that the aircraft was back again over land.

"Error? Why is that?" asked the Deputy.

"Well, sir, they were not talking to an air traffic controller, which meant they were most likely on intercom and transmitted inadvertently. In fact, they had zero radio transmissions with anyone, and as you know, that's rare. Even unheard of. We were able to get their position and match it up to their transmission, and we have them flying around the airport in Zhangye, at the Gansu airstrip," Mark explained.

Robert pointed up to the screen. "Here it is on the map, sir. Borders the desert, up here in the middle of nowhere. Makes sense, so that locals couldn't take pictures. Test fly a bird up there all day long, and no one would see a thing."

"Emily, your viewpoint? Do you have anything to add?" the Deputy asked.

"I'm impressed at the Rivet Joint scan, sir. Although it gave a negative return on the radar signature to see what it was, I read they did pick up the pilot's or copilot's fitness tracker," Emily told the Deputy.

"WHAT? His fitness tracker? On his wrist? What, the commercially available ones for the wrist that talk to the smartphone via Bluetooth? Well, I'll be...not sure if I'm impressed that the jet was invisible on radar or that you could read his fitness level."

"Yes, sir, not only using Bluetooth, but the device can receive GPS signals," Emily said, smiling, "Helpful if you're a runner. We are already working with the cyber team to tap into the commercial provider to see where he's been running, walking...even sleeping. It could also give us his pulse, his sleeping habits, and depending on how he uses it, his caloric intake and water."

"No shit. Huh. That's incredible," the Deputy said.

"Furthermore, sir, the ROCK crew recorded their encrypted GPS navigation using our satellites. *Ours*, sir. They must have figured that their encryption was solid, and we wouldn't know. Well...we know. We have their times, locations, and best yet, their *speeds*," Robert continued.

"Speeds? Wow. OK, what are we talking about here? Mach two...two point five?" asked the Deputy.

A knock came at the door, and Jason, the Deputy's assistant, entered. "Excuse me, sir. DNI's office on the phone. Wants to talk...ah...North Korea, today's Hill hearing, and next week's ceremony over at the Pentagon," Jason shared.

Calvin Burns sighed, looked at everyone, and smiled. "I'm sorry, I have to take this, guys." Calvin stood. "I'll be back shortly."

Oh, brother, Emily thought, *another delay*. With Ford at the game and how late she was, it couldn't be helped. Ford would be fine without her for a bit longer and most likely was enjoying the game. If the director of National Intelligence, the DNI, calls for you, you have to take it.

"Well, we have time to kill. I'm going to check the reports from Fort Meade. Let's see what NSA has," Mark said, heading toward their cubicle area.

The National Security Agency was responsible for global monitoring, collection, and processing of information for foreign intelligence and counterintelligence purposes. It was possible they intercepted a signal from the area that was not picked up by the aircraft. Mark also thought to check the flight reports again, to see if any new ones were published since they last checked.

Scrolling through, nothing was new in three locations on the websites. He checked a fourth, scrolling his mouse down to the end of the page to see if there was anything to catch his attention. Mark squinted, focused, and then slowly smiled ear to ear.

"Hey, you guys, come here, take a look at this! A navy P-3 Orion crew out of Myanmar found a needle in the haystack," Mark said.

Emily came over and looked over Mark's shoulder, eyes opened wide, with a look of surprise on her face. "Does this match with what you guys had earlier?"

"Whoa. Better. This shows a potential aircraft with...*six hundred degree temperatures*? What the hell is that? Aw, man...this also shows the actual phone numbers from the phone on our stealth jet. The pilot, or someone else, had his phone powered up and it was communicating with the cell towers. This also shows all the calls, texts, and e-mails the person made," Mark explained, looking at the links available that connected all the cellular data.

Over the past four years or so, the Chinese telecommunications industry had exploded and expanded rapidly. While some communities and villages struggled to have electricity and running water, millions of citizens had smartphones. This enabled them to not only stay connected with family and some current events but allowed unique options such as telemedicine and digital currency. The same concept had worked successfully in places like India and Ghana. Chinese corporate strategists saw the opportunity and started building cell towers across the nation, enabling the technology.

"Bollocks...that's a hot aircraft skin temp, yes?" Emily asked, but the men didn't answer.

Robert nodded. "Speculative, because it's only a potential

aircraft. The win in the cards could be the phone data."

"Let's take a look at who he's talking to," Emily said.

US Consulate, Linshiguan Rd, Wuhou, Chengdu, China

Chris came back to 143A, put down his pad, and turned to Vic. "What do you think, Vic?"

"Well, he was as calm as a cucumber. As you know, we get some walk-ins who are freaking fruitcakes, and others are peeing in their pants. This guy has nerves of steel. Even sarcastic. Not showing any tells. Up front with his boss's name, which validates who he is, in a way. Files show he also has a robust US travel past, according to the DHS and state department databases," Vic said, sharing his observations.

"Wonder what he knows. What does he have to tell this Ford Stevens guy?" Chris wondered.

Vic was able to search some other databases from the computer terminal in the room. He ran Wu's fingerprints through IAFIS and the new NextGen system, and Wu's voice through an analysis system. They turned up nothing. "He's negative on prints and voice recognition," Vic announced.

The FBI's Integrated Automated Fingerprint Identification System, or IAFIS, is a national fingerprint and criminal history software system that law enforcement officials can check to solve crimes and catch criminals, terrorists, and other bad apples. The system provides automated fingerprint searches, background-search capability, mug shots, legal records, image storage, and electronic exchange of fingerprints. Criminal histories are also stored there, as well as crime scene shots, scar and tattoo photos, and physical characteristics like height, weight, and hair and eye color, in addition to aliases. One-stop shopping for the FBI.

"Got it. What about the Janken cameras?" Chris asked.

The new Janken camera system was developed from a Japanese robot that was originally used to play the game of rock-paper-scissors. It was a high-speed camera that measured Wu's eye movements and human reflexes. The recording was then uploaded into a computer and verified things like the shape of Wu's hand, the angle of his wrist, and micromovement of the fingers, to verify if he was telling the truth.

Janken also measured Wu's micro expressions, recorded his distress, and searched for his eyebrows being drawn up toward the middle of the forehead. This movement would show short lines across the skin of the forehead, adding data to tell if Wu was telling the truth. Same thing with eyes and eye contact, in addition to speech patterns, sweating, stuttering, hesitating, rocking, rhythm, or erratic arm movements. The system captured it all.

"From what I can tell, this guy is for real, Chris. Janken reported negative results, too."

Wu sat in the room for at least ten minutes alone. Then his phone vibrated, notifying him he had a text. He looked at the text message coming in and smiled after seeing it was from Ford. Wu read it and put it down on the table. *The timing is excellent*, he thought.

Wu stood up in the meeting room and walked toward the

door. Placing his hand on the doorknob, he tried to rotate it, but it was locked. He turned around and walked over to the two-way glass and tapped on the window with his index finger twice. He motioned for Chris to come back into the interview room again.

"Our guy is up and around...wants us. Maybe he's having second thoughts, huh? Something's up," Vic said. "Hey, I'm on board with his request. This is interesting to me. Let's see what this guy wants with Stevens."

"All right, let's see what the captain is up to," Chris said.

Chris exited the small room, went down the hall first to grab two cold sodas from the refrigerator, and then entered the interview room again where Wu was seated.

"Yes, Captain Lee, what is it?" Chris asked, offering him a cold soda as he opened one. Chris's soda move was pure psychology at this point, a technique he learned while training in the Camp Peary course at Williamsburg, Virginia. In social psychology, this "reciprocity" social rule was where we should repay, in kind, what someone else has given to us. Someone will give back to you the kind of treatment they have received from you. The rule of reciprocity translates that we are obligated to repay favors in the future, and Chris was hoping the soda, or pop, was opening the door for information.

"I found Ford. I know where he is," Wu blurted out.

Chris laughed because it didn't take long for Wu to speak. "You do? Where is he?"

"Washington, DC. He is attending your NHL Washington Capitals hockey game. Right now. He is seated in section 101, row M, seat 1. Behind visitors' bench."

How the fuck does he know that? Chris did not know what to say and thought that this guy Lee had his crap together. "Thank you, Captain Lee. I'll be back. Let me continue looking into what our options are. Would that be all right?"

"He's at a hockey game, not sleeping there for the weekend. You don't have *that* much time," Wu answered.

Chris left Wu and went back into room 143A. He gave a thumb's up sign, pointing through the glass to Wu, and told Vic, "Get a load of this guy Lee."

FBI Supervisory Special Agent Vic Damone recently finished a three-year tour at the Washington field office, the WFO, just this past summer. Vic worked in the counterintelligence division in the Asia directorate and knew the DC streets and National Capital Region very well. He put his head down, nodded, and then looked up at Chris, after thinking of the Verizon Center's location in proximity to the WFO.

"Just an idea, but the Verizon Center is at F Street and Sixth in DC. Our WFO is at F and Fourth. I could call over and follow up with the paperwork later. Let me call the SAC or ASAC in the NCR Squad and—"

"What's a sack?" Chris asked.

"Oh, the SAC? SAC means special agent in charge. Pronounced 'sack'. Sorry with the acronyms. I guarantee we got an agent in the National Capital Region squad who's a special events liaison to the Verizon Center."

Each FBI field office had a designated team of FBI agents to liaise with their professional sports team or teams, in addition to the sports facility that hosted them. Sometimes it was a retired special agent who was employed there, or a retired police officer, but there was always someone who once wore a shield.

"Let me make a couple calls, all right? At a minimum, the boys in the counterterrorism division will be in the office still, and we can have a few guys go meet Stevens at his seat at the Caps game in a few minutes. A favor. From me," Vic suggested.

"Huh. Really? How long would it take to get your guys together?" Chris said.

Vic looked up at the world clock, saw it was early evening, and laughed. "Normally, this would take a week turnaround for something like this. They would only spring into action if it were, say, a time-sensitive counterterrorism threat. But...my guys in the old office are either still there at work and wrapping things up, or most likely getting ready to go to the hockey game themselves. You know, going out for a beer.

"Are you sure, Vic?"

"Forgetaboutit. One call to da WFO and we *may...may* have Stevens in minutes."

Chris thought about it and figured he had nothing to lose. If this was small potatoes, he lost nothing because it was free. If it was big, if Lee was a big fish, then they all had plenty to gain. "Let's verify Stevens's cell number so we can locate him and see if he's even there at the game. If your guys get a StingRay location hit, and Stevens is sitting there eating his Cracker Jacks and drinking a cream soda, you're on."

"Yeah, yeah, right," Vic answered.

Chris cracked his knuckles and thought some more. "OK. Yeah, OK. Do it."

Verizon Center, NHL Hockey, Washington Capitals vs. Calgary Flames, Washington, DC

Ford Stevens loved the excitement of hockey, the fanatical fans, the adrenaline of the players following the puck, checking one another, and the electric feel of the indoor arena. Even as a young kid playing street hockey, he loved the winter sport then just as much as he did now. The Caps were always his favorite team, most likely ever since his father's job with Shell Oil brought him to DC to live on a few occasions. Even when they weren't in DC, they were sometimes in locations that had hockey teams with a robust fan base, like Calgary, Canada.

He scanned his phone screen into the Verizon Center entrance using the mobile ticket QR code system and walked into the arena along with thousands of others. Entering on Sixth Street was convenient for both people watching and pregame viewing, which was why Ford chose this entrance. The Capitals marketing team had players signing autographs, leading to the fan team store for merchandise, leading to the beer booth stands. Ford stopped into the fan team store, looking for a little stuffed animal for Emily, but he did not want to carry it around the arena if she wasn't there yet. Embarrassing, he figured.

Ford bought an Old Dominion Lager draft and made his way to section 101. The players were not on the ice yet, but the pregame music was blaring, and kiddie hockey players were doing circles around each goal. The floodlights were circling, and Ford could feel his organs move to the strong bass music. He loved it.

A hockey fan, white male in his forties, alone, squeezed into his row and sat down a few seats over from Ford around seat 4 or 5, wearing a #8 Alexander Mikhailovich "Alex" Ovechkin Caps hockey jersey. He and Ford exchanged hellos. More people filled the seats both in front of him, as well as in back of him, before the game started.

Ford was reflecting on the fire back at Ellsworth, now that he had a free moment, thinking of what the outcome would be from the board. He continued to be quite bothered by the incident and was hoping that they wouldn't pin the mishap on him. After all, he did sign for the aircraft, meaning he owned it until he signed again to return it. Certainly, there was nothing he could do to prevent the ground mishap, and *it was* an accident, but the Air Force did not always think like that. Someone was always responsible.

Ford sat thinking for about ten more minutes when he was interrupted by something in the aisle next to him. Two men in their forties wearing navy-blue suits, physically fit, appeared next to his seat on his left and stood in the aisle. At the same time, the man with the Caps hockey jersey sitting a few seats down who just squeezed past Ford, stood and walked toward him in the row. In total, three men surrounded Ford in a few short seconds. *Who the hell are these guys*?

"Sir, are you Ford Stevens?" asked one of the men in the aisle.

"Maybe. Who the hell are you?" asked Ford in return, not wanting to identify himself right away.

"I'm FBI Special Agent James Collins, and this is FBI Special Agent William Roberto. Next to you is Special Agent Gary Klein." Collins opened up a folded black-leather wallet from his jacket pocket that encased his credentials, his creds, which included a tin shield and an identification card that read "FBI" in large blue letters.

"Are you US Air Force Captain Ford Stevens?"

Some of the fans were more concerned that they could not see the kids on the ice, so they started to lean around the men standing. The loudness of the people in the seats and pregame music contributed to others in the crowd not seeing and hearing what was going on.

"Yeah. I'm Ford Stevens. Why?"

"Captain Stevens, would you please come with us? We would like to ask you a few questions in another room here at the Verizon Center. It should only take about fifteen minutes," Agent Collins said.

Ford thought about what his options were and immediately figured it must be related to the ground mishap. *Oh, boy. Perhaps there was a connection with the snowplow driver and criminal activity.* "All right. I have a friend coming to meet me. My girlfriend. I need to get back here to the seat in no more than ten or fifteen minutes."

"It won't take long, Captain. Thank you."

The FBI agents did not say anything to Ford as they escorted him up the aisle. Ford was sure people thought he was being arrested. The lead agent led them down the hallway past the counters selling food and drinks, and into the Verizon Center

Corporate Suites section. The retired FBI agent who worked Verizon Center law enforcement liaison unlocked this suite for them since it was not being rented for the night. Two of the suited agents entered the room, then Ford and one agent in the hockey jersey in trail.

Ford was still wondering what the heck the FBI wanted with him. He had traveled all around the world, with his family and with the military, and had never had an issue with law enforcement. "Am I under arrest for something? Is this related to the snowplow driver?" Ford asked.

"Not exactly," Collins answered.

The FBI agents did not answer and looked at him eye to eye. The silence was deafening. There were 18,500 ice hockey fans screaming at the top of their lungs outside, music blaring, but Ford could hear his heart beating.

"Do you know anyone in China?" asked Agent Collins.

Ford squinted his eyes. "China? Yeah. I used to live there. My father had a job with Shell Oil, and we lived there when I was a teenager. Why?"

"What else?" Agent Collins asked.

"Don't answer a question with a question. What do you mean 'what else'? What is it you're looking for?"

"We're asking the questions here, Captain."

"Spit it out then. What do you want?"

"Do you know someone named Wu Lee? Captain Wu Lee?"

Ford just about melted. *What's going with Wu?* He looked at all the agents now in the eye. "Of course I know Wu. He's one of my best friends. Why? Is he all right? Is he in trouble?"

More silent treatment from the FBI agents. Ford noticed this guy Collins was doing all the talking, while the others observed. The other suit, Roberto, took notes on a small pad and Klein, in the hockey jersey, just looked Ford up and down.

"Not exactly," said Agent Collins.

"Then you three Keystone Cops better tell me what the frig is going on, or I'm getting the hell out of here. Quit the good-cop, bad-cop bullshit routine you learned at Quantico and spit it out already," Ford said, obviously agitated by the way they were questioning him. The three-to-one ratio was uncomfortable, too, and, of course, done on purpose by the agents.

"Your friend, Captain Wu Lee, entered a consulate in China not too long ago, asking to speak to a US intelligence officer. After some folks there talked with him, it turns out his request was only to speak with you, by name, using a secure video teleconference," Collins explained.

Ford closed his eyes. He remembered the Wu texts now and the e-mail he did not read. He grabbed his cell phone to see what the unread e-mail was. "Wu did?" He did not receive an answer. Ford quickly took out his phone and read the e-mail about Wu's sister. *His sister?* It was starting to make sense somewhat, but plenty of details were lost on him. "What does he want to talk to me about that he couldn't text, or e-mail...or call me about?"

"He didn't say, and we aren't speculating. Whatever it is, though, it must be big, if he is risking being a walk-in to a US consulate," Special Agent Roberto answered.

Ford thought long and hard about what Wu was up to, but there were so many combinations running around in his head that to guess would lead to nowhere. *What on earth does Wu want?* And the sister thing really puzzled him.

"Yeah, so...what are we doing about it?" Ford asked. "We have a hockey game starting any minute, and I have my girlfriend meeting me here. Am I talking to Wu or what?"

"Our consulate point of contact asked us to verify that you were even present at the game and to verify that you know this Lee guy," Collins said, "and we've already contacted them and are waiting to see what they want to do next."

"Well, I'm here. I don't know how the fuck you knew I was here, but I am. I've verified I know him. Get me a secure video chat or whatever you're calling it. Let's get this bullshit dog-and-pony show on the road, or I'm sitting back down."

"Calm down, Captain."

"Look, just hurry the hell up."

Defense Intelligence Agency, Washington, DC.

Robert combed through the cell-phone report and could see the calls this specific phone placed and received, the e-mails sent and received using a Yahoo account, and the texts sent and received. It was a gold mine of data that would normally take hours but with the aid of computers was going to take just minutes. The cross-mapping of data associated with the phone number would easily be laid out in a picture form, like a mind map, and displayed on a PowerPoint slide for briefing purposes.

"Look at this. The phone was at all these towers, here, here, and all the way over here," Mark said, pointing to a map that displayed where the towers picked up the phone. "If I hold up this pen, like this...check this out. Like a straight line."

Emily took a good long look at it now. "The cell phone must have been inside the aircraft, or in his pocket, when he was flying. As the aircraft came closer to the tower, the signal was picked up," Emily said, looking at the time and date stamps from just one day of data. "Sporadic hits from altitude, but they're there."

The speeds of this aircraft were like nothing they had ever seen before. To fly this fast would mean the aircraft would have to have very special engines, a sleek design, and climb to abnormal altitudes normally not seen flown by manned aircraft. While the cell data was only an indication, the accumulation of information they were coming across was painting a picture of a remarkable aircraft.

Robert was scrolling through the raw phone numbers and saw that he, or she, did not call that folks. What Robert did notice were a few phone numbers to and from the United States.

"This guy is in contact with someone in a 605-area code," Robert said, looking at Google. "That's South Dakota—Rapid City."

Emily immediately perked up. "Really? That's where my boyfriend lives. He's an Air Force B-1 pilot up at the Ellsworth Air Force Base."

"Ooohhh, Emily has a *boyfriend*..." Mark teased her. She gave him a dirty look and was ready with a comeback until Jason walked in.

Jason stood outside their doorway and told them that the Deputy was finishing his call with the DNI. Mark replied that they would all meet back in the conference room in a few minutes, and they would be ready.

"Stop teasing me, Mark. You'd get a girlfriend one day if you wore more than that Nationals jersey with cut-off sleeves and a turned-around baseball hat," Emily snapped back at him, humorously. "Get rid of the man bun. Shave once in a while. The unshaven look is so...so George Michael of the eighties."

"Ouch," Jason said, listening in to the banter.

Mark and Emily began walking back to the conference room together, with Emily laughing at Mark and his choice of dress. Robert stayed behind just a few seconds longer, looking at the phone number report and wondered why a Chinese pilot was in constant contact with someone from Rapid City. The chances of him calling a relative were slim, and Robert hit Google for the demographics in the event the Deputy asked. Last census had 68,957 residents in Rapid City, and only 1.2 percent were Asian. Robert also acknowledged to himself that an assumption was that the potential Chinese pilot was calling someone else who was Chinese. That's only 204 people if this pilot was calling another Asian. Either way, with only sixty-eight thousand people, he'd have answers in seconds from the cell phone records software database.

"Yo, this China pilot guy has fifty-six texts to the Rapid City citizen, just this month alone!" Robert yelled in.

Robert was waiting for the software to cross-check the

name on the cell phone in China and receive the report. Certainly, the metadata argument was playing out in the United States press regarding the collection of US citizen data, but overseas, it was a different story. It wasn't a want, but a need. The Chinese number was registered to provider China Unicom Limited, with the customer named Wu Lee. He then read the Rapid City, South Dakota, 605 area code number to see what the person's name was. This provider was Sprint, and the customer was named Ford A. Stevens. Both street addresses were included, in addition to their billing payments.

"Who the hell are Wu Lee and Ford Stevens?" Robert said quietly. He punched up the Stevens cell number into the software to see who Ford Stevens was in contact with, just to cross-reference the Stevens cell with their database. *Perhaps the Stevens number was connected with other known associates?* Robert thought.

"Let's go, Robert," Mark yelled from the meeting room to the cubicle area, "Deputy will be here soon."

"OK, two more minutes!" Robert yelled back.

Robert then pulled up the current status page, just to see if the Wu Lee cell phone was powered up and being tracked by a cell tower. He pulled up Google Maps and fed in the connection from the phone network that could display active phones. The phone he was looking for turned up blue in color on the screen as a dot.

"He's *inside* a US consulate," Robert said aloud. "What the hell?"

Robert then pulled up the same Google Maps program and

searched for the Ford Stevens phone, just to see if that was powered on. While that program was working and searching, he went back to the known associates cell report from earlier, to see the Stevens phone number list. That would take a few more seconds.

He switched back to the map.

"Hold everything. Crap! Are you freaking kidding me? The Stevens phone is not only powered up, but he's at goddamn Verizon Center!" Robert said.

"He's here, Robert. Deputy's here." Mark yelled, laughing, from the meeting-room doorway, when he really wasn't. Mark just wanted to hurry Robert.

Robert was able to log into the slides from where he was in the cubicles, updated the slides in the meeting room remotely, and hurriedly walked down the hall with the new info. The rest of the group waited for him to arrive.

Jason arrived two seconds later and saw the team waiting patiently. He leaned on the doorway.

"Sorry gang...looks like the Deputy wants to call the director to brief him on the call he just had with the DNI. He'll be just a bit longer," Jason announced, then turned away and went back down the hall.

Robert came in excitedly. "Mother lode! Let me bring you guys up-to-date with what I just found. I cross-referenced the raw data and got names and locations for the Chinese pilot and a new connection for the Rapid City, South Dakota, number. Wait till you hear this. Our Chinese pilot is named Wu Lee, and I have his phone located and powered up at the moment. No shit, he is sitting *inside* the US consulate in Chengdu, China," Robert told them.

"Shit almighty. He's inside the consulate right now?" Mark asked.

"Wait. It gets even better. The Rapid City 605 area code cell we found is owned by someone named Ford A. Stevens."

Emily looked at Robert with horror. "What names did you say?" she asked.

"Wu Lee. Chinese guy. And Ford Stevens. Ford A. Stevens. Spelling is S-T-E-V-E-N-S. I tracked Stevens's powered up cell phone, and, believe it or not, he is right frickin' here in DC at the moment. His ass is right over at the Verizon Center. Right goddamn now," Robert said, excitedly.

"Why? Emily, you know these guys?" Mark asked, puzzled at her facial expression.

"Bugger me. *Oh my God*," Emily said.

"What is it? Emily? What is it?" Robert asked.

"Ford Stevens. *Ford Stevens*. That's my boyfriend. Ford Stevens of Rapid City. He's the pilot I just told you about. Wu Lee is his best friend. Yes, I know these guys. Ford is visiting me this weekend, and we are supposed to go to the Capitals game tonight. Right now. He's there waiting for me right bloody now," Emily said, bothered by the recent news.

"You have *got* to be shitting me," Mark said.

Jason came down again. "Two minutes."

"Emily. Are you fucking for real?" Mark stared at her. "Does Ford know who you are? How well do you know this guy? Wait a second. What...what's he doing talking to the *Chinese*,

Emily?"

Part 4

Deceived

Verizon Center, Washington, DC

"HEY. I JUST RECEIVED A TEXT THAT WE'RE GOING across the river to DIA headquarters. They have a video teleconference room available," Agent Collins announced.

"Aw, man," Ford said aloud. He asked if he would be missing the game. "Frigging great."

"Yup, let's go," Agent Collins told him as they walked through the crowd, exited the Verizon Center to a black sedan with tinted windows that sat curbside. Collins shot down Sixth Street, got on I-395 heading north. They passed Nationals Park Stadium and crossed the Anacostia River to I-295 south on the Frederick Douglass Memorial Bridge. The trip wasn't more than ten minutes at this time of night.

As Ford sat in the backseat of the sedan, his mind was racing. He wondered if Emily would be all right without him being there at the game and what she would think. *This better be good, Wu.* Ford looked at this watch and figured this wouldn't take more than thirty minutes or so. Then back to the game. Ford just stared out the window and watched the US Park Police Bell 412 turning its rotors on the pad.

Radio station WMAL 105.9 FM was tuned in and playing *The Truth About Money with Ric Edelman*. Ford had actually read a few of his personal finance books, but he wasn't interested in hearing about mortgages and retirement advice at the moment. He took the phone out of his front pocket to call Emily. As soon as he pressed her number, he hung up. Ford had second thoughts about bothering her, especially since she was called back to the office after hours, so he went the texting route. *It would take longer to explain than to just do this and get it over*. He opened up the text icon and started writing.

Ford: Emily, I'm running late for the game. Stuck doing something but will be there. Will explain. Love, Ford

"Based upon your situation, your cash reserves should be at least twelve months' worth of spending, twenty-four even better," Ric Edelman told a caller on the radio.

Ford was barely listening as he looked away from the phone and outside the window again, down at the reflections on Potomac River and into the night.

US Consulate, Chengdu, China

"Captain Lee, your story checks out regarding Captain Ford Stevens. He admits he knows you," Chris told Wu, standing near him in the room at the consulate.

"I told you he would. Will we get to talk soon?" Wu asked, coughing. "Also, if it's not too much trouble, thank you for the soda, but may I have some water?"

"Of course. We'll get you some water," Chris told him. "Are you feeling well, Captain Lee?"

"Actually, no. No, I am not," Wu answered. He then

deliberately delivered the news. "I'm actually...dying...of cancer," Wu said quietly and emotionless.

Chris sat silently, looking at Wu. He didn't know what to say. It suddenly made the interview much more humanitarian.

"And please, keep that between us. My superiors are not aware of my disease."

Chris was sure Vic was watching, but his own life flashed before his eyes. Wu was so young. "Captain, I am truly sorry to hear that," he said slowly and as sincerely as he could.

"Please call me Wu." He paused. "Just now. You're the first person I've told."

There was a knock from outside the door, and Chris walked over and knocked back. The door opened, and water appeared. Two bottles with blue American labels.

"Thank you for sharing that with me, Wu. Is there anything I can do?"

"No, thank you. My mouth is just so dry. Arranging for the teleconference is just the beginning. When we talk, you'll see a bit more. A bit more of why I am here."

"Yes. And how do you know Ford Stevens anyway?" Chris asked, as he watched Wu take another set of pills for the pain.

"The Stevens family lived near us in our apartment in Beijing. Ford is my age. He might be thirty now; sometimes I forget his birthdate. Anyway, when we were teenagers, we did everything together. The Stevens family lived there for five years. We rode bikes, played ball, laughed, and chased girls. We explored the city and countryside together. You know—teenager stuff. His family was wonderful to me. His father was like the father I never had. My father died when I was young."

"Oh, I understand. Your relationship goes back a ways," Chris commented.

"Mr. Stevens brought the whole family and me out for the day to go white-water rafting, north of Beijing in the mountains. I was quite scared of water at the time and fell out."

"Out of the raft?"

"Yeah, out of the raft. It was my first time being on a raft and also first time wearing a life jacket. Wasn't aware you have to *attach* the strap. I rode the river without a life jacket on, fell out, and started to drown. We all ended up in a circular motion in the river, called a whirlpool. The family in rafts and me in the water."

"Wow. That kills people sometimes."

"It nearly killed *me*. I had banged my head on a rock or something and was facedown in the water. Ford jumped in and pulled me to safety on the shore." He coughed a bit more. "It was something I will never forget."

"The whirlpool almost got you. Well...he sounds like quite a guy," Chris said.

The meeting room door opened, and Vic told Chris and Wu that they were going to use the video teleconference system down the hall, in the ambassador's meeting room. Since he was at the embassy in Beijing, Vic made arrangements for a window between DIA headquarters and them, beginning in a few minutes.

"Vic, this is Captain Wu Lee. Wu, please meet FBI Supervisory Special Agent Damone."

"Haya doin," said Vic, as he extended his hand.

"Hello, Supervisory Special Agent Damone."

They stood up and walked toward the doorway. Wu stopped in his tracks and turned to face Chris. "Ford is quite a guy. I owe him. I owe him my life, which is related to why I am here."

Defense Intelligence Agency, Washington, DC

Emily cleared her throat quietly. "Guys, I have known Ford Stevens for years. I trust him completely. And no, he does not know what I do for a living. He only knows of my cover job at the IMF, and that's it."

"Do you know Wu Lee then?" Robert asked, somewhat suspiciously.

"You're so *gormless*. Yes, Robert, I do know Wu Lee," Emily answered sternly. "He is Ford's best friend. I have never met him."

"I'm sorry, Emily. No harmful intent in the question. Just wanted to ask. This is all going so quick," Robert said, as meaningfully as he could.

Mark wondered what other types of connections there were and things they were perhaps missing. He looked at the computer and then off at the wall.

"Robert, did you say you could check that cell phone's e-mail? Lee's e-mail?" Mark asked.

"Yup, sure can. Let me pull it up," replied Robert, sitting at the keyboard, but looking up at the wall screen.

More scrolling through databases and numbers until he found the Wu Lee cell again. He was able to see the apps, calls placed and length, and e-mails. It was like he had the phone in his hand.

"What was that e-mail right there, that one right there above your cursor?" Mark noticed, pointing up to the screen with his finger.

"It's a Yahoo account. Looks like...ah...a medical report of some type. It's from a nurse at a hospital," Emily said.

Mark looked at it closely. "We have a medical doctor downstairs on the watch desk in the operations center. I'm pretty sure she is from the National Center for Medical Intelligence...from over at Fort Detrick, Maryland. How about we get her up here?" Mark said, calling downstairs to ask. He leaned over the table, grabbed the black landline phone, and placed the call.

Erin Clifton, MD, was assigned to the headquarters for national security reasons just like this and was upstairs in minutes. The National Center for Medical Intelligence was part of DIA, and they monitored, tracked, and assessed a full range of global health events that could negatively impact the health of the country. Dr. Clifton was part of the Maryland team and on assignment to headquarters as the medical expert in forward-leaning medical intelligence. The center's rich set of missions revolved around producing intelligence products on topics such as infectious disease and health threats, pandemic warnings, military medical capabilities, and biosafety. They also dabbled in topics such as force-health protection, which covered infectious disease risk assessment, environmental health risk assessment, and a blood safety index. This evening, though, Dr. Erin Clifton was there to do an analysis of foreign medical records discovered by a DIA team.

No traditional long white lab coat in sight, but wearing a blue business suit and sporting larger than usual DKNY silver eyeglasses, Dr. Clifton jumped into the subject and took a good look at the medical report. She scrolled through it, nodded, and took off her glasses. "My assessment of this patient is very difficult to ascertain because of the written language barrier. Certainly, I could provide way more of an opinion if this report were in English, but as it turns out, these images...these scans, are universal in any language," Dr. Clifton said.

"We can easily get them translated later or tomorrow, Doc. In the meantime, can you interpret what the scans say? Is that possible?" Mark asked.

"Yes, I can read them. Unfortunately, I can see that this patient is not doing well. This gentleman has extensive pancreatic cancer and is most definitely terminal. You can see from these CT scans...here. And here. Has this gentleman passed yet? Because if not, it's coming soon. Just a matter of two months or less. He's functioning now, but in about six weeks or so he'll be in a bed."

"*Sod off*! No, actually, we think he's still flying as a pilot. In China," Emily said.

"He is? A *pilot*?" Dr. Clifton asked, surprised. "Not for long. As I just said, he's not going to make it past two or three months. Also depends on when these images were taken last. You know, currency of the scan. Can't see a date. Was it this morning or a month ago? You have to consider that. If you get it translated, the date will be in there."

She looked at the screen again and explained the numbers on one of the pages.

"See this here...and here"—she pointed with her pen to the screen—"this is a prescription for painkillers. This patient is feeling the pain of the cancer, and the medical team gave him a prescription. Pills aren't going to cut it, though. Can't believe it's not morphine...most patients here in the States get an intravenous drip and are bedridden. They are also jaundiced. You know, their skin and eyes take on a yellow tone. He also won't be hungry...won't be eating. If this cancer has spread, as most cancers do, and it hits his brain, his balance and gait will be also off. His speech slurred. Just not himself at all."

"Understand, Doctor. Thank you," Robert added.

"If you need any further help, I'm here until six, when my tour ends, and then I head back up to Fort Detrick for the week. Call me up there if you need anything else. Here's my card," Dr. Clifton replied, handing out her blue-and-white business card to the room.

Everyone thanked her as Dr. Clifton left the meeting room. Mark could not believe what he was hearing, nor the information they'd found. He reviewed the story line in his head and was fascinated. They found a Chinese pilot, flying some new and fast aircraft, who has terminal cancer, with only a few months to live. *Was this happening?*

Robert, Emily, and Mark stopped in their tracks and looked at one another. The room was quiet, except for the whir of the heat coming through the ceiling vents. The computer fan could be heard, too.

"Cancer? I don't recall Ford ever mentioning that news," Emily said quietly to the team.

Just then Jason came and opened the door a bit, and behind him was the Deputy.

"So sorry, folks. I had the DNI on the phone, then a back brief to the director. Things that the three of you have to look forward to when you get to the SES seat," Calvin Burns told them.

"Yes, sir, we understand. No apologies needed," Mark said, making a hand gesture.

"Then my final but quick call. I received word from the operations center downstairs. Seems the FBI is bringing over a US Air Force pilot to use one of our teleconference rooms in a few minutes. One of the consulates in China had a walk-in who says he knows the pilot and wants to talk to him. An American. Well...can't make this stuff up. So, where were we?"

Robert, Emily, and Mark stared at the Deputy but remained silent for a moment.

"Team. Where were we?" asked the Deputy.

"Sir, what did you just say? They are bloody bringing him here?" Emily asked.

"Yeah, yes, seems so." He paused. "Why?"

"Is the pilot named Ford Stevens? And the Chinese walk-in named Wu Lee?" asked Mark.

The Deputy turned to Jason, and he gave a hand gesture and wiggled his fingers. He put his cheater reading glasses on to the tip of his nose, while grabbing a document from Jason. Deputy Burns scanned the middle of the report and looked away and up at Mark.

"Actually, yes." He looked above his reading glasses, sporting a puzzled look. "Those are the names. How the hell did you know that?"

Inbound to Defense Intelligence Agency, Washington, DC

The black Crown Victoria sedan traveling southbound made the right turn off the I-295/South Capitol Street service road and into the main gate at Joint Base-Anacostia Bolling AFB. The gate guard checked Collins's creds, then waved them through the main entrance on Malcolm X Boulevard. Ford had no idea that DIA headquarters was on an Air Force base, although he did know of the place from being a military pilot. Nothing caught his eye on the drive in, but he did see a Marine Helicopter Squadron-1 Sikorsky SH-3 Sea King do a low pass, inbound to their facility behind DIA.

The DIA headquarters was just one of the many units and tenants aboard the base. From HMX-1, the rotary-wing executive fleet used to transport the President and Vice-President. The White House Communications Agency, responsible for the global communications requirements for the President, were located on the base. The white roof-topped aircraft of the squadron were usually assigned to the executive transportation mission, while the all-green ones were used for US Secret Service and press support. New airframes included the Boeing V-22, replacing the Vietnam War-era Boeing CH-46 Sea Knight.

Collins drove the sedan to the DIA underground parking

garage off Brookley Avenue and parked it in one of the open executive parking spaces that sat empty. Everyone's doors opened at the same time, and Agent Collins led the way over to the elevator.

Ford pulled his phone out again and thought of texting Wu, but since he would be talking to him in a few minutes on this video teleconference, he thought, *Why bother*? He also checked for a reply from Emily, but there wasn't one.

On arriving upstairs, Collins directed them to the operations center. "Let's lock up our phones here in this locker area. Captain Stevens, you keep your own key. No phone allowed inside," Collins announced.

Collins texted Vic Damone in China and told him they were there at the DIA parking garage building entrance with Ford. Vic replied back that they were prepared and ready.

"Captain Ford, this is where we part. Best of luck," Agent Collins told him, and they shook hands.

Ford nodded, "OK, thanks," and kept walking and following the escort from the operations center. "Let me know how the Caps are doing while I'm in this windowless building without a freaking phone," Ford said with full sarcasm.

The escort officer from the operations center did not know who Ford was personally, but he did know he was an Air Force captain after checking his ID card and addressed him with the proper protocol. Ford was offered a restroom break, which he took.

Ford exited the men's room and made a turn to follow the escort officer again down the hallway. He saw three civilian employees at the end of the hallway, walking toward the same meeting room he was heading for. Looked to be two men and one woman from a distance. He slowed down his pace and looked at the woman a bit closer at the end of the hall coming toward him and tilted his head sideways in amazement.

"*Emily*? *What*? What are you doing here?" Ford said, as puzzled as he has ever been.

"Hello, Ford," Emily said, coming over to give him a hug.

"I don't understand. Why...why are you here? Aren't you supposed to...be at work?" Ford asked.

"Ford, things are not as they seem," Emily said, stepping back a bit, "let me explain."

Mark and Robert came down the hall and stood off to the side but close enough to observe the moment. They could tell right away this was going to be awkward.

"Go away, Muppets. Give me a bloody minute or two," Emily told Mark and Robert.

"Yeah, yeah..."

"Ford, I need to talk to you." They pulled to the side for a bit of privacy. Emily started out slowly and quietly. "As you know, my name is Emily Livingston. But. I have something important to share with you. I...do not work for the IMF."

Squinting, Ford stared at her, wheels turning, deep in thought. He shook his head, attempting to understand what she was saying. "What? What is it?"

"I am an intelligence officer from the United Kingdom. An operations officer. I am a member of Great Britain's intelligence agency, what we call the Secret Intelligence Service, known as

MI6."

"MI6? An *intelligence* officer? What the...you *lied* to me all this time? I don't know what to say. I had no idea."

"Ford, it doesn't change us. You and me. We are still the same. I love you. The only thing different is my source of pay."

"Emily. You lied to me."

"Ford, you have to know I was going to tell you. I was, Ford," Emily attempted to explain with full emotion not normally shown at work. "Ford, it's me. You know the MI6 mission is clear, like yours is. Mine just happens to be secret. We work secretly overseas. I develop foreign contacts and gather intelligence that makes the UK safer. I was not allowed to tell you until we...we were serious. And we are now."

"What do you do for them?"

"Well, I help the UK identify and exploit opportunities. I help our team navigate risks to our national security, our military...our economy. I work across the globe to counter terrorism, sometimes to prevent the spread of nuclear and other weapons. And I work with a team, like these guys from DIA, to help protect *both* of our countries. Ford, please don't let this come between us."

"That's...that's pretty cool, I guess. The finance and banking gig is fake, then?" Ford asked.

"Yes, it is. The IMF is my cover. A story. People think I work there so I can maintain my status in the event I am needed to do certain things to obtain information," she said, smiling. "I'm glad you are not upset."

"This is a lot to comprehend, Emily. I guess I'm not upset,

no, as I do understand what it takes to be in MI6. Actually. Ah, actually, I'm impressed," Ford replied, stunned.

"Thank you, Ford." Emily stood on her toes to give him a hug and kiss.

"I love you, too, Emily. Look, *no more surprises*. Anything else I need to *know*?" Ford said with a combination of love and starkness.

"Well, yes. I work here at DIA in DC as a liaison. I'm assigned to work on the China team, which, ironically enough, led us to you."

"To *me*? Oh. With this thing with Wu?"

"Yes, Ford. Allow me to introduce you to the rest of our team," Emily said.

Ford did the usual handshakes with the other members of the DIA team, but he wasn't totally there. *Was I being played? Years with this girl and her job was a lie? Aw, man. How did I not know?* Things had always been so easy with Emily, as it was like hanging out with his best friend. Ford was beginning to think she might be "the one" until this new situation, but now, he was not so sure. *Does she really love me?* So many thoughts were competing in Ford's mind, and now there was something serious going on with Wu.

Jinniu Qu, Chengdu Shi, Sichuan Sheng Air Base

The Devil Dragon sat in the hangar, nose first, like an animal with its nose buried into its mother's body. Warm and comfortable, the Devil Dragon rested with beauty, kept clean and maintenance-free and coddled by her team. Her tail barely made it through the hangar doors, both in length and height. This was a Lieutenant General Chen design, so that most hangars in the country could hide her whenever they landed. It kept tourists, spies, citizens with cameras, and satellites from space, at arm's length.

Lieutenant General Chen, full of alcohol and roaming around the hangar, was all over the ground crew, micromanaging and getting in their business. Because he helped oversee the design and building of one of the most radical aircraft in the world, not only did he take great pride, but great personal ownership. It was *his* aircraft, *his* speed records, *his* covert dragon of magnificence. This hands-on oversight, mixed in with the alcohol abuse, extended to the pilots, too, which was why Wu hated him breathing down his neck so much.

The ground crew, flying around the country, ahead of the Devil Dragon when possible, set up shop at a new airport nightly. It consisted of auxiliary power units on wheels that provided electricity to the jet when its own engines weren't running. The ground crew flew with spare parts, such as engine fuel filters, oil, hoses, and avionics, as well as whole racks of extensive and rare metal tools for unique, nonstandard titanium aircraft skin. They also carried with them an array of aircrew gear, from helmets to flight suits to kneeboards, ready to push the aircrew to greatness. Lieutenant General Chen made sure the whole maintenance team, as well as the Devil Dragon herself, was completely expeditionary, something he learned as a student at China's National Defense University.

Nearly as important as the Devil Dragon to Chen, was his dual pursuit of another star in achieving his next rank of four stars. Everything Lieutenant General Chen did was related to the new development of the aircraft, which he foresaw as his ticket to achieving rank. In his mind and plan, pleasing the political and uniformed leadership above him was the ticket to success. If he couldn't get the star, Chen thought, he would be a shoe-in candidate for a politically appointed position in the party's senior leadership. Unfortunately, he chased these simultaneous and multiple goals on the backs of the folks below him.

Part 5

Disclosure

Defense Intelligence Agency, Washington, DC

ROBERT TURNED ON THE AUDIO FOR THE SCREEN and was able to bridge and connect the equipment to the consulate. The encryption was tight and high-end, and the room, as well as the people on the call, were all cleared.

The team entered the teleconference room from the hallway, talking about Ford's relationship with Wu. They were not talking for more than thirty seconds before the live feed started to come in from the consulate. Ford sat at the end of the table facing the camera and screen. Emily, Robert, and Mark were seated at the table and off-camera.

"Chris, Robert here in DC, how do you read?"

"Four by four. All good."

The camera inside the consulate moved off Chris to Wu, who was sitting with an emotionless face, staring at the camera.

Ford looked up at the screen and saw Wu. He immediately noticed his coloring and weight loss. He smiled but knew something wasn't right. *Oh my God*, Ford thought.

"Jojo rising, Wu," Ford greeted him.

"Jojo rising, Ford."

"Wu. What's going on, buddy? What—why are we here, why are we meeting like this? Why didn't you just fly here or give me a call to talk?" Ford asked.

"Ford, it is so great to see you, my friend. How are you?" Wu asked.

"I'm fine, just fine," Ford replied but knew this wasn't a time for small talk. "Wu, ah...you have contacted the DIA and me, for something I determine is extremely unusual. I've known you for what, fifteen years? What are you doing?" Ford asked, probing a bit more aggressively than usual because of the situation.

"Ford, yes, a bit unusual, but I think you'll understand here in a moment," Wu said, taking a drink of water and swallowing. He closed his eyes longer than normal. When he opened them they were glassy, near tears. "I am sick."

"What do you mean? You have a cold?"

Wu turned away from the camera, a tear streaming down each cheek, then turned back to the camera again.

Aw, man, he's crying. I've never seen Wu cry before.

"No, Ford," Wu said and waited about five seconds. "I have cancer, Ford. Terminal cancer." Wu didn't say anything else for a few brief moments. "It started in my pancreas and spread."

A pin drop could be heard in the silent room.

"Oh my God, Wu," Ford said quietly and emotionally, his own eyes filling up with tears. "How—what...what did the doctors say?"

Wu swallowed. "I am nearly stage four. Went to the doctors over the past few months. They kept telling me it was nothing. Take some aspirin. Played it down. I went two times. Even went to the ER. Then one day I finally get a CT scan, and it's everywhere. The cancer is everywhere. Liver. Lungs. It's all over, eating me up."

Emily rubbed a tear from her face and her nose with her hand.

"Wu...Wu. I am so *very* sorry," Ford said. "Wu. Are you being treated? How...how long did the doctor say you had? How many months?"

Ford couldn't help notice the extensive jaundice and his weight loss. *It made complete sense now.* He mentally braced for the answer but knew in his heart it couldn't be that long. Wu just did not look good. He did not look healthy, and he was trembling.

"I have two or three months left. If I am lucky, four months," Wu replied, closing his eyes. "Most patients this far along are bedridden and on morphine. I've been taking these...these painkillers by mouth. Because of my robust health and fitness before getting sick, I have somewhat of an advantage for day-to-day living," Wu shared. "That's how I can still fly, for the moment, that is. No one knows."

Ford noticed out of the corner of his eye that Emily was

really upset and crying now, and that Robert and Mark were taking notes on their pads. Also, a man Ford did not know had come in the room unnoticed and was sitting listening. It was DIA Deputy Calvin Burns.

"Wu, is there anything I can do to help? Look, I will take some leave and come there to help you. Is anyone...helping you at the moment?"

"Actually, Ford. I do need help. I need *your* help, your personal help."

"Anything, bro. Anything. What can I do?" Ford offered.

"Please allow me to explain why I am here today." Wu cleared his throat. "You and the US military are most likely not aware that we have developed and been actively flying, a new secret aircraft."

Mark and Robert looked at each other, then over at Deputy Burns. Emily banked her hand gently from side to side to Ford and shook her head in a no fashion, giving the message that they did not know that much.

"The new aircraft is the H-18. A stealth bomber," Wu said slowly, "built in secrecy to replace the Xian H-6K."

"Stealth bomber? Aren't you still an H-6 pilot?"

"No, not exactly," Wu replied, coughing to the side, covering his mouth.

Wu was at the end of the meeting table in a swivel chair facing the camera, and Chris was in front on the teleconference gear. Vic was sitting near him. No one else from the consulate was in the room.

"I am the lead pilot on the H-18," Wu said, sipping from

the bottle that Chris handed him.

Chris sat back down and looked at Vic then back to Wu.

"The aircraft...we call her...the Devil Dragon."

Wu saw Ford turn his head to look at others in the room. Then Ford nodded his head in agreement.

"All of this will be important in a moment, so please allow me to continue."

"OK, buddy. Take your time and go ahead."

"First, the description of the jet, so you are aware of the impact of this information." Wu cleared his throat, took another drink of water, and then continued. "The range on the jet is over ten thousand kilometers, ah, sixty-two hundred miles. The Devil Dragon can carry a payload of eighty LS-6 precision-guided glide bombs and six CJ-10A cruise missiles. The overall size is smaller than your B-1B and closer in size to your C-130 Hercules but unbelievably fast. Fast, like world-record fast. We can also carry the supersonic antiship missiles, YJ-12 and YJ-100, to take out your aircraft carriers. I won't even get into the nuke capability yet. All of this is possible without being detected on your radar. The jet was designed to arrive at your front door in complete silence. Unannounced." Wu looked down at the table, then up again at the camera and screen area. "We were so confident and advanced in our testing, that we have already had it in afterburner quite a few times and at max speed. Also, we took it outside China airspace."

"*You did*? Where have you flown it?" asked Ford.

"We've already been eastbound across the East China Sea, across South Korea, across southern Japan, and south to Okinawa.

And back," said Wu, just beginning to share the true capacity of the Devil Dragon. "If we're hauling with some speed, it takes me as much as a hundred and eighty miles to turn her around."

Calvin turned around in his seat to look at the scrolled Asian map behind his seat and glanced at the immense geography Wu was explaining.

"That's pretty momentous. I'm pretty sure the United States, South Korea, and Japan didn't detect you, or we would have heard about it," said Ford.

"Ford. Look. Before I die in the coming weeks or month, or whatever, I have a special request. It is the reason I have contacted you in this manner," said Wu.

"OK, what is it? What is your request, Wu?" asked Ford.

"I want us, you and me, to steal the H-18 Devil Dragon stealth bomber from China. My desire is to deliver it to the United States," Wu announced.

Both meeting rooms were quiet, and no one was taking notes now. All eyes were on Wu and Ford.

"Holy shit," Mark said, transmitting over the video teleconference from DC to the consulate.

"Ford, you and I both know...that I have a true love for the United States. After growing up with you and your family, and your dad always taking me under his wing and visiting so many times, I feel I have an obligation to support the country I love and respect. I do not love or respect China. I do not like or respect my political and military leadership," Wu explained.

Wu thought about NFL football games, the Miss Universe pageants, his trips to the shopping malls, the open debates about politics and elections in America, and the way the stock markets operated. To him, America was the land of opportunity, built by immigrants who started off with farming, then manufacturing, and now technology. Wu loved America and his extended family. Wu was comfortable with his decision and thought about how to tackle it, but he needed a hand, especially in his medical condition.

"I have some ideas on how to get the jet out, but I need to talk with you and your military and intelligence team on some of the potential gaps. How to do it. And it goes without saying that time is the most important, because of my health."

Ford was floored. He thought about Wu's health and how frail he was, and now here he was talking about him getting in to China, most likely unannounced, and flying out undetected. There was no question, though; Ford was onboard with the decision. He would have taken off in that jet tonight, if given the opportunity.

"And so I do need your help, Ford." He coughed. "You, and only you, for my final flight. No one else. Our goal of flying together, from when we were kids. We do it," Wu said, with a more positive tone, a certain happiness. It was as if he released the burden of keeping it a secret for so long.

The room stayed quiet on both ends for what seemed liked forever, but Deputy Director Burns stood up and broke the silence. He walked over to Ford, placed his hand on his shoulder, and pulled up a chair next to him. The Deputy was in the camera frame now.

"Hello, Ford and Wu, my name is Calvin Burns. I am the Deputy director of the US Defense Intelligence Agency. It is nice to meet both of you."

"Hello, sir," Ford and Wu said at the same time.

"Wu, I am truly sorry to hear of your health issue. My father suffered from the same disease, and I understand what you are up against. Please know that I'm thinking of you at this difficult and challenging time. It pains me."

"Thank you. Thank you, Mr. Burns," Wu replied.

"Your offer is most impressive...the one regarding the H-18 Devil Dragon aircraft. While I cannot give you any details on the *how*, because we have not planned anything yet, I can assure you that we are grateful for your generous offer. I know it will be dangerous, and risky, and may lead to loss of life."

Ford looked at the Deputy. "We can do it. Absolutely. We can do this, sir," Ford said aloud with complete confidence. Ford was a forward-leaning, hard-charging officer, eager to fly and most enthusiastic to fly an adversarial aircraft like this one. He would be the only American to ever pilot something like this, at these speeds, and the thought of stealing it with Wu thrilled him. It would be an unbelievable opportunity, not only to fly this thing, but to help Wu.

"I understand, Ford. I'm sure you both can," the Deputy said, with the tone of a wise and older father figure, as he placed his hand on his arm.

Calvin Burns knew this was a lot to process in a short amount of time. Not only did he need some time to think, some white space to really think this through, but he valued his team's input. The Deputy wanted to hear what they had to say out of the earshot of Wu. He thought for a moment, and although they were under a time crunch, he decided a few minutes chatting privately was what they needed.

"What I would like to do, Wu, if it's OK with you, is go around the room here in Washington, DC. We have a few analysts sitting around here to support this effort, and I would like to seek their opinions. Then over to Chris, sitting there with you, then finally, Ford."

Ford was immediately thankful that his opinion was being sought but not a second later was taken back that they were going around the room. *These are analysts! They look at things I do, and Wu does, and all they do is crunch data, maybe write a report!* he thought. *What is there to discuss? Make a plan, and let's do it. Let's fly this thing out. Is there even a chance we won't do this?* These thoughts quickly went through his head.

"Ah, yes. Yes, sir," Wu said, sounding a bit surprised to know there were others in the room.

Wu, familiar enough with American culture, was fully aware they were going to talk about him and his proposal. He wasn't offended, and he knew he was asking a lot of the United States and of Ford. The only thing bothering him now was that he'd been in the consulate for a while now, and if for some reason someone was keeping tabs on his arrival time, it would potentially be an issue.

Robert immediately double-checked the green light on the equipment, verifying that no outside agency or individual was attempting to tap, or penetrate, the call. He was somewhat caught up in the moment and wanted to ensure the encryption was fully operational. The last thing they needed was the Chinese government listening in on their plan before it even began. The light was green, and Robert let out a big breath.

The Deputy put his head down then looked up at the group. Glancing around the room, he smiled and nodded. He thought about the developing story and how the original tip-off came from a potential missile launch. Calvin Burns had been around the block a few times, but this topped it. *What the hell was going on? How did the Chinese get stealth jet plans and, worse yet, fly the thing without us knowing? And over Korea and Japan for joyrides, over sovereign airspace? That took balls the size of Detroit. Damn*, he thought.

"Robert, could you please mute us?" asked the Deputy. "We'll be back with you in a few minutes, Wu and Chris."

"Yes, sir," Robert answered and did as asked.

"Well, this is a rapid and unique chain of events," he said, standing up and putting the reading glasses on his forehead. "I've never experienced this one before. Let's go around the room. Be honest in your opinion, and no bull. Robert, let's start with you," the Deputy said. The Deputy gave off the aura that he was disappointed, that this was something they missed as a DIA organization but was going to be a bright prospect as well.

Robert reviewed his notes on the yellow legal pad. He held a doctorate from George Mason University in psychology, so there was no question that he did a personality profile on Wu right in the room. The hard data backed him up.

"I did the normal twenty-five questions to profile him, which I can dig deeper into later. Out of the gate, I do trust this guy, ah, Lee. I ran his voice through the software, and he's telling

229

the truth. I'm sure the FBI over at the consulate did as well. Came back as negative." Robert paused and flipped to the second page of his notes. "He was telling the truth on his medical condition and meds, which was verified by DIA medical doctor Erin Clifton when she was with us earlier."

"What's your assessment on his personality profile? Is he capable of pulling this off?" the Deputy asked.

"Sir, I've got a tentative report already sketched out. From what I heard, Wu seems to be resourceful, action oriented, and someone who is in an excellent position of responsibility. His desire to take control leads him to make things happen, and he resists being labeled by peers and senior leaders. He's a self-starter, well educated, and well read. The details and routine of regular flying most likely bore him, although he can review details for Devil Dragon with ease and—"

"Wait. Bored to fly, but OK for flight test?" Mark asked.

"Yup. He most likely pushes his buddies hard and can be a pain in the neck to an adversary. And a supervisor. Wu seems like a critical thinker. He's articulate, matter-of-fact, and hands-on, but in a good way. The Chinese selected him years ago as a military pilot for a reason. He just enjoys moving through life. Fast. Once a position is dull to him, he may move on to another. This may also translate to his personal life with women. I know he is single. I would also say that he may regularly rebel against the rules, which is why he came to us. He is unhappy with Communist China and its policies, so that makes sense. Wu is a natural leader and decision-maker, which is why I can see him as a test pilot. I say some of his main assets are that he is self-disciplined, confident, and convincing."

"Thank you, Robert. Very extensive. Anything else?' asked the Deputy.

"All that from a conversation on VTC?" Ford asked.

Robert ignored Ford's comments at the moment. "There is, sir. I also ran his voice through the software to see if it matched one of the pilot's voices from Rivet Joint. It's a hundred percent voice vocal range match." He looked around. "Regarding pulling this off, after some careful planning, yes, I think we are a complete go, this is a go...a mission."

"OK, thank you, again, Robert. Emily, what do you think?" asked the Deputy, still eager to hear opinions.

"An honest self-assessment of myself is required," she stated, already acknowledging her bias toward the situation, which was the true sign of a professional because of how close she was. "I am somewhat torn because of my relationship with Ford. Ford and I have been dating for years, sir. Would I want him to go on a clandestine mission like this, one where he may not return? No. My feelings are lukewarm because I am biased. But I will add that I do trust Wu Lee, not only because of this interview, but because Ford Stevens vouches for him. And certainly I trust Ford. To me, this mission to me is a full go. Let's do it."

"All right, Emily, thank you. Dating, eh? OK. Honest? I appreciate your opinion. Mark. You're up."

Mark had his Green Bay Packers hat on and turned around, sporting his five o'clock shadow that looked like a small beard. The cut-off sleeves of his green football jersey were on full display, hidden earlier by the hoodie he was wearing. Mark looked like he was ready to attend a fantasy football meeting, and here he was, ready to give his assessment of most likely one of the largest covert aviation operations in US history.

"If I were a neutral observer, coming into this cold and reviewing the facts, I would still feel the same way. Bottom line, I think this mission is a go." Mark stood and started walking around the table in the room. "If we split up the mission into three parts, rather four parts, we would have to start off with getting Ford cleared by the Air Force Reserve. We know what that bureaucratic headache could be. Then he has to get trained up in a minimal amount of time. On what? I don't know just yet. We generate a plan to get him in there. Another plan to get him out."

Mark looked up at the screen and saw Wu bent over and coughing. Others in the room looked up to see the same. They saw Wu retrieve a small bottle from his pocket, take a pill out, insert it into his mouth, and take some water.

"And then phase last...where are we bringing the jet to, and what do we do with it? I think getting it to the mainland United States is the real challenge here, but we can really put some brainpower toward this and come up with a solid plan. Bottom line, I am a go," Mark concluded.

"Thanks, Mark. Ford, you're next. Fully understanding you are not at DIA, nor an analyst, just tell us what you think. Plain English," asked the Deputy.

Ford gathered his thoughts before speaking, something he learned from a mentor back at the Navy squadron. He quietly let out a long breath. In his nose, out his mouth. "Yes, sir. Thank you. This flight is a go. No question. Based on what Wu has shared with me tonight, and many years of friendship across Asia and North America, there is no reason to doubt his intent. I was not aware you had other data, including something from a Rivet Joint crew? And you guys have a medical doctor here?" *Those were pretty remarkable facts. Guess that's the intelligence business.*

"And that was one hell of a personality assessment. I think...not only are we helping a true friend, both personally and professionally, but we are capturing something that may rightfully be ours. How do we know, based on history, the Chinese didn't steal the drawings and plans and whatever else from an Air Force computer or a defense contractor? You know...cybertheft? Anyway, I'm rambling. Bottom line is I am a go. I'm in. I'm ready."

"Got it, Ford, and thank you," said Deputy Burns. He asked Robert to unmute the room and waved with his hand on screen for Chris to unmute on his end. "Thank you, Chris. We just went around the room here for some initial impressions and analysis, but I wanted to ask you. Do you have anything to add?"

"Only that Captain Wu Lee has shared his story with me, from the present back to his days with the Stevens family. There is a whirlpool river rafting story that is impressive. If I understand correctly, it was when, as teenagers, Wu and Ford went white-water rafting. Wu nearly drowned. Ford jumped in the rapids and saved his life. The story does not contribute to the task at hand but provides background that their bond is strong and long lasting," Chris added.

Ford smiled at the story coming to the table. He nodded his head, looking down at the table, then up at Wu's face. That was also the day of the aircraft flyover, the day they made a pact that they would fly together. "All true," Ford added, "we nearly lost Wu that day when we were kids. We also learned that day we both wanted to be pilots. Couple of Chinese fighters came down the river north of Beijing, doing a low-level. They were in trail...scorching speed. Wu and I decided there on the spot that we were going to fly."

Chris waited respectfully until Ford was finished. "Sir, based on the information that I have so far, I think Captain Lee is legitimate. Not sure what you discussed over there, but this seems like we could pull this off. The risk is worth the reward."

"Thank you, Chris. I appreciate your thoughts," said Deputy Burns.

He waited a moment before speaking again. He wanted to absorb everyone's comments and review his own assessment in his mind. There were glaring gaps on the *how* portion of the plan, like the blowback from the Chinese government and fallout from the Lieutenant General Chen, but it was worth exploring. Calvin was sure of it. "Wu, I am going to turn this case over to Mark, our lead for the China area. I know that he and his team, along with you, will generate a solid plan for you and Ford. They will keep me informed. I wish you the best of luck in your health, and I look forward to meeting you one day soon. Again, Wu, thank you very much for your kind and generous offer. Hang in there," Calvin Burns said. He stood and left the room.

The Deputy and Mark said good night and shook hands. Mark then stepped into the camera frame.

"Wu, my name is Mark, and I am a DIA analyst on Chinese aircraft. I work here in Washington. It is a pleasure to talk with you today."

"Hello, Mark. You specialize in Chinese aircraft? Huh. What did you think of the Chengdu J-20?" Wu asked, being a smart aleck. Wu knew, as did everyone there, that the J-20 fighter looked exactly like the USAF F-22 Raptor. "Sorry, Mark. I know and you know how we got ahold of those manufacturing plans. Yes, looks exactly the same, I understand. A copycat. I am sorry."

"Thank you, Wu. Perfectly, all right. Please know that I, along with the team, will generate a plan in the next twenty-four hours. Is there any way that you can come back to the consulate tomorrow?"

Mark could not help but consider how they would get in regular contact with Wu. They needed encrypted communication, for starters, and coming to a US facility might not always work.

"Well, the flight schedule is very fluid and not generated by me. It is generated by Lieutenant General Chen. I cannot guarantee that I can come in."

"OK, OK. That's what I thought. Chris, can you hear me?"

"Yeah, Mark, I am right here."

"Can you hook him up with the Peanut app?" Mark asked.

The Peanut app was an application downloaded onto a smartphone that provided private, encrypted, and secure texting. Known in shorthand as "the Peanut," the download automatically installed encryption software that protected the communication between the phone and whoever was on the other end. The standard encryption, called "Pretty Good Privacy" or PGP, was the latest standard. It provided end-to-end data encryption.

The Peanut, born in the medical community for medical

professionals, was designed to chat with patients. It was HIPAA compliant and had an ISO 27001 certified infrastructure, it gave health-care systems, private medical practices, and hospitals secure communication, along with PIN protection, two-factor authentication, and remote lock-and-wipe capabilities. What worked in one industry, was easily transferable to work in another.

"Absolutely. I'll set him up before he leaves."

"Thank you all. Looking forward to talking again soon. See you, Ford," Wu said, as he got up from his seat.

"See you, buddy," Ford said.

Mark pointed in Wu's direction on screen. "Hey, Wu, one last question. Are you wearing a fitness tracker right now?"

Wu slid the sleeve up his right arm, showing it for display. It was black in color and on his wrist.

"Yes. Here. Why?"

"Just wondering. Thanks," Mark replied. That was Mark's last gut check to verify that Wu was their guy. It made sense, considering the info they grabbed from the surveillance aircraft. Mark just wanted to have that last check, just in case they were being played by Chinese counterintelligence. Mark felt more comfortable after seeing it.

Everyone at DIA headquarters looked at the empty chair on the screen where Wu sat. Seconds later, the screen went blue, and the connection terminated. They were all saturated with the information and events of the day and exhausted. Emily turned to look at Ford, and he winked. *Cocky pilot*, she thought and smiled, shaking her head.

"See everyone bright and early in the morning. Planning for OPERATION WHIRLPOOL starts tomorrow," Mark announced.

The Dubliner, Capitol Hill, Washington, DC

Sean Patrick O'Halloran, manager of the Dubliner, was working the front door along with his bouncers this evening. A steady crowd of young Capitol Hill staffers were there after work, along with the usual lobbyists from K Street. Conor Malone was playing live tonight, and he and his band were setting up their musical equipment to entertain the crowd with Irish acoustical music.

Michelle Boyd, the DIA foreign-missile analyst and former Capitol Hill liaison, stepped up to the dark wood bar top, put down her Givenchy leather satchel knockoff, and took out cash to pay for her Kilkenny Irish Cream Ale. She looked around the bar, seeing some faces she recognized from coming here for so many years, but did not say hello to anyone yet. Michelle was waiting for her cousin, Jessica Esposito, staffer on the Senate Select Committee on Intelligence, to arrive.

Jessica Esposito and Michelle Boyd were first cousins, growing up together in Central Pennsylvania since birth. Jessica, also a former resident of Lewisburg, Pennsylvania, had an upbringing similar to Michelle's and held the same resentment toward the snooty and well-to-do kids in and around Bucknell University. Jessica, too, graduated from the University of Scranton and was attracted to the Department of Defense as a career. At first, Jessica attempted to join the Air National Guard out of Harrisburg and follow in her father's footsteps. Her father, a senior master sergeant in the Pennsylvania Air National Guard's 103rd Special Operations Wing, was an engineer in their EC-130J Commando Solo. Jessica always felt comfortable in and around the wing as a kid, going to work with her father from time to time, getting rides in the aircraft, and she made it a goal to join once she graduated from college.

Unfortunately for her, during the medical physical as a navigator applicant, Jessica was found to have tritanopia, or blue-yellow colorblindness, a nonwaiver disability that would keep her out of an aircrew position. She did, however, land a ground-officer position with the Pennsylvania Air National Guard in security forces. This blood bond between the girls explained why Jessica would risk talking to the senator about the DIA auditorium.

Jessica said hello to Mr. O'Halloran on the way in and beelined it over to the bar through the crowd. You could hear Malone and the band tuning up their instruments, and "test, test, one, two, one-two-three" repeated over the mic a few times.

"Hey, Michelle. What the heck? What the hell is going on?" Jessica started in with Michelle upon her arrival.

"Hi, Jess. Grab a beer. Then we'll move down there to those stools. Those guys are leaving soon," Michelle told her, nodding down to the end of the bar.

Michelle thought about how she should tell her cousin about the DIA auditorium meeting from earlier. After all, Jess had a clearance, and she knew to be careful outside of a protected and cleared area. She worked the same issues that Michelle worked, just in a different location. Michelle thought through the issue of just telling her everything, disclosing everything she knew to her on the potential missile, or stealth aircraft, or whatever it was, just to get it off her chest.

"What'd you get?" Michelle asked, as they sat on two stools toward the end of the bar.

"What else? A Guinness. And I'd love to chat again with that new hottie bartender with the Irish accent. His name tag says 'Kiernan.' He's from Shannon. Hmmm-mmm," Jess replied, checking out the bartender behind the bar.

"Well, thanks for meeting up, Jess. I'll explain everything. Jess, work is just eff'd up. I don't like where I am...and, I just don't think I will get promoted where I am. The office politics stink. I know it exists everywhere, and there is no getting around it. But I don't like it," Michelle disclosed.

"Yeah, I got it. I understand. The power and politics are everywhere. Just seems like in DC, it's magnified. What...what went on at this auditorium thing? The senator was fired up at the Deputy. I'm sure you watched or heard about it. I mean, the Deputy didn't like it, I could tell," Jess asked.

"Well"—Michelle took a sip of her beer—"we had this missile-related hot topic that came up over from Buckley. The SBIRS guys. And we did a few hours of work on an anomaly and were in an auditorium brief with the Deputy. Made the slides, did the research, even had a rehearsal brief. We were all there. All of a sudden, one of the aircraft analyst hotshots stands up and starts mouthing off," Michelle said, getting heated as she relayed the story. "This guy, wearing some funky clothes and a man bun with wrestling shoes...he didn't even look like an analyst. Anyway, he basically interrupts the Deputy and my boss. No facts. No homework. Just started in as the good-idea fairy, taking the spotlight from us. From our team in missiles!"

"WTF. What did this aircraft guy have to say? What desk was he from? What's his name?" Jess asked.

Just as Michelle was going to share the whole story, as she'd decided earlier, her sixth sense kicked in. She certainly knew they weren't in a SCIF and that the Dubliner was not an appropriate location to discuss such classified topics, but she was mad. Michelle never disclosed any work stories, but her emotional state, plus alcohol, had her fired up angry.

"The guy was from the..." Michelle started out, and before blurting out the words *China desk* or *missile flashes* or *possible China stealth bombers*, or the whole thing she had on the tip of her tongue, she kept her mouth shut. Something wasn't right in the bar, especially with the crowd. "It's not important right now, Jess. We can discuss it another time."

"Nah, we can talk now. Are you sure? You seem pretty excited about it," Jess said, taking another sip from her beer.

"Positive. Perhaps when we are back at work one day. OK?" replied Michelle.

"Well, Senator Ricks wants a full follow-up from him next week. I've ignored Jason at the moment with additional details, but we'll have to get them on the schedule," Jess said, referring to her office at the Senate Hart Building.

Michelle was flush with emotion and nearly broke out in

tears. *What the heck was I thinking,* as her entire career flashed before her in her mind's eye. Michelle just realized she nearly disclosed a top-of-the-pyramid, intense secret of the United States in a Washington, DC, bar for all to hear. Michelle sighed, looked down at the bar, and was relieved she disclosed nothing. It was a close call. "Anyhow, what are you doing for the holidays? Going home?" Michelle changed the subject quickly, learning from her near-disastrous mistake.

US Consulate, Linshiguan Road, Wuhou, Chengdu, China

Chris stood up and pressed the up-arrow button on the wall to raise the white projector screen then shut down the power to the projector in the room. He also put the computer to sleep and walked back to the table where Wu was standing. Chris thought about the events as quickly as he could and realized this was a heck of a proposition. It was nearly overwhelming to him.

"Wu, again, I am very sorry to hear of your health. I hope that we can help. We do have a regional medical officer, who is an American medical doctor who could look at you. Another physical. He's at the embassy over in Beijing, and I could have him come here tomorrow if you think that would help," Chris offered. Chris didn't know if he was available, or even in China at the moment but thought it was a nice gesture.

"I'm comfortable with what I was told. At the hospital. No one in the Chinese Air Force knows, as you heard. The scans show the mass and the spreading cancer. I believe, in America, you say that a picture is worth a thousand words. Yes?"

"Yes, we do. You're correct," Chris nodded.

"Then the images I have from the hospital say it all. There are black blobs on the image where there should be healthy tissue. If you combine that, along with my pain, how I look, how I feel, and the blood work, I've got the cancer. I can certainly fly for now, but we know in the coming weeks I won't be able to," Wu said. He tried not to be negative or bitter, but it came out like that. "I'm sorry. My intent was only to share my situation, not share my sorrow."

"Captain Lee, I really do understand. No apologies needed."

Vic came over from the doorway in the room to where Wu and Chris were standing near the meeting table. He was holding a plate of nachos from the vendor in the basement and offered it to Wu, but Wu wasn't hungry for that.

"Thank you, but no. Ah, umm...would you happen to have any chocolate chip cookies?" Wu asked Vic.

Cancer patients, especially at Wu's advanced stage, could not keep down much food due to limited appetite. Some cancers, like ovarian, pancreatic, and stomach cancers, cause the loss of appetite by affecting metabolism. In Wu's case, his pancreatic cancer had caused his spleen to grow and push on his stomach, causing him to feel full. Even when Wu had eaten only a little bit of food, his body generated ascites, which is a build of fluid in the abdomen that creates a feeling of being full. The cookies, high in sugar, were simple energy to fill a craving. Plus, he could keep them down.

Vic departed and returned quickly with cookies for Wu.

"Wu, just a review, keep the Peanut up on your phone. When you connect to a cell tower, you'll always be connected and encrypted to us and Ford. Just make sure you have the green light on the icon, and we're good for encryption. All right?"

"Yes, yes. I'll connect it right now," Wu said. "Why does it think I am a doctor?"

"Because the app comes from the medical community. It's OK. Wu, I think to get you out of here today, out of the consulate, we'll put you in the van downstairs in the parking garage. I'll take you out into town, drive around for a while, and then drop you off within walking distance of your hotel. Most likely near the shopping area, the mall, where you would normally be this time of day. Sound like a plan?" Vic said.

Vic was concerned about counterintelligence, and the what-if scenarios were flowing through his mind. If someone on the outside saw him come in, someone on the inside working as a local national, or someone following him, were all what-if disaster scenarios.

"Yes, sounds good. I certainly am fatigued, but before I leave, I do want to relay some additional requests to you." Wu drank more water to rid the dry mouth. "Or to the US government. And have them considered by your leadership. Would that be all right?" Wu asked.

"Ah, sure. Absolutely. What are they? What are you interested in, Wu?" Chris asked.

The hair on the back of Chris's neck stood up. Right away, Chris thought it was odd that Wu asked for additional information through a set of requests after the camera was off. Because only

Ford knew him personally, and Chris only spent a few hours with Wu, he thought for a moment that it could be a ploy by Lee. *Was Lee Chinese intelligence?*

But Chris and Vic were not amateurs; they were graduates of the best intelligence and military schools. Not only did they have the formal education to bring in a walk-in and interview him successfully, they had the operational experience to go with it. Chris's notes went down the counter-human-intelligence checklist, which reviewed and covered the detection of hostile sources within an organization, including moles and double agents. His notes reviewed MICE, the acronym for money, ideology, comprise/coercion, and ego. Textbooks and his experience always described these as common reasons people broke the trust of their government and told secrets, told about their work, or discussed why they would join certain organizations. Wu fell in perfectly.

FBI Supervisor Special Agent Vic Damone, alumnus of both the New York and Washington field offices, was no stranger to this world, either. Most Americans knew of the FBI in law enforcement, tackling the Mafia and bank robberies, or tracking down terrorists after September 11, but they are mostly unfamiliar with the FBI's role in espionage. Vic's psychological assessment in his written notes, which he planned on typing up and sending to the FBI headquarters, reviewed the reasons Wu was offering up the jet. Based on Vic's work in the past, especially with the Russians, it was always smart logic to question, sometimes silently, a walk-in's financial situation, extreme political views, potential blackmail, extensive need for approval, or intolerance of criticism. The history books were full of cases that fell under this logic, especially from former FBI agents who turned to the Soviets, like Earl Pitts and Robert Hansen. Either way, Vic understood Wu's motivation for his operations disclosure: political views, love for America through the support of the Stevens family, and being terminally ill.

Wu was thinking of a few last-minute items regarding pulling this off. He figured he would ask for a few items close to his heart, since he did not have that much time left. What was important to Wu would also be important to Ford, and he wanted to make sure Ford was taken care of in some capacity. There were also a few other things on Wu's mind.

"Let's sit and discuss, please." Wu extended his hand back toward the chairs at the meeting table.

Defense Intelligence Agency, Washington, DC

Emily woke in her room, and Ford in his, and they met in the lobby to drive over in her LapisLuxury Blue Mini Cooper Clubman and parked on the north end of the headquarters in a near-empty parking lot. The lot was normally overfilled with employees searching for spaces, but on a weekend, hardly anyone was at work, especially this early in the morning. Mark's red '57 Chevy was already there, parked at that annoying angle that took up two spaces, as if he thought the lot would be full and someone was going to ding his door.

"Ford, why aren't you talking to me about this mission?" she asked.

"I don't know. I'm just reviewing the events in my head. It's a lot to take in. Not only the mission, but Wu's health. I've never experienced something like this before."

"Are you scared?" Emily asked.

There was a long pause. "Yeah, I'm scared. I'm really scared. Confident about flying, but there are so many moving parts. And my best friend is dying of cancer on top of it."

She leaned over and put her head on his shoulder. "I'm here for you, Ford. I understand, love. I really do. Just talk about it with me...so I can help you." Emily hugged Ford for the longest time. Ford had a tear coming down his cheek. The emotion of the moment, combined with the unfolding of the whole story, finally hit him.

"I'm afraid and brave at the same time, Emily." Ford wiped his cheek. "I am mourning the future loss of an extended family member while thinking about his request. But I want you to know...I love you. A lot."

"I love you, too, Ford."

Emily and Ford walked into the cubicle area to see Mark and Robert hunched over their computers, drinking their Starbucks, and talking about the morning news cycle.

"Well, well, well. Good morning," Mark said, holding up his coffee as if he were toasting. "Got you guys a few coffees over there on the table."

"Thank you." The couple walked over to the center office table, which was full of everything from spare plastic forks to extra packets of ketchup to outdated magazines. Extra food was always available on the table, too, and this morning was no exception with the bagels provided.

Mark spun around in his seat. "Let's get right into this. Ford, you are already cleared at the top-secret level. We'll have WHIRLPOOL be designated a formal operational code name and have the security folks grant you the level over at Air Force Reserve. Would that work?" Mark asked.

Ford thought about it and nodded. "Yeah, that should work. We'll have to work on orders, too. Ah, at least in the front office of the chief of Air Force Reserve. Cannot imagine them allowing me to stay onboard unless some calls are made with a by-name request. I'm standing here now because I'm on leave, but it'll never be approved long-term without some firepower from above. Like your Mr. Burns calling over, maybe," Ford answered, thinking of the bureaucracy in his organization.

"Yeah, done. We can worry about that later," Mark said, wanting to switch gears. "Let's take a neutral look at the facts we have so far, and then after that let's do some brainstorming on the three phases that I mentioned yesterday. First off, does anyone have any reservations now that they've slept on this?" Mark asked the team, sipping on his coffee and looking around the group. They were all sitting now in a circle, having moved their seats, consciously or unconsciously, to a collaborative setting. None of the group members said a word.

"Good, no reservations. How about CI? Is anyone questioning this op from a counterintelligence perspective?" Mark asked again, but no replies. "This morning I read the reports from Chris and FBI Vic over at the consulate, including their psychological profile. This adds to Robert's assessment. Everyone thinks this is a legit mission and a go," Mark continued, ensuring that the decision-making was by consensus. Mark wanted to ensure all voices were heard, which was why ample opportunity was provided to speak freely. He also knew this was the early morning, on a weekend, so ideas would not flow as easily as in another more reasonable time of the day. Classic unusual suspects.

"You guys are a tough crowd this morning. Like the first pew in church," Mark said aloud as he got up to add some more sugar to his coffee from the community table.

"Stick it up your arse, Mark, it is bloody early, after all. We are all on board with the plan. Just need to wake up a bit and work on the details," Emily commented, sipping her coffee and really wishing it was English Breakfast Tea.

"So, let's break this problem down. First, we have to answer some critical questions to provide the context. This will require brainstorming. Robert, you're our scribe, so pull over that whiteboard and the dry-erase markers," Mark directed, taking the leadership role.

Robert pulled over the wooden-framed, two-sided, academic whiteboard. He started to put the date on the board with one of the black markers, only to find it was dry. He dumped that one in the trash and used the purple one instead.

"First question...let's brainstorm on phase one. How is Ford going to get *into* China? Brainstorming only, so no negative comments. All ideas are valid. Go."

For a few seconds, there were no ideas coming. The room was pretty quiet. Robert started. "Commercial shipping vessel."

"Cruise ship," Mark offered. "Ah, a crossing from a border country."

"Commercial airline...as a passenger," said Emily.

Robert was busy writing everything down under a heading of "Into China." Ford thought it was refreshing to see, using old-school board and markers, thinking back to his early flying days. The squadrons were all using PowerPoint slides, which he thought took away from the expeditionary nature of flying. The younger pilots were concerned with the look of the slides and who they were briefing before a flight, rather than the content and quality of the information in the brief itself. Perhaps it was a generational thing, Ford thought, considering baby boomers, Gen X, and Gen Y/Millennials could all be in the same air wing together.

"Back of a military jet," Ford said.

"Piloting a military jet," Robert offered.

"Shite! A private jet crew member!" Emily yelled, laughing.

"Through Europe or India...or Nepal...or even Burma. On a train," Mark said.

About twenty seconds passed without any more ideas. They went around the room one more time, and all their ideas were written out on the board. The concept was still in Mark's head that Ford had to *infiltrate* China because if there was any leak of this, and sometimes there was in clandestine activities, Ford would be captured for sure. Mark did not want that on his hands.

"Nice. Nice. Let's tackle some of these ideas and cross off the ones that will most likely not work. Without looking at the list again, we all have to keep in mind that we have a timing issue, meaning that we don't have a lot of it because of Wu's health. Our doctor verified his records, as we know, so we only have days or weeks to pull this off," Mark said.

Ford looked strangely at Mark. "What doctor? I know you mentioned it briefly last night, but what doctor?" he asked.

"Ford, we electronically intercepted Wu's e-mails recently and saw the medical records that the hospital sent him. We had our DIA doctor review the records to ensure that Wu was telling the truth," Emily told him.

"What, you don't trust him?" Ford asked, questioning them. "Look at the guy. He's sick, OK?"

"Ford, we understand. At the time, we did not know Wu and only had raw intelligence without analysis and context. We believe him," she shared. She placed her hand on his, whispering to him, "It will be OK, love."

Mark paused for a moment. "We certainly need Ford there sooner rather than later. Wu has three months, maybe two, right? The second phase, which we can talk about next, is once Ford gets in there, we have to link him up with Wu and the Devil Dragon. A rendezvous."

Robert stepped away from his writing on the board. He looked at the list twice. "The train and shipping ideas most likely won't work, but again, I am brainstorming. They seem to be too slow for this mission."

Mark stood up and walked over to the list. "He should not take commercial jet travel because his name will be all over the manifests. If we get caught doing this and a link is made to the United States, our DIA fingerprints will be all over it. Pretty sure that method is a no-go and won't work. It leads folks directly back to us, something we don't want."

"I could fly on a military aircraft, say a C-17 mission, under the premise of embassy support or USAID mission. Or into another country close by," Ford offered, but he changed his mind quickly. "I guess that would only get me so far. How would I get from Taiwan—or Korea or even Japan—across the water? That idea won't work, either."

It was quiet once again, and Emily kept reviewing the list. Then an idea hit her. "Hey. I got it. I kind of like the business jet idea. How about he flies over on a business jet as a passenger and gets out at the airport of destination? We control the point of departure."

"His name would still be on the manifest, and he would have to clear customs. We could...always give him a cover with a fake passport. Would that work?" Robert asked.

"Wait a minute. *Hold everything*," Emily said, standing and putting the palm of her hand up and making a stop motion. "How about we send him on a business jet, but he exits the aircraft early...before landing?"

"*Before landing*? What do you mean? Like, parachute out?" Mark asked, sitting up in his seat.

"*Yes*!" Emily answered, looking over at Ford. "He's a well-qualified parachutist, er, skydiver. Jumps regularly, both military and civilian trained. Right, Ford?"

"Yeah, sure, yeah, that...may work. Absolutely. I've got a hundred and sixty-seven jumps. Been doing it since high school," Ford said, thinking about how to incorporate it into the op.

Mark looked at the board again. He grabbed the marker out of Robert's hand and drew a basic airplane. "How about he departs the aircraft in a wing suit?"

"Bugger me. A *what*?" Emily asked.

"Yeah, a wing suit," answered Ford. "Yeah, yes. Yes. Impressive idea."

Using a wing suit versus a parachute added surface area to the body, which enabled a pretty good increase in lift. This newly created additional surface area was designed with fabric under the arms and between the legs, and made the jumper look like a birdman, or batman. Some have even said a jumper looks like a flying squirrel. Ford could glide through the air horizontally, then deploy his parachute, and could steer using the parachute toggles and control the path to land. It would allow Ford to fly laterally for miles to the left or right versus coming straight down.

"Ford could jump out, fly laterally—horizontally—and land on the airfield with Wu and the jet," said Mark. He drew a line out of the hand-drawn jet on the board, to the ground.

Robert looked at the simple diagram. "Huh. How far can you go laterally?"

"I think the record is sixteen miles, at least...figure ten miles would be a good ballpark," Ford offered.

"That's a hell of a capability. We can always get you down to the SEAL teams in Little Creek for practice," Mark said, as the plan was starting to formulate.

Emily liked the idea, and it reminded her of her operational days back in the UK when she had to pick up some SAS troops on a mission using a commercial boat in the Celtic Sea.

"I think we would have to have Wu bring the jet to a favorable airport for the linkup. Wu maybe could generate...like, a fake diversion and force a landing at an unplanned airport. He could generate a bloody fake maintenance issue, perhaps, in which he absolutely has to land the Devil Dragon. We could help him choose an airport, one with limited military security, like perhaps a commercial airport with a well-published flight schedule," Emily said. Her wheels were turning, reflecting on past operations.

Ford considered the plan so far. "Most of the time, I'm jumping out of an aircraft that is configured for jumpers. Proper speed, doorway, drop-zone area—you know, the usual stuff. Pilots are familiar with the procedures. This sounds like a pretty good plan, but business jets don't exactly open their doors in flight, right? They would get ripped off, and they'd have some explaining to do with Chinese customs. How do we get around a pressurized cabin, oxygen issues—depending on the altitude—in an aircraft where doors don't normally open in flight? How would we get around that?"

"Ford, that problem may be a problem for mere mortals and commoners. Not us! How about we borrow a business jet and have it modified down at Gulfstream. Down in Savannah by the boys in Special Missions. Maybe they can modify, or make us, a door in the rear. At the bottom rear," Mark pointed to his drawing on the board. "Bottom portion of the aircraft lowers, like a ramp. The ramp door opens, Ford jumps out, and the door comes back up to close. We can ask Gulfstream Special Missions to modify it so that it does not look like it was modified from the inside or outside."

"You're just going to 'obtain' a Gulfstream 550, or 650, or whatever, have them cut a hole in the airframe, and let us fly it out? Come on. No way," Ford said, doubting the plan.

"This is the DIA, Ford. You need a jet, we get a jet," Robert said.

Robert, Emily, and Mark looked at one another and at the same time said in unison, "Corning."

Corning Incorporated, of Corning, New York, is a manufacturer of glass, ceramics, and related materials, used for industrial and scientific applications. Through the years, Corning corporate had befriended the intelligence community and helped on a number of research and development projects. From time to time, Corning CEO John Abbott had lent the jet to DIA for operational missions, generously contributing to national security in his own humble way. Corning Inc. kept their Gulfstream jets at the Elmira Corning Regional Airport, a quiet, county-owned public airport in Chemung County, New York, about seven miles northwest of Elmira, New York, and eight miles east of downtown Corning.

"Robert, call up to CEO John Abbott at Corning and see if their six-fifty is available. I'll call the Deputy at home and see if he can call in a favor to ole Reggie at Gulfstream in Savannah. Depending on what's available and when, we'll go down there later today or tonight and see what the art of the possible is," Mark said.

"Just like that? We are going to walk-in with a borrowed fifty-million-dollar jet and get it done?" Ford asked, being a smart aleck, snapping his fingers.

"Just like that," Mark snapped his fingers. "Ford, you're stuck in rules and policies, man. Rules constrain. They cloud your thinking, dude. Think outside the box." He pointed at Ford and laughed. "Kids, pack your bags. We're going down to the Low Country," he announced.

Zhangye, Gansu Airstrip, China

Wu and Liu were finished preflighting the aircraft and ready to do some high-speed flight tests on today's mission. They already completed their paperwork with the engineers and maintenance, filled out the performance cards for their kneeboards, talked to the ground crew about any issues with the jet, and were nearly ready to strap in.

All pilots have a predictable routine before taking off, no matter where they live. For some, it might be inspecting the same portion of the engine on preflight checks, or rechecking the weather one last time before leaving the building, or even saying a small prayer. Two of the most important routines ever include double-checking the fuel and going to the bathroom, no matter what country they're from.

Wu and Liu were no different. Liu had a ritual of drinking coffee either in the hotel or at the airport before every flight, mostly for the caffeine, especially with the odd hours they were flying. Wu's only habit was to hit the airport restroom, and this morning he did with a purpose. It was an opportunity for him to throw up, yet again, while having a bit of water and two more pain pills.

Wu glanced down into the pill bottle and saw the last two pills left in there. He shook the pill bottle lightly to make them move around a bit and could actually see the bottom of the container. Wu looked in the bathroom mirror and thought about his sunken face with his weight loss, in addition to his awful coloring. He splashed water on his face and acknowledged how bad he looked, but he felt strong. Wu also mentally reviewed a few options for getting Ford in here, but he did not have much thinking time to devote before his takeoff in just a few minutes.

Wu and Liu walked together out to the jet, listening to the hum of the APU, the auxiliary power unit, supporting electricity to the aircraft. The APU was whirring, throwing power into the jet until it could start its engines and provide its own electricity. A small gasoline engine powered a generator, which provided 28.5v DC output voltage, 3,045 cranking amps, and two hundred amps for the Devil Dragon's prestart operations. But most important, the air pressure generated by the APU meant that they could spin the turbines of the main engines fast enough to get them started.

The advanced avionics suite, such as the encrypted radios, satellite communications, global navigational equipment, and modern radars, in addition to the intercom, at a minimum, required ground power. So did the air conditioning, which was often overlooked by engineers because it was not a sexy component to build on an aircraft. What was laughable to Wu over so many years as a pilot was that most aeronautical engineers had never flown, so they did not have a clue what it was like to be in a greenhouse-like cockpit with 110 degree temperatures outside. On the inside, temps could easily pass 140 degrees, making the engine start of any aircraft, an issue.

Wu and Liu started her up this morning, ops normal, quickly taxied for takeoff prior to sunrise, and away they went. Wu was able to dump the visit to the consulate yesterday so he could concentrate on his mission today, knowing if he didn't, the United States and Ford would never get the jet. This technique of parking issues in one's life was called compartmentalization, and most pilots were able to put topics of importance in the back of their minds to concentrate on the flying task at hand. As an example, Wu had compartmentalized their radio screw-ups to deal with the larger issue of the gear problem. At the moment, Wu's task at hand was to measure acceleration from one airspeed to another, looking at the full momentum of the throttles through military power and into afterburner. Liu ran the stopwatch for time measurement.

Liu was tuning certain frequencies into the radios as they flew westward across China so that they could monitor air traffic. Wu and Liu never transmitted on the frequency on purpose, because no air traffic control organization knew they were there. There was no flight plan filed, no squawk assigned to appear on radar, and no flight following from radar controllers. Or almost no one. Wu knew the Americans were monitoring him in some capacity now, but he didn't think twice about it.

Liu was also busy completing takeoff and climb-out checklists while dialing in altitude bugs, stepping them up like a staircase to a predetermined altitude. The bug, when dialed to a certain altitude, meant the jet would level off at a certain altitude with the autopilot in the on position. Upon arrival at flight level

510, or 51,000 feet, Wu turned the jet from the western portion of China, where they were at the moment, and faced east.

"Heading zero eight zero, five-fifty knots," Wu announced.

"Roger. Head is down, copying numbers. Area is clear. Ready to commence maneuvers," Liu replied.

Today was nothing more than a simulated drag strip in the air, a straightaway of open airspace with good weather that allowed them to open her up. See what she was about. The Devil Dragon would be flown as fast as a man could go, and Wu was ready as a pilot, but he knew with time that his medical condition would wear him down. Wu pressed on, continuing to suffer in silence, and did not let Liu know of his slight discomfort, but how he wished he was healthy to enjoy the flights once again. Either way, the worst thing that could happen would be for Liu to find out about his health condition and report it directly to Chen.

Wu sat in the left seat and moved the throttles forward a bit more with his right hand, inching them toward the front of the jet. His hand was able to control all four engines on the throttle quadrant with ease and could move them forward smoothly. His scan came inside to see the engine oil pressures and temperatures, and all checked in the green. Ops normal. His left hand on the stick was able to change the pitch of the nose, because as the jet changed speeds, the attitude in reference to the horizon changed. Wu wanted to maintain altitude, and he had a small thumb wheel to trim out the jet easily, especially at these wild speeds.

"Passing Mach 0.78...0.85...0.98...1.1," Liu reported as the jet passed the speed of sound without as much as a bump. To the

The Devil Dragon Pilot

outside world, a sonic boom could be heard, which may have sounded like rumbling thunder to the Chinese villagers some eight miles underneath them.

The speed of sound, first broken by US Air Force test pilot Charles "Chuck" Yeager in 1947, was always a historic and unique measurement of aircraft speed and performance. The Devil Dragon flight test today was measured in dry air, as it was in 1947 at 45,000 feet in Yeager's X-1. The temperatures up high today would determine the Devil Dragon's Mach number. For example, if they determined the outside air temperature today was 20 degrees Celsius, they would travel at 1,126 feet a second, or 768 miles per hour, to achieve the speed of sound. For them, it was 667 knots because aircraft measured airspeed in knots, or nautical miles per hour. At those altitudes, though, it would be more like – 20 degrees, so the Mach number in knots would be much lower. On their kneeboard cards were paper charts, which also took into account atmospheric pressure and density altitude so they could generate future charts for the flight manual they were authoring.

Wu and Liu were at supersonic speed now and up high in altitude with nothing coming past their windscreen. It felt like a simple and uneventful Sunday drive in Dad's wood-paneled station wagon. Wu slowed down the jet and flew for two minutes at an even Mach 1.0 at FL 510. Everything was in the green. He then pitched the nose up to climb, and the next item on their card was FL 550, or 55,000 feet, at Mach 2.0.

"Looking for flight level five-fifty at Mach 2.0," Liu announced, reading off their kneeboard card.

The Devil Dragon leveled off at 55,000 feet, and Wu kept

the throttles forward. They were at Mach 2.0 in just a matter of seconds. Passing through Mach 2.0, the jet again was smooth, and nothing was felt inside the cockpit. Liu made note of the test at the lower altitude and wrote down the temps outside the aircraft as Wu reduced the throttles to maintain the 2.0 they were looking to maintain. At this speed, it would be easy to continue on to Mach 3.

BING. BING. BING. FIRE. FIRE. A computerized female voice came over the intercom.

Wu and Liu looked inside the cockpit for the issue right away. "I don't see what component is on fire. Where is it? What's on fire? What's on fire?" Liu asked.

An onboard fire that a pilot cannot control is one of the worst and most serious things that can happen to any aircraft. Depending on where it is on the aircraft and which component is burning, it could be a disaster.

"Calm down, Liu. Calm down. OK. Let's go one hundred percent oxygen, ON," Wu announced, which was nothing more than flipping a lever for both pilots.

Wu looked at the gauges in the cockpit and saw that engine number two temperatures were abnormal. The temperature was high, and the pressure was low.

FIRE, ENGINE NUMBER TWO. FIRE, ENGINE NUMBER TWO. FIRE, ENGINE NUMBER TWO.

The female voice once again came over their helmets, as Wu scanned the instruments. Wu was already calculating that the next normal procedure would be for Liu to declare an emergency over the radio, while he maintained safe flying conditions by concentrating on the jet. Flying a secret jet complicated things because he wasn't on a flight plan, was not being tracked by radar, and could not really land just anywhere.

"I'm going to pull the throttle back to idle to see if it goes out. Confirm engine number two is at idle?" Wu asked.

"Concur, Wu, go ahead," answered Liu.

"Shit, we still got a problem. Nothing happened," Wu replied.

"What do you want to do?"

"I'm pulling the T-handle for engine number two. Confirm my hand is on engine number two T-handle?" Wu asked Liu.

"Whoa. OK. Confirmed."

"Pulling."

Wu pulled the handle, which shut down the fuel valve to engine two between the fuel tank and the fuel pump, therefore shutting the engine down immediately. He then put his hand up to the fire extinguisher and placed the switch down. This sprayed the engine area with halon gas, robbing the engine area of oxygen, ensuring that even if the fire was still going and burning outside the engine, inside the engine compartment, it would extinguish. No oxygen meant no fire.

An aircraft engine fire in the Devil Dragon, like most airplanes, could easily spread to the wing or fuselage, resulting in a mishap. The heat from the fire could cause distortion of the wing, affecting the aerodynamic lift, aircraft fuel, hydraulic, and electrical systems, and eventually compromise the physical structure of the aircraft, leading to loss of control. At these speeds, a swarm of mosquitoes on the wing could cause a mishap.

If Wu and Liu successfully contained the fire, there was still risk that the fire might reignite, and a plan to land the jet as soon as possible was needed.

As the jet slowed down through the Mach numbers, the jet shuddered like a car on an exit ramp coming from the highway. It wasn't anywhere near violent or uncontrollable, but you knew it was there. Wu maintained control of the jet the entire time, remembering the fundamental saying—aviate, navigate, communicate—when facing an emergency. It was something all pilots were taught at the beginning of flight training and lasted a lifetime.

"Liu, look, we need to land. We both know we need to land. We can land immediately or take a chance and continue to destination on the remaining three engines," Wu said, scanning the other engine instruments for any secondaries. "I don't see any secondary fires."

"We are eight minutes from the civil airport at twelve o'clock...Korla Airport. Radar shows Korla has three commercial aircraft in pattern, waiting to land. They are all on final. Two Air China jets and a China Southern jet. Runway in use is twenty-two, length is ninety-one hundred feet," Liu replied. Liu knew this was a tough decision and let out a breath.

Wu considered landing right away and thought about what would happen on landing in this case. Their jet was most likely damaged, but not much. The fire looked contained and should be out. Everything else was ops normal, and although they couldn't finish their test, he was comfortable.

"Wu, what do you want to do? You need to descend now

to make the airfield. NOW. What are you deciding?"

Part 6

The Plan

45 Bistro Restaurant, East Broughton Street, Savannah, Georgia

THE GULFSTREAM CORPORATE WEEKLY DINNER was being held at 45 *Bistro* this week, and the usual gang from customer service and marketing always hosted a splendid meal. Aircrew from all over the world flew into Savannah, Georgia, for semiannual training, as did new owners, technicians, and anyone else affiliated with Gulfstream for the week. It was their special night out, all expenses paid, to show their appreciation for the business they gave Gulfstream. Each week the location rotated to another fine dining experience, and 45 Bistro was an excellent choice for this fine evening, located in the Marshall House Hotel just five minutes' walk from the famous River Walk, full of scenery, bars, and more restaurants. The historic hotel, rumored to be haunted since being built in the mid-1800s, had previously served as a hospital, treating yellow fever for soldiers of the Union Army during the Civil War.

Sitting in one corner of the restaurant with his back to the original 1851 brickwork was an unusual and boisterous patron. Reggie Bryant, President of Gulfstream, was the special guest at tonight's early evening dinner, a rare occasion, considering his travel and work schedule. Reggie had just ordered his meal, laughing with the visiting aircrew, when his smartphone vibrated.

"Burns, you old dog. How the heck are you?" Reggie

answered, seeing it was Calvin Burns calling on his caller ID. They were both Savannah State College alums, former roommates and fraternity brothers, and Reggie did not want to ignore the call. It was about four months since they last talked, and Reggie was always willing to talk to his good friend. He was also always available to the organization he represented, as the US government was a large customer with deep pockets. In addition to being patriotic, it was good business for Gulfstream.

"Good. Good. I hope I'm not bothering you," Calvin said, ever so respectful of his time.

"Brother, anytime is good for you. I'm at a work dinner, but let me step over here toward the doorway, make some room, here. These pilots at this dinner are getting loud and rowdy already! Goddamn these pilots, always yelling...carrying on. Anyway, how's the family?" he said laughing at the energy and fun in the room.

Reggie was already up and walking over to the doorway. He glanced outside at the wooden awning over the sidewalk. The aircrews and other guests were already into their third drink and getting louder by the minute. The domestic and international pilots and others were visiting the Savannah facility to do their semiannual pilot training in the simulators, or to pick up a new jet, or even attend crew resource training. The costs associated with a new jet could be around $67 million, so the least Gulfstream could do was take everyone out for a fun dinner.

"Everyone is terrific, my friend. All healthy and good...and I hope yours are, too. Hey, sounds like a fun evening, but look, ah, Reggie. I'm sorry to bring up business this fast, but I need a favor.

I need a time-sensitive, work-related favor."

"Sure, sure. What is it?" Reggie asked.

"We have a special need—a rush job. It'll require some work on a jet we're borrowing, and the timeline is much faster than usual. Special Missions. The request is...uncommon."

"Great. Love it," Reggie replied, laughing. "Just bring her on down to SAV. Not sure what jet you're using this time, but we can always get you one if you can't locate one. Even a used airframe, Calvin, we have them available. Our Special Missions team can do it. We can make it happen," Reggie said, with a tone of reassurance.

"Your airframes guys will be busy. Can't say what we are looking for at the moment...um, on the phone, but it is not a normal request. Your engineers would have to be present at the face-to-face meeting, too. We have our eye on a G650ER from one of your customers. We've been in contact, and it's available. I'll have my guys down tomorrow. Can I have them come see you?" Calvin asked.

"Yup, just have them call first to ensure they get on my schedule. I'm in Savannah until Wednesday, then on to Appleton, and then our Long Beach facility. Happy to help you, Cal," Reggie answered.

"Thank you, Reggie. If you weren't hosting your weekly dinner, we could chat about Kathy and your girls. I'd love to hear how South Carolina State is going for your youngest. I know you're busy, brother. Thank you."

Reggie ended the call and thought about the request. Different, although no different from when they made modifications to other three-letter agency Gulfstream jets from DC. Like the time DIA wanted a radar hidden in the nose of a G500 back in January. And the StingRay cell-tower device they installed in the vertical tail section last year in another aircraft for the DEA. All the three-letter agencies came to see Reggie and the Gulfstream team because they were the gold standard. There was no better business jet on the market. Fast, glossy, high-end, and luxurious, their jets delivered folks and their equipment nearly anywhere in the world with style.

Zhangye, Gansu Airstrip, China

Wu knew that any aircraft fire was a serious situation, nearly always life threatening, and almost always meant land as soon as possible. That meant right *now*. He'd had engine fires before, along with similar "smoke and fumes in the cockpit" emergencies and was comfortable with these time-pressurized dangers. Wu was selected for this testing because of his coolness under pressure; he understood he was testing a newly developed, high-performance jet and *sometimes* these things happened. Wu was calm under the gravity of the situation, while Liu was *way* edgier. Wu could pick up on it.

"Liu, we'll be all right. We're not burning still because there are no other indicators in here. We're green across the board. Look outside. I'll bank the aircraft as we slow down, and you tell me if we're trailing smoke," Wu told him over the intercom, in a soothing voice that demonstrated style under pressure.

Liu wasn't that experienced as a pilot flying unknown jet aircraft, as he was primarily here as an observer and reporter of flying statistics to Chen. Sure, Liu was a rated pilot, but he was more the general's informal pet and politician than one of the guys in the squadron.

"No trail, Wu. No trail. No smoke in sight. Only the usual thick segmented contrail...our donuts on a rope," Liu reported, breathing a bit heavier than normal. His face was full of sweat, at least the portion that was exposed above the bridge of his nose and outside his oxygen mask. Wu's sixth sense was still spot-on.

The donuts on a rope exhaust, extremely rare and unique, were the shock diamonds, also known as Mach diamonds. They were a formation of standing wave patterns that appeared in the supersonic exhaust plume of the Devil Dragon's engines when it was operated at high altitudes. The diamonds were formed from a complex flow field and were visible due to the abrupt density changes caused by standing shock waves. What was unique about the Devil Dragon was that they didn't come out of all four engines, which was one of the Devil Dragon's most unique, secret features. It only came out of the two outboard engines.

Wu knew he was taking a gamble on this decision. Certainly, the miles of wires embedded inside the cockpit, wings, and airframe, connecting generators, alternators, and batteries to components, all made of toxic materials, could have easily burned. They connected electricity to all the lights, weapons systems, navigational components, instruments, and radios from the fuselage to the tail to the wings. The fire could also spread rapidly from the 5,000 psi high-pressure hydraulic system, easily spraying fluid out, cutting wires, hoses, and even some internal aircraft skin. Even worse, the multiple fuel tanks full of straw-colored jet fuel and fumes could instantly burn or explode in just a matter of seconds.

Wu's goal was twofold at this point. First, he needed to calm Liu down and reassure him all was good, and second, get him back to Gansu where they left from. Wu thought carefully about how to approach this scenario, because it would also be excellent timing for him personally to get back to the consulate. The icing on Wu's cake would be saving face with General Chen in bringing the jet back to the field they left from. Most likely, the ground crew wasn't even packed yet back into the Y-9 from this morning's launch, and they were still present on the ramp.

The ground and maintenance crews were under enormous pressure from Chen, too, and Wu understood that. He was sympathetic to them building and fixing a new jet that had no records, no history, and no formal maintenance manuals to troubleshoot issues. At times, they made the Devil Dragon maintenance seem easy, and at other times, it was apparent that they suffered from the difficulties of excessively dusty conditions being so close to the desert. The extensive travel, the constant secrecy, and the pressure of the flight schedule all played into the high mission-readiness demand. Making matters worse for everyone on the team was when the hours flown for the month dipped, and then Chen was all over everyone.

From this geographic position and altitude over China, Wu looked to the south and could look down into what was the ancient seventeen-hundred-mile old silk route through Pakistan, almost reaching the saltwater port that shipped Chinese freight on wooden ships all over the world. From this high up, he could see for three hundred miles, with a dark sky above and brown, green, and blue earth below. For centuries, it was the link for Asia to connect with the Middle East and beyond. These days, China was leading the world in mining precious metals, like copper, and Wu knew the historical significance of the route as he looked to the right. At the moment, though, Wu didn't care about history, as he turned his head forward again and drove the jet eastbound.

"Listen up...here's our plan. My decision is we are going back to Gansu Airfield. Plot me a course for the field. No need to land below. Satisfactory?" Wu announced, making a decision as aircraft commander but seeking some buy-in from Liu.

"Yes, ah, yes, yes," Liu said. He began to punch in the way points to the flight computer's GPS. Liu verified their course was laid out on the colored moving-map display in front of them. A white line was plotted on the screen from their current position to Gansu. "Turn to zero-one-zero, 458 miles to go."

"Coming left, turning to zero-one-zero," Wu replied, flying the aircraft manually. Upon rolling out, Wu flipped on the autopilot switches between their seats. He verified the course, airspeed, and altitude were set correctly, then made notes on his kneeboard for the engineers on the speed tests they completed. Plus details of the fire, of course. Wu would also be able to check the electronic flight records, as much of the information was recorded onboard the aircraft and downloaded to his smartphone for data transfer upon landing. This electronic maintenance and performance record helped troubleshoot the jet on its return. If the jet were staying in Chinese hands, the electronic records suite would be especially helpful during the weapons portion of flight testing.

On this flight, though, they would not be able to fly as fast as they wanted due to the loss of an engine, but it was still fast enough. The Devil Dragon wanted to fly, and the more flight time Wu accomplished on her, the more he realized how efficient the design really was. Slowing her down, even with speed brakes for drag, flaps, and gear, was a chore. Rule-of-thumb flight calculations would slow down an aircraft sixty knots for every second of deployment of the little speed brake doors. Not this bird. The thin wings and aerodynamic shape helped it slice thru the air with ease, and it seemed like she could fly forever.

In 1964 a Soviet mathematician who generated the stealth concepts by publishing "Method of Edge Waves in the Physical Theory of Diffraction" in the *Journal of the Moscow Institute for Radio Engineering*. He wrote that the strength of a radar return is related to the aircraft edge configuration of an object, not its size. With the current flight computers to aid the aerodynamically unstable aircraft, the sky was the limit.

The nose, body, and wings made it glide like the old SR-71 and U-2 that Lockheed's famous Skunkworks team of engineers used to produce some fifty years ago. The acrylic windshield, which was a combined canopy with quartz, could withstand the impact of any bird strikes in the air and 600 degree Fahrenheit temperatures. Off the sides of the jet came the shockwaves, generated by the different angles of the airframe. It flowed better than any aircraft designed by China and was definitely at the same level with those of the United States. The unique air intakes on top stabilized the clean air, allowing the supersonic flow without choking with turbulence. The air had to be slowed down to subsonic speeds before entering the jet in order to produce the thirty thousand pounds of thrust per engine. Over five thousand sensors provided real-time feedback to the flight computers, demonstrating the high technology that China had.

Wu thought about the visit to the consulate yesterday and wondered if the latest fire would help him in his rendezvous with Ford. *He wondered if Liu actually considered a secondary, divert airport, or an unscheduled landing, because of the fire?* Wu slowed down the aircraft in the descent checklist, but his mind was wandering, for sure. He worked the landing checklist with Liu and performed a number of different items inside the cockpit before lowering the gear and flaps, but he was thinking hard now. *How could we land someplace else...because when Ford comes, he will fly in Liu's seat? Would Ford have to kill Liu to get him out of the seat or aircraft itself?* Wu was a pilot, not a killer of an innocent fellow pilot. *What would Ford have in mind?*

"Good speed. Flaps fifty percent," Wu announced.

Wu did not want to have to take Liu out. *Maybe a gunshot wound? Maybe push him off the hotel balcony?* Wu shook his head slightly, talking to himself in his mind, answering that those ideas wouldn't work. He coughed a bit but still maintained control of the aircraft in the descent.

"Sorry, yeah, good speed. Gear down," Wu said, instructing Liu to put the handle down to lower the gear.

Wait a minute, Wu thought. *Got it.* He figured he had a

pretty good idea brewing on what to do with the jet and how to get Ford on board. He simmered the idea some more but was less than a minute from landing. Centerline was good, runway was clear. He repeated in his head...*aim point, airspeed, aim point, airspeed.*

Would this new idea work?

"Cleared to land," Liu announced over the intercom.

Mid-Atlantic Region, United States

The Gulfstream Special Missions Program Office was the bull's-eye for modifying business jets. About two hundred Gulfstream-built aircraft supported governments and militaries around the globe, including jets being flown for executive transportation, airborne early-warning systems, and even in support of open-ocean coastal surveillance. Beginning nearly fifty years ago, Gulfstream had served all five branches of the US military and other government agencies. From training astronauts to fly the space shuttle to special electronics/signals intelligence to target towing, Savannah had been part of it.

Gulfstream's Special Missions Program Office was stocked full of program managers, engineers, and pilots, all with a unique understanding of and expertise in solving the most demanding aircraft requirements. The highly skilled, experienced technicians for interiors, exteriors, avionics, and heavy metal structures do detailed modifications to the aircraft, along with an extensive aerodynamic analysis and computational fluid dynamics to determine the proper placement of the modification. Reggie and the Savannah team took great pride in coordinating and designing aircraft modifications, as well as the install of their state-of-the-art equipment.

The US Army C-12 King Air taxied onto the ramp at the Fort Belvoir Army Air Field in Northern Virginia and picked up Ford, Robert, Emily, and Mark for their trip to Savannah. Just to the southeast, and close to the airfield office, was the tarmac to drop off and pick up VIP passengers. The two chief warrant officers wasted no time getting them on board for their two-hour flight to the Savannah Airport in Georgia.

The quick flight to the south was uneventful, and the four of them napped nearly the entire way. The murmur of the two prop-driven, turbine engines were at the right frequency to enable a quick snooze, refreshing the DIA team for their upcoming meetings. Savannah Airport handled private business jets, the massive Gulfstream complex full of new hangars and ramps, the Georgia Air National Guard C-130s, and commercial air traffic. The warrant officer pilots parked in front of Gulfstream Aerospace on the north end of the airport, just off runway 1/19, and a nine-passenger, three-row, blue-and-white golf cart pulled up greet them.

"Hey, y'all. Welcome to Gulfstream," said Barbara "Babs" Ferry, of the Gulfstream customer service team. Ford, Mark, and Robert all noticed her pretty, long blond hair, cute southern accent, tight blue Gulfstream polo, and white miniskirt. And curves. Babs looked to have more curves than a mountain road in the French Alps. Emily noticed the reaction from the boys on her team more than anything. Ford was quick to look away, then whispered to Emily that he wasn't looking.

"Sure you weren't," Emily replied, knowing him better.

They all got into Babs's golf cart, and she drove them up to the customer service counter. Babs showed them inside where free snacks and cold drinks were served. There were meeting rooms available, showers, a small gym, computers and printers, a flight-planning room, large leather seats and couches to relax in, and enough aviation and news magazines to fill a bookstore rack. There was also a whole wall of the continental United States in aviation charts, from Seattle to Miami, showing all the highways of the air, called airways, from one coast to the other.

"Thank you, Babs. We appreciate your fine hospitality," Mark said with a huge grin, knowing that Babs was hired there for a reason. The only thing Mark said to himself was, "No wonder Gulfstream is number one."

"Wish y'all could have been here last night. We had our weekly dinner out in town and all them boys came out. All them boy pilots are real nice. Had a real fun time, too," Babs said.

"Slag, I bet they did," Emily said aloud.

Slag was another one of Emily's British terms, this one meaning "promiscuous woman."

"I'm sorry, sugah, what was that?" Babs asked, not hearing Emily's snide remark.

"I said I bet everyone had a great time. Well, anyway...we are here to visit your corporate offices. Mr. Reggie—" Emily started then got cut off.

"Oh my Lord. Oh, my. I had no idea you were here to see Mr. Reggie. I'll call up there right now in a jiffy," Babs said in her

Georgia peach accent.

Mark and Robert looked at each other and smiled. Emily stuck her finger into Ford's rib cage. "What?" Ford said, laughing. They were all silently making fun of Babs, her hair, her accent, her outfit, and other parts of Babs, but she had no clue.

Babs walked them, red pumps and all, over to the corporate office where Reggie's personal assistant greeted them in a more businesslike way. Ms. Linda Grey brought them into Reggie's office, where they sat at his conference table inside his office. Linda told them that Reggie was still out on the manufacturing floor looking at paints and interior woodwork and would be with them shortly.

They sat at an enormous wooden table, surrounded by attractive high-backed black-leather chairs. Reggie's outsized office had an entire glass wall that faced the manufacturing floor, where the final assembly of Gulfstream jets in that hangar were visible. He also had a private bathroom, a separate couch and coffee table area, a bookcase spanning an entire wall full of books and mementos, in addition to an impressive lineup of hand-carved jet models on pedestals. Some of them were Gulfstream jets, and others were military aircraft, which must have been Reggie Bryant's first career.

"Look at this." Ford held up a C-130 model and nodded to the framed photos on the wall of a younger Reggie Bryant in his flying days. "Pretty cool. He's a pilot, too."

"Probably helped him get up here. To the fat-cat suite," Mark said.

"It did! It did help me!" Reggie entered unannounced,

laughing at Mark's comment. A large man, full of personality, was eager to say hello to his DIA friends.

"I'm sorry, Mr. Bryant. No harm in saying fat-cat suite. Please take it...as a compliment," Mark said.

"Stop, Mark! All good between us. All of us. Gulfstream is one hell of a team, though, and I am lucky to be here," Reggie said, using his personality to make everyone feel at home. "How is ole Calvin Burns doing? He's a rascal, that Cal."

"Good, sir. Very good. He sends his best," Ford answered.

"Terrific to hear. One of my best friends, ole Cal Burns. Wish we lived closer. In a jet, it's fast to just zip up the coast, but...life gets in the way. You know?" Reggie replied, reflecting on how busy he got. "So glad to meet all of you. S, my boy Calvin called me and said you guys have something up. A special—or unique—request is how I think he phrased it. How can I help you?"

"Well, sir. We've borrowed a G650ER from Corning, one of your customers. They fly a newer 2016 model. Not that many hours on her, and only a few international trips so far. Mostly to Asia, about eleven trips to China, to be specific," Mark said, as the lead.

"Yes, yes. I know the aircraft. I know the CEO, too. They are lending it to you for a work mission?"

"Yes, sir. They are. Dates are good for whenever we need it. So is their loaner flight crew of two pilots. And so that leads us to you."

"OK, keep going," Reggie said with excitement.

"Thank you, sir. We're excited. We'd like to know if you

could build something for us. Modify the 650 airframe. We are interested in a ramp," Mark started to explain.

"A *ramp*. For real?" asked Reggie.

"Yes, sir, a ramp. Like your C-130, from your previous career," Ford added.

"Ohhh, now we're talking. You want a ramp in the rear of the aircraft that can be lowered and raised."

"Exactly. While in flight. One that would allow someone to exit the aircraft in flight."

"Hmmm. That is interesting."

"Then raise the ramp, and the interior and exterior would look like there is no ramp," Mark added. "Airframe and seats and carpet...ops normal."

"Ha! You guys are into some funky shit up there in DC!" Reggie said, leaning in his seat, laughing, and holding his belly with both of his folded hands. "Ole Burns got you guys going *good*! Going *good*!"

"Well, Reggie, can you bloody do it?" Emily asked.

Defense Intelligence Agency, Washington, DC

"Jason, would you come in, please?" the Deputy asked, motioning with his hand to come in his office.

"Yes, sir," Jason entered, carrying his steno pad and pen, ready to take action, as any staff officer would in Washington.

"Have Mike Klubb come in from Missiles. Is he still out there waiting?"

"He is. He's solo, as you asked."

"OK. He's not on the Outlook schedule, correct? Nothing written down?"

"Yes, sir. Correct."

"Between us, Jason, is his neck tie above his bellybutton, real short over his front porch stomach?" Calvin Burns nodded his head. "Never mind. Send him in. Thank you."

Mike Klubb, the briefer from earlier in the auditorium, came in and stood by the Deputy's table, waiting to sit down. He was pretty sure he was here in the Deputy's office as a follow-up to the brief but wasn't sure because Klubb and his team usually got ample notice on read-aheads, editing slides, and rehearsals. Nothing like that this morning.

"Hi, Mike. Thanks for coming in. I'll only take a few minutes of your time, as I know you are busy," the Deputy started right away. "The Buckley detection that you originally worked the other day was indeed not a fluke. There was something there. We have secondaries that prove there was an object—you know, other sources from collection assets."

"Sir, wow, that's great, sir. The team and I, we're ready! You know, we can do it. We can do anything. And the team—"

"Hold up, Mike. Let me finish."

"Yes, sir. Yes, sir. What was it?" asked Mike, eager to hear what it was, especially since he and his team initially spent so much time on the project.

"Well, that's why you're here this morning." The Deputy got up from his desk and walked over to where Mike was standing. Calvin was still wearing his reading glasses. "The detection was not an anomaly." Then, there was silence.

"I don't, umm, I don't understand," Klubb said. "What...what was it then?" Beads of sweat were forming on Mike's forehead, and he had to take out his handkerchief to wipe.

"Mike, it's compartmentalized, Mike. I can't read you in, and...I can't tell you," said the Deputy, lowering his head to look above his reading classes, like an old-school college professor. This was something he learned when he was a young junior assistant to a former chairman of the Joint Chiefs of Staff under President Clinton. Theatrics.

"Oh, I see," Mike said, somewhat startled that the Deputy not only got up to talk closer to him, but his tone and volume were different. Mike's hands were nearly wet with sweat now, as it sank in that he was way up in the Deputy director's office, about a gazillion pay grades above his own.

"It's sensitive, Mike. I'd like to tell you, but I just can't. I respect you and the team enough that I wanted to tell you in person. So, let's drop the topic and not freely discuss it anymore. Are we all right with that?"

"Ah, yes, sir. Yes, sir, of course," Mike said, nodding fast. He wouldn't breathe a word of it to anyone now, especially being up here in the Deputy director's office. In fact, Mikey was downright scared. "Zip. Not a word, sir. Not me."

They shook hands, and the Deputy gave him a small gold and multicolored DIA challenge coin to thank him for his efforts. Mike looked at it and was thankful for the opportunity to visit with the Deputy. *In his office.* He had never been up in his office before, and he was happy to add the coin to his robust collection back in his cubicle area. Mike then turned and made his way toward the doorway.

Military challenge coins usually depicted an aircraft or piece of equipment, the unit's name, location, and perhaps a senior leader's name. The tradition has been around for some time and has extended to outside the military, and was now in organizations like law enforcement and fire departments. If you didn't want to buy the whole bar a round of drinks, you made sure to bring at least one coin out to the bar with you. The legend was that someone could coin check you, meaning they ask to see your coin. If you did not have one on your person, standing there among friends and mates without a coin, it was your turn to buy a round.

Using an old-school police detective trick, the Deputy called out Mike's name just as he was ready to depart the office doorway. Calvin knew this trick because Mike's guard would be down, and it was a great move to get that one last piece of information that may have been held back or not released previously in a meeting.

"Hey Mike. Thanks again for your hard work and the work of your team. By the way, what is the name again of the person on your team who used to work on the Hill?" the Deputy asked, truthfully not having a clue if there was someone or not. It was a directed question, and the Deputy was completely fishing to see what answer Mike would provide. Line in the water.

"Oh, sir, that's Michelle Boyd, sir. Yeah, she used to be the liaison to the Senate. The, ah, the committee. She was sitting just behind you during the last auditorium brief. Put in a lot of work on this project. Michelle is from Pennsylvania and her cousin is Jessica—"

"Oh, that's right. Got it. Thank you, Mike," answered the Deputy, cutting Mike off at the knees. "Have a great day."

As Mike left the office, Calvin Burns sat down and put his reading glasses on his desk. He rubbed his eyes for a moment with both hands, then took out his pen from his suit pocket. He wrote down this woman's name on a yellow sticky pad and considered the potential connection with this Michelle Boyd and the Hill. Because the Deputy had the liaison job when he was much younger in his career, he knew the way the relationships worked. Calvin Burns easily made the link. There was *no way* that anyone on the Hill could have heard about the auditorium brief without a phone call and connection from someone actually sitting in the room, leaking the details to someone on the committee. *Hell, that's how I used to do it!* The only real way would have been Michelle Boyd contacting a staffer there and then grabbing the senator's ear. Calvin circled her name on the yellow sticky with his pen.

"Bingo."

Gulfstream Corporate, Savannah, Georgia

Reggie didn't answer Emily's question but got up from his table, still chuckling, and walked over to his office doorway to talk to his longtime personal assistant, Linda.

"Linda, can you have Rose and Arnold come on up, please?

Have them join us?" asked Reggie. He turned back toward to group at the table, then turned about again to Linda. "Hey, also have them bring the 650 models. And load up the CAD! Thank you!"

Reggie sat back down, entertained with the DIA crew. They still didn't know if Gulfstream could help them or not. They trusted Reggie but were feeling the pressure.

"Rose is our Senior Vice-President of engineering, and Arnold is the Senior Vice-President of the Airframes and Power Plants. I've called them in because they are our experts. From what you have asked from us so far, I'm pretty sure we can do this, but let's talk to them. I only work here," Reggie said, ending again with deep laughter, clasped hands over his large stomach again.

The two Gulfstream vice-presidents came in, both wearing casual golf shirts and sporting tans. The tans were rare this time of year up north, but in the Low Country, it was a regular sunny day. Reggie did the introductions, and the DIA team explained the situation and their request. The VPs both knew what the federal government meant to Gulfstream's bottom line. Plus, if Reggie called them in to the suite, it was important to them.

Arnold from airframes immediately went to the room's computer, logged in, and pulled up some of the internal and external diagrams for the 650. They had some exceptional, whiz-bang, 3-D CAD diagrams that allowed rotation of the aircraft on the screen in all sorts of directions.

"Right here?" as Arnold used an electronic pen to mark up the computer image of the jet on the screen. "Here to here is where you want the ramp? Comes down like this, then back up?"

"Yes, sir. Exactly. We need it there and in the interior, the seats and carpet...they need to return to their original positions. In the event that the aircraft is boarded on arrival and inspected, it can't look like it has a ramp," answered Robert.

"Could we modify the crew door?" Reggie asked, thinking that it might be easier to modify.

"Hmmm. No, we can't, Reggie," said Rose from engineering. "The aerodynamic forces at these speeds would tear it off. Because it's in the slipstream, it would also affect the knots. Too much drag. When you have the ramp, it's in the rear and out of the slipstream. We'd have to run the sim, but I'd be willing to bet the pilots would get some yaw out of it, too."

"Well, you're the customer, Mark," Arnold jumped in. "Is this what you guys were thinking with the ramp right here?" Standing up, he walked over to point on the screen on the wall. "And it would open and close like this?" He held his wrists together and flapped his hands like an alligator's jaws. He repeated the motion twice.

"Perfect. That would be terrific. We also have the other request. It's to be opened internally, but no switches or wiring that show we have a ramp. We understand that may complicate things for your electrical system on the jet," Mark answered. "It's for our operational security."

"Nah, easy. We have a Gulfstream app for that," Rose answered.

"Really? An app?" Ford asked.

Ford was used to military aircraft, so the commercial

technology was just on the edge of being beyond his thinking. The military aircraft he flew were certainly modern and high-tech but designed to fight in an expeditionary fighting environment. At Gulfstream, it was about customer convenience and luxury, so an app on a smartphone made complete business sense.

"Sure, we have an app just for each aircraft. By tail number. The aircraft has its own Wi-Fi system that the aircrew and passengers can connect to. From anywhere around the aircraft, you can connect. Passengers use it for entertainment or business. If the pilots have the password, they can control a number of things from their smartphone," Arnold answered.

"Are you kidding me?" Ford asked.

"No, no kidding, Mr. Ford. We'll have to use the onboard aircraft electrical system for the ramp motor, but perhaps wire it in through the pressurization system. When you decompress the cockpit, power is applied. It will allow you to use the app and will activate the actual on and off switch for the ramp motor. On inspection, no one would question why there is a circuit-breaker switch that leads to pressurization. Normal ops," Rose explained.

"That would work great. Yes, fantastic," Mark answered.

Rose and Arnold looked at each other. They seemed happy to be working on a project like this one again. Ford couldn't put his finger on it, but there was a combined casualness and confidence that he did not expect. To modify a jet was a big deal to him, but not to them.

"We both know that Corning jet well. It comes in for inspections and upgrades about once every month for their first year, at our expense. They use it up there in overcast, cold Central

New York to ferry around their folks...their executives and retirees. They call it a 'shuttle run,' I think. Flies the Lexington, Hickory, and Wilmington route, if I remember correctly, then back to Elmira," said Rose.

"That's pretty respectful that they allow you to use it. Beautiful jet. If I remember, it was tail number November seven-eight-eight Charlie Golf?" said Arnold, turning his head slightly to remember the blue-striped paint job.

Mark thought long and hard and was amazed these guys knew their customers well enough to recall tail numbers. He guessed that when you spend a year building a machine that perhaps you think of it as one of your own, and then it leaves home. *Impressive.*

There was a pause in the conversation.

"So, we are in somewhat of a...jam on the timeline," Mark said. "How long do you think it would take from the time the jet arrives to your facility?"

Another long pause, then Reggie turned to Rose for an answer.

"I think we could get it done, in and out, in about three or four days. We have all the parts here, as well as the labor. No need to ferry up to Appleton. Would that work for you?" answered Rose.

"That would work phenomenally for us," said Mark. "Thank you."

Hilton Head Island, South Carolina

The meeting ended, and Linda escorted them back to the corporate waiting area. When they were alone, Ford suggested that since his parents lived nearby, they could drive about forty-five minutes over to their area in Hilton Head Island, South Carolina, and meet for dinner. Everyone was happy with the idea, and they made their way on to Route 17 and Highway 278 in a Gulfstream loaner car.

The Low Country of South Carolina was stunning, with its striking array of waterways that included an ocean, rivers, a sound, eclectic creeks, and rich salt marshes. Hilton Head Island is a resort town just twenty miles northeast of Savannah, and about ninety miles south of Charleston. Its twelve miles of beachfront on the Atlantic Ocean make it a popular vacation destination for many on the East Coast.

Robert drove the Nissan Ultra loaner while Ford sat shotgun and navigated. Mr. and Mrs. Chad Stevens decided to meet the group at the Skull Creek Boathouse Restaurant, near the Hilton Head Plantation, directly on the Skull Creek Intracoastal Waterway. The Boathouse, on the waterfront and next to an actual warehouse that houses boats, had an outdoor bar complete with a year-round thatched grass roof, a multitude of flat-panel televisions, and a robust schedule of outdoor acoustic guitar players. The atmosphere was exactly what the team needed to rehash where they were with the plan.

From the backseat, Mark, ever the backseat driver, was always on the go, talking, pointing, and active. Sometimes people thought he had ants in his pants, like a kindergartner, but it was just his personality.

"Looks like phase one, the entry, is coming together. We should head up to Corning in the morning to have the chat about the jet, but I'm happy that it is not only available but our ramp can be made," Mark commented, now that they had a few minutes alone to chat.

Emily was in the backseat, relatively quiet. She had been more of the thinker today, not saying much but backing up the team on decision-making. Mark usually made his decisions by consensus, in that he usually asked all of them for their opinions before going final. She was also the true critical thinker of the group, using her high emotional intelligence that got her into MI6. She was also the woman behind the man, providing the special nurturing and encouragement that Ford was going to need.

"Phase two," Emily said, with a half a second pause. "We need to get Ford back to skydiving, so he is familiar again. Also, get him into a wing suit."

"Ford, what do you think?" asked Robert.

"Hold up everyone. Wait a sec. Wait a moment, please. I'm looking up something on Google Maps. I suggest we also take a hard look at airfields on the China map again," Emily added, while looking at the east coast of China on her smartphone.

Ford turned around in his seat. "I'd like to get a jump in with the guys from the teams as soon as possible. I'm also about a week out from flying, from physically sitting in the cockpit. Not rusty, but it's a perishable skill. If not, perfectly OK. Perhaps a simulator flight or two over at Andrews or wherever, just to get back in the saddle."

"We can do that. Sure," replied Mark.

Ford continued. "We also still don't know the performance parameters of Wu's jet, and it would be pretty damn helpful if we could replicate some of it so I know what we are dealing with. Weights, speeds, power plants, takeoff and landing data. If we can," Ford added. "Fuel is a big one, too. If this thing takes some weird hybrid fuel, and Wu lands someplace that doesn't have it, it complicates things. Most engines can take most fuels, but who knows with this thing?"

Robert pulled the sedan into the restaurant parking lot, which was full of islanders eating and drinking for their night out on the town. After parking the car, Emily and Ford were able to walk together slowly while Robert and Mark went ahead. Robert and Mark went to the bar first for a beer, and Emily and Ford walked toward the pier alone.

Emily held his hand while Ford checked out the waterway on Skull Creek. He then looked at her and planted a kiss, something he had not done in a while because of the pace of their situation.

"You OK, Ford?" she asked.

"Oh, yeah. Fine." He glanced at her, then down at the ground. "I'm just thinking about Wu again. You and I never really talked about him much, but he truly was close to our family. He was the best. Still is the best, I mean. Unfortunately, I'll have to tell my parents tonight."

Emily looked out at the water. "I understand. I never told you this, but I lost a girlfriend in college. My roommate of two years. She died over the course of a few days from meningitis. I was heartbroken. So, I do understand, love. But you know you can't tell them, your parents, about the op, right?" Emily said. She wanted to be sympathetic, yet ensure Ford understood the ways of the intelligence community. He held a clearance, but something at this level was so dynamic, so important and sensitive, that a reminder was necessary.

"Yeah, yeah. I know that. I'm sorry to hear of your friend from college. I had not heard that before. It's just tough, you know," Ford answered, looking at the fishing boat coming back from an afternoon's catch. "My parents know I fly and do things like this around the globe. They'll just be upset at the upcoming loss of Wu. Wish they could have seen him. Maybe they will, depending on where we land and the timing and all."

"I want you to know I love you, no matter what happens, Ford. The pace will pick up, and we won't have that much alone time together. I'll do whatever I can to support you on this mission and get you back safely," Emily said, hugging him hard.

"I love you, too. Thanks for the support, Emily," Ford answered. "Keep up the love, and maybe we'll start dating."

"Start? Well, OK, but then I'd have to stop dating all those other pilots. Hey, cut that out, fly boy," Emily teased him.

They walked inside and saw Mark and Robert at the bar, watching highlights of the college football games. The square bar inside was jammed, and Ford looked around for his parents. Since they weren't there, he took a look out back. Peeking through the glass pane to out back, he spotted them sitting near the outdoor bar. Ford doubled back to grab everyone and led the way outside to the patio and bar area.

The Stevenses stood up and hugged Ford. "Good to see you, son. You look just great. Not a scratch on you from the fire last week!" said Mr. Stevens.

A waitress dropped off menus for the latest guests at the same time but did not ask for additional drink orders yet.

"We are so happy that you were able to come down and enjoy this beautiful weather with us!" said Marion. "Sunset from here is priceless. So. Ford...please introduce us!"

Robert looked closely at Mr. Stevens and thought that he had met him someplace before. He couldn't really remember a location or an event, but yes, he had met him or worked with him in the past.

"Mom, Dad, of course you know Emily. And this is Robert. And this is Mark." Ford said, as each person shook hands and exchanged greetings.

"Mr. Stevens. Have we met before? You look very familiar to me," Robert asked after the introductions.

"No, I don't believe we have. I'm retired from Shell Oil. Lived around many places in my career. Where are you from?" Mr. Stevens asked.

"Around. Moved around as a kid because my dad was army. Then I was army. I work now in Washington, DC. Defense contractor," answered Robert.

"Oh, I see. Well, perhaps I look like someone you know," answered Mr. Stevens. Except that he did recognize Robert from the past. He could not remember either, but he was pretty sure he did. He kept it to himself and didn't let on. Maybe it would come to him later in the dinner, as he sipped his Palmetto Ale microbrew.

Ford took a sip of his beer and looked at his parents. He gave them a half smile and considered what he had to tell him about Wu. He knew it would be tough. "Mom, Dad. I have some news to tell you about Wu."

"Ole Wu! How is he doing? We haven't heard from him since Christmas!" Marion commented. "Both boys, pilots," as she pointed to Ford. "We've known Wu since we lived in China many years ago. These guys were kids and now both pilots! And look at them now."

"Mom, well, Wu is very sick. Very ill. In fact, terminally ill, Mom."

"My gosh, what happened?" his mom said.

"He is? God...well, what's going on?" said Mr. Stevens.

"Wu and I, er, met on a web chat with a camera. You know, on the Internet with the computer. He told me he has cancer. Pancreatic cancer. He only has about three months to live, at best."

"Oh, my. Poor Wu. He was like another son to us. Another boy in our family. And his mother passed away a few years ago," Mr. Stevens said quietly, sighing. He held Marion's hands. "He doesn't have anyone else. No family."

"Is he being taken care of? Is the medical community in China making him feel comfortable?" asked Marion.

"I'll see. I may be seeing him in the coming weeks, so perhaps I can take care of him before he passes. I'm pretty upset about it, but if I can get out of work and burn up some leave, I'll go over."

Robert and Mark exchanged glances, not knowing if Ford was going to blow it. They were sure that his parents would not know a stealth bomber from a crop duster, but that wasn't the point. Ford was sworn to secrecy until death and beyond, and the exchanged glances were precautionary.

"We have heard so many great things about him. It is a terrible shame that he's come down with this disease. So young, too," Emily added. She looked at Ford and put her hand on his arm. "We know you'll do your best to go there and take the very best care you can of him."

Marion started to cry, and she wiped a tear away with a tissue from her purse.

Ford thought about the logistics of the trip and how much his parents were going to ask him about the details, but they didn't. Slowly, the subject changed, and the table was off on something new to chat about. Everyone talked over dinner and drinks, got caught up with one another, and the rest of the dinner table conversation was warm and entertaining.

After dinner, they made their way to the exit on the far side of the restaurant. Ford led the way. As he turned around to make sure everyone in the party was following and navigating OK, he saw his dad and Robert talking quietly and closely. Ford had not seen that before and wondered what they were talking about. They were standing and not following the rest of the group. Ford thought that was weird because they had just sat for a few hours talking.

They said their good-byes, and Ford and the crew got into their car to head over to the hotel. Inside the car, the topic went from the beaches of Hilton Head to their mission.

"What were you and my dad up to back there?" Ford asked Robert, pointing with his thumb back toward the restaurant.

Robert was driving again, and Ford sat in the backseat just behind him this time around. Robert made the right turn out of the parking lot and back to Highway 278 for the Hilton Head Omni Hotel.

"Oh, just talking college football. Turns out he is a University of South Carolina fan, too."

Ford immediately thought that was strange. *Dad doesn't like college football.*

Zhangye, Gansu Airstrip, China

Normal flight operations in any sane flight department or military flying squadron would have you declaring an emergency over the frequency for a fire, as pilots were taught worldwide. From a solo student in a Cessna 172 to a Boeing 777 captain, when an emergency happens and you've troubleshot it as much as possible, you declare the emergency for special handling to the airport of your choice so that the fire department is waiting for your arrival. Unless you are piloting a secret stealth bomber that doesn't officially exist, in which case, you don't tell a soul until you land.

Wu and Liu rolled to a stop after landing safely and parked

the jet where they'd just left from. The ground crew was shocked to see that they were back, and Wu and Liu could tell from their pointing that there must have been some fire or smoke damage visible on the airframe. The director of maintenance and the chief engineer both came out to see Wu. Luckily, no Chen yet.

"A fire? You had a *fire*?" the chief engineer asked, but it was more like yelling.

The Chief was mad at something the jet did to them, for heaven's sake, Wu thought. *We didn't cause the fire, we put it out.*

"What happened?" he asked again.

"We were running the planned flight profile past 2.0, and we had indications for a fire. Oil pressure dropped. Temps were high, in the red. Smoke and fumes in the cockpit," Wu explained. By now the maintenance guys were all standing around, listening in. "Pulled the T-Handle, shut her down. Number two."

"What else? You have avionics problems?" asked the director of maintenance.

Liu perked up. "No, sir. Nothing else."

"Why didn't you land earlier?" asked the engineer.

"We discussed that option, but since the fire was out and you were all still here, we decided to continue a bit farther and come back to you," Wu said. He hoped that was enough to forestall a browbeating.

The chief engineer and the director of maintenance looked at each other and were appreciative. Landing that far out would only delay the repair, and who knew what kind of additional parts they would have to fabricate to get her back on the flying schedule.

"You were right, Lee," the chief said, "you bring her here." It nearly pained him to say it, but he did. "Good job. All right everyone...get her in the hangar, NOW!"

"Thank you. Liu was a great copilot. Tremendous help. Was there the whole way, right in the checklists," Wu added, breaking a smile among men who rarely did.

Wu wanted to get back to maintenance as soon as possible, so he downloaded the mission from his smartphone into the computer database in the hangar's portable computers. He spent some considerable time writing up the details for his postflight report, in enough detail for even Chen's questioning. Who knew what kind of questions he would have, but after talking with engineering and maintenance, Wu was satisfied.

Wu was exhausted after the flight and just wanted to take a shower at the hotel and rest. He wasn't hungry, but he did crave some sugary snacks. Perhaps even some cookies, if available. Wu passed through the lobby of the hotel where he was last evening, so he knew where the vending machines were. He looked over the lobby chairs, the small bar and restaurant, and the front desk, but what he wanted were those machines. Easily located, he stood in front going through the options and smiled into the reflection. What caught his eye again was how aged he looked in the reflection. He put in some yuan, selected all sorts of snacks for his junk-food dinner, and headed up to his room for some more meds.

Wu got into his room and let out a long breath. He pulled out his smartphone and attempted to write a text to Ford. Looking at the screen, he saw that the traffic light icon was in the red, although the Peanut was installed. He shut down, then restarted the smartphone. Looking at his screen again, he saw he had a green light. It was pretty cool technology. *What doctor or nurse thought of this little software?*

DIA Operations Center, Washington, DC

The Peanut app transmitted as easily as two middle-school teenagers gossiping about a classmate, and the communications satellites picked up the signals as if Wu was using a home Wi-Fi in Seattle and attempting to get a local website. The texts, along with all the Devil Dragon apps information from the phone, went from Wu's hotel Wi-Fi out to the computer structure of China Telecom and then right over to the ops center. The entire sequence, along with full encryption, was only seconds. Because Mark Savona and crew were going to be off the grid awhile and traveling, he arranged for all the team's texts to arrive to the watch officer first.

The report from Wu's phone generated an automatic report titled "OPERATION WHIRLPOOL" and sent the entire raw content to the DIA Operations Center at Bolling AFB. The amount of data in the report was quite large and consisted of additional e-mails, locations, websites visited, and aircraft performance reports going as far back as the initial flight. The attachment in the e-mail had a day/time stamp of just four minutes ago, and the watch officer on duty was fast on his feet to make the phone call. He looked up the point of contact who needed the information and was surprised to see it was the Deputy himself.

"Jason Cohen, sir, this is the watch officer, Major Scott Howard. Your boss has a priority message here that just came in. Want me to run it up?"

"Yup, bring it up. Thanks. Make sure it's sealed," Jason said, since he wasn't cleared for whatever the contents were.

Jason immediately went in to the Deputy's office, and Major Howard hurried up to the Deputy's office.

"Sir, you have a priority message coming up from the watch officer. A Major Howard."

"Hmm. Thank you. Who is it from?"

"Unknown at the moment."

Just then, Major Howard entered the foyer of the Deputy's office.

"He's here now, sir. Want me to send him in?" asked Jason.

"Yes, please. Have him come on in."

Major Scott Howard entered the room and greeted the Deputy. The Deputy took off his badge so Major Howard could identify the Deputy and write down his number on the back of the badge. He checked the clearance list for this message and the Deputy was on it.

"Good to go, sir. Here you go." The major handed the paperwork in the locked, cloth pouch to the Deputy.

Calvin Burns sat at his desk, unlocked the pouch, and took out the report on OPERATION WHIRLPOOL. He opened the heavy folder and saw 212 printed pages of data, a majority of the pages full of numbers in columns. The dates and times were there, in addition to longitudes and latitudes, or the positions of the aircraft. It displayed airspeeds in knots, converted to miles per hour, outside air temperatures, and altitudes of the vehicle. It also gave, in number form, their navigational route, where they started, and where the flight ended. It showed engines numbered one through four and their performance data, including engine oil pressure and temperature, fuel tanks and their levels, in addition to their temperature. The weapons data was empty, which showed they had not started testing the aircraft yet as a weapon of war. A host of information was important to an analyst who would not only enjoy reading the report but relish reading it more than once.

Calvin also noticed the shutdown of the number two engine during the last entry, which was just dated hours ago, seeing the engine instrument numbers increase in temperature. He ran his finger across the page, turned it to the next, and on 210–211, he saw it: FIRE. *Oh, shit*, he thought, *Wu had a fire*.

"Jason! Get me Mark Savona on the phone!" the Deputy hollered.

Near the Omni Hilton Head Oceanfront Hotel, South Carolina

The Omni Hilton Head Oceanfront Hotel was a terrific waterfront resort, recently remodeled and decorated beautifully. Robert drove up to the hotel parking lot on the south side, and they walked into the small general store inside the lobby so Mark could reload on his coffee fuel. Judi from the lobby at DIA wasn't here to make him his special drink by facial recognition, so he was forced to order like all the other ordinary customers.

Ford grabbed a table for them, and everyone but Mark sat. He arrived shortly with a round of decafs and sat down with him. As he was stirring his drink, his smartphone vibrated. The screen read, "Work—Big Room."

"Hey, ops center calling. Check it out," showing the phone to the table. "Hello. This is Mark."

"Mark, this is Big Room. What is the initial of your last name?" asked the caller.

"S, as in Sierra," Mark answered.

"And what is your code number?"

"Seven, four, seven, six, five, two, T, U."

"What is your code word or phrase?"

"Bryce Harper. Washington Nationals."

"Thank you. Please hold for a call from the Deputy."

Mark placed his hand over the phone. "Deputy is calling," he told the table. Mark checked to ensure they were green, and they were.

The gang all looked at one another, then Ford looked at his watch.

"This guy ever sleep?" asked Ford.

"Mark, Calvin here. How'd things go in Savannah today?" asked the Deputy.

"Good, sir. All good. Thumbs up on the request. Reggie sends his best," Mark answered.

Mark thought about telling him they were heading up to

Corning tomorrow but decided not to. The Deputy called him, not the other way around. No reason to bend the boss's ear if he was calling him.

"OK, good. Reason I am calling. Our friend. He had a fire. Fire on number two. Looks like all OK. But, just wanted you to know for planning purposes. Certainly more details when you get back," the Deputy said.

"Whoa. I see. OK, sir. Thanks for the call. We're heading up north past you tomorrow to see your other friend. Should be back to you in the evening."

"Got it. Tell him I said hello, and please pass my sincere thanks. Safe travels and see you then," answered the Deputy. He hung up.

Mark disconnected the call on the phone and looked down, then at Ford. "Ford, Wu was flying and had a number-two engine fire. Deputy received the report. He didn't say how, but it must be the Peanut relay. Wu landed safely, and the Deputy said more details upon our return."

"Bloody hell," Emily exclaimed.

Robert was thinking that based on Peanut's performance in the past, the report must have come from the ops center, then to whoever requested it. The Deputy must be the most senior person on the list to be notified, he thought.

"Shite," said Emily.

"Shit is right. Well. Those things happen. Engine fires are somewhat normal, and you just shut it down and hope other components of the jet didn't catch," Ford said.

"Are you for real? A fire is normal?" Robert questioned.

"Not normal, but we get a lot of stuff thrown at us, and a fire is just on the list of all sorts of crap that can go wrong," Ford answered. Ford kept silent but remembered a flight crew just last month had to eject out of an F-15 due to an engine and fuselage fire. Ford also didn't even know if Wu had ejection seats, about which he made a mental note to ask.

"On nearly every single flight I have ever been on, something breaks. Something gets damaged or doesn't work anymore. Not surprised. It's a machine, no different from your washer or dryer at home," Ford added, trying to explain the similarities to nonpilots.

"I'll remember that next time I'm flying home on British Airways to Heathrow," Emily said.

They walked out of the general store and made their way back to the front desk. Getting room keys, they met one last time to touch base for the morning flight to Elmira/Corning Airport to check out their chariot. The Corning G650ER was waiting their arrival.

Mark gathered them around one last time for the night. "Check out at 0600, takeoff at 0700. Taking a Citation jet up to Elmira. Breakfast is available here starting at 0530. Good?" Mark asked.

No questions, so everyone started off for their rooms. They all got on the hotel elevator, and Robert and Mark got off on floor two, while Emily and Ford rode up to floor three.

"Quit looking at my bum. You go to your room, I go to mine." Emily winked at Ford.

"Come *on*. Ohhh, all right. Good night, Emily."

Sunshine Hotel, Shandan, Gansu, China

Wu got in his bed and slept for what seemed like a week. He woke up after a few hours, a bit refreshed, and grabbed his smartphone. Wu propped up his head on the pillow and placed the phone on his chest. He verified the Peanut app was on there and connected, and it was. Green light. It looked like a real traffic signal hanging from a wire like in America, which had red, yellow, and green lights on it. His was green, so he started to write his text message to Ford.

Had a number two engine fireee yesterday (we have four engines). I am okk, but jet was damaged. I think its minimal damage and will find out today. Compressor stall?

New idea—I will bring jet to China east coast airport under a falsee maintenance problem. Can you meet me there\Monday? Time is wasting and I am not feeling any better. Check out hong Kong, Beijing, Shanghai airports. Large airportss at night will add to the confusion on my end with local air traffic c0-pilot and boss.

Elmira/Corning Regional Airport, Horseheads, New York

The white US Army Cessna Citation business jet taxied to parking on the ramp at Atlantic Aviation, the fixed base operator company at the Elmira Airport. Atlantic Aviation provided fuel, oil, and other services to the business jet and general aviation

303

community. Emily got off first. She immediately noticed the damp chill in the air and tightened her coat up a bit. The freezing temperatures, snow and ice on the ground, and the overcast skies were a shock compared to yesterday at Skull Creek and the warmer Savannah climate. Ford, Robert, and Mark walked down the jet stairway after her, and all felt the same way about the classic Western New York weather. Typical Mark—he didn't even have a coat with him.

The customer service folks from Atlantic walked them from their lounge area, next door to the Corning corporate hangar. John Abbott, Corning chairman and CEO, was there to greet them, wearing his crisp dark business suit and white shirt, the uniform of Corning. He had been with Corning, Inc. nearly his whole adult life, except when he went up to Boston to attend business school, in addition to the Corning business road trips that were required to climb the ladder.

"You must be our friends from Washington," said John Abbott. "It's a pleasure to meet each of you. Please come into the hangar office."

The DIA team walked into a ground-level meeting room that was decorated like any other high-end room they had been in, except this one was outfitted with leather recliners, some flat panels, and a pool table. There was a wet bar over in the corner, in addition to an eating area, a stove and microwave, a full-size black refrigerator, and large wine cooler.

"This is part meeting room, part pilot lounge. Where our pilots relax between flights, flight attendants prepare meals, prep the jet..." John explained.

"Thank you for hosting us, John. And thank you for the use of your jet again. You and Corning have been most gracious through history, and today is no different," Emily said, with her thick British accent.

"Oh, a Brit?" he said, giving her a special smile. "Well, yes, it's the least we could do. Corning has, over the years, supported the IC and the military, and we are glad to help the national security team. My father served in the Army Air Corps during World War Two, and I've always been very patriotic."

"John, thank you again for the loan on the jet. I'm Robert, the one who called you on behalf of Deputy Director Calvin Burns." They shook hands once more.

They sat at the table in a circle and munched on the sandwiches that were already set out.

Robert opened up right away. "John, per our conversation, and if it's OK with you, we'd like to borrow the jet for about a week. Borrow your crew with the jet...modify it at our expense down at the Gulfstream facility, fly it to China, and return it. Safely."

John shook his head while he rubbed his chin. "I see. OK. I have a flight department full of pilots. Most have been here over fifteen years, some closer to thirty. You can have anyone you want. They are all qualified in the 650, worldwide."

"Sir, hello, my name is Mark Savona. Nice to meet you again. We met a few years ago at a social function at the Corning Museum of Glass. A fund-raiser. It was under another, eh, mission for DIA. Anyway, sir, thank you again," Mark said, as he cleared his throat. "What we are looking for is for your crew members who not only can fly but can understand the...sensitive nature of what they are going to do. Be respectful of the mission they are about to embark on."

"You mean keep their mouths shut," John said.

"Exactly," said Mark. "Please allow me to introduce you to US Air Force Reserve Captain Ford Stevens, one of our military pilots."

Ford shook hands with John.

"Wait, are you flying our jet, too?" asked John, eyeing Ford and thinking that he wasn't part of the original deal in the phone call from Robert. "I'd have to check with our insurance folks if that is covered."

"No, sir. Not exactly. I'll be a passenger on the jet. Solo. Your jet and crew will be delivering me to China," Ford said, speaking up to paint a picture for John, since it was his $50 million jet.

"Ohhhh. Who am I to question the DIA?" John said laughing. "What do you need us to do? Want me to select a crew for you? Visit the jet?" He stood to look through the window into the hangar. "She's right out there inside the hangar. The hangar doors are closed, and it's warm inside, so you could look around if you wanted."

John thought ahead about his team of pilots and had two guys in mind. They flew frequently to China, knew Savannah, were very familiar with the 550 and 650 series jets with Gulfstream, and were trusted representatives. John had known them for close to twenty-six years and knew not only their spouses but their kids.

"Yes, that would be splendid. We would love to meet

them," Emily said, looking toward another room where two pilots were looking at a table that was barroom height and had a piece of Plexiglas over it. They were busy with paperwork, filling out some forms as they used a calculator to compute something.

"Andrew, Lurch, you guys have a second?" John yelled inside to the two pilots.

Andrew Fitzpatrick and Jeff "Lurch" Baker were very experienced pilots. Both pilots exceeded twelve thousand hours of flight time and were commercial pilots type-rated in over a dozen different aircraft types between them. In addition, Lurch was a retired US Marine Corps AV-8B Harrier pilot who earned his call sign back in the squadrons, and Andrew was a civilian pilot who worked his way up the aviation ladder by flying bank checks at night.

"Andrew, Lurch, please meet our friends from DIA. This is Emily, Ford, Robert, and Mark," John said, as he did introductions. The pilots walked from the doorway over to the table in the lounge.

"Hello, hello. Nice to meet everybody. How can we help DIA?" asked Andrew. "Mr. Abbott told us earlier you may need to be flown someplace."

"Again, thanks, Andrew...and Lurch. Yes, we need, first off, absolute sensitivity to us being here. Complete secrecy. Complete sensitivity. In fact, before we go any further, you also need to know that this mission does involve some high risk. And as a result, we can compensate you each ten thousand dollars for your time. As a bonus. All we ask is you sign a nondisclosure form, which obligates you, for life, to never disclose this event," Robert explained.

"Ohh, reminds me of the Flying Leatherneck days! Love the excitement. I'm in," Lurch said.

Both men took pens from their shirt pockets, read the paperwork quickly, and signed the documents. This wasn't the first time they'd flown a DIA mission, but it would definitely be the first one of such a unique nature.

"I'm Mark, and thanks. Thank you. So here's what the plan is. This gent right here is Ford Stevens, and he is an Air Force pilot. He has flown fighters and bombers, balloons and gliders. He's also a parachutist. Only thing he isn't, is an astronaut. The three of you will fly to China with Ford as your passenger. Upon reaching a certain geographic location, one of you will lower a custom-made ramp that will soon be installed by Gulfstream in the back of your jet, and Ford will jump out with a parachute on. You two pilots will continue to fly, land the jet in China, and can carry on with your business as usual," Mark said.

There was silence in the room.

"Corning would need to cook up a standard business trip, which they have surely done before, to make it look normal," Emily added.

"That's pretty cool," Andrew said. "What kind of a ramp?"

"You two gents"—Mark nodded to the pilots—"along with Robert, will take the jet down to Savannah tomorrow, where they are waiting to modify the rear of the jet. We just came from there, and the CEO has his top folks standing by for you guys to arrive. They even remembered your tail number. Gulfstream is going to cut a hole in the airframe to make a ramp that will lower for Ford to exit, then retract, all without anyone noticing the mod in the airframe," Mark said.

"Extraordinary. Wow. Well, we're prepared to support. We can leave when you're ready, Robert," Lurch said.

John Abbott stood up and made his way toward the window, looking at the jet sitting in the hangar. She was parked in there, stairway down, and the hangar doors were still closed against the elements. The bright lights suspended in the ceiling made the glossy white floor electrifyingly bright, helping to illuminate the large space. On each side of the Gulfstream were red, portable toolboxes, along with a few carts on wheels that held laptops, spare parts, containers of fluids like hydraulic and engine oil.

John suggested they all take a look at the jet up close, just to ensure it was the right choice for their mission, before they ended the meeting. He led the way, bringing everyone out through the length of the meeting room. John and the pilots were far enough ahead that the DIA crew could get in a second of mischief. Mark pretended to throw a billiard ball at Robert on the way out, and Robert threatened him appropriately. Then, Ford took a pool cue stick and hit Emily on the butt, which she pushed away with her hand and told him quietly to cut it out.

"Keep it up, Ford. Keep up your shenanigans, and I'll never kiss you again," she told him with sarcasm.

The Gulfstream 650ER was much bigger than any of the DIA team expected, with a few "wows" overheard by John as he stopped in front of the left wing of the white jet. Painted on the nose at a forty-five-degree angle were two thick stripes of blue, one baby-blue stripe and one Navy-blue stripe, representing the corporate logo colors of Corning. Painted on the tail section in baby blue was the official tail number of the jet, N788CG, used on all written flight plans worldwide for radar identification and flight following. The transponder also emitted the tail number, transmitting to all radar systems its altitude, airspeed, and heading, helping air traffic controllers keep them safe in congested airspace. The pilots also used N788CG on the radio frequencies to talk with the controllers verbally.

"*This*...is November 788 Charlie Golf," John said, pointing his arm out, presenting it to the DIA team like he was a game-show host. Mark laughed under his breath and whispered to Emily, "*Weirdo*...just kidding." Andrew and Lurch stood over near John, beaming with pride at their newest jet in the Corning fleet.

"Andrew, why don't you share some of the facts about the plane, so our friends know what they are dealing with?"

"Yes, sir. Happy to," Andrew answered, clearing his throat and stepping out a few feet in front. "This is the flagship jet at Gulfstream, bought by Corning recently. A 2016 model. It has ultra-long-range legs at top speeds. It recently logged the longest nonstop flight in the airframe's history, with a trip of eight thousand ten nautical miles. It traveled from Singapore's Changi Airport to McCarran International in Las Vegas with four passengers and three crew, at an average speed of Mach 0.85."

Ford was impressed and raised his eyebrows in amazement. "Very cool," he said aloud.

Andrew walked around toward the stairs, and the DIA team followed.

"You can see in the rear that we have two large and powerful engines. They provide an efficient thrust that can power us around the globe with the fuel burn needed to not have to stop and gas up. Certainly it could depend on the winds at altitude and overall weather, but it's a gem to fly. Let's jump inside," Andrew commented as he led the way up the stairs.

"This special cabin reflects the ultimate plan of arrangement, function, and efficiency, with the tech for the executive passengers, as well up there in the cockpit, ah, flight deck. Think of 'high-speed performance,'" Andrew said, sitting in the cabin in a large white-leather seat. Everyone followed and took a seat.

Displayed on the shelves that lined the fuselage were fresh fruit, some large coffee-table art books, vases of freshly cut assorted flowers, current fashion magazines in French, unread copies of the *Financial Times*, *Wall Street Journal*, and UK's *The Telegraph*, as well as crystal glasses for drinking. A pop-up flat-panel screen was making its way vertically upward from a pocket, displaying the Corning logo on its screen, as well as a menu of sorts. There was also a galley that rivaled most kitchens in private homes, complete with a wine refrigerator, more fresh flowers, a wine rack, and tremendous food storage capability.

Each captain's leather chair could rotate, and each section of chairs in the cabin could face one another as needed. There were also portable tables that pulled out from the wall, hidden behind beautiful woodwork that lined the cabin bulkheads as far as the eye could see. Robert and Mark sat looking in awe at the elite cabin, sitting on the long leather couch, complete with

Corning embroidered blankets and pillows.

"Ummm, we don't have any of this in our jets," said Ford, which made everyone laugh.

"Understand, Ford," Andrew said, amused. "This fuselage keeps the jet ovoid-shaped and not perfectly round. That's why it gives us big guys the shoulder and headroom needed in either the rear, here, or up front. I don't have to hunch over when standing. Take a peek outside."

Robert and Mark leaned behind the couch at a circular window. Ford had his own, as did Emily.

"Those big clean wings and the T-tail in the rear are aerodynamically engineered by our friends down in Georgia to provide a mixture of speed, distance, and range, and the takeoff and landing performance needed for worldwide flying. Those large Rolls-Royce engines I pointed out earlier give it the kick you'll feel on takeoff."

Ford gestured with his hand. "Some of my buddies fly corporate charter and fractional, you know, after getting out of the Air Force. They've said that the cabin air helps them recover better from jet lag...better than when we flew together in the military jets. What's that about?"

Lurch was standing between the cabin and the cockpit. "Yup, way different from the jets I flew and you fly now, Ford. These panoramic windows provide ample natural light, where perhaps sometimes in one of your bombers, you're hidden behind the electronics. Mr. Abbott and the other execs we ferry at Corning only breathe one hundred percent fresh air that is replenished every two minutes while airborne."

"Huh. We don't do that," Ford said.

"Of course not!" Lurch said, spoken as someone who once wore the green military flight suit. "They design these jets for comfort and style. You're all about mission first and dropping weapons. This cabin is pressurized to less than thirty-three hundred feet at initial cruise altitude at flight level four-ten. Reduces the jet lag, as you can imagine. And quiet...like a baby's room, too."

Andrew motioned for everyone to take a look up front in the flight deck. A big, tall man, he easily fit in both the cockpit and captain chair on the left side of the aircraft. He was able to power up the aircraft avionics and show the multicolored panels that displayed all the common flight instruments, such as the heading, attitude, and airspeed indicators. The HUD was very modern, displaying the flight data just like Ford's F-18 from his Navy days. They even had a FLIR camera that displayed images onto the HUD, peering through most low-visibility days and nights to see the runway clearly. The HUD system, called Enhanced Vision System and Symmetry Flight Deck, changed the way Corning flew and allowed the pilots to get down lower and safer when attempting to land.

Ford thought of all the cockpits he'd been in, and nothing looked like this one. Many military aircraft had a combo of old original gauges with needles that were mechanical by design, with *some* glass screens. This jet was all computerized and modern, with an attractive digital cockpit that had all touch-glass screens. Even the active control side sticks worked a fly-by-wire system and looked terrific to fly. "This is one hell of a bird. I wish I was flying one, instead of jumping out of it," Ford said as he looked at Mark and Robert.

"Maybe in retirement?" answered Lurch, referring to himself, a retired military pilot.

Ford felt the vibration in his pocket that a text was there and looked to see who it was. He opened up the text app and saw it was from Wu. Ford read it, then told everyone the news.

"Wu verified the news we heard last night from the Deputy. Has some new ideas for us, which we can discuss later. Just wanted to let you know," Ford said, putting the smartphone back in his pocket.

"We actually need to get going, then," Mark said, ending the tour. "Robert, I can see you are in great hands. Andrew, Lurch, thank you very much," as he shook their hands in the cabin. "Mr. Abbott, sir, thank you again. Please know Mr. Burns sends his best."

"You're very welcome. God speed and see you all again soon. Take good care of her. Safe jumping down in Oceana, too, Ford," Abbott said, and he patted the jet's bulkhead with his hand.

Gansu Airfield, China

"What do you mean, fire? A fire? Is that jet damaged? What happened?" Chen looked up from his desk. He was chewing on an unlit cigar, and his temper was growing. He pushed the seat away from the desk and stomped over to the chief engineer.

"What the hell is going on?" Chen asked, pointing at his

chest. "What happened? Are we delayed?"

Chen did not want to lose the aircraft, and he completely blew off asking about the health of the two human pilots who were flying her. His mind went directly to the Devil Dragon, the Spratly Islands, the political leadership, and the uniformed leadership. The idea of possibly blaming him for a potential disaster was his worry. The pressure was mounting on him to perform, and he sure as heck was going to apply pressure on the team below him so he could get his way.

"General, here is Captain Lee's report. Looks like a simple compressor stall took place on one of the push engines. Minimal damage. We are working on the airflow intakes now, and it should be turned around for tomorrow evening. Captain Lee wrote in his report that he could make up the missed tests due to the fire on the next flight," the engineer answered, hoping it would satisfy the unpredictable general.

"You better be right," Chen boomed, looking at the paperwork for not more than two seconds before physically throwing it back at the engineer. Papers flew in a variety of directions, and the engineer picked them up quickly. "Get out of here. I want them up flying again as soon as possible."

Chen looked up at a wall chart that displayed the current progress of the jet on a calendar timeline and the proposed timeline for the future. Compared to other flight test programs, this one was aggressive, advanced, and difficult to execute in complete secrecy. Weapons testing was next, and that required detailed coordination with ordnance ranges, ground- and air-based radars, and other Chinese jet fighter aircraft, as needed.

What complicated things was the constant moving of the operations office environment, such as computers, wall charts, and maintenance items used to track an aircraft program that had to be moved each time they set up shop. Moving ordnance and the men who worked on those issues would complicate the potential success in the coming months. Sure, the general had an office back at headquarters in Beijing, but he personally traveled with the Devil Dragon in what could be summed up as an appalling case of micromanagement.

Chen had dreamed about becoming a four-star general ever since his colonel father took him to the army offices and barracks a child. Colonel Chen even let young He Chen ride old armored tanks around as a kid, which led to Chen's desire to serve in the military. He Chen, as a young man, remembered the souring relations between China and the Soviet Union while his father explained the border clashes in 1969 to him. His father, working armor issues for the People's Liberation Army, facilitated new tank plans at one point that could match the Soviets, which eventually led to the development of the Type 69 tank.

He Chen, even as a teenager, was mesmerized by the fact that capturing or stealing another country's technology and equipment could give him an easy advantage. He learned that you could incorporate some of the stolen technologies into your *own* technologies, as his father did from capturing a Soviet T-62 tank. It was during the 1969 Sino-Soviet border conflict when the elder Chen and other Chinese forces were able to capture a Soviet T-62 tank. The stolen tank was inspected, and some of its gear and capabilities, such as the Soviet Luna infrared searchlight system, were directly copied and installed into a new Chinese Type 69 tank design. This lesson of illegally acquiring something stuck with the younger Chen. This young lesson of his eventually led up to acquiring the plans to build the Devil Dragon.

Chen was mentored, groomed, and educated to be a four-star general, and was told by many senior leaders through his career he might be, or could be, the *one*. The lucky one, the blessed one, the chosen one, to lead the Chinese military into the future. It was just so unpredictable, though, to get to that senior level, that any slipup, or hint of a slipup, or even a perceived issue, could mean disaster for him. Thirty-four years of service would go down the drain because of a misperception in the Air Force, a leaked story in the news, leaked womanizing, or an actual event that happened on his watch. It was because of this drive, this determination, and the constant pursuit of rank and status, that this Devil Dragon project, engine fire or not, would *never* fail while he was in charge. Chen would find a way to be successful, or else.

Oceana Naval Air Station, Virginia

The army Citation jet was on approach to runway 5 Right, the long twelve thousand-footer at Naval Air Station Oceana, when Emily looked out the window to see all the F-18 Hornets lined up on the ramp. They were in line, all pointing in the same direction, looking like gray soldiers from the Civil War.

"Is that what you flew, Ford?" she asked Ford, pointing down below the right window of the Citation.

"Yeah, that was my Navy carrier tour. Loved flying that little jet. Enabled me to fly as a single-seat pilot again, like in pilot training. Went to the carrier, fully qualified. Visited maybe a dozen countries. I was able to do about a hundred landings and takeoffs from the ship," Ford answered, reminiscing about the days. "Completed a full workup and a Med float. Fantastic squadron life. It was fun."

"You were a carrier pilot, too?" Mark asked, not knowing this portion of his past. Robert wasn't with them because he was ferrying the Corning jet from Elmira to Savannah. "What else don't we know about you, kid?"

"Stop. I'm not keeping secrets," Ford said, laughing. "Yeah, I can land on ships, too."

As he said that, the jet touched down at the air station and rolled down the runway. Emily looked out at the window, staring. She was quiet again, using the free time to think about the second and third phases of the challenge they had with Wu and Ford.

"Carrier pilot," she said to herself. "Carrier pilot," she whispered. "Hey, carrier pilot!" Emily said a bit louder.

"Yeah, a carrier pilot. What are you all fired up about?" Ford said.

"No! Bloody hell!" Emily exclaimed.

Mark turned in his seat, which did not rotate like the fancy leather ones on the Gulfstream 650. "What is it?"

"Carrier pilot! Ford is fully qualified to land on *carriers*!" Emily said loudly. She pushed Mark in his shoulder sitting in the seat in front of him.

"Yeah, so what?" Mark asked, not seeing the connection.

Mark was impressed, but as an aircraft analyst, he had met hundreds of carrier pilots before. "I'm impressed, really, but why are you freaking out about it?"

"Shut the front door! What if...*what if* when Wu and Ford get a hold of the Devil Dragon, they fly eastward out into the Pacific and land her on a carrier? Any Chinese aircraft won't be able to fly or search that far out to sea, and we could recover the jet in secrecy. Capture the jet using the carrier to land on!"

Mark's eyes lit up. "No crap. Are you kidding me?"

Ford nodded with a smile. "I knew I was with you for a reason, Queen Emily. That is one hell of an idea."

Mark took a sip of his Starbucks. "I love it. We'd have to request one of our Pacific Command ships sail in the vicinity of our choosing, but that shouldn't be a problem. The Deputy could always call the admiral. Yes. Yes. Hell of a freaking good idea, Emily."

"Thank you," Emily smiled and winked at Ford.

Ford rubbed his face and chin. "I'd be eager to hear from Wu how strong the gear is on the jet. That landing may not be pretty. It's not a carrier-based jet, and we land pretty goddamn hard. Plus, the sea state of the ship comes into play. It bobs and weaves, pitches and rolls with the waves," Ford explained, holding his palm down, showing how the ship could move in open seas.

"Hmm. You'd be hundreds or even a thousand miles out to sea. No runway in sight. You had *better* land her," Mark added.

"Thanks for the vote of confidence, Mark. Dirtbag," Ford replied. "Look, I can land her. Might be an issue for speed, descent angle, and potential collapse of the gear once we hit, but if we can find the ship out there with the limited navaids, we can get her down."

Emily looked at the parking spot they were pulling into with the Citation they were on. It was at the base of the airfield tower, and a uniformed Navy captain was waiting for their arrival out on the ramp. Dressed in green-tinted camouflage that looked different from other US military-green uniforms, the captain sported a dark green trident on his chest, symbolizing he was a Navy SEAL. A SEAL was a Sea-Air-Land commando, specifically from Naval Special Warfare. He was there and waiting to greet them and arrange for Ford's parachute training.

Emily thought aloud some more before the cabin door opened. "How about this. After you land, have the Navy pull her to that airplane elevator and hide the Devil Dragon in that hangar. That, ah...hangar deck I've visited before. Good size. That way the Chinese imagery satellites won't detect their most prized possession sitting on our ship," she said. "That's called *evidence*."

"That's a damn good idea. I don't remember the ship elevator dimensions that well. But if Wu said that it is smaller than the C-130, that aircraft wingspan won't fit in there," Ford added, trying to remember the layout.

"Please. We could fly out some welders to meet you guys upon arrival. We could just cut those bad boys right off, fit her in the hangar deck," Mark said. "Just cut 'em off."

"You have welders at DIA?" Ford asked, raising his eyebrows.

"Kid, you'd be surprised what we have access to. Now get out outside and meet this SEAL," Mark said, laughing and pointing with his coffee.

"Carrier, huh? No shit," Ford said, grabbing Emily's hand on the way out of the Citation.

They stepped down the stairs to the tarmac to greet the SEAL.

"Hello, Captain Peoples. I'm Mark Savona from DIA. How do you do?" Mark introduced himself.

"Please call me Gabe. Nice to meet you, Mark." Captain Peoples extended his hand to Mark.

Captain Gabe Peoples, commanding officer of Naval Special Warfare Group 2, was the senior leader of East Coast SEAL Teams 2, 4, 8, and 10, based out of Little Creek Naval Amphibious Base, Virginia. Located near Norfolk, he had a variety of men scattered across the world, completing both training and real-world missions. He led some of the most motivated set of goal setters in the world, experts at fighting in the sea, air, and land.

Mark did the introductions again, as he had done during their last few visits. Everyone followed Gabe Peoples into the base of the air traffic control tower and into flight operations for the air station.

"I am aware that you would like to jump with one of the teams down here for practice. Very unusual request. Could you tell me some more so I can determine how to help you?" he asked without a smile, as they sat down in a cold and uninviting flight-planning room. It was just the opposite of what they had experienced at Corning and Savannah.

"We are working a tier one intel community mission, solo, outside of JSOC. A requirement exists to get one of our pilots, who is an experienced parachutist, back to jumping to make him current. He needs experience in a wing suit," Mark explained.

"Under what authority? This is a pretty steep request. You'll use some of my guys for training. Burn up a few hours of fuel on my bill. Disrupt our training schedules and our prep for deployments. Again, I don't know. You're asking a lot."

"We work directly for the principal Deputy director of DIA."

There was a deadening pause and then a smile from Captain Gabe Peoples as he looked at everyone, especially Emily.

"Calvin Burns?"

"Yes. Yeah, Calvin Burns," answered Mark, nodding. "You know him?"

"Oh, why didn't you just say so? I've known Mr. Burns for years. We've done plenty of work with him. It was always real world, no training requests like this one, but, yeah. Sure, we can do this," replied Gabe Peoples.

"Great. Thanks for the support. As I said earlier, this is Air Force Captain Ford Stevens," as Mark pointed to him at the table. "He is our military pilot assigned to DIA. Ford has some one hundred jumps—closer to two hundred? Either way, he needs wing-suit experience. Needs to learn to fly laterally for an insertion."

"Sounds interesting. An insertion, eh? Maybe you need our guys on this? You know what we are capable of in the teams, right? I could assign a platoon, you know, to help," offered Gabe.

Part of it was out of kindness, and part of it was relevancy. The teams were always in competition with other high-speed units like Delta, Army Rangers, US Marine Corps Force Recon, and sometimes even FBI Hostage Rescue. Then, depending on the sensitivity of the mission, Delta Force and Team Six are in the mix. Everyone competes for the missions, which translates to competing for the money. The unit that gets the nod gets the work, then gets future money out of tight budgets for cool gear, cooler training, and travel expenses. Even in a nonprofit military world, there was a fight for cash.

"We appreciate your offer, Gabe, especially because our organizations work so closely, but this is a relatively sensitive mission. There are some sensitive and unique State Department twists to this op, and only Ford is participating. Solo." Emily grinned at him, hoping he would back off while she used her beauty to their advantage. She knew the pitch from the special operations boys because they always wanted to get involved. Even back at home in England, the SAS were the same.

"So be it. I understand," replied Gabe. He looked at his green bound notebook for a second. "Let me make a call. We may have a jump going this afternoon. Hang on a few minutes, will ya?" Gabe got up from the table, left the room on his phone, and talked in the foyer area for ten minutes or so.

Gabe returned to where the others were still sitting. "You're in luck. We have two jumps going out today. First one is a MH-47D Chinook water jump with the 160th SOAR. One of the platoons is taking "Gunnar" the dog out, plus some boats. That involves an oil tanker ship takedown. Not too sure that helps you. Second jump is a C-17 Globemaster to both a water and land LZ. No, sorry, a C-130. High altitude, low opening. We never discussed if the mission dictated that or not, but I guess we could always discuss it with the flight crew in the brief...of, ah, of what you wanted," Gabe explained.

"Thank you, sir. Let me think for a moment and see if it fits the profile of our op," Ford said, as he wrote in his notebook with a pencil.

Ford considered his options for jumping for the day. He was calculating the altitude when he would come out the rear of the Gulfstream, which was most likely already in the descent to land. Tough to judge from a meeting room where they couldn't talk in front of the SEAL. By Ford's calculations, they would be at least forty-five thousand feet and in a descent. The G650 would need about one hundred miles to descend from that altitude. Take into account the wing suit that could laterally fly about ten miles. So, he thought, he would have to have the Gulfstream make an approach to its destination that flew within at least ten miles of where Wu was going to be.

"Sir, if it's not too much trouble, could we chat in private for a moment?" Ford asked.

"Absolutely. I'll be right out here. Take your time," Gabe said, as he walked out of the room and shut the door.

Ford explained his math and used a whiteboard to draw out what he was thinking.

"Wu's text said he was thinking of an east coast airport. That matches what we have come up with for the aircraft carrier course of action. But we need to come up with specific airports, because it will make a difference on the jump math. If the Gulfstream is heading to airport *x* and Wu is way out here at airport *y*, it will never work.

Mark got out his iPad and pulled open Google Earth, remembering what Emily said in the car during the Hilton Head trip. He opened it to eastern China and zoomed in and out. Both Emily and Ford sat on either side of him, looking at his screen.

"From what I see so far, one option could be to head south to the Bay of Bengal. Pick up the carrier down south here, to the east of India. Sail home like that," Mark said, pointing to that option on the screen.

"What about down here, off Okinawa?" Emily asked.

"Well. Hmmm. Another option would be to still take Wu's idea of an east coast airport." Mark paused. No one said anything. "Wait, here's a scenario. The Corning jet routinely flies to Beijing, right? Beijing is ninety miles north of Tianjin. Simple...on the way in to Beijing, you jump out. OK, OK, let's do this. On approach to Beijing, the Gulfstream will be overhead Tianjin, or close to it, on the descent. Copy?"

"Yeah, keep going."

"We ask Wu to bring his jet into Tianjin. Ford, you jump out of the Gulfstream as you're descending into Tianjin. The Corning jet continues to Beijing. Easy. You meet Wu in Tianjin," Mark explained.

"Wu did say in his text that he could fake a maintenance issue. Force the jet in there." Ford paused for a moment. "We are just going to bring her in there in broad daylight, though?"

"The airports are aligned pretty well. Even if the winds aren't correct for landing to the north, the Corning crew could ask for that runway anyway, then circle around to another runway,"

Mark said.

Emily spoke up. "You do have a point, Ford. Why would Wu want to bring a secret jet in there, into a crowded airport? It will have to be at night. Maybe if it's at night, the confusion of a commercial airport could work in our favor," Emily suggested. "How about this. Ford, once you land, you create some type of disturbance. A smoke-and-mirrors diversion that focuses the entire airport to look in one area, while you swap seats and fly off with Wu in another area. What would work?"

"Hmm. What would work for a diversion?" Mark asked.

"Got it. I could start up an aircraft and taxi it into something to cause a ground mishap?" Ford offered.

"No, that requires keys, potentially exposing you. Also requires you to escape out of another jet without you getting caught in the fire," Mark said, shooting down the idea.

Emily perked up again. "Hey, got it. Got it. This may...work. We give you a handheld laser that is normally used to identify targets when using night-vision goggles. We get a strong one from the boys in R&D, like a class 4 science fiction kind. The strong shite. Invisible to the naked eye but creates a shite storm. We get one that creates heat. You get yourself in a position to squirt the laser at the sprinklers inside an aircraft hangar. This sets off their fire suppression system, you know, white foam, with the fire retardant. It'll blow millions of gallons out into the hangar and ramp. Complete bloody chaos. All sorts of havoc," Emily suggested.

"Girl. You still got it going on. Another hell of an idea," Mark told her. "Awesome."

"How big is this laser?" Ford asked, thinking he'd have to have a big backpack full of electronics and batteries.

"As big as a pen," Emily said. "Fits in your pocket."

"That is some cool shit."

"Dude, come on. Please. This is DIA. Anyway, look here," Mark said pointing to the image on Google Earth. "Naturally, the fire department will roll out after the alarm sounds. That means the firehouse will be empty. You, Ford, wait near the firehouse until they leave. Hide out near their facility. We ask Wu to park the jet there, engines running, and you get in. He can tell his copilot buddy they are parking in that spot for an emergency."

Ford was really thinking the plan was coming together. They had some great ideas and the backing of the highest levels of the intel community and government. He was feeling comfortable with the courses of action laid out.

"I'm liking it. Yeah, yeah. Let's do it. Why don't you guys work on some of the details, and I'll wing suit it up with the SEALs?" Ford said, nodding toward the door.

"Be safe. See you, kid," Mark said.

"See you, Ford. Have fun," Emily replied.

Ford opened the door and saw Gabe. "I'm up for the HALOs with the Herk, sir. Today. When do we go?"

Tidal Area, Virginia

The Air Force Reserve's 328th Airlift Squadron of Niagara Falls, New York, flew C-130H2 Hercules aircraft. The four-engine, turboprop aircraft, originally designed with a pencil and slide rule in the 1950s, could fly anything and everything from vehicles to combat troops to special operations forces. New Herks continue to roll off the Georgia assembly line even today. The workhorse of tactical cargo, the C-130 has done everything from fly in the Blue Angels to landing on aircraft carriers. The two Niagara pilots, a flight engineer, a navigator, and two loadmasters, taxied the Herk to the ramp at Oceana Air Station to pick up the squad of twelve SEALs from Team 8, plus a rubber F470 combat rubber raiding craft, or Zodiac.

Niagara's 328th had a rich history of real-world missions, and the SEALs enjoyed flying with the reservists because they either had gray hair, or no hair, meaning the aircrew was overdosing in experience. When you jumped, you wanted an aircrew who knew what the heck they were doing, and the SEAL squad felt relaxed flying with them. The 328th had flown plenty of special operations teams and parachute forces, especially since they have been conducting aerial transportation since the China-Burma-India theater from 1944 to 1945 and, later, troop carrier training from 1947 to 1951. The Niagara squadron also deployed to Southeast Asia during the Vietnam War and knew how to handle guys from the teams.

Ford was also on the tarmac, mixed in with the squad from SEAL Team 8. He looked just like they did at a glance, except his clothing and gear was a bit different. Assigned to be with an experienced wing-suit jumper, Captain Gabe Peoples partnered Ford with an E-8, a senior chief by rank, to ensure he got the wing-suit training he needed.

"You ready, sir?" Senior Chief Special Warfare Operator

Bobby Tosca yelled over the roar of the C-130 taxiing to where they were standing, in addition to hooking up his oxygen mask for prebreathing. "You look good. Any last-minute questions from our orientation class from earlier?" Tosca's title, used solely by SEALs, is the corresponding rank of a senior chief petty officer or master sergeant.

Ford shook his head no. He was reviewing the plan, going over the details for the jump altitude today at thirty-five thousand feet and ensuring that his gear was properly set. The brief earlier in the day consisted of the flight crew from Niagara, the leads from SEAL Team 8, and included crucial things like weather, winds, other aircraft in the area, emergency procedures, and drop-zone conditions.

Ford was wearing a flat-black wing suit, gray-black helmet, and a tinted visor, in addition to donning the MFF ARAPS, or military free-fall advanced ram air parachute system. He was also carrying his personal oxygen supply, connected to a gray oxygen mask that connected to his helmet.

Their jump today was considered a HALO, pronounced *hay-low*, which was a high-altitude–low-opening jump. The HALO ARAPS provided a multi-mission, high-altitude parachute system that allowed military members to jump as low as thirty-five hundred feet, up to today's max height at thirty-five thousand feet. Their plan called for breathing oxygen for thirty minutes prior to the jump, which they were getting ready to begin, just to get rid of any nitrogen in their bloodstreams.

The wing suit provided Ford the lateral distance he needed, while the rest of the team was aiming for a separate, sister-water drop zone a few miles away. Only Ford and Tosca were hitting the land-drop zone today.

Since Mark arranged with Gabe about acquiring some additional gear required for the mission, at DIA's expense, Ford figured he'd better use it today for practice. His first option offered, almost like a new toy, was the Electronic Automatic Activation Device, or EAAD, and it would allow an automatic activation of the parachute if either of them was unable to deploy the parachute at the designated altitude. Ford considered it but didn't accept because of the added extra weight.

Ford was also sporting a personal navigation aid, a navaid, which was a moving map displayed on a screen that he wore on his wrist. It provided in-flight navigation, winds, weather and previously uploaded mission-planning capability, which allowed him to concentrate on the jump itself first. This navaid allowed Ford to free-fall and glide in the wing suit and while under the canopy to continue to track and locate himself, steering directly to the intended drop zone. Ford's navaid system used an encrypted GPS that integrated multiple satellites and would be usable in Asia.

The last item that differentiated Ford from the average civilian parachutist was his oxygen mask. Since they were jumping today above thirteen thousand feet, they wore the new parachutist oxygen mask, or POM, rather than the MBU-12P mask issued to basic military parachutists. The POM provided Ford with a terrific range of vision, as well as an unobstructed range of motion, ensuring the oxygen reached his body at such dangerous altitudes. It also allowed him to communicate by talking to other teammates over a common radio frequency, but they didn't plan on using that feature today.

The Herk stopped taxiing a few hundred feet in front of them, all four of the T-56 Allison turboprop engines roaring. Just after the loadmaster lowered the ramp, he waved in the guys from Team 8, carrying the Zodiac in first. Both loadmasters were outside the aircraft now, headsets on and wire cords trailing, to stay in contact with the rest of the aircrew. The Zodiac did not have an engine attached to the rear, but it did have one fastened down to the interior of the small boat. It also had a parachute that would not only deploy but steer onto the middle of the drop zone with pinpoint accuracy due to the self-steering parachute attached to a GPS device. The device, called JPADS, for joint precision aerial delivery system, would bring it right down to its intended target using GPS satellite navigation.

Senior Chief Special Warfare Officer Bobby Tosca also had, on his body or inside the raft, a backpack, a radio, hundreds of rounds of ammo, an HK416 rifle, and a harness full of pockets that carried everything from rifle magazines to grenades to a first aid kit. Because he was not doing a regular simulated combat jump with the rest of his squad from Team 8 and doing the special wing-suit jump today, he couldn't wear anything else. If he did, it would interfere with the aerodynamics of the wing suit, which was not lost on Ford.

Another aspect that Ford was familiar with, but certainly not an expert on, was the weapons. He was a pilot, not a ground firearms expert. So Tosca gave Ford the once-over on the Heckler and Koch HK416 assault rifle, which was based on the AR-15 platform. Ford recognized it immediately because it looked like a smaller M-16 rifle, but he still need an orientation. Tosca said that the designers of the HK416 thought of this smaller rifle as improvement over the Colt M4 that was a new issue to the US military. Tosca even showed Ford the short-stroke gas piston system, native from another Heckler and Koch product, called the G36. Ford nodded yes to the lesson but as an aviator he had nothing beyond a basic understanding and laughed to himself about it.

Ford made another mental note, too, because besides not knowing about the rifle, he knew even less about the engines and landing gear on the Devil Dragon. He'd also be jumping in pretty light on basic military survival gear, inserting himself illegally into China, with near zero gear, via a parachute. This wasn't the time for Wu to play "I have a secret." On further thought, he'd definitely want to know before he left US soil for planning purposes.

The ramp on the C-130 remained down, touching the ground, even after the rest of the team was on board. Engines were still going, gray exhaust trailing and blowing with force out the back and then dissipating down the flight line. Ford and Tosca boarded last and were eyed by the Niagara loadmaster. The loadmaster was busy talking into his headset microphone, most likely busting their chops due to their unique-looking wing suits. Ford could only imagine what the loadmaster was telling the rest of the Herc crew about how funny they looked. The loadmaster pointed to the two last positions near the doorway since they were heading out first, signaling that was where to sit.

Today's military free-fall operation was the perfect training ground for Ford's mission. It was also a typical SEAL team jump that they used to deploy quickly and quietly, compared to a complete conventional static line jump that the army would most likely conduct. The army had a chute that opened up as soon as they departed the side door of the aircraft, and the procedure was usually performed by having hundreds of jumpers out the door in the same time window, over a lengthy drop zone of a mile or more.

The Niagara C-130, using "BISON 82" as their call sign, took off and departed from the runway on the way up to altitude. BISON 82 climbed and climbed, taking about thirty minutes for them to get to altitude and cruise awhile, especially so the aircrew could complete their checklists up front between the pilots, flight engineer, and navigator. Just as important, they needed to get their aircrew oxygen going, too.

As the navigator gave the pilots a solid approach to the insertion point over the Suffolk, Virginia, drop zone, the flight engineer ran the checklists for decompression and oxygen, among other things, to prepare the Herk for the jump. The flight engineer then signaled to the loadmaster over the intercom headset to lower the ramp. Between the noises, freezing temperatures, smell of exhaust from kerosene-like fuel, and rush of outside air, all communication between the jumpers and the loadmaster was done by hand and arm signals. The teammates did have intrateam radios but were not connected to the aircraft. Because of the two separate missions going on with the wing-suit training and the tactical jump, and that Ford would be doing the real mission solo,

Ford and Tosca had zero comm gear.

The loadmaster signaled to the jumpmaster SEAL to verify that their helmets were fastened, to unbuckle seatbelts, and to double-check personal oxygen. Ford and Tosca signaled OK. The loadmaster gave the two-minute signal as well. At this point, the jumpers unplugged the oxygen hoses from the aircraft system, then plugged in to their own oxygen tanks.

Then, the loadmaster raised his arm, which told the jumpers they should stand up, which they did. A few more seconds went by. The loadmaster then raised his arms straight out with his palm up at the shoulder level and touched his helmet. This told all the jumpers to move to the rear of the aircraft. Some shuffled because of their heavy packs and gear, while Ford and Tosca moved effortlessly because they weren't hauling anything but themselves. They were also sitting in the far rear of the Herk, closest to the ramp.

BISON 82 was bringing them near the insertion point, and Ford and Tosca stopped at the hinges of the cargo ramp. The rest of the SEAL squad, complete with their packs, Zodiac boat, rifles, ammo, communication gear, and other strange tactical items Ford had never seen before all moved to the rear of the plane. Ford could not hear much because of his helmet and earplugs but did hear some of the SEALs yelling out of motivation just in back of him.

This was always the point when Ford had butterflies in his stomach. It never prevented him from jumping, but it was more of a nervous excitement. His neighbors and friends, ever since high school, always laughed and criticized him for jumping out of a perfectly good airplane. This was the moment, though, and he was ready. Ford said under his breath that they must be seconds away now, but it seemed like days.

Up in the C-130 cockpit, the navigator was talking with the pilots on the proper insertion point. Giving them one- or two-degree heading changes for accuracy, the navigator was verbally telling the pilots to come left or a little right and verifying their altitude and airspeed. At the precise moment, the navigator gave the command to the copilot to flip the light.

"Green light!" yelled the navigator.

"On!" replied the copilot. The copilot reached his right hand over to his right console and flipped the silver toggle switch to the on position, putting in motion a series of events that could not be reversed, even if tried.

Ford and the other jumpers could not hear any of the BISON flight crew, but they stared intently at the light system above the ramp, waiting for the red light to change to green. It was all Ford and Tosca needed to see. Green light! This was it!

"GO! GO! GO!" yelled the jumpmaster and loadmaster, and off the ramp they went.

Ford and Tosca leaped off the back of the ramp and into the thin, freezing air. Ford's arms were extended out and slightly to the rear, as his wing suit material under his arms filled up with air. His legs were spread apart, too, with the same airflow that forced them open. The wing suits had a large piece of material between the feet that looked like webbing on a duck's feet; it helped bend back their legs slightly at the knees. Their bodies were in belly flop position as if they were about to hit the surface of a swimming pool. Ford and Tosca were free-falling, fully separated from the C-130 and literally flying like an airfoil. They both fell straight down initially and then climbed for a few moments above the height of the aircraft as their aerodynamic foil acted like the wing on an aircraft, creating lift. This extra lift was what provided a wing-suit flier to move through the air laterally like an aircraft wing, rather than fall straight down like a standard jumper.

The SEALs and Ford, falling from BISON, could not be seen on a ground radar system. For the purposes of OPERATION WHIRLPOOL, this was the perfect insertion method. Until their parachutes opened, in fact, they could not be seen by observers on the ground or pilots of friendly or enemy aircraft. It was the perfect silent entry.

An altimeter, which was worn on their right wrists and closely resembled a large and bulky watch, determined their height above the ground using air pressure. On their left wrist was the GPS-based navaid. Both altimeters were set up with alarms for chute opening at thirty-five hundred feet. This would provide the rapid descent they were seeking, the lateral glide path for the insertion, as well as the minimal parachute time just gliding through potential bad-guy territory.

Ford noticed how different the wing suit was in cutting across the earth, only because he was able to pass relatively close to some clouds. The FAA rules in civilian jumps did not allow him to parachute close to clouds, but today under the military rules, he could enjoy the ride a bit. He wondered whether, if he was closer to the ground, say from a free-fall base jump off a tower or a mountainside, he would be able to see the terrain and trees go by his eyes. He also kept an eye on his instructor, Tosca.

Ford looked down at his GPS moving-map display on his wrist and saw he had already flown laterally 8.3 miles, with another 1.2 miles to go. He double-checked his height on the altimeter at forty-six hundred feet. *Looking good*, he thought.

Just another few moments and he would pull his rip cord. The wind was howling around his ears, continuing to be piercingly loud with the rush of air going by despite his earplugs and helmet. Ford looked down again at his altimeter and counted down silently. *Three seconds. Two seconds. One second. Pull.*

The parachute came out of the packed compartment on his back, with the top of the chute filling up with a bit of air. Ford waited to feel the jerk. Waiting...waiting. He glanced upward and saw that the chute was not as full as he was used to seeing. The risers went up into the air as the chute jerked his shoulders with only a small degree of tug, but nowhere near what he was expecting. Ford placed his hands on the risers, but he could tell something was off. He didn't feel the tightness on the material like he had so many times in the past. Ford bent his head back to look up again, only to see his worst nightmare. His chute was not fully inflating with air.

An awful feeling came across Ford instantaneously. Normally the chute would fill up with air and reduce the rapid descent by now. Ford would be able to steer with the risers toward his landing spot in the drop zone. Instead, he continued to fall as the chute malfunction continued to get worse. Ford struggled as he passed through twenty-one hundred feet. He was rolling now in the air, struggling with straps and material and the bewilderment of the situation.

Passing through eighteen hundred feet.

Ford twisted and turned his body attempting to unravel his main chute.

Passing through twelve hundred feet.

Ford wasn't calculating his time, but he sure knew he was only moments away from hitting the earth. Depending on the Virginia air density and his body weight with his wing suit and parachute on, his rate of descent was about twenty-two to twenty-four feet per second. Only moments left.

Passing nine hundred feet.

He struggled and struggled and just could not unravel his main chute. *Emergency,* Ford said to himself. Ford only had seconds to go until impact. *Shit. Shit. Shit.* In his mind, Ford thought only one thing: *Right frickin now...need to fix this right now.*

Rapidly passing through seven hundred feet. This was it.

Suffolk Executive Airport, Suffolk, Virginia

Mark wanted to get Robert, Emily, and Calvin Burns on a conference call prior to getting Wu on the phone. He dialed Jason to inquire about the Deputy's availability, and the Deputy was available in an hour. Mark then dialed Robert.

"Robert, Mark here. Before we start talking, verify your Peanut is up and you have a green light," Mark asked.

"I'm green. Verified," Robert answered. Some machinery

and cutting was heard in the background on the floor at Gulfstream.

"Good to go on my end. What do you have going on with her?" Mark asked, careful not to describe too much, just in case the call's encryption was penetrated. It had never happened to the Peanut software, but you couldn't be too careful with an op like this, he figured.

"Going well. She's inside, which is where I am now. Can you hear them working? All cut out, pistons inserted and fully mobile," Robert reported.

"Already? Those guys are fast," Mark said.

"Yeah, the interior guys are working a solution so one of the guys up front doesn't have to get up out of the seat after the package is dropped off," Robert said, referring to one of the pilots not having to get up to move the seats back to their original positions. The package term was Ford jumping out the back.

"Understand. Ford is out right now with our mutual friends, practicing. We'll see him in a few minutes. Emily is here with me, too," Mark said. He glanced down at some notes he had been writing down. "I'm going to text you a number. Call the number in about forty minutes. That's our conference call number. Got it?"

"Yeah, got it," Robert replied.

"I'm off. Talk soon," Mark said, then pressed the red icon to hang up the call.

Mark was thinking of Wu, who had not contacted him in a while. He had hoped he could make the call, considering he had not even asked him yet.

"Yo. Yo, Emily," Mark yelled over to her, standing inside the foyer of the Suffolk Executive Airport fixed-base operations building, the FBO. An FBO was a commercial business located at an airport to provide aeronautical services to airport customers, such as fuel, tie-down, parking, aircraft rental, maintenance, and flight instruction. The Suffolk building was not larger than a convenience store and had more of a mom-and-pop storefront feel than a large aviation corporation.

"Yeah, Mark?' Emily answered, coming over to the old maroon chairs he was sitting in by the window.

"Could you text Wu, ensuring your Peanut is green, and see if he can dial in to a conference call with us in about forty minutes? I'll text you the number now," Mark asked.

"Certainly. Ford should be done with his jump then, too."

Emily held her smartphone in her right hand and was able to tap the icons and letters without clicking her red colored nails on the screen. Her tips were all that were required.

She started typing.

Emily: Wu, this is Ford's friend, Emily. Can you make a conference call with us? He will be on the call, too. We are also aware of your latest development. If so, I can send you the number. Thanks.

Emily put the phone back in her pocket and looked out the window at the chutes opening in the distance. She knew Ford would be landing very shortly. Then, a vibration from her phone.

Wu: Hello, Emily. Yes, I am in my hotel room. I can talk then. Will call. Send me number. Wu

Emily smiled.

Sending now. Talk to you soon. Emily.

"Mark, we're on. Wu confirmed from his hotel room."

Over the Suffolk Executive Airport Drop Zone, Virginia

Ford had no time to waste. Not even bothering to check his altimeter because he already knew how close to death he was, Ford made a split-second decision to ditch the first parachute and separated it from his body. He did his best to roll over facedown and moved his hand to pull the rip cord for his reserve chute.

Passing six hundred feet.

The risers were fully extended as Ford looked up to see his parachute canopy fully inflated with air. The risers felt tight in his hands.

Passing 450 feet.

Ford was just moments away from hitting the ground. He calmed down, maintained his bearing, and was able to glance out at the horizon to see where he was. Off in the distance, Ford saw Tosca and reassured himself he was close to the proper drop zone. He quickly looked at his GPS and triple-checked.

Passing three hundred feet.

Ford said to himself that he was *not quitting...no way...it's not my turn to die...this better fully open.*

Only 250 feet to go.

He pulled down on the risers to swap his canopy speed with a bit more air for the flare, which slowed down his rate of descent tremendously. He was in the flare. Ford was nearly down to the ground and landed relatively gently. He was able to do a small run, then a quick trot. Ford came to a complete stop, got down on a knee, and took a breather for a second. He sighed and started reeling his chute into a ball so the wind didn't fill up the chute again and drag him across the ground.

He looked around to see where Tosca was and saw he was walking toward Ford. He arrived at Ford's position, smiling, as he pointed and nodded at Ford's primary chute already on the ground and near the both of them.

"Secondary chute? *Motherfucker*! You must have had one hell of a time up there. What the *hell* happened?" Tosca asked.

"Primary didn't take. *Holy shit*. Didn't capture any air. Rolled around in it until just a few hundred feet above the ground. Then I was able to get my hand around and...yank...ah, yank the secondary," answered Ford.

"You are one lucky son of a bitch. Hoo-wee. *Fuck*! I love it. Can you believe we get paid to do this shit?" said Tosca, laughing.

Ford nearly died, and here the SEAL was laughing at the situation. Ford was not nervous, but he was indeed sweating, thankful that the secondary chute worked. It was only the second time he had ever had issues with jumping. "Yeah, all this and a paycheck. Well...the wing suit kicks butt, though. Yeah. That was one hell of a ride."

"Yup. Welcome to the club. I knew you'd like it. Well, sir. You made it," Tosca said, smiling at Ford. "Let's do it again."

Conference Call

Jason looked at the electronic Outlook schedule and dialed the conference call number that Mark had given him. Wearing a starched white-collared shirt and cuff links, he sat in a clean and air-conditioned executive office. He most likely had never spent a day out in the field. A tone was heard, announcing his arrival on the call. He was the first one in the virtual room.

Down in Suffolk, Ford had walked into the lounge area, carrying his chute, and saw Mark and Emily huddled together over the phone.

"Yo! How's it going?" Ford asked.

"Dude! How'd it go? You made it," Mark said. He looked back down at his phone. "Suit worked well?"

"Suit, terrific. *Chute*? Had to use the secondary. My primary failed to open."

"Really? Ford, are you OK, love?" asked Emily.

"Yeah, yeah. Fine. Secondary was good to go. I have to tell you...it was scary for a moment, but the wing suit made it worth it. Fantastic ride," Ford said, as he put his hand on her shoulder.

"Jason, Mark here. I'm here with Emily and Ford. Just moving to a little room here at the airport. I'm in the green. Robert should be on shortly," Mark said. He stood and waved everyone over to the jumper classroom where the ground lessons were given. It was quiet and provided just the atmosphere for the call.

"Got it. I'm green, too. The Deputy will pick up once Robert gets on," Jason told him.

Emily and Ford sat next to each other at a small gray metal

table with six chairs. Mark sat at the head. He placed his phone down in the middle and put it on speaker. They heard a tone; Robert was checking in.

"Robert here, in the green, anyone on?"

"Hey, man. Yup, nearly all here. Waiting on Wu," Mark said.

Another tone.

"Hello? Hello? This is Wu. Anyone on here?"

"Hi, Wu, this is Ford. Yes, we nearly all on here. Just waiting for Mr. Burns to pick up."

Jason walked in and told the Deputy everyone was on the line and suggested he pick up when he was ready.

"OK, Ford. Hello. Jojo rising," Wu said.

Everyone in the little classroom smiled and looked at one another. They could tell by the tone of his voice and his saying their little phrase, that the engine fire Wu had must not have been that bad.

"Jojo rising, Wu. You doin' all right there?"

There was some noise on the speaker, and no one said anything. No reply from Wu, either.

"Hello. Mark, you on the call? This is Calvin Burns."

"Yes, sir. Hello. In the room with me are Emily and Ford, and, ah, from Savannah is Robert, and from afar is Wu," said Mark, opening up the meeting.

"Great. Thanks for dialing in everyone. Mark, go ahead," the Deputy said.

Emily stood up, walked over to the whiteboard on the wall, and picked up the black marker. She wrote the words "Phase

1, phase 2, and phase 3," with vertical lines separating the groups. Perhaps it would help the team's thinking in sharing the plan with Wu, as well as the Deputy.

"Sir, the premise of our call today is to share where we are to date and discuss the plan since we all last met and talked. As a summary, we've split up our plan into phases. Phase one is getting Ford into the country. Phase two is linking Ford up with Wu. And Phase three is getting the Devil Dragon out of the country and into a safe location," Mark said. He was looking up at the whiteboard while talking into the phone, and Emily was writing away.

"Understand," replied the Deputy.

"Sir, for phase one, we have borrowed a Gulfstream 650ER from our friends up at Corning. We were all up there in Elmira, and Robert stayed with the jet. He then brought it to Savannah where it sits at the moment. Gulfstream, via your friend Reggie, has bent over backward to make modifications to the jet for us. Of course, Reggie says hello."

"Reg-gie, my man! Oh, sure. I knew he would take care of you," Deputy Burns replied.

"So...yes, sir. He did. We generated a plan to cut a hole in the fuselage and make a ramp in the bottom rear of the bird that will open up at altitude. This ramp will allow Ford to parachute out of the Gulfstream using a wing suit," Mark said.

"A ramp and a wing suit? Wow. *Really*?" Wu said.

"Yup, we're coming to help, buddy," Ford answered.

"Sir, the G650 will start its descent with the international flight plan destination listed as Beijing. On approach to Beijing, the Gulfstream will be overhead Tianjin Airport. With the appropriate timing, Ford will jump in order to parachute into Tianjin. Wu, for you, the plan is to get the Devil Dragon into Tianjin Airport. Can you do that?"

Wu thought about it. "Tell me more."

"Yes, of course. Ford, again, you'll exit the jet descending into Tianjin. You'll use the wing suit to laterally maneuver into the airport. From there, the Corning jet continues to Beijing for a normal landing. We don't see the Gulfstream jet again."

Wu spoke up. "Yes, I can get in there. I know the area pretty well...and the airspace," Wu said. He thought some more, then coughed a bit. "What I'll do is...stage a fake maintenance issue. Maybe another engine fire or hydraulics issue. Something that makes us land unexpectedly. My copilot will ask plenty of questions. Ah, although we had a real fire this last flight, there was no major damage. I'll come up with something that will force us to land, and I'll select there."

"Great. OK. Ford, you'll land as close as you can to the airport firehouse and—" Mark said.

"Firehouse? Why there?" Ford asked.

"Wait, we'll explain. Once you land and get settled, combat crawl to a position where you can see inside the commercial hangars. We'll show you where they are located. Emily, over to you," Mark said.

"Hello, everyone. Ford, you'll crawl or move from your position pretty easily for nighttime operations and get a good solid view of the hangars for China Air. They are in enormous white hangars with massive doors that are usually wide open. You can't miss the bright lights on the ramp and..."

"Hold on. Where did you get these pictures?" asked Ford.

"Google Images," Emily replied. "I'm half kidding. Some are purchased from Geo-Eye, the maps from NGA, and the runway photos here, here...and this one here were taken from passengers flying on flights and posted on Facebook and obtained by Google."

"Wow. Pretty good pics. Yup, I can see where to go...pretty good on there. Thanks."

"So, Ford, you'll use a class-four laser to paint heat on the fire sprinklers. Now, it is invisible to the naked eye, so we'll give you a mono night device to see. It's a dangerous laser, so don't be pointing into your eyes. It's not a flashlight. Spray the laser energy on the fire sprinklers...the heat...it will set them off. The hangar will then completely fill up with foam...the, ah, fire retardant. That's the distraction for the op," Emily said.

"Interesting. OK, keep going. I like it," the Deputy weighed in.

Mark was up at bat again as the briefer. "Wu, you bring the jet in on Monday after sunset. Get in there and squeeze in between the airliners. When you get there that evening will decide everything. You'll have to text Ford somehow when you're coming in so he knows when to set off the sprinklers. Then, after landing, taxi over to the firehouse and do the crew swap," Mark continued to explain. Emily was writing on the whiteboard.

"I'm confident you will hear us arriving, but yes, yes, I can do that. General Chen won't make it fast enough to our location to detect anything. When we've landed someplace unannounced, and we eventually contact him, it takes hours for him to arrive," Wu said. Wu was also thinking about his Liu, his copilot, and what the plan was for him. "On another note, what were you thinking for my copilot, Liu?"

"I've thought of that. Do you have access to eye drops?" Robert asked.

"*Eye drops*? What kind of question is that? The little clear container? Yeah, we have that here. The ones you put in your eyes to get red eyes clear, right?" Wu replied.

"Yes, those. Put a good amount of those clear and tasteless drops into a drink before takeoff. He'll feel some stomach grumbling. Midway, he'll have an issue. When you land, he'll have to hit the bathroom as soon as possible for quite a while. The guy will have some severe bowel problems. I'd expect that he'll have to run into the empty firehouse to use the toilet right away. It works out because the fire company and all the fire fighters will be out responding to the hangar foam fiasco. The firehouse leaves their bay doors open, so your copilot could walk right in," Robert said.

"That's the end of phase one. Phase two is getting Ford in the jet, taking off, and departing to the east. Ford, you're up," Mark said.

"Wu, Ford here. What you and I will do is depart the airport and head east, really southeast bound. We'll go feet wet over the water and climb high. Depending on the fuel state and winds, we'll go high as we can. I'll do my best to prebreathe, but I won't have a pressure suit. We'll have to talk about aircraft performance here in a few minutes."

"High and southeast. OK. We are landing in South Korea? Or Japan?" Wu asked.

"Well, not exactly—" Ford answered.

"No? What then? We won't have that much fuel to reach Hawaii," Wu said, already not liking the idea. "Plus, by the time Chen figures out what is happening, he could contact chasers and cause some major issues. We could get pursued by J-31s." Wu could not imagine executing the plan by taking off into nowhere land. It was all water after that, and they could never make it. *Perhaps Ford thought they could since they hadn't discussed most aircraft parameters yet.*

"Wu, allow me to weigh in. We are already in contact with our combatant commander for that area of the world, US Pacific Command. That's a US Navy admiral, a four-star, who leads all US forces in that area of the world," Mark explained. "The US Pacific Command statistics were staggering. They had thirty-six thousand military and civilian personnel, along with twelve hundred special operations personnel assigned. This area of the world consisted of thirty-six nations, including five of the seven US treaty allies. In addition, five of the world's declared nuclear nations were present, and seven of the world's ten largest standing militaries. On top of this complex environment was a language barrier, a geographic area consisting of thirty-two hundred languages."

"Yes, I am aware," Wu said, now curious why he was bringing this up. "I live here, remember?"

"Yes, Wu, sorry. Yes, we know. PACOM is moving an aircraft carrier for us, about two hundred and fifty miles southeast of Okinawa. Ford, as you know, is a fully qualified carrier pilot.

He'll bring her down to land on the ship," Emily said.

"*No kidding*? Wait. What?" the Deputy said. The tone of his voice showed both surprise and pride.

"Wow. I...I have never been to the carrier. That's a great idea. Yes, I like that," Wu said.

The Deputy sat in his office, arms folded, thinking about the carrier idea. "Hold up. Hold up. Hang on a sec. I have big concern here. We want to take a foreign, a foreign aircraft, with no *tailhook*, onto a US carrier? That could do a lot of damage. I need to do some definite push back because I think it's an absolutely crazy idea. The Hill would have a field day with this, not to mention the Secretary of Defense. Brilliant, but crazy."

Mark didn't answer him just yet and wanted him to mull it over a bit longer. This push back was unexpected.

The Deputy sat on his end with his arms folded still. "Ah, look. This is doable, but not as safe and probably effective as sneaking it into Okinawa or some other US base in the Southeast Asia and Pacific area. Even Guam has climate controlled hangars for B-2s where you could hide it...those things should at least be considered before the carrier idea."

Mark was pleased that Wu was on board but not so sure about the Deputy. It was important to him to have buy-in from both, especially since Wu was taking such a high risk.

Some time passed with complete silence. "Yes, sir. I understand your—"

"Mark. Wait a second. Again, excuse me. I trust you and the team. If this is your plan and you tell me it's going to work, then...then let's do it. Go for it. It's a risk for sure, but...OK, continue."

"Got it, sir. Thank you. The, ah, USS *Abraham Lincoln* could be in that vicinity in as early as two days from now. In fact, everyone, listen up. That's what we are shooting for on the timeline. Ford just completed his orientation wing-suit jump earlier today and is scheduled to go back out for another two jumps...with his little squirrel suit, and so the plan is ready," Mark said. "Are there any questions related to the plan before we get into aircraft performance?"

"Mark, this is Wu," Wu said. Mark chuckled quietly, as he clearly knew who it was. "The Devil Dragon wingspan is just shorter than your Boeing 737...and a C-130. Will it fit on your carrier's roof...your ship deck?"

"Yup, sure will, Wu. You'll clear the right wing on the vertical island of the ship by a few feet. No issues there. What we are concerned about, though, are your Chinese satellites. It's possible that they could see the Devil Dragon sitting on the flight deck. So, our plan is to fly out our welders to the *Abe Lincoln* tonight. Upon your arrival, they will cut off the wing or wings so we can get the jet onto the elevator and hidden in the hangar deck. Underneath," Mark said.

"This is amazing. I can't believe this is going to happen. I'm grateful," Wu said, coughing.

Mark wanted to include one last item on code words. "We don't want to transmit that much about anything over radios, so let's use two simple code words. Ford, when you land in your wing suit, text me the word *NATS*. Then, when you are ready and inside the Devil Dragon to take off, text me *METS*. These simple code words prevent a long explanation over the phone, text, or radio. Keep it simple."

Ford nodded, then covered his face with his hands after hearing the rough sounding cough again. It sounded horrible. "How is your health, Wu? How are you feeling?" Ford asked in a concerned tone.

"Ford...I'm getting a bit worse, but I can fly. I can still hide it because it looks like I just have a cold. But...I'm nearly out of pills. My stomach and lower back are just in pain all the time. My lungs are on fire, and I'm coughing up blood. Headaches. Not eating much, either. My time is just so...limited. If I weren't coming to see you, I wouldn't be able to fly more than one or two more times," Wu admitted.

"We understand, Wu. We really do. Emily, Mark, can we discuss an hour-by-hour timeline now?" Ford asked.

Emily drew the timeline across the board from left to right. It had takeoff times from Savannah to China, landing times for Wu, and landing times for Ford. It even had the carrier window and when it started and ended.

"Wu, Mark here. Bottom line. Can you make it to Tianjin Airport two days from today? We are ready to help. Just so you know, we named this op after you. It's called OPERATION WHIRLPOOL."

"Yes, I can be there. And your operation name is great, too. That whirlpool was a hell of a trip. So, yes, I will be there," Wu answered, sounding like he at least had some spirit left in him.

"Awesome, Wu. A few questions regarding the Devil Dragon. Will I have use of Liu's helmet?" Ford asked.

"Yeah, he'll most likely leave it in the cockpit when he gets out to use the restroom in the firehouse. That way we can talk over the intercom from the time you sit in the seat, all the way out," Wu answered. "If not, just wear yours from your jump."

"Tremendous. Next, what type of engine performance are we talking about? In fact, we don't even know your speeds, engine specs, or any real technical data. And your landing gear. Is it strong enough to land on a ship, or should we expect some issues?"

"This might be hard for you to comprehend. But. We can do Mach 5 on our ramjet engines. We've got the ability to do Beijing area to Europe in three hours, cut from a thirteen-hour flight. We can hit Paris from Beijing in two hours and thirty minutes," Wu said.

"*Mach 5*? How did you design ramjet rocket engines? Hypersonic speeds?" asked the Deputy.

"*We* didn't. You did. And the Brits helped. We...ah...reallocated your plans," Wu replied.

A ramjet was no ordinary jet engine. It was still air breathing but used the aircraft and engine's forward progress to squeeze the incoming air without an axial compressor. The ramjet cannot produce forward thrust at zero airspeed, and they couldn't move the Devil Dragon from a standstill with just ramjets. *These Chinese brilliantly had two types of engines on the same aircraft!* said the Deputy to himself. *Freaking brilliant!* The Devil Dragon required an assisted takeoff from two standard jet engines, and then once they had some forward motion, the remaining two ramjets took over to kick in the required speed. All they needed was some air. The Devil Dragon ramjets were very capable at supersonic speeds approaching Mach 5, but their testing for future aircraft already had Chen drooling about speeds of Mach 6, or close to forty-six hundred miles per hour.

"Ford, can you translate that engine speak for us a bit?" asked the Deputy.

"Yes, sir. As the Devil Dragon's airspeed increases, the effectiveness of her engine starts to drop as the air temperature in the engine inlet increases due to the compression." Ford looked at the DIA team, and they gave him smart-ass looks. "And so, sir, as the inlet temps increase and grow to reach the exhaust temperature on the back of the bird, less energy can be extracted in the form of thrust. What that means is that the Chinese engineers and research dudes figured out that to produce a characteristic amount of thrust at higher speeds, the Devil Dragon's ramjet engine had to be engineered so that the incoming air is not compressed as much. And, ah, look, the air flying through the combustion chamber is still moving at mind-numbing velocity and...will, basically, be supersonic. It's a freaking hell of an idea."

"So let me get this straight for us nonpilots. You have two regular jet engines for takeoff? Once you get some air flow, like down the runway, the two additional ramjets start-up...for the high-airspeed flight. Four engines total?" asked the Deputy.

"Yes, sir," answered Wu. "That's exactly how it works."

"Thank you, Wu, and oh, thank you, *Professor* Stevens," Mark said sarcastically. "Hold up. Hang on, man. I don't understand something. The heat must be intense upon landing.

Wu. These are amazing airspeeds. How are you working the ground handling then? Isn't that too hot for your ground folks?" Mark asked.

"Well." Wu cleared his throat. "We learned from the Concorde, the SR-71 Blackbird program, and even from the open sessions in Glasgow, that the temperatures—"

"*Glasgow*? What's that?" blurted the Deputy.

"Mr. Burns, open source is a terrific thing. They let anyone in. The American Institute of Aeronautics and Astronautics Hypersonic and Spaceplanes has an annual conference. We attended. They talked about lessons from past hypersonic jet programs. Things like how to handle new tools, missing rivets, maintenance turnarounds, broken inlet parts, and delaminated panels...items that ground crews have to deal with when we land. The PLAAF learned a lot of these things at conferences, which contributed to the Devil Dragon. Free admission, too."

"I'll be damned. First the stealth, now speeds. Shit. We gave it to them on a goddamn silver platter," the Deputy said slowly and very quietly. Then, much louder, "Wu, what else can you do with her?"

"Well, sir. Total sensor package. Stealth. Speed. Combined with tons of munitions. Can fly in complete congested airspace, like yours, Russia...India. Targeting pods. Antennas embedded in her skin. Radar for air and ground. We can sweep the entire electromagnetic spectrum or jam it, if needed. We can act as a vacuum and scoop it all up but be invisible. Chen also talked about the upgradeability on future bombers and something else that was hushed that I don't even know. Oh, and lasers, too," Wu said.

"Whoa. That's some aircraft. *Future bombers and lasers?* How many Devil Dragons are there?" Ford asked.

"I really don't know," replied Wu. "As far as I know, just this one. But, I have heard him discuss something called Black Scorpion and scramjets, so maybe there are plans for the future. I just don't know. You have to realize that Chen is demanding and always thinks things through. He also trained up two other pilots who were cleared to fly her, but I was the one selected."

"Oh, boy. Black Scorpion? That's gonna be an issue. What else did you learn from the United States, Wu?" replied the Deputy.

"Um, well, we learned about your stealth jets from *Have Blue*, *Hopeless Diamond*, and *Senior Trend*, and we—"

"Wait, Wu, the beginnings of the F-117 Nighthawk?" the Deputy interrupted.

"Yes, sir. From Amazon books. And believe it or not, from your Smithsonian Air and Space Museum at the Dulles Airport. And the Internet, of course, computers," Wu said, coughing.

"Did you say museum?" asked the Deputy.

"Yeah, and, sir, did you know that on display in Ohio...at your Wright-Patterson Air Force Base Museum, sitting in the open, all in the same hangar, you have a U-2 Dragon Lady, an SR-71 Blackbird, an F-117 Nighthawk and a B-2 Spirit? All in the same location? Chen couldn't believe it. He had college students take the detailed pictures, if I remember correctly. You in the United States, ironically enough, sought out Chinese college students to attend US universities and then paid their tuition money with US dollars and grants. Chen laughed at the opportunity. All the college students did was drive to Dayton for him from Ohio State University with their smartphones. And your government paid for it."

There was silence.

"Oh, and your downed aircraft," Wu added, as if the museum story wasn't insulting enough.

"*Downed aircraft?*"

"Yes. If I recall the story correctly, you were using F-117 Nighthawks over...um...the former Yugoslavia in Operation Allied Force. Serbian radar detected your jet when your pilot opened his bomb bay doors. He was shot down, and...ah...and both the Soviets and China grabbed the wreckage."

The DIA team all exchanged glances.

"That's how we learned about the iron ferrite coating to absorb the radar. And your slippery fuel, what you call...I think, JP-7? It was all over the wreckage. I heard it barely smelled, which threw off the science and technology people."

The Americans invented the hypersonic and stealth game know-how many years ago. The Area 51 gang had designed and tested the technology on bench tests, had a few mock-ups and demonstrators, and since 1959 were flying the SR-71 Blackbird way back then. Along came the 1970s and 1980s with the design of the F-117. This news today, though, that China had taken the extra step faster than the Americans, learning from history and doing something about it, was breathtaking. Area 51 had terrific standoff and security, but it was rare to keep the Chinese out of their electronic and computer records. *No wonder we're behind...Chinese did their homework. And cyber. Damn it!* thought

Calvin.

Wu continued, coughing. "As a follow-up on the gear...I can't be sure of the landing gear required for your ships, but it's not built like your naval aviation jets. It's for runways. If I remember your History Channel episodes, we'll slam down pretty hard," Wu said.

"History Channel?" Emily mouthed to the DIA team.

"Mark, can you relay via your networks for the *Lincoln* CO to have the barricade up and spray the landing area with foam? The chance of a mishap here is pretty high, and since we don't have a tailhook, we don't have a snowball's chance in hell of stopping without it," Ford asked.

"You got it, kid. Consider it done," Mark replied.

"I'm also concerned about the avionics of the jet, Wu. You'll never get our encrypted ship TACAN channels or the instrument landing system on the Devil Dragon, so I'll have to hand carry something that provides some type of satellite navigation," Ford added.

"No, we receive all the signals. All of them. X and Y channels on TACAN. We have the GPS moving map, and...we can see all your navaids from the ships," Wu said, without skipping a beat.

"Wait a second, those are all *highly encrypted*. How can you receive *those*?" asked the Deputy.

"We got 'em, Mr. Burns. This jet has the keys to all your high technology. The cyber teams in China have worked hard over the past few years, and Chen has been aggressive on capturing intellectual property from the government, military, and private sectors. We can see you, but you can't see us. Only way for you to see the Devil Dragon is visually."

"That is just amazing," Robert said. "All our technology firewalls and US Cyber Command, and the Chinese walk through the front door."

"Yes, open source. Free admission," Wu said, like he was referring to an admission ticket at Disney World.

Ford was thinking that for some reason if the navigation avionics did not work, there was no way for them to know the location of where they were. He was somewhat uncomfortable with the idea of going that far out to sea, in the blind. The wristwatch GPS from the jump would have to be the plan B.

"Mark, I'll have my smartphone with me, as well as Wu's. Certainly, a moving map from the wing-suit jump will be close by. Maybe as the first backup, NSA and the *Lincoln* could ping us for a position. It would make me feel better. As a second, maybe a visual from a nearby pilot. If there are any guys in the area, they can call in with a pilot report, a PIREP, as we go by," Ford said.

Mark quickly wrote down all the requests in his notebook, and Emily copied them down on the whiteboard. They did not want to miss anything, especially since they were so close to executing the mission. The plan was really starting to come together after discussing it and looking at the big picture on the whiteboard.

"Any other last minute items?" Mark asked. No one said anything. "Wu, we won't chat or text again until you contact Ford as you are inbound to the airfield for the Ford swap out. Maybe use the code word JOJO RISING. I don't know. You're good with that? We'll have doctors on the ship, in addition to the infirmary, to help you upon arrival. Yes?" Mark asked.

Wu took a swig of water from his plastic water bottle and swallowed one of his remaining pain pills. He was nearly finished with the first of the two prescriptions. No one could see him on the conference call, but he was pleased with the timeline, especially since he was running out.

"Yes. I'll be there," Wu said, clearing this throat. "Thank you." Wu terminated the call.

"I cannot believe we gave the Chinese all the components to build this thing," the Deputy started out after Wu hung up. "Right under our noses. Our sweat. Our test flights. Our dead test pilots over the years. All our engineers and years of flying out west. *Really? Open source conferences? The Dulles Air and Space Museum?* They came right in, like Robert said, right through the...the motherfucking front door." The Deputy was angered and his tone and volume changed. "We gave it to them on a silver platter. I mean, the Wright-Patt Museum? Who the *fuck* approved putting four of our stealth aircraft on display? What's next, public libraries? You have got to be shitting me. They got the blueprints off our backs, did their homework faster than we could, and...and we're paying the price for being such an open nation. Damn it!"

Mark had never heard the Deputy curse and lose his composure like this before. The DIA team could also not see that the Deputy threw his notebook across his office. No one dared to answer his rhetorical questions.

Defense Intelligence Agency, Bolling AFB, Washington, DC

"Jason!" the Deputy called inside.

"Yes, sir."

"Have Michelle Boyd get her ass up here. Don't go putting it in writing, either. She's one of Klubb's girls...a missile analyst. I want you in here, too, so have her come up here to talk to you, then, bring her butt in here," Deputy Burns instructed Jason. "Now."

"You got it, sir." *Oh, man, he is fired up* thought Jason, as he called for Michelle to come down to his office. Michelle did not read into the call and came up to see Jason right away. She was not carrying anything in her hands and nearly pranced in to see Jason. Her involvement with the committee phone call seemed like forever ago, she had not thought about it since her night out with Jess at the Dubliner.

"Hi, Michelle. Come on in. The Deputy wants to talk to you," Jason said.

Her face immediately felt flushed and turned red with complete embarrassment.

"Oh, I thought I was coming to see you, Jason." She knew exactly why she was in there but now wasn't sure if the FBI was inside to arrest her for partial disclosure back in the bar.

"Follow me, please," Jason said. Michelle followed behind and had near zero reaction time to formulate a plan. Jason knocked twice on the wooden office door. "Sir, Michelle Boyd here to see you."

"Send her in, Jason," Deputy Burns said, as he came out from around his desk.

Michelle walked in just behind Jason.

"Ms. Boyd, come in. Don't bother sitting, as you won't be here long. I know of your bullshit involvement with contacting the Hill recently regarding my hearing. Yes?" the Deputy said, rolling the dice. He really wasn't 100 percent sure if she did it or not. This was the moment where she could deny it all, or come completely clean.

Michelle stood there and at first did not say anything. She was silent.

"Michelle?" Jason said, a bit loud.

"Yes, yes, sir. It was me," Michelle admitted.

"I don't care what your reasons are. I don't care what your politics are. Not completely sure what your connections are on the Hill. But...if you don't want orders to frickin' Timbuktu, you are going to fix this. Understand? Am I clear?"

"Yes, sir. I am so sorry. When I placed the call, I was just calling out of anger. Our missile section wanted the nod to do something good for DIA. We wanted the credit, and it made me mad that Mark Savona, that aircraft analyst, came in there and started in and—" Michelle attempted to explain.

"Hold it, hold up." The Deputy waved his palm around in the air. "I don't want to hear your bullshit excuses. Bull crap! You know what you did was wrong. I have every right to throw your goddamn ass out of here and strip you of your clearances. You'd never work in national security again. You'd be stuck working at the IRS, or worse, DHS. So shut it and grow up."

"Yes, sir," said Michelle as she started to cry.

"Call over to your source on the committee, have her march in to see the senator, and tell the good senator that it was nothing. False report. Turn it off. OFF!"

"Yes...sir," Michelle said, sobbing now.

"I'll consider this mess done, then. Come and see Jason later today after you make the call. Jason, yes?"

"Yes, sir," they both replied.

Calvin thought for a moment and then changed his mind. There was no need to come back and report to him. "Wait a second, wait a second. Don't bother calling," as he put his hand up in the air. "I am confident you will take care of it. Clear? Now get out of here."

They both walked toward the door, and Calvin knew he'd unloaded his anger. "Hey, Michelle. Hold it again."

"Yes...yes, sir?"

"Look. This situation is one of the largest missions in DIA history. You wouldn't have known that when you made your call, but I know now. This has grown into a major event. A major national security mission. It doesn't get any larger than this. There is a big mission with details that would blow your fucking mind. So, we keep this topic and conversation between only us. Understand? Classified. Not a breath to anyone."

"Yes, Mr. Burns."

"Now get the *hell* out of here."

Gansu, China

Wu pressed the red icon on his phone to hang up and was overcome with emotion. He sat on the desk chair on his hotel room and held his face in his hands. Wu cried; he cried hard. Tears streamed down his jaundiced skin from his red eyes. He was emotionally shot, and he did not want his life to end so early. The roller coaster of denial, then anger, and now sadness was taking a true mental and physical toll on him. He looked and felt like total hell and was happy the jet was being worked on today so he could take a breather before taking off again on his final flight.

He used the time wisely to reflect on his tremendous life and was thankful for the opportunities his mom set up for him when he was young. The opportunity to study math, attend college, and achieve a prestigious position in the Air Force was every boy's dream. Wu was reviewing his life in sequence, thinking about his father when he was a young kid. Although he was not a man of religion, Wu wondered if he would see him, along with his mother, again. Perhaps above all the emotions he had felt already, the strongest emotion felt was his loneliness. He wanted someone to hug him, to hold his head, to take care of him, to just tell him things would be all right, like his mother used to do when he was a young boy. He missed her, too, and let another round of crying come out of his body.

Wu took out his phone again and decided to text Vic at the US consulate. He made sure the Peanut was attached and in green.

Wu: Vic this is Wu Lee. Just wanted to make sur you relayed my final requests to Mark and if not it is necessary you to do it today. Things are happening soon. Very soon. Than you

Gulfstream Hangar, Savannah Airport, Georgia

Robert was lying down on his back on the white, glossy floor of the large aircraft hangar and looking up at the belly of the G650ER, along with the certification process specialist, an electrical engineer technician, and an external loads engineer. They had flashlights and were shining the light on the external seal where they just finished making the rear ramp.

Robert rubbed his palm on the lip of the ramp, which was evident if you were looking for it but terrifically camouflaged from the outside. He crawled out from underneath, thanked the technicians, and walked inside to chat with the pilots.

"Ramp looks good. Want to try it out for me?" Robert asked, pointing his thumb back inside the hangar. Robert walked back to the jet, and the techs were still there, as now were Reggie, Rose, and Arnold, the Gulfstream leadership team. The electrical engineer technician handed Lurch back his cell phone, complete with the new Gulfstream 650ER app installed. The tech verified the aircraft's Wi-Fi and password, and showed him the up and down options.

"OK, here we go!" Lurch yelled outside the cabin door to the floor, wanting to ensure no one was down below.

Lurch pressed the down button, and the two rear seats slid to the outside of the airframe on rails, as did the carpeting. The floor and ramp of the jet lowered to the hangar floor.

Vrrrrrrr ffffft.

They could hear the motors lowering the ramp down on the pistons, and there was just enough space for Ford to slide down on his butt and jump. The glossy white floor was now easily seen.

"Well. I'll be dipped in shit. Check that out," said Lurch, as he spit some chewing tobacco into a Styrofoam coffee cup.

"Very impressive," Robert said, sliding down on his butt to simulate how Ford would do it for real. It worked. Robert slid right out of the back of the G650 and walked around outside to the stairs.

"Hey, put it back up," Robert yelled inside the jet from the outside. He then walked to the back of the jet as the ramp went up.

Vrrrrrrr ffffft.

No evidence of a ramp at all in sight. Robert then walked up the stairs and saw the seats were just as they were before they started.

"Friggin' great. This is incredible," he said, happy with the work Gulfstream did in such a short time.

"You like, eh?" Reggie said, laughing and once again holding his belly with both his hands.

"Works like a champ. Say, Ford will be here later and prepped for departure in the morning. Any last minute questions, Lurch?" Robert asked.

Lurch already had his pre-mission planning meeting with Andrew. They were all supportive of the flight. "None that I can think of. Let's get a test flight under our belts. Work out any kinks.

If she works, it's a go...let's launch," Lurch replied.

"Thanks for your help and support, Lurch. This means a lot. Appreciate your efforts," Robert said, as he shook his hand. "Reggie, thank you, sir."

"Go give her a test flight. If ops test is good, Godspeed," Reggie replied, giving Robert a hug.

"If she's good, you leave in the morning. We'll get Ford back down here," Robert announced.

Rendezvous at LAX Airport, California

Mark arranged for Emily, Robert, and himself to rendezvous at Los Angeles International Airport, LAX, before heading to Hawaii together on a commercial flight. Robert flew in from Atlanta, while Mark and Emily flew in from Dulles.

"Hey, welcome to California," Mark said to Robert as they met at Terminal 7 to board the United Airlines flight westbound. Robert looked like he'd been up for days.

"Thanks, Mark. Guys back in Savannah did a bang-up job. Real nice work. Engineers and techs built it just like we designed, and we tested it yesterday afternoon. Worked terrific," Robert said, then putting his head down for a drink at the fountain.

"Impressive. Well, Ford's ready. He did his practice jumps yesterday. Had a bit of an issue with his primary chute, but all good on the secondary. He loved the squirrel suit...the wing suit. Looked like a fruitcake, but it works great," Mark said.

Emily listened in as they walked in the terminal, stopping at the Gordon Bierch Restaurant near their gate. "He was way below a thousand feet when it opened. Yanked the secondary chute and made it," she added. "His remaining jumps were normal."

They sat down and looked at the menu, then quickly ordered a few drinks. Mark was already thinking of the logistics of landing in Hawaii and then getting out to the aircraft carrier. His phone was already in his hand, and he scanned through the numbers until he reached the DIA Operations Center and dialed.

"Listen, I'm concerned that we are going to be talking in a public place about this stuff, so let's watch one another. No one around when we talk, especially on this call I need to make, good?" Mark told them.

"You got it, boss," Robert replied for both of them.

Mark already had the phone to his ear. "Hey, Mark S. here. I'll give you my ID in a sec. Need to be patched to US Pacific Command Operations Center." He covered the phone and whispered to the group about ordering off the menu.

"One moment, sir," replied the watch officer on phone duty. "I can see your caller ID, and you're coming up as green in the computer. I'll connect you now."

"Thank you."

"PACOM, this is DIA Operations Center. Sending you a call from Mark S. Go ahead, Mark."

Mark listened in until it was his turn to speak. "Good afternoon, PACOM. Mark from DIA calling for the admiral. He is expecting my call." He pulled the phone off his ear and glanced at the screen again, ensuring he was green on the encryption. He covered the phone with his hand and whispered, "Emily, get me a burger and a Golden Blonde, please. I'm waiting for the admiral."

Emily did as requested as they waited for the admiral.

"Hello, Admiral. Mark from DIA calling," he said quietly in the crowded restaurant.

"Hi Mark, how are things coming along?" asked Admiral Matthew McDevitt, the Pacific Command Theater commander.

"Good, sir. Very good. Just wanted to touch base verbally with you on the plan. Your aide has it in an e-mail, but big picture, we are coming now via commercial flight to Honolulu. The command is picking us up for the G IV flight to Kadena in Okinawa, then a C-2 Greyhound flight to the *Lincoln*. The package will arrive sometime tomorrow night to the *Lincoln*."

"Understand, Mark. My aide has been keeping me informed. My J3 tells me we're a go, but as you can imagine, I have issues. A few issues. So, you nonflying DIA types have planned to just have them come in here and land her? Look, I'm all for supporting your mission. Supporting DIA. Certainly grabbing her, but to use a ship to do it is near excessive risk."

Mark remained silent due to operational security, or OPSEC, as he was in the corner of a public restaurant.

"My J3 also tells me to trust your pilot and also to trust you, so I'll still approve it, but I want your pilot doing everything he can to make it safe. Do I have reservations, Mark? You bet your ass I do. But, I understand it's a...mitigated risk...and I'm a risk taker. So. Any issues, call my aide again and we'll troubleshoot," said the admiral.

"Thanks, sir. Appreciate your help and support on this. The Deputy sends his best," Mark said, nodding his thanks to the waitress who dropped off the beer.

The admiral cleared his throat. "Mark, you never know what's going to happen out there. As I just said, I'm a bit uncomfortable with them zipping around the pattern without a tailhook. Not unheard of, so we do have a plan in place. But for Christ's sake...they are going to come running out of the China airspace like a rabbit being chased by foxes. Fighters could be all over their asses. Missiles. Electronic warfare gear blasting crap all over the goddamn place. Who knows? No matter what, the *Lincoln* CO is going to be prepared, so I just need to warn you now, things could get dicey. I'm ensuring *Gettysburg* is around to protect *Lincoln*. And the *Lincoln* CO is sending up at least a section of F-18 Hornets, at a minimum, to protect the ship. I'll also have a few F-22s out of Kadena."

"We understand, sir. Ah, I've also talked with your J3 about the portion of the plan that involves the airdrop," Mark said, looking at Emily.

Emily threw a look to Robert and whispered, "*Airdrop? You know anything about that*?" Emily looked at Robert. He shook his head no.

"OK, Mark. Take care. Safety, got it? Out," said the admiral, as the call ended.

The waitress came back again, this time dropping off some appetizers that they ordered. Emily waited until she left and took a swig of her wine. Robert held up his beer, and they did cheers silently without a verbal toast. They all knew what they were happy about so far. Mark ensured his phone was disconnected and waited until they were completely alone.

"What's this airdrop you and the admiral just talked about?" Emily asked quietly.

Mark thought about their location and made a decision to talk quietly at the airport restaurant. Because timing was so sensitive, and they had none to waste, Mark took a chance talking about the mission in the restaurant. He rolled the dice talking outside of a secure area but was comfortable with his decision because it was so fluid and dynamic. For them to pass a one-minute bit of information, they would have to locate a secure room at the nearest facility, most likely the Los Angeles Air Force Base.

"Look, this isn't necessarily the best place to be talking about this stuff, so I'll make it quiet and quick," Mark said nearly whispering. "While I was sitting in Suffolk, it hit me that we needed some type of diversion out at sea. A Devil Dragon *wreckage*. If Chen is the bastard that Wu makes him out to be, he's going to be pissed off with a capital P. That weasel will want proof that his jet landed someplace or crashed. So I contacted the embassy in Tokyo and got a hold of the FBI LegAtt. They are getting two corpses from the Tokyo morgue to—"

"*What*? For *what*?" Robert asked with emotion but also whispering.

"Hear me out," Mark said quietly as he put up his hand. "This is an old Second World War move, straight out of the playbook. It's like—"

"Operation Mincemeat?" Emily asked.

"Well, yes, exactly," Mark replied.

The World War II operation, named Mincemeat, was a

real-world and successful British disinformation military plan that was part of a big deception plot to shield the invasion of Italy from North Africa. Mincemeat helped influence the German leadership that the Allies were going to invade Greece in 1943 instead of Italy, which was the real plan. The disinformation was accomplished by persuading the Germans that they had, by total luck, captured classified papers giving details of military operations. The papers were located in the pockets of a corpse intentionally left to roll up on the shore in Spain.

"History lesson, eh, Mark?" she replied, smiling.

"Yup. Worked then, may work now. The embassy doctor oversaw the transfer of two DBs for science, you know, dead bodies. Ones that already had blunt force trauma damage, in addition to severe burn marks. They were from the train crash that we saw in the *Washington Post* two days ago. They were already severely damaged...no marks, no fingerprints...not even a face. Just had to find the same blood type Wu told the guys at the consulate," Mark explained.

"What are the details?" Emily leaned in even closer to hear the rest of the story.

"The legal attaché from the FBI picked up the DBs from the Tokyo morgue. Bureau worked a favor from the local police. They went over to mainland Japan, to Yokoda, where there are Herks. The Thirty-Sixth Airlift Squadron out of Yokoda loaded them up, and some Defense Department friends put them in damaged Chinese flight suits with no markings"—Mark took a swig of beer—"along with some fuel, oil, JOGAIR aviation sectional charts, and a fake Wu Lee wallet. This package will be airdropped at sea to simulate a crash. Location will be in the shipping lanes of the Philippine Sea. A passing commercial shipping vessel will pick them up in a day, maybe two, at the...at the most," Mark said.

Mark had also thought long and hard about where to drop the dead bodies at sea, which he did not really elaborate on due to their airport location. The commercial shipping lanes running in this area of the Pacific were some of the busiest sea traffic in the world and would be a perfect spot for their drop. It was just a matter of time before a ship spotted the debris field and picked up the two bodies. From there, it was just a phone call to get a hold of a nation's coast guard, then the Chinese government, which would hopefully explain where their missing jet was.

"Bloody hell!" Emily said quietly. "Lovely idea!"

Savannah, Georgia

Ford woke up early after a quick nap and not sleeping well, and walked over to the window facing the paper mills to the north, red rooftop lights blinking bright in the dark morning sky. He looked down at the Savannah River to see their reflection in the water, sipping his Hyatt Hotel room's coffee. Ford checked his phone and saw a text from Mark.

Mark: Chief and Deputy Chief of Air Force Reserve personally cleared you to fly from Pentagon and Georgia. Deputy Burns called them. You are on special assignment to our team. Take good care and see you soon.

Thank God, Ford thought. *Red tape cut just like that.*

He showered, got dressed, and went down to the hotel

breakfast buffet, where he ate as much as he could before getting an Uber car to the Gulfstream hangar over at the airport. In his carry-on luggage was his tactical gear, consisting of a Sig Sauer P226 handgun, an HK416 rifle, backpack parachute, his GPS and altimeter, laser, black wing suit, gray helmet and oxygen mask, and a small oxygen canister.

He had taken up the Hyatt's offer of a personal hygiene kit from the hotel, so there was no need to have his own. Robert left him a garment bag at the front desk last evening that consisted of the weapons he had acquired from the Georgia Air National Guard that shared the runways of the Savannah Airport. It also consisted of a change of clothes, including a newly purchased business suit to wear on the jet. This was just in case of the remote chance that someone spotted him getting on the jet, he wanted to blend in as a Senior Manager or Executive Vice-President. Today, he looked like Mr. Ford Stevens of Corning, Inc., and made his way over to the airport.

"Wheels up in twenty minutes, Ford. Ready to go?" Lurch said, turning around in the cockpit to see Ford standing there, looking at the G650 glass flight deck in awe. The space was large enough for Ford to fit in there as well, peeking over their shoulders to see everything inside and outside the jet. It was completely lit up, and their flight plan was displayed on one of the four large Symmetry Flight Deck multifunction glass screens that took up the entire dashboard.

"Let's do it. Make it happen," Ford replied and turned around to walk over to the wide, open, and empty cabin section of the jet.

"Take a nap, Ford. We'll wake you over the Pacific in a few hours. Or just before your mission," Lurch told him.

"Will do. Fellas, thanks again. We couldn't pull this off without your help," Ford said, respectful of their time and trustworthy efforts.

Ford turned to head back to the cabin and could hear Andrew doing the tail end of the pilot brief. "Lurch, final portion of the departure briefing. We're full on fuel, near max weight of 103,600 pounds. Includes the National Business Aviation Association...ah...instrument flight rules reserve fuel. One passenger today. Max operating speed of Mach 0.925, but filed for 0.88, and V1 takeoff speed is 120 knots. Navaids are punched in for the departure. Radar altimeter is set for an emergency return. No hazards or terrain on the climb out. All emergencies per standard operating procedure. Ah, weather is good en route. Destination is cool with fog and mist. ATC routing is always in question once we get farther west. We're a go," Andrew briefed. They taxied into position, held for a moment, and then received clearance from the tower for takeoff. Lurch pushed the throttles forward as the Rolls-Royce engines came alive with full vigor, and away they went.

Ford missed flying over the past week or so and was looking forward to getting back in the seat. He stopped walking rearward past the cabin entrance and looked again at the luxury surrounding him. The welcoming cabin was just gorgeous, and it combined the airy high-end interiors of a Ritz-Carlton Hotel while airborne. It consisted of an attractive-looking sleeping area, complete with a queen sleeper bed, crisp white sheets, and a feathery pillow. Ford also had access to a whole host of fresh fruit, cheese trays, salads, bottles of Silver Oak Cabernet Sauvignon wine, a multitude of choices of in-flight entertainment, Wi-Fi, and a moving-map display that showed their location on earth. The jet could sleep ten when flying a much shorter leg or seat a total of nineteen in the smooth leather captain chairs and couches. While the jet could go as far as seventy-five hundred miles, today's flight at 7,335 miles could easily fit eight passengers. On this flight, though, Ford was in the cabin solo. *Who has it better than me?* he said to himself.

He climbed into the inviting bed, prepared for him by Gulfstream corporate customer service as they did for all their customers. Ford laughed. *Wonder what the squadron mates would say if they saw me now, all pampered and ritzy?*

Their flight plan, filed with the FAA over a computer during the preflight brief, had them flying over Atlanta, Little Rock, Denver, San Francisco, then south of Adak, Alaska, over to Sapporo, Japan, direct to Seoul, South Korea, an overflight over Tianjin, and finally landing in Beijing. The 7,335-mile flight was expected to take eleven hours and eighteen minutes according to the flight software, which did not take into account winds at altitude, the reduction in airspeed for the descent, nor the radar vectoring from air traffic controllers to land. They flew the filed plan at Mach 0.88 at fifty thousand feet, which was near the G650ER's max cruising altitude, and so far, they were able to get that out of the aircraft with ease.

The jet made Ford giddy because he wasn't used to this much luxury. He had been in military business jets, which Ford thought were nice, but this was completely over the top. It was almost comical to him how the top 1 percent lived. He finally did relax, and by the time he closed his eyes for a nap, they were at altitude over Oklahoma and steadily on their way to the Asia Pacific region. Compared to the noisy B-1, the quiet ride in this jet was complete pampered luxury.

Kadena Air Base, Okinawa, Japan

The US Navy C-2 Greyhound that performed carrier onboard delivery, or COD, was already turning engine number two on the ramp as Mark, Emily, and Robert came out of the terminal building, carrying their bags and rolling their small suitcases. They just landed in the G IV from Hawaii to Okinawa and were ready to press on to the carrier. The DIA team used the flight time to nap, attempting to catch up on the jet lag. A flight-suited crew member of the USS *Abraham Lincoln*'s C-2 crew was there to escort them on board and to the ship, compliments of the ship's captain.

"Welcome aboard! Sorry to yell. Let me get you some headsets," shouted the C-2 aircrew chief to the three of them as they buckled in.

Mark started to sit then stood up quickly to shake the hands of the pilots. He waved in thanks for the mission as he and the other two appreciated the ride out to the carrier. Mark turned to return to his seat and got a solid whiff of the exhaust from the Allison T-56 number-one engine, just starting on the left wing.

"Chief, they up yet?" the copilot asked, just as the three were putting on their vests and headsets.

"Yes, sir, all three passengers up," he answered.

Mark forgot that the headsets were not voice activated, so he started talking, but his voice did not transmit. He then pressed the button to talk, located on a small black box located on his cord, connected to his headset. As he did it, the chief closed the door, and the noise of the engines was muffled a bit.

"We're here," Mark said over the intercom, giving a thumbs-up to the crew. So did Emily and Robert.

"Nice to meet the three of you. So, not sure who you guys are, or who you know, but we were diverted from Seoul to Kadena to get you. We have another sister aircraft picking up VIP passengers down at Naha, Okinawa, in a few hours," the aircraft commander told them.

"Yup, appreciate the lift very much. Thank you," Mark said with complete sincerity.

"Yes, thank you, boys," Emily added.

"Whoa, a Brit?" the copilot said. Both the pilot and copilot turned around in the cockpit to see if the face matched the accent. It did, and they looked at each other with complete amusement and smiles. "Well, welcome aboard. I'm Ginger and this is Piglet," said Ginger from the left seat.

"How long is the flight today, Ginger?" Emily asked.

"Man, she is a freaking hottie. Dude, did you see that butt? Look at her..." said copilot Piglet, by accident transmitting it to the whole aircraft versus just the pilot on intercom. "Crap. Sorry."

"That's OK, Mr. Piglet," replied hottie Emily.

"We should be landing on the *Abe* in just over an hour," Ginger replied. He slapped the copilot in the upper arm with his right hand, telling him to shut his mouth. Ginger covered his headset and yelled over to him, "They are guests of PACOM, you dipshit. The admiral. Shut your mouth, dummy."

At about forty minutes of flight time, the headsets were full of chatter from a variety of voices. From inside the aircraft, the crew was performing the descent and prelanding checklists that consisted of everything from the cabin pressurization to harnesses.

"Hey, passengers. Not sure if you have ever landed on a carrier while at sea, but we will be approaching the ship soon. Ensure your harness is locked. As we come down in altitude, we'll be talking to her and listening to commands from the landing signal officer, the LSO," said Ginger. He looked at his watch. "I'd say about twelve more minutes or so."

"Got it, Ginger. Thank you," Mark said. He moved the black knob lever located near his right hip to the forward position. He leaned forward in his harness, and he no longer had freedom of movement. Locked.

The C-2 zoomed by the right side of the carrier at one thousand feet of pattern altitude, at 220 knots, preparing for the procedure called the "overhead break." Robert leaned forward and looked out his porthole and could see in large white letters and numbers "CVN-72," along with white lightbulbs, painted in the vertical island. The ship looked tiny from that altitude, but he knew it was gigantic. It was the fifth Nimitz-class aircraft carrier, and Robert always loved seeing the ballet in progress on the flight deck—all sorts of moving aircraft and helicopters and a variety of personnel doing things all at the same time.

"What are all the colored-shirts doing down there?" Emily asked, seeing the same view Robert was seeing.

The crew chief came up, pointing to a little laminated handheld chart he had to explain just that. It described the deck operations, with a few warnings.

"The deck of the USS *Abraham Lincoln* looks like chaos, but things are very controlled and coordinated. Upon landing, your escort officer will take care of both you and your bags. Please follow his or her instructions and we will explain everything upon landing. We welcome you to the Abe!"

Below the opening paragraph on the card were photos of the different colored shirts the sailors might wear on the flight deck, with a small explanation of what they were.

Purple—Aviation Fuels
Blue—Plane Handlers
Green—Catapult and Arresting Gear Handlers
Yellow—Aircraft Handling Officers
Red—Ordnance
Brown—Air Wing Plane Captains

Ginger and Piglet received permission from the air boss to make the left turn in front of the ship, yanked the yoke to the left, and turned in a hard and tight angle of bank turn opposite the direction of the ship. They got dirty with gear and flaps, and double-checked all their instruments to be sure they were turned up to the ship frequencies. They were now abeam the island, and Ginger, in the left seat, kept his scan active to ensure just the proper angle to begin both a turn and a descent toward the rear of the carrier. Ginger looked out his window as he had so many years ago when he learned to fly the T-34C Turbo Mentor with VT-28 at Naval Air Station Corpus Christi, Texas. He extended downwind a few more seconds to give him the proper separation between himself and the rear of the ship. One last scan that the gear was down, hook down, and flaps were 50 percent.

"PROVIDER 32, you are cleared to turn. Call fuel state and souls on board," said the *Abe* air traffic controller.

"*Abe*, PROVIDER 32. Six souls. 3.2," Piglet reported back.

"Roger, PROVIDER. Winds 220 at 22. Call the ball."

Ginger kept the turn in to line up the aircraft visually with the moving aircraft carrier. They were turning on to final approach, with both Ginger and Piglet looking at the approach end of the ship, in addition to the Fresnel lens that was used to determine the aircraft descent angle. All the landing navaids were tuned and working properly, always a good backup to a visual approach.

"PROVIDER has ball," Piglet called out to the *Abe* over the radio.

"PROVIDER 32, you are cleared to land."

"Roger, PROVIDER cleared to land," replied Piglet.

Robert, Emily, and Mark swayed back and forth with the aircraft as the pilots up front made minor adjustments to the aircraft. The water was coming closer and closer to the window, and if they did not know they were landing on a ship, it looked like from the rear of the aircraft they were going to landing on the water.

"Ginger, Buttercup here at LSO. Continue. Looking good, my friend. Keep her coming down," said Buttercup, a fellow pilot who was working as the landing signal officer. He was there to talk down the pilots, keep them at ease during the landing process, and provide them input for altitude, attitude, airspeed, and safety.

"Good altitude. Continue. Spot-on. Add a bit of power, looking low," Buttercup said, in a calming and serene voice.

"Roger," Ginger replied, concentrating on the approach.

Mark leaned over a bit, and he saw Piglet place his hands at the base of the throttles, just below Ginger's right hand. Ginger was moving them ever so slightly, and Piglet looked like he was just supporting him.

"Keep her coming. Looking good. A bit more power. Power. Almost there..." Buttercup said.

The C-2 slammed on the deck of the carrier, and everyone was pressed hard into their harnesses. The engines went from a low roar at what seemed like idle, to full power, making enormous noise. Ginger went to full power on both his engines upon landing, just in case he missed the ship's deck or a wire. They were no longer airborne, but the aircraft was moving still a bit on the deck.

Ginger pulled back the throttles once he was assured they were safe on deck, and the aircraft leaned back a bit. The ship was moving at a steady fifteen knots, and the airplane bobbed and weaved with the deck of the ship, cutting through the clear blue water of the Pacific Ocean.

"Good trap, Ginger. Welcome back," Buttercup said. "OK, three wire."

Every single landing on the deck of a ship for a pilot was graded on a scale of no grade to four and corresponded to one of the four wire steel cables strung across the approach end of the ship. The pilot's goal was to catch the number three wire with his tailhook, but catching any of them meant you landed. Even if you made a perfect landing, the best you could do was "OK" on the grade sheet. Nothing like keeping the egos in check.

"Roger, Buttercup, thanks," Ginger said.

"PROVIDER, you are cleared to taxi. Follow blue-shirt instructions for starboard parking. Welcome home," the ground controller told them.

Mark, Emily, and Robert looked at one another with smiles. They gave thumbs up signs to one another. Mark thought that in just a few short hours, Ford and Wu would be doing the same thing.

"That was cool as heck. Bloody hell! That was cool!" Emily crowed.

"Civilian guests, welcome to the USS *Abraham Lincoln*, international waters, Pacific Ocean. Your first hook. Congratulations. All right, follow me, please," the crew chief instructed them, and they exited the C-2 Greyhound to see the floating city.

Sunshine Hotel, Gansu, China

Wu returned from the Chinese drugstore, located near the Sunshine Hotel, where he purchased eye drops. He also realized how out of breath he was, which disturbed him because the distance was so short. In his room, he located his flight-suit pocket to put the drop bottle in, then took out his smartphone for flight planning. The flight-planning app aided Wu in his flight for later today, which was to be the speed test that they missed because of the fire.

Wu looked at his flight-planning software and punched in the numbers for his planned route of flight to the Xining Caojiabao Airfield, dragged the icons across China on a map, and saved the file. He would be able to upload the planned route into the jet's navigation software upon arrival, which made it easy to transfer data both before and after a flight.

Wu had been back in his room for a few minutes, but he still breathed heavily and sweated profusely. He got up from his desk and slowly walked into the bathroom to splash water on his face, finally coming to grips that the simple walk to the drugstore practically exhausted him. Because the cancer had taken over his lungs, as evident when he spit blood into the sink, his tumors had spread to the lymph nodes and made him wheeze. Wu told himself it would not be long now, swallowed, and closed his eyes to concentrate.

Wu opened them, walked back to the desk, and sat. He typed out the secondary profile, this time from Gansu to Tianjin, total distance of 948 nautical miles. Wu thought for a moment and cracked a smile at how short that was for the Devil Dragon.

He shook his head from side to side and figured he would have to take the jet out to the northeast to simulate the flight test, and come around to the Beijing and Tianjin area on the turn back to the west. Wu opened up what looked like Google Maps, and a blue line showed the potential flight path.

Wu then changed to the satellite imagery and looked at the firehouse on the airfield. Seemed easy enough, he thought, since he was just off the taxiway near the western runway. Depending on what direction they were landing, he figured they would be fine with the plan. *Pretty smart*, he thought, and he wondered who specifically generated the idea.

Wu gathered his flight bag and overnight bag, as he had done so many times before, and mentally said good-bye to the hotel room. He had hoped he would never see it again, as he always thought of the nice hotels he had stayed in during visits to America. From the MGM Grand in Vegas to the Yellowstone Hotel at the national park to the Hollywood Hotel in Los Angeles, Wu felt very lucky to have stayed at so many nice places. He would not miss the Sunshine Hotel.

Meeting in the dining area as they did before every mission, Wu and Liu dropped their gear and went over for some food and tea. Wu grabbed the table they'd eaten at a few times in the past and sat. Liu sat, didn't say much, and got right up again for the buffet.

Wu calmly looked around and saw that no one was near him or looking in his direction. He slipped his right hand into his flight suit pocket near his right calf and pulled out the clear bottle of eye drops.

"You want any tea?" Liu asked, startling Wu from behind, not even seeing him arrive back at the table. Wu immediately dropped the eye drop container back into his pocket.

"Yes, yes, very nice. Thank you," Wu answered.

Liu dropped off two teas in cups and saucers at the table, and Wu was shocked that he nearly got caught in the act. *Shit!* he thought. He was already feeble physically and mentally, and here the mission would have been over before it even started. Wu made a note to pay better attention.

He dug his hand back into his flight suit pocket and was able to grab the eye drops again. Unscrewing the cap with both hands under the table, Wu placed the container in his left hand, looked around to see Liu over at the food, and squirted. He put a few seconds of the clear and tasteless liquid into Liu's water and teacup. The container was nearly empty, so he put the cap back on and placed it back in his pocket. Done.

After eating, they made their way to the airport and into the hangar where the jet was being prepped for their flight. Wu put his gear under the wing, as he always had, and was going to walk inside to talk with the chief engineer and the chief of maintenance and check the weather. Upon entering, though, there was an unexpected visitor inside the maintenance offices, hunched over the counter with a crowd standing around him in silence. Chen was here early.

Over the Sea of Okhotsk, Western Pacific Ocean

Andrew, Lurch, and Ford were all awake as they flew over the Sea of Okhotsk, near the Kamchatka Peninsula and Kuril Island. Still at flight level five hundred, they were making great time and were just over an hour out from the drop zone.

"Hey, we'll have to get on one hundred percent oxygen in a bit...flush the nitro out," Lurch announced to them. Nods came back.

The moving-map display depicted them perfectly on the navigation map in the cabin, and the primary one the crew was using up front had excellent resolution and clarity. Ford looked outside at the terrain off the right wing to ensure it matched, and it was difficult to tell from the declining daylight and altitude.

Ford sat down in one of the captain's chairs, reviewing his four-step process in his preflight meditation. He started a seven-second inhale through his nose, held it for eight seconds, and then exhaled for eight seconds. He did this for a few minutes, which helped clear his mind of distractions. Ford's thinking was also positive, concentrating on his breathing, going through the mental rehearsal of opening up the ramp, scooting down, jumping off, descending, and landing. He did this multiple times, and this generated positive energy, wiping out any negative thoughts that perhaps may have lurked prior. Ford also repeated, "I can do this...I can do this," continuing the cycle as he did before every flight, and relied on it as his secret to his success.

Ford pulled over his parachute backpack to his lap, checking out the primary and secondary chutes visually. He looked them over to make sure they were packed correctly, ensuring there were no tears in the material when he loaded them into the jet hours ago. Turning to his weapons, Ford decided to insert the magazines, checking that they were on safe, but he did not put a round in the chamber. Chief Tosca from SEAL Team 8 showed him how to strap the HK416 rifle to his upper leg so it would not interfere with the aerodynamics of his wing suit and also showed him how to stow the handgun. He hoped he would not have to use either of them, but at least he was prepared.

He glanced over at the Gulfstream moving-map screen again and saw how much distance they'd traveled since he last looked just moments ago. They must have a heck of a tailwind at their current altitude because their ground speed was impressive. *Better continue to get ready*, he thought. *There's only one chance to get this right.*

Ford took off the white business shirt he was wearing and folded it neatly to pack for the pilots to carry out of the jet. Next were his dark suit pants, and he put them in the same place. Out came the olive-drab flight suit, size 46R, complete with Velcro and pockets, but no name tag or squadron patches, and he slid into it. He then reached into his leg pocket and placed the class 4 handheld laser, and zipped it up tight. Next was his smartphone, and he started to type out a note to Emily but decided against it so there were no messages going through the foreign cell towers and servers. He had no idea if the Wi-Fi on the jet went to foreign or friendly satellites and wasn't going to start asking questions this late in the game. It would be OK on the ground, but there was no need to announce his arrival to anyone. Last part of the suit-up process was the wing suit, which fit him as perfectly as the practice jump completed the other day, and he put it on over his olive flight suit.

Lurch turned around from the left seat to see where Ford was and yelled for him to come forward.

"Yeah, what's up?" Ford asked after coming up front to the pilots.

"Stevens, we have a fucking problem," Lurch said, getting his attention immediately.

Gansu Airfield

"Captain Lee," Chen said, in his booming voice. "Lee. You do not look good. You look sick again. Maybe I should get one of the other two pilots to train up."

Wu's knees felt weak just hearing him say it. He knew he looked terrible. He felt rotten, but he needed this flight. *One more flight to go*, he thought. "Sir, hello. I am just fine. Just watching my weight, exercising regularly. Losing some fat, sir. Top shape," Wu replied, attempting to downplay. He even smiled at the general.

"No. I have the flight surgeon coming here to take a look at you. I want him to see you before you fly. TODAY."

There was no getting out of this one. The doctor from aviation medicine who handled all the pilots was most likely already present in the area. Wu would have to think long and hard how to pull this one off so he could fly. "Yes, sir. Of course."

The general's aide approached Wu and told him the doctor was in the building behind the hangar, only about a ten-minute walk. They had a temporary exam room all set up for physicals today, and the aviation medicine team had physicals lined up for the day. Wu knew his thyroid and glands in his neck were as big as golf balls, and once that doctor touched him, it was all over. He needed some type of a distraction.

"Which doctor is it today?" Wu asked Lieutenant Bai Keung, the aide.

"Doctor Xi Kong is here, sir. He is in that building back there, room one-four-seven, a temporary clinic," Bai replied.

Wu took his time walking over there. *Motherf'er.* He thought about how to get out of this one. *How about detaining the doctor in some capacity? Nah, that would not work.* He had to think. *Think! What were some options?* Wu slowly reviewed a number of ideas as he walked more slowly than usual toward the building. *Perhaps tell him there was a terrible accident with his wife or kids? That won't work either...there would be a paper trail on his departure, and he'd get caught in a lie. Need something clean...no trail. Wait! How about a building fire?*

"Good day, Captain Lee," said the nurse who traveled with Dr. Kong.

"Hello. Nice to see you," Wu replied.

The doctor was reviewing some charts and standing at a counter located at the entrance to the building. He was wearing a long white lab coat, glasses, and was about fifty-five years old with thinning gray hair. "Captain Lee, sir, I have been expecting you," Dr. Xi commented.

"Hello, Doctor, Lieutenant Keung just asked me to come find you. Scheduled for a physical today I understand?" Wu asked. Wu saw just what he was looking for on the counter of the makeshift clinic, about two feet from him. A pack of cigarettes and a lighter were sitting there, unattended. *A perfect grab*, Wu said to himself.

"Yes, you go that way. The nurse will take care of you," Doctor Kong said, showing him the way by pointing with his arm.

Wu set his notebook down on the counter for a moment, and with his bottom hand, he lifted up the lighter and the notebook together. It was perfect timing because one of the medical supply personnel came right in from outside to grab his cigarettes. As Wu walked away, he noticed the young orderly was searching the floor and counter area for his lost lighter. *Got it*, Wu said under his breath.

The nurse showed Wu into a makeshift exam room, clean enough to pass for a clinic room at a temporary airfield for pilots and maintenance teams. There was a long exam table on wheels, a large counter, plenty of cabinets, a trash can, and a weight scale. The walls were white, with no windows or artwork and glass jars of items like cotton balls and tongue depressors. Old-school medical clinic supplies...*not much here...crap*!

"Please undress and slip this on, Captain Lee. I'll weigh you in, and then the doctor will come in for the exam," the nurse said. She handed him a green medical gown.

"Yes, yes, of course," Wu replied. He was thinking there was no way this little exam was going to prevent him from taking the Devil Dragon and freedom. Wu had to make this fire happen, or he was in an official and certified major shit storm.

"These are your slippers, and here is your specimen cup for urine," said the nurse, putting the cup down on the counter.

"You do have to go, yes? Urine? I'll be back in ten minutes."

The nurse left the room, and Wu felt he had only five, maybe ten minutes, at best. *Got to make this shit happen now* he said in the empty room. He immediately got up off the table and started searching the cabinets. Wu bent over and rifled through the bottom ones as rapidly as he could and found they were mostly empty. Just a few plastic bins, some staples, alligator clips, an old mouse and computer keyboard, tampons, and some old yellow faded printer paper. Not much for him to work with. Wu went through the top cabinets, and they were full of folders, some ink cartridges, a can of old hair spray, and masking tape. He had nothing and was near frantic. *Shit. Shit. Shit!* Wu did not have much time.

He looked up at the ceiling and noticed they were drop down tiles. Wu pulled the seat over and stood up on the counter, popped the ceiling tile up, and looked around the crawl space with his eyes, searching. That's when the idea hit. *Hairspray!*

Wu quietly climbed down and grabbed the old yellow printer paper he saw. He put it up in the ceiling and did three trips. He filled his flight suit pockets with the tampons, stuffing them in his pants. On the last trip up, he noticed the old-style, building mineral insulation, the kind that burned easily. *Perfect,* he thought.

"Captain Lee, are you almost ready?" asked the nurse. She knocked on the door.

"No, no. Not exactly. Can you give me just five more minutes? Just wrapping up a call with the leadership. Thank you," he replied while standing up on the counter.

"Oh, my. Yes, of course. Take your time," she replied.

Wu got a hold of the hairspray and held it up above the ceiling titles. It felt heavy, so he was pleased that it must have been pretty full. He lit those cigarlike tampons like torches and chucked them as far as he could in one direction. Then he repeated the same thing in another direction. And another. And then some more. He had at least a dozen flaming tampons going, all accelerated with gorgeous, flammable hairspray.

Wu then did the same thing with the yellow pads and placed them in the ceiling just above him, and they, too, immediately took with flame and smoke. Wu sprayed the entire area with a purpose, like he was using a flamethrower on steroids. Full effect with determination. The flame sprayed with a vengeance about three feet and reached the far ends of the crawl space that he could never reach if he were to crawl. Wu was giddy at his progress. It was almost fun, knowing this was his ticket out.

Wu was lucky that hairspray was available, mainly because the polymers in the solvent made it flammable. Combined with the propellant gas of propane and the solvent of an alcohol binder, it was the perfect combustible mix. Wu had in his hands a personal beauty product that any woman of the world would use to keep her hair in place. Except for today, though, when Wu held a personal aerosolized sprayer that was an exceptional incendiary device.

The room did not start to fill up with smoke just yet, but he quickly replaced the ceiling tile so it did not look like he was the catalyst for the fire. He waited and listened, and heard nothing outside the doorway. No sprinklers or fire alarm yet, either, but he was sure that the fire was raging up there. *The tampons he threw first and the farthest must be a goddamn inferno about now*, he thought. *Where the hell is the fire alarm?*

He dropped his flight suit to around his waist and took off his shirt. He was immensely embarrassed at the jaundice and his excessive weight loss, so he quickly put the shirt back on and decided to take his boots off. That way it would look like he was in the process of undressing.

RING. RING. RING. RING. RING. RING.

The fire alarm was finally going off, and he realized in his room that there were no fire sprinklers. Wu flung open the exam room door with full theatrical effort, and the entire hallway was full of smoke and the ceiling at the far end and across the hall was fully engulfed. The nurse ran toward him.

"Captain Lee. There is a fire. Are you OK? We must leave right now!" the nurse yelled.

"Yes, yes, let's go!" Wu ran out, holding his flight boots in his hands. "Let's go!"

Outside the building, people started pouring from every door. People were even coming out of the first-floor windows. The older building was dry, not up to modern code, and was engulfed in flames quickly. The building did not have that many people inside, and the senior doctor present was Dr. Kong. He conversed with his staff and verified that all the patients and medical folks were out. Dr. Kong then approached Wu in the crowd of people.

"So sorry, Captain Lee. Certainly we can reschedule another time. Would that work with your flying schedule?" he asked.

Wu secretly rejoiced and sighed to look somewhat bothered. "Yes, tomorrow will work if we must. I will come back tomorrow morning for the exam, depending on the flight schedule," Wu answered.

"I'll let General Chen know of the situation right now. Sorry again, Captain Lee."

Wu turned to walk away toward the flight line and hangar, and by now the entire one-story makeshift clinic was engulfed. The sirens could be heard in the distance as the fire fighters made their way over to the clinic building.

On the way in, Wu spotted the aide, gave him a nod, and then made his way toward the Devil Dragon in the hangar. Wu could tell she was all ready for flight since the covers were off the air intakes and engine nozzles, and the ground crew was polishing the canopy windscreen for improved visibility. Wu picked up his flight and overnight bags and climbed inside the cockpit to set up for the flight. He saw Liu was already up there.

"Hey, Wu, ah, I got a little stomach issue brewing but nothing to cancel the flight for. Must have been the hotel food," Liu reported to Wu.

Whoa, that eye-drop stuff works. "Understand, Liu. Thanks for telling me. If it's not an issue, I'm ready to go, then, if you are," Wu commented.

Just as Wu was getting ready to buckle into his seat, he saw General Chen march out of the maintenance offices and over to the nose of the Devil Dragon. He waved for Wu to come down. *Oh, boy*, Wu said under his breath.

Wu climbed out of the seat and reviewed in his head if he let on about anything regarding the plan. It would be near impossible that he or anyone in Chinese military or intelligence would know of the plan, but you never knew. *He could have easily slipped up, though.*

"Yes, sir?" Wu asked.

"I got my eye on you, Lee. Something isn't right," Chen said to him.

"What's that, sir?" Wu asked. He could smell alcohol. Again.

"I don't know. You have been acting strange lately. I am usually right," Chen said, as he rubbed his chin. He then shook his head. "When you land, you come see me. I want to talk to you about this jet. We are at a crucial point in the flight test being complete and the politicals and generals want a final flight test report. Weapons testing is next. You are to generate a final written report on the performance of this jet soon. Liu will help. I'll approve it. You understand?" Chen told him.

"Yes, sir. I will make myself available," Wu told him, just to get him off his back.

"You go," Chen said, waving his arm from the nose of the jet to the flight line, making a get-going gesture with his hand. "Lee, I'm not taking my eyes off you."

Wu turned around for the last time, knowing he would never see Lieutenant General He Chen again. He walked back toward the Devil Dragon in silence and without a smile. Wu reviewed the years of flying there, the opportunity to take up fast machinery among the clouds, up in the air...but to also suffer harassment by someone who was a miserable son-of-a-bitch micromanager and an unstable raging alcoholic. Wu would not miss him, nor this suffering communist country. Then, another idea hit him, and Wu cracked a mischievous smile. He might have cancer and be fragile, but if he could pull this one off, it would be the ultimate screw-you message to Chen. Wu knew since he wouldn't see him ever again, he might as well do this one last deed. This last act, unrehearsed and off the cuff, would be the ultimate revenge on his way out the door.

Wu took out his notebook from his flight-suit pocket and walked back inside to the maintenance office. He pretended to look at the computer that stored the flight records, hours, and engine information. Then he pretended to look for a prior flight plan, calmly scurrying around the quiet office. What Wu was really hunting for was Chen's coffee cup. It was always located near his general officer hat, cell phone, and red-covered notebook, and it was Lieutenant Keung's job to fill it and keep it warm. *Found it!*

Wu was sure no one was looking. He casually glanced around again, noticed that he was just about alone in the office. Only a young airman clerk was there at the far end of the office, typing. The airman's back was turned to Wu, and the timing would never be better than at this very moment. Down in the right pocket of his flight suit, Wu again located the small bottle of eye drops, unscrewed the cap, and unloaded the rest of the bottle into Lieutenant General Chen's cup of steaming coffee. The eye-drop bottle was now completely empty; he was sure of it, squeezing has hard as he could to get out every drop. It was his last feat of rebellion, and he was blissful.

Part 7

EXECUTE

Entering China Airspace

"WE HAVE A FUCKING PROBLEM? WHAT IS IT?" FORD asked, replying back to Lurch.

"Beijing Center says they are landing to the south at Beijing Airport. We are north, and that means it's a near straight shot in to the runways. *Damn it to hell.* That means they will never vector us around to the south, and we'll never fly over Tianjin," Lurch said.

"Umm, *yeah*, that's an issue. Huh...OK. Ah. My recommendation is...that when you get handed off to Beijing approach, you either hope for a runway change or just ask to be vectored to the runway we need and do a circling approach. Pick one of their fifty something STARs. Tell them you need it for company training. A check ride," Ford suggested.

A STAR was a standard terminal arrival, a highway in the sky to align aircraft up to specific runways for landing.

"Yeah. Excellent idea. Yup. That sounds good. We'll try that," Lurch said, facing front again inside the cockpit. Andrew nodded. "Good idea, kid."

A circling approach allowed the flight crew to use the instruments inside the cockpit and what they could see outside. Then at a certain altitude and location when they saw the airport runway, the pilots could steer the aircraft by circling around to the other runway to land. You had to have the weather clearance, meaning nearly no clouds, or at least higher clouds above the ground level. Ford's idea meant the jet could approach the airport in Beijing from the north, then do a circling approach, steer around in a circle, and land. It was a completely normal request and shouldn't turn any heads with the radar controllers.

"What's the weather at Tianjin?" Ford asked.

Andrew had already printed it out on a little flight printer they had in the cockpit. He turned and handed it to Ford so he could read it.

Wind	*from the S (190 degrees) at 2 MPH (2KT)*
Visibility	*5 mile(s)*
Sky conditions	*partly cloudy*
Weather	*Mist*
Temperature	*41 F (5 C)*
Dew Point	*35 F (2 C)*
Relative Humidity	*80%*
Pressure (altimeter)	*30.30 in. Hg (1026 hPa)*
ob	*ZBTJ 0000Z 19001MPS 3000 BR SCT019 05/02 Q1026 BECMG TL1400 2800 BR*

"Thanks. Good enough for a jump," Ford said. He reread it,

acknowledging the cold temperatures, the mist, and the clouds in the area. *Sure wasn't Savannah.* Not an issue, but definitely chilly.

"Thirty minutes till drop window, Ford. I've got the smartphone out for the ramp. Looking good," Lurch said.

Ford shuffled up, shook the pilots' hands, and thanked them again.

"We are depressurizing soon, so going on oxygen up here. Give me a thumbs up when you are on yours," Lurch said.

"I'm already on the air!" Ford yelled back. Ford took off the little aircraft oxygen mask and slipped on his helmet. He then connected the mask to his helmet with the two bayonet clips that attached the mask to his face. The mask covered his nose, from the top of the bridge and around his mouth, making a tight seal. His oxygen was flowing, and he had a good hose connect with the G650ER oxygen system. It was another mod that Robert at Gulfstream made so that Ford didn't burn up all his own portable oxygen. As Ford lowered his clear visor, he gave the thumbs up to Andrew and Lurch.

His ears popped as the cabin depressurized, and Ford read the altitude both off his wrist and the in-flight entertainment monitor. They were descending at about nine hundred feet per minute, a bit faster than the standard five hundred feet per minute, but nothing cosmic. Ford looked outside, saw the setting sun to the west, and kept his breathing calm and regular. He closed his eyes to focus. He focused on his breathing again, in through his nose, hold, out through his nose.

"FORD! TWO. MINUTES." Andrew yelled from up front through his clear, plastic mask. "RAMP. COMING. DOWN!"

Ford disconnected from the aircraft oxygen system and switched to his personal oxygen tank. He had a good blow of air, and the portable bottle was in the green. Ford gave another thumbs up.

Lurch looked at his smartphone on the right console, sitting and waiting to transmit its signal. He had the app open and hit the green button for the ramp to lower. He pressed it with his thumb. Nothing happened. He looked at the antenna coverage for Wi-Fi in the jet, and it had no coverage bars. Lurch could not believe his eyes. *What the heck was going on? No mother Wi-Fi bars!* That meant the ramp could not lower!

Ford looked up front, and he saw Lurch leaning over the center console in between the two pilots. Ford thought that was weird. *What was he doing?* Ford then saw him drop the phone.

Lurch sat there for a moment, then unbuckled and got out of his seat. He looked at the phone again and saw he had full bars while closer to the middle console where it sat on the floor. The different position in the cockpit enabled the Wi-Fi signal to reach without an issue. He sat back down, buckled in, and hit the green button. The whir of the motors was heard, pumping life into the pistons and gears on the ramp, and the frigid air from outside seeped into the cabin as the rear seats began to move.

The rear cabin seats flipped outward again, just as they did in the hangar in Savannah. The carpet went with it, and the floor lowered to expose the atmosphere and frigid—20-degree-Fahrenheit air. It was loud inside the Gulfstream now, and Ford could easily see the ground lighting, in addition to feeling the cold on his exposed face. His flight gloves protected his hands, and his oxygen mask covered a majority of his face, but it was still glacial cold. Frostbite was definitely an issue, but his polypropylene knit undergarments should keep it away.

The Gulfstream was still descending as planned, passing through twenty-seven thousand feet. Ford looked at his GPS moving map on his watch. They were at a good altitude but still not close enough for him to reach the airport with the wing suit on. Still at seventeen miles laterally, and he wanted ten miles to be safe.

"ONE. MINUTE. ONE MINUTE!" Lurch yelled from up front, holding his index finger up.

Ford gave another thumbs up, got down on his butt, and slid slowly toward the hinge in the floor. He looked outside and it seemed like it was getting darker by the second due to the combo of the clouds, mist, and deep setting sun. Ford looked at his GPS map again and read that he was still 14.4 miles laterally and getting closer to his window but not there just yet.

"GO! GO! GO!" Lurch yelled. "GO!"

Shit! Ford said into his mask. *Now?* He checked his GPS map again and saw he wasn't in his ten-mile window. He was nearly two miles off his mark at 11.8 miles, but if the guys up front said to jump, he had to go. Beijing approach was vectoring them anyway, and this was as close as he would get. This was a mitigated risk, and he hoped he could make up the distance in the air, but he wasn't sure. *Shit! Go now or wait?*

"FORD! NOW! GO!" Lurch yelled again.

Ford was faced with the dilemma of not making the drop zone because he would be short on the distance. *The world record was closer to sixteen miles* if he remembered correctly, so it *was* possible. This entire op relied on him. The decision was all Ford's, and he had to make it and make it right now.

From the cockpit, the autopilot was on and the Gulfstream jet was practically flying itself on the way down. Lurch turned around from the front right seat, then Andrew turned around in the left seat, and they faced the cabin, both looking aft.

The rear of the jet was empty. Ford was gone.

Inbound to Tianjin Airport

Ford left the Gulfstream exactly as he wanted, and his body sailed through the freezing air flawlessly. The black sky while wearing a black wing suit camouflaged him perfectly, and not a soul on earth could see or hear him coming. He looked down at his watch to check his altitude and it was winding down normally, as it always had. Ford then checked his GPS, and he was moving toward his bulls-eye destination nicely, so there was nothing to be concerned about just yet.

The helmet protected his head, keeping the loud wind-whoosh sound away from his eardrums, which were still adjusting to the rapid changes in air pressure. The clear visor did the same, helping to prevent his eyes from tearing up. His oxygen mask had a tight seal, the temperatures were warming up as he got closer to the ground, and Ford was confident in the jump so far. He didn't detect any health issues with the high altitude and lack of oxygen, but he sure noticed the pollution.

He sailed down and outward for a few short minutes, and

pondered if the Gulfstream was getting ready to land in Beijing by now. Ford also speculated about Wu's health and the rest of the mission. *Amazing how the mind can wander when you're skydiving.*

GPS had him on target to make the drop zone, despite the longer distance. He would make it. Ford checked his altimeter, and it looked to be about another thirty seconds before he would pull his chute. The lights of the city were getting brighter, and the ambient light bounced off the smog, clouds, and mist. *The mist sure helped his camouflage*, he thought. *Or was it the nasty smog?*

Ford reached for his rip cord at two thousand feet and pulled. The black streamers extended into the dark sky, followed by the black canopy that filled up with air. To Ford, it was a handsome sight. He placed his hands on the risers and had the excellent steering capability he expected. Looking down at the ground, Ford looked for familiar landmarks from his map study in the brief. The main runway was lit with arriving traffic, and he saw the city easily. Next, in his field of vision were the blue-colored taxi lights, then the rotating airport beacon on top of the air traffic control tower, flashing white and green, in sequence every few seconds. He spotted the firehouse on the southwest corner of the airfield, which was located near his drop zone, and there were no ground vehicles or taxiing aircraft to witness his landing. The drop zone was clear.

He turned into the somewhat calm wind on his final approach, pulled the risers to flare, and jogged a few steps onto the uneven ground. Ford nearly fell and tripped, as the ground he was on was full of mud, holes, and sporadic grass mounds. He got down on a knee and was able to reel in his black chute easily into a ball. He lay down for a moment to listen and look and be sure that no one saw him.

What caught Ford's attention wasn't what he heard or saw just yet, but the awful smell. He must have landed close to a water treatment facility, because the smell of human or animal waste was strong. So intense that Ford thought perhaps he was standing in it. The satellite images he studied with Mark showed this was just an empty field, surrounded by a fence. No treatment plant in sight. *What is that smell?*

Ford stood up so he could see the large hangar and wound the parachute as tight as he could into a smaller ball. He heard a deep stomping noise behind him, three or four times in the row, pounding the earth. It was a deep thump each time. *What the hell is that?* Ford slowly turned to see what it was. It was intensely dark in this area of the airfield, so he wasn't sure. Then came a snort, like something breathing very heavily. The snort sound was moving...and got closer, and then another stomp. Now the ground seemed to getting pounded by...*hooves?* He'd landed in an animal pen!

An ox, with a full head of horns, was coming into view, angry that Ford was disturbing him. He came charging at Ford. Ford froze, then turned to the small white fence to his right that he noticed on the way in. *You got to be kidding me!* He just about peed his flight suit and had to make a run for it, as it was his only option. Ford sprinted as fast as he could while wearing the wing suit but was restricted because of the gear he had, in addition to the material that linked his legs to fly. He also had to carry his balled-up parachute. *Holy shit.* Ford got to the fence and was able to slip one leg through the fence quickly and then the other. The ox nearly got him before he was able to crawl through the horizontal railings. *"An ox? Really?"* Ford whispered to himself.

He was on his way to a clear viewing area to observe the open doors of the commercial jet hangar on the airfield. By staying low, he made his silhouette a lower profile than by standing straight up and was able to use the tall grass to his advantage. The *Miscanthus sinensis*, or Chinese silver grass, was a species of flowering plant in the grass family, native to eastern Asia throughout most of China, Japan, Taiwan, and Korea. This grass was longer than allowed at US airports, which provided Ford the camouflage he needed to do his work.

The manmade cement drainage ditches on the airfield allowed Ford to maneuver to a viewing position in order to squirt his laser, too. Once in his concealed position, he lay face down on the ground and took out his smartphone. He turned it on, covering the dimly lit screen with his hand. Ford checked for good cell-tower coverage, then for a solid Peanut with a green light. No messages yet, so Ford lay down in the prone position and waited. The only thing he did was type the code word for a successful landing and sent it to Mark.

Mark: NATS.

The only other texting to Mark would be when Wu landed and they were ready to depart, and he would transmit the code word, *METS.*

Gansu Airfield

The bright afternoon sun was long gone, but the very faint pink sunset was plenty of sunlight for them to perform their mission at altitude today. Wu and Liu had their test cards for the flight on their kneeboards and were ready to taxi the jet for takeoff. Wu was not as reflective as he thought, but he did take a moment to peek over to his left on the taxi to see the smoke dissipating over the clinic. *Close call*, he thought. *Closest call ever*.

It was a custom in aviation worldwide that the pilots wave to the ground crew and maintenance who help them prepare for departure, usually in the form of a wave with a hand or salute—a simple gesture of thanks for the help in the departure. Wu and Liu did the customary wave to the team today, but he also noticed that a few hundred feet down the line and off to the side of the taxiway sat a black General Motors Cadillac CT6 sedan. It was *the* black Cadillac.

Standing out front, overweight, sloppy, and cranky-looking, was Lieutenant General Chen, observing the aircraft he helped build, while always chasing, always clinging to the dream that the military and party would select him for that fourth star. Chen stood with his aide, drinking coffee, the same coffee, hopefully, that Wu fixed for him. Liu waved at the general as they went by, performing the usual custom, but Wu did something very unusual. He taxied the aircraft on the yellow centerline, and instead of just passing Chen, Wu completely stopped the jet. Wu did not wave and did not say anything. He stared Chen down, through his dark visor, giving him the ultimate poker face that demonstrated Wu had the upper hand. Wu shook his head ever so slowly, back and forth, thinking of what a piece of shit Chen was. Wu was glad to finally see the last of Chen and get on with the land of baseball, mountain biking, unpolluted air, hot dogs, and clean beaches with boogie-board waves. Chen stared back and turned his head slightly sideways, wondering what Captain Wu Lee was up to. Wu released the brakes with the top of his feet on the pedals and moved the throttles forward again as they continued with their taxi for takeoff.

Liu was completing his checklists on the right side of the cockpit, punching in the destination for Xining Caojiabao Airfield, when Wu realized he forgot to stage the engine wiring in the back of the jet for a simulated fire. The medical clinic crisis had distracted him. *That's a big issue*, he said to himself. *Shit. I will have to come up with something while airborne.*

Wu looked to his left and right before getting on the runway. Once in position on the runway, he stopped the jet again by pressing the brakes on the top of the rudder pedals. He advanced the throttles to full power. "Let's check the thrust-to-weight ratio today, Liu. Get ready to hit the clock for me. Here we go. Ready in three, two, one." *The plume of flame coming out of the rear must be a specular sight*, he thought, as he released his brakes, and both pilots were pushed back in their seats with vigor and force. The airspeed built up quickly while they ran the jet down the runway. All four powerful engines were roaring.

"V1, Rotate," Liu said, as Wu pulled back on the stick.

"Gear up. Flaps up," Wu ordered, as the jet roared with thundering power.

Wu kept the aircraft close to the runway as he built up promptly built airspeed. The runway was long enough, and there were no obstacles to be concerned about off the departure end of the runway, so he kept it low while the gear and flaps came up. The Devil Dragon was designed so that once air was being forced into the other two ramjets, they did an autostart and produced enormous power immediately. This explained how Wu was able to scorch the jet across the deck, approaching four hundred knots, in what was just seconds. Once they reached toward the end of the airport fence two and a half miles from start, Wu announced to Liu, "Stand by to climb and hit the clock. Pulling Gs. NOW! TIME!"

Wu pulled back on the stick with his left hand, and the jet went vertical into the air, climbing to the heavens.

"Tiiiming," Liu announced. He hit the digital stopwatch on the dashboard for timing and struggled to talk as his body was forced back into the seat. Liu struggled to stay awake, preventing a pass out by performing the HOOK maneuver. Wu wasn't that far behind in his frail health state and was barely able to perform the HOOK breathing. The HOOK maneuver, a breathing technique, forced blood to the brain. They were looking for how many thousands of feet they could climb in a minute. The fastest climb rate was set by the American F-15C Eagle years ago, reaching more than sixty thousand feet a minute. Wu wanted to beat that, so he thought, *why not try today on his last flight?*

The Devil Dragon wanted to climb. Her engine instruments looked good and in the green, and all other flight instruments looked ops normal. Wu had the jet at near 90 degrees nose up, and they continued to lean back in their seats like they were riding in the Space Shuttle *Discovery*.

"Fifteen seconds at sixteen thousand feet," Liu announced.

Wu did the quick math and that was only about sixty-four thousand feet a minute. He made sure the throttles were in full afterburner, giving the jet the extra kick of raw fuel being poured into the engines.

"Come on! Thirty seconds at 35,750 feet," Liu said over the intercom.

Wu was pleased at the rate of climb now, sure he could beat the climb record. At this point, he wasn't sure if the Americans could see him fly this skyrocket up like this, but he didn't care, either. This was pure fun. Wu did not know enough about their surveillance and maybe would have cared in the past about certain countries, like the Russians, seeing him doing this maneuver so close to the border, but today, he didn't give a hoot.

"Forty-five seconds at 52,250 feet. Go! Go!"

"Make sure...you make a note...of those...numbers," Wu said, thinking he could show Ford.

Wu tiled his head back a few degrees and since he was upside down, he could see the curvature of the earth and pink glow through the canopy. It was a stunning sight, one he had not seen before from this angle. He then looked straight out again and started to see the sky fade from orange-yellow to blue-indigo to black. Wu reflected that this was most likely the last time he would have this view in his life, and at that moment, his never-ending stomach pain suddenly ceased to exist. Wu was at peace at this moment, in bliss. His entire life flashed before his mind's eye, and he felt at harmony with his illness. It was a strange feeling that Wu had never felt before, and he was prepared. Wu was ready for what was to come, and he was at peace.

"TIME! One minute at 71,400 feet," Liu announced. "Nice. I'm pretty sure that is a record. Maybe we beat the F-15!"

Wu nodded, "Yeah." He was leveling the jet now at seventy-three thousand feet and was already thinking of his dilemma of getting the jet over into Tianjin in the east. *Think, Lee!* He pulled back the throttles below full military power and only to about a third of the way forward. No need to burn up the fuel at the moment while running some after-takeoff checklists.

Wu went through the aircraft systems in his head, as he did when he was a test pilot student. Nearly every aircraft he was a student on or flew had the same five core systems that made it fly, and the Devil Dragon was no different. They were known in the pilot community as HEFOE. HEFOE stood for hydraulics, environmental, fuel, oil, and electrical systems, and any one of them could take down an aircraft, especially if the system emergencies were combined.

Wu looked down inside the cockpit at all the gauges, the moving-map display that showed where they were exactly over the earth, then at the clock. *HEFOE. HEFOE.* Wu repeated it a few times to himself and thought hard about generating a solution while airborne. *Got it!*

"Coming right," Wu said. This was Liu's cue to look out the window and clear air traffic. It was very doubtful that anyone else was up this high, but nevertheless, the procedure was to look.

"Clear right," Liu said.

Wu was absolutely sure to observe where Liu physically put his head to look, to actually see where his eyes were scanning when he cleared them for the turn. He was comfortable with where Liu's head placement was, because it was crucial for what was about to happen next.

On the Ground, Tianjin Airport, China

Ford was belly down in the tall grass and ditch, and he was sure no one could see him. The tall grass was key, plus he was in a lower elevation on the airfield that protected him from both the light wind and from being seen. Just to his right was a large flat metal grate that allowed water to drain off the runways and into the city sewer system. Connecting to this section of the airport were the same large cement half pipes and tunnels used to transport drainage water from the far end of the airport to where Ford was.

Ford used the starlight and ambient light from the hangars and city to inspect the metal grate, and he touched it to check out its strength and weight. Ford straddled the steel and was able to lift the top of it off with both hands and take a look inside down into the dark hole in the ground. It had steel rung cemented and built into the sidewall, and appeared to lead down below into an underground sewer system. Maybe if he needed to escape and evade, this hole might work; however, there was no reason to descend farther. It looked like a superb location to stash his parachute and wing suit, though, and he arranged the gear so he could dangle them downward from the first rung. He felt the steel rebar step with his hand, embedded into the concrete, and jerked it hard to ensure it was solid, and it was. Ford then slipped out of his black wing suit, which now smelled like ox dung, and hung it up from the step. He also took his balled up black parachute and let it hang down into the drainage hole, tying it on the first rung as well. Ford moved the steel grate cover back to its original position and was satisfied with the concealment part. Now came the wait. Ford made a mental note that if Wu ran long and into the sunrise and daylight hours, he might have to make the sewer hole a temporary home.

Ford squatted down and returned to his belly-down position from moments earlier. He made sure his P226 handgun was on safe, as well as the HK416 rifle, and that both were clean from dirt and mud. He strapped the rifle back to his back and the handgun in leg holster, ensuring that each weapon had a round in the chamber and was ready to fire if needed. As he slipped the P226 into his holster, he could hear in the distance the faint sound of multiple police sirens. They were getting louder with each passing second, and he crawled back up to the mound to look around to see if they were heading in his direction. Wearing his olive-drab flight suit, he was still pretty camouflaged, so he felt comfortable blending in. *Shit, they are coming over here. Police cars? What the hell? Can someone see me?*

He watched two white police sedans with flashing blue lights race in his direction. Ford was definitely pissed off and, frankly, shocked that they could be coming for him. He was confident no one could have seen him, but there they were, coming in his direction. The first police sedan passed his hiding area completely, and Ford could tell that at their rate of speed, this first police car was not coming for him. This white sedan whizzed right by. Ford let out some air and was a bit more relaxed.

The second police car seemed to be a potential problem, though. This second sedan was not as fast and did pass him but stopped about fifty feet in front of him and sat. *Crap!* Ford thought, and he immediately scurried down the incline to the steel grate where his items were hanging. He quickly pulled off the steel grate and laid it next to him so he could pull it over himself as he crawled down into the hole and stood on the rungs. Ford then pulled the grate over his head to hide.

Ford was angry and shook his head in amazement. *All this way, and now I'm going to get locked up in a Chinese jail by some airport cops? No frickin' way.*

In the Air, Inbound to Tianjin Airport

"Coming back left," Wu announced and looked to the left to clear himself, "clear left." He brought the jet back to the east, just comparing the turn rate and capability at their speed of 540 knots at seventy-five thousand feet. It was always good for them to write down their maneuvers for the engineers, but in this specific case, it was for show only. Only Wu knew no one would see this data, except the Americans. Wu looked at the digital map again on the dashboard and saw how far east they were progressing, so he put in the final turn to the right to head south, the turn that would start the beginning of the end.

"Let's get some speed on her today. Open her up. See what we can get, Liu. Ready?" Wu asked. Wu figured this was the final flight, and he had nothing to lose. He wanted to go out on top, his rules, his experience, and this was it. Right now.

"We're clear straight ahead. Go."

Wu pushed the throttles forward into afterburner, and all four engines pushed them into their seats. There were no reference points by looking out the windows, but by the airspeed and Mach indicators, they were hauling the mail.

"Mach 1.7. 1.9. There's 2.0. Keep her going."

The jet hummed along across China, smooth as silk, with Wu taking in the view and the speed. For today, he was going to be the fastest man alive.

"Mach 2.6. 2.8. 3.1. Faster than a bullet now, Wu. Keep going. Don't sneeze with your hand on that stick or we'll disintegrate in the atmosphere."

"Yup. Still going strong. Will do."

"Approaching Mach 5. Unbelievable. This jet is something else. Stand-by...stand-by...there it is. Mach 5.0! Wu, that's about three thousand miles per hour."

At this speed, it would take Wu at least 180–200 miles to do a simple turn. He was already determining the location and speeds to get the jet down but did want to relish their accomplishment.

"Yeah, Liu. Pretty cool," Wu said casually, but on the inside, he was screaming with joy. *Goddamn, that was fun!*

Wu brought the throttles down toward idle and let the Devil Dragon slow down a bit. It would take a solid few minutes to not only slow but change altitudes since they were so high up. Looking down at the airspeed, Wu saw they were already down below Mach 2.0, which was what he was scanning for. The jet continued to slow down, and Wu wanted to get slower to make the plan happen.

"Clear, right?" Wu asked as he prepared to turn the jet.

Liu turned his head to the right, looking away from inside the cockpit as he did just a few minutes prior. *This is it, now or never.* It was at this precise moment that Wu slid his right hand slowly off the throttles and down to below the throttle quadrant to the four fuel control switches for the engines. They were hidden from the normal scan of the cockpit, and Wu was near certain that Liu did not even know they existed. Blocked by human factor design during the construction of the jet to prevent an inadvertent touch, he counted by feel for the four switches, from left to right.

Silently, Wu counted, "One. Two. Three. Four." Wu doubled back and found the second switch, second from the left, for engine number two. He cycled it OFF, quickly, then ON again. This small, half a second movement of the toggle switch, would force the landing he wanted. Wu knew that even with the full twenty-nine-step air start process, it would be a bear of a task to relight in the air at any altitude. The electrical fuel pump shut down immediately, as did the fuel control valve that meters fuel to the engine, cutting off all fuel to the number two engine.

WHOOP. WHOOP. WHOOP. PING. PING. PING. WHOOP. WHOOP. WHOOP...

"Engine number two flameout. Engine number two

flameout," a female computer voice came over their helmets.

A multitude of red and yellow lights lit up on their warning panel, with a bright sequence of flashing lights all over the dashboard. The oil pressure needles dropped into the red. Fuel pressure dropped into the red. The jet yawed to the left slightly, an aerodynamic phenomenon that is felt when thrust is lost on one side of an aircraft and not the symmetrical other side. They were losing some airspeed.

"What happened? What is it?" asked Liu, excitedly.

"We lost engine number two. Get the checklists." Wu ordered. "Aviate-navigate-communicate. Looks like that damn engine number two again. Instead of a fire this time, she flamed out."

"Holy shit. Guess maintenance didn't fix it after all," Liu wondered out loud, as he buried in the checklist for a relight. Wu was pleased that Liu was thinking like that because it took the responsibility off him at first. "OK, I'm in the checklist for an engine restart. Step one throttles back..."

The lights were still flashing, too many to count, and seemed chaotic. Wu pressed the warning light to stop the flashing, and all the lights that once flashed remained illuminated. It reduced some of the overwhelming sensation that something catastrophic was about to happen.

"Hold it. Hold it. Hold on a second on the air start. Look, Liu...I am really uncomfortable now. This jet was supposed to be fixed and it's not. Two major issues in two flights. Engine two is a lemon. We've had a fire and now complete flameout," Wu let it sink in. "We're landing. I'm not going all the way back to Gansu, either. We're landing as soon as possible."

"What? No, no. Are you sure? Won't General Chen be mad?" Liu asked.

"I'm sure he will be mad. At this point, it's not about emotion, it's about facts. We need to save the jet. For the love of our Air Force, we must save the jet. Landing someplace, then calling maintenance to have us fixed, is the best move. The safest move," Wu announced, glancing at the moving map he'd lined them up for Tianjin Airport covertly.

Liu sighed. "OK, OK, I'm in agreement. Have to use the bathroom desperately, so it does help me. I'm ready to go in my flight suit."

"Don't do that. We'll land shortly. I'm looking over there to the south. Look at the map. Southeast of us, beyond Beijing, is Tianjin. The airport," Wu pointed out the area with his finger at the screen. Liu nodded. "We'll do a penetration descent, an unannounced arrival, and land next to the active on the dark, parallel runway. Lights out. I've been there before, so I know the airport, and we'll park...at, ah...at the southwest side of the field. The firehouse. No passengers, no lights. We can sit until the maintenance jet arrives."

"No coms with center? Or approach, or even tower?'

"Nope. Unannounced. Liu, come on. You think we should *broadcast* to the world the Devil Dragon exists? We are low paint scheme, flat black, no visible lights. No flight plan. No squawk on the transponder. Tower *may* see us coming in, but if we time it correctly, we can fit right in between the commercials. Maybe even use their unlit runway."

"OK, Wu...your call."

"Yes. Prepare for high-speed penetration," Wu announced, then yanked the throttles back to idle and nosed over the jet. Their altitude was rapidly unwinding on the altimeter and the airspeed was climbing. Their vertical speed indicator was pegged and unreadable, as they dropped through the atmosphere like a rocket ship. Wu's ears were playing games with the popping, as were Liu's, shaking their heads and opening and closing their mouths. Sonic booms were transmitted though the atmosphere, and they rode her down as they zoomed through the sky.

"Descent checklist," ordered Wu. Wu wasn't sure if Liu was nervous about the strange landing site, his bowels, or what Chen would say, but Wu was picking up his vibe. A flameout was enough to throw off the best of pilots, and if you flew your entire life in a single-seat, single-engine aircraft, a flameout without an immediate engine start meant only one of three things: crash, eject, or land immediately.

"Let me check my smartphone to ensure the jet is talking to the app correctly. Want to make sure maintenance can troubleshoot this for fixing. You have the controls."

"I have the controls," Liu said.

Wu took out his smartphone and simulated that he was using it as he told Liu. He typed in a text message to Ford and hit send.

Ford: JOJO RISING, four minutes.

"I've got the controls. We are good on the engine app, all data transferring ops normal," Wu said, then taking a look at the

420

digital moving map. "OK, Liu, get me to fifty miles west of Tianjin, twenty thousand feet. Currently passing forty-one thousand feet and still in the descent. Work up the waypoints. I'd like to land from the north to the south and squeeze between Beijing."

The aircraft was still groaning from the loss of the engine, despite Wu muting the warning lights. Every so often, another warning light would come on again, and Wu would silence it with his hand. Losing an engine was no small issue, and it was only Liu's second time. Liu was also suffering with his bowel issue, and he shifted in his seat uncomfortably. He needed to hit the bathroom since what seemed like hours ago. He had to go, and go now.

"Wu, I can get you a waypoint closer. I need to land. Can I program you a waypoint closer to fly, and you can burn off the airspeed in some tight turns?" Liu offered. Liu knew that airplanes can reduce their airspeed by turning tightly, and the Devil Dragon was capable of doing that. Normal aircraft flying in class A airspace above eighteen thousand feet were not regulated to a speed in knots, but as they got closer to their airport, a speed restriction was required. Because the Devil Dragon was not seen by radar and no one knew it existed, there were no limits, and therefore, the pilots had a license to steal. Since they did not have to follow the class C lower-altitude airspace rules, they could easily exceed the two hundred knot speed restriction.

It was completely dark now, and Wu was speeding along as he rapidly continued the descent, now at nine thousand feet at twelve miles, 580 knots. He made some turns to bleed off the energy and was tempted to drop the gear, but at these speeds, the gear doors would rip off. He wanted to wait until the last possible moment because with the gear hanging, acting like a hard-point weapon system, something would return on the radar echo with controllers watching. It wouldn't cause that much of an issue, but a few swings of the radar would detect *something* was there and alert the radar controllers. He was also aware of the thunder they must be producing, echoing across the city suburbs rapidly.

"Four miles. 430 knots. Twenty-five hundred feet. Wu, you're still too fast," Liu announced. The lit runways were in easy sight now, as well as the dark runway. The dark runway was magnified by looking through the forward-looking infrared heads-up display, allowing full sight of the darkened runway.

Wu shook his head, thinking this damn jet is just too fast. They were now at one thousand feet and in a tight turn at three miles out, just in front of the approach end of the runway.

"Pulling Gs, hold tiiigghhtttt..." Wu announced as they pulled a left 6-G turn that compressed them into their seats. Wu did a complete 360-degree turn, and they were now at one mile with the gear up, finally slow enough to drop the gear. Still, no one could see them, but Wu was sure that they were making some unbelievable noise down below. There was no way a high-performance military jet could do a 6-G turn at a thousand feet to bleed off airspeed without waking up a few sleeping babies below in the city of Tianjin. The thunderous roar set off car alarms and caused people to look outside and into the sky from their high-rise apartment building balconies.

"Wu, we are at one mile. Drop the gear already!" Liu nervously yelled out.

On the Ground at Tianjin Airport

Ford waited in silence with the steel grate over his head and heard the second police car screech his wheels and peel off. *They left.* He gave it a few solid seconds, waiting as quietly as he could. Then his phone vibrated twice. What timing, he thought. Luckily his ringer was off. Then a second vibration. It was a text message.

Ford quietly climbed out and put the grate back on the hole. He slid on his belly up to the position he had earlier and saw that the police sedan was gone, and finally realized why the second car stopped. Ford was near a taxiway that crossed a runway. The first police sedan most likely had clearance from the tower to race cross, while the second police sedan had to wait for the Air China jet to finish his landing. After the Air China Airbus rolled past the sedan, he could continue on the police call.

Ford pulled out his phone and read the text from Wu:

Wu: *JOJO RISING, four minutes.*

Whoa, Wu wasn't kidding around, he thought. At the same time, off in the distance to the north, Ford could hear an outlandish, deep grumble that sounded like nothing he had ever heard before. It wasn't the usual turbofan of a Rolls-Royce or Pratt and Whitney engine sitting on the wing of a commercial airliner. It had guts and sounded mean. As the seconds clocked by, the deep growl of the engines made Ford's insides vibrate. This was an intense sound. The rumbling roar reminded him of being near the concert speakers when he saw Metallica years ago at

Giants Stadium. *What in the hell is that? That has got to be Wu*, he thought, and he turned his one-eye, night-vision goggle toward the approach end of the runway. It was at least two miles away from where Ford was, but he could see a dark object in the sky at the approach end of the runway with no landing lights on. *Yup, gotta be Wu.* It was coming toward the airport, getting bigger with each passing second. *Look at that thing.*

Ford didn't have time to sightsee. He took out his laser and aligned it with his night vision device, and looked through the monocle at the target. Ford switched to the non-night-vision portion, as the hangar lights were washing him out and he couldn't see that well. Ford searched the ceiling of the large, open hangar doors that housed Air China jets. There was a surplus of maintenance folks working on two aircraft tonight. On the right side of the hangar was an Airbus A319 with all the engine compartment doors open and propped up, which appeared to be fully broken down for extended overhaul work. To her left was a Boeing 777 on jacks, on what looked to be a brake job. Ford continued to scan the hangar, looking at the back wall, and again where it met the ceiling. After about fifteen seconds, he spotted the metal sprinkler heads, and they all came into view now. Just like when he was firing the M9 Beretta in small arms training, he took a deep breath, let it out, and held it, shooting the laser to hit the sprinkler target. He moved it around ever so slowly, and after five to eight seconds, the show began.

The sirens and lights started flashing inside the hangar, and Ford could hear the alarm bells from his position. With his naked eye, he could see the white foam shooting from highly pressurized foam guns located all over the hangar. It looked like a ski resort was shooting manmade snow out of its snow guns because a small mountain of foam promptly filled the hangar floor. *Like a bathtub filling up with water.* The employees were under it now, scrambling and running outside on the ramp, and the foam was easily above the wing level on both jets parked inside the hangar.

The deep rumble of the Devil Dragon was getting closer, and the timing seemed to be perfect. Ford turned his head to see Wu again but could not locate him. His attention was diverted from looking for Wu when the firehouse, the closest building to his staging area, came to life. The doors of the firehouse went up vertically and opened, as the lights on the fire apparatuses lit up. Ford could see the fire fighters getting into their boots first, then putting on their large coats, and finally donning their fire helmets. The driver of each apparatus pulled out in front of the firehouse and waited a moment for everyone to get on board. Once the firefighters were on the engine and truck, they pulled out and hurriedly drove over to the hangar. Little did they know that an unknown aircraft was landing on the same dark runway that they would be crossing to reach the emergency.

Tianjin Binhai International Airport, Runway 16 Left

"GEAR DOWN. GEAR DOWN! Flaps one hundred percent," Wu commanded. He was sure that the landing gear coming down would give their position away on radar, just like a wing holding an external weapon, so waiting until the last possible second was smart business.

"Roger, gear down, flaps down!" Liu announced. Liu saw the speed was good, but their landing speeds for their weight made them fast. He quickly checked the runway length again and was happy it was an eleven-thousand-footer. The problem was that since they were faster than the 139 knots landing speed, Wu had to use aerodynamic braking, holding the jet off the runway as long as he could. He traded airspeed for altitude and delayed the main gear from touching the runway, gliding just on top of it. They landed long, about a third of the way down the runway.

At the end of the very same runway, 16 Left, a major problem was brewing. Wu looked ahead in his normal landing scan and saw that the fire department was rolling two fire engines or trucks out of the firehouse. The first one was following the second one, and they were crossing the runway directly in front of them. Wu planted the main gear on the runway, already at idle with the throttles. *They are going to the hangar!* Wu remembered silently.

"Speed brakes," Wu said, in addition to practically standing on the jet's brakes. *We're gonna be hot.* Wu was rolling the dice with these two fire engines. Wu was too slow to take off again and too fast to come to a complete stop. They were on the final rollout of a dark airport, on a dark runway, in a flat-black secret jet, and only seconds away from slamming into the back of the local fire department.

Wu moved his feet to steer the Devil Dragon to the left side of the runway and hoped he wouldn't drag his left wing on any obstacles. By doing this, he could effectively steer around the moving second fire truck, which still was on the runway. At a minimum, the Devil Dragon's right wing would pass directly over the fire fighters' heads, and at everyone's speeds, they would only *feel* the air.

WHOOSH! The jet went past the second fire truck, and the fire fighters didn't see or feel a thing. They most likely heard the roar of the jet go by at idle, but they were busy looking at the foam burying the two commercial airliners inside a hangar where there appeared to a fire.

"After-landing checklist," Wu told Liu, as Wu pulled off the runway and taxied in the dark to the front of the firehouse.

"Roger...close call there, Wu," Liu said, as he ran through the checklist to raise the flaps, monitor the ground controller frequency, and do some other cockpit chores.

"Look, Liu, I'll call General Chen and explain to him what's going on. I'll park here temporarily, let you out to hit the bathroom, then we'll park over there," nodding to large open space. "You'll hear me pull away."

"Thanks, Wu. I have *got* to go to the bathroom. See you in a few minutes."

"Hey, ah, leave your helmet here. No need to take it in the toilet with you," Wu said, starting to lead the way for Ford.

"Yeah, unplugging my helmet and off intercom."

"See you around, Liu," Wu said, reflecting to himself that he would never see him again.

"I'm just going to the bathroom. You're saying good-bye like you're leaving," Liu said.

Liu was off the intercom and down and out of the jet in seconds, running to the firehouse. Wu watched him run off into the darkness and toward the two open bays where the apparatuses parked.

"No, Liu...I *am* leaving," Wu said aloud.

USS *ABRAHAM LINCOLN*, 243 miles SSE of Okinawa, Japan

Mark, Robert, and Emily sat in the Combat Direction Center, the CDC, looking at the radar feeds for the ship, radar feeds for other ships in its sailing party, and a variety of flat-panel televisions that aired the news.

"Sir, something here you should look at. Want me to put it up?" the Navy petty officer working the intercepted radar repeater for Tianjin Airport. The Navy was able to tap into their feed and watch the air traffic for all the runways and vicinity. Airport traffic inbound was to runway 16R, or 16 Right. Each target showed the name of the aircraft, its speed, direction, and altitude, depicted on the screen. Except one.

"Yup, put her up," said *Lincoln* commanding officer Captain Chuck "Muddy" Waters, an F-18C Hornet pilot and fully trained naval aviator and aircraft carrier ship captain.

"Sir, this is a short recording of the radar feed from the Tianjin class D airspace just moments ago. Note all the commercial traffic lined up and landing on the right...ah...runway 16R. I'll fast-forward it for you. Then, look at this. Here and here"—he pointed to the left runway—"you see a blip here at pretty good speed. No transponder for the aircraft identifying itself. Then another blip and the radar sweeps. An object looks like it's doing a turn...you know...a rapid turn to burn off airspeed. No other data displayed. Then another blip when the radar sweep comes around again, and you can see it slowed down a bit. Target is now over the runway, then...it's gone, as if it landed."

"Thanks, Petty Officer McGarry," said Muddy, turning to face Mark. "Your guy, Mark?" asked Muddy.

"Sure looks like it. While I don't want to get into properties of stealth and minimal cross section, that would be about when we see him. Coming into land. How old is this recording?"

"Air ops, how old is this footage?" McGarry yelled inside to the far end of the CDC. A voice yelled back, "Six minutes."

"Six minutes, huh? OK, that's about the window. Nighttime, just after sunset, was the window. Depending on the turnaround with our pilot getting in, and flight time to us, we may see them within the hour," Mark said.

Emily looked at Muddy and decided to throw in her opinion, now that the Devil Dragon seemed to have landed. "Captain, I know you talked with the admiral. May I suggest the barricade going up sooner rather than later? Certainly, we don't want to meddle in your ship's activities, but this aircraft flies at a high rate of speed, and we hope they will slow down to appropriate landing speeds. We both know we only have one chance to retrieve her."

"Yes, Emily, absolutely. The admiral and I discussed that, and I concur with his uneasiness. His concern. I'll have our crew start working on it right away." Muddy nodded to the executive officer, known as Big XO, standing over to the side and listening in. "Got to tell you, though, landing on the ship without a tailhook is downright fucking scary. That's why we have one—to stop. Your guy, Stevens, never did it without one, I'm sure, so he's relying on our little volleyball net to catch him. Like catching a fish in a net. Very nonstandard. Just want you to know we could either catch him successfully, or have a raging fire on our hands. Your Stevens better be one hell of a pilot."

"Thank you, Muddy. We understand. Yeah, he is one hell of a pilot. On another note, I also know you have your sprinkler nozzles available for foam. Do you apply that beforehand?" Emily said, looking at the captain and then the XO.

"Usually, our deck crew uses the aqueous film forming foam, or AFFF, to put out an aircraft fire *after* an aircraft develops an emergency on the flight or hangar deck. Ah...let's go with the foam *if* something happens, not before. I don't plan on something happening, though. If your Ford Stevens guy is carrier qualified, as you say he is, he'll get her down on the deck. The barricade will do its job."

Robert was more quiet than usual and was able to absorb everything coming in by watching and listening. The carrier intrigued him, and he was impressed by the ship and the dedication of the crew. Robert also noticed on the weather radar screen that rain was coming.

"Is that going to be an issue?" Robert asked, pointing to the green and yellow blob, signifying moisture, about fifty miles ahead of the ship's path. "A few years ago, rain brought down one of our B-2s in Guam. Stealth aircraft are great, but they are a tricky bunch. Not saying that will happen tonight...just thinking through things."

These guys ask a lot of questions, Muddy thought to himself. *More than the usual visitors out to the ship.* "As it gets closer, we can take a look. Not sure if your jet is all-weather, but ours are. Traditionally, the Chinese have built and flown all-weather birds, so if I had to make an educated guess, it would be all right. The secondary question is the sea state, ah, how much the *Abe* will pitch and roll, making it a challenge to land," explained Muddy. "At night, no less."

Over the ship's loud speaker system, the 1MC, announced:

"Flight operations in fifteen minutes. Case three weather conditions. FLIGHT OPERATIONS IN FIFTEEN MINUTES. Case three weather conditions. Rotary and fixed wing operations."

The XO came back in and handed Muddy a folder with a cover sheet on it, meaning it was classified. He read it then looked up at Mark. "Have a message here for you from the Deputy director of DIA. Name is Calvin Burns. Know him?"

"Yeah, we work directly for him. What does he say?" Mark acknowledged.

"Says here, 'DIA Operations Center sent message traffic that three cell phones were detected in the middle of the Tianjin Airport. Two phones just off the runway in front of the airport firehouse and one a close distance away in the grass between the two main runways, runways 16L and 16R. Southern end of the airport.' Want me to keep reading?" Muddy asked.

"Please do. This is our only confirmation so far," Mark replied, excitedly.

"Grass-area cell belongs to US citizen Ford A. Stevens. Firehouse-area cell belongs to Chinese citizen Wu Lee. Second phone, Liu Nie, registered to Chinese Telecommunications Company. Then Deputy Burns added, 'Keep up the good work.'"

"Well, this will be beastly," Emily turned to Robert and Mark.

Just as Muddy finished reading, Mark's cell phone, connected to the ship's Wi-Fi, vibrated. He took it out to see who the text was from.

Ford: NATS.

Tianjin Binhai International Airport, China

Ford crouched down and ran as fast as he could from the grass depression to the Devil Dragon. It was purring loudly with its engines at idle, no lights visible, and looked much smaller to him than the B-1 that he was used to walking up to. *Wow, this is a freaking cool jet.* He approached the jet from the left side, hoping to see Wu in the pilot's seat, and saw a figure sitting there with a helmet on but could not make out Wu's face. Ford had to remember that he would look a bit different since he last saw him in person due to the weight loss and was ready for the shock of seeing his best friend suffer.

Ford stopped his run and crouched down on a knee before going any closer. He lifted his right hand and crept around in his left shoulder zippered pocket for two yellow foam earplugs. The sound of the Devil Dragon was deafening, and he would need them before going any closer. He squeezed them and placed them inside each ear. Only waiting a few seconds for them to expand in his ear canal, it enabled him a few moments to look at the jet from afar. Ford was, no doubt about it, impressed with the look of her. It was sleek and aerodynamic, with unique curves to the entire fuselage and two air intakes that shoved the air into the four engines. It looked like a hybrid between the Lockheed F-117 Nighthawk and SR-71 Blackbird.

Wu saw Ford and started waiving his hand in front of the canopy to come closer. Ford ran across the wide-open ramp and stopped under the jet. Just prior to climbing the vertical ladder that extended down from the cockpit, behind the nose gear, Ford stood and looked at his phone on last time. He typed out a fast text to Mark and hit send.

Mark: METS

Maybe seven minutes went by since she landed, and Ford was finally reaching the inside the cockpit. Wu was unbuckling and ready to turn around and get out of his seat, when unbeknownst to them, Liu had finished his business in the bathroom at the firehouse.

Liu stood in front of the open firehouse doors, hands on his hips, and watched the dark figure run from out of nowhere, wave to Wu, and then stop under the jet. *That's strange...who the hell is that?* Liu thought. *This is most peculiar.* Liu then saw the glow from a cell phone for about five seconds before it was put away, and the guy climbed aboard into the jet. *That's my aircraft!* he said to himself. Liu was incensed, wondering who the heck knew they were there and who would know enough to climb aboard. Liu started to make his way over to the Devil Dragon.

"Wu, it's me, Ford, buddy!" Ford yelled, as he reached the top of the ladder and entered the cockpit. Wu had already placed the parking brake on the jet and was out of the pilot's seat and waiting to hug Ford. They embraced a quick and tight hug. Ford noticed the noise was not as loud up in the cockpit, and they could talk at near normal levels. It was hard to see though, since the cockpit lighting was set for night flying and dim.

"Hi, Ford. So very happy to see you. Thank you," Wu said, putting his hand on his shoulder. "Take this seat and this helmet. We gotta go right now. We don't have much time." Wu climbed into the left seat.

Ford looked around in the cockpit, saw the glow of the glass instruments, and put one leg on the copilot seat on the right and held the helmet and mask with his left hand. Suddenly, out of the corner of his eye, he saw movement from the hatch area in the floor, the cockpit entrance. *Someone else was climbing aboard the jet?* Unexpectedly, it was Liu coming back from the firehouse.

Liu had already swiftly bustled up the ladder and into the cockpit and wished he had his QSZ-92 pistol on him. In his right hand, though, Liu had his Gerber LMF II combat knife, sharp with a four and seven-eighths-inch blade and a six-inch handle. Liu pulled back to strike at Ford, attempting to stab him, but Ford pushed off the copilot seat with his leg and jumped to the side to avoid the blow. Liu attempted to thrust forward again, and Ford, completely startled, blocked his thrust with the flight helmet.

"Wu, start taxiing! Go! Go! Now!" Ford yelled.

Liu was astounded that this man in the cockpit knew Wu's

name. *Remarkable*, he thought. Liu again went at Ford, this time connecting with Ford's left shoulder, giving him a good slash through both the Velcro and flight suit material. Ford was bleeding through the flight suit, but not enough to cause him to stop fighting. At that instant, Ford had to make a decision. Either his life was going to be taken or this copilot's, because this guy wasn't letting up.

Ford's college football skills came into play when he decked Liu like he was a red-shirted sophomore. Ford was now on top of him, striking him in the face with his fists and pinning his left hand, which held the knife. Liu lost his grip on the knife, and both men felt the jet move out of its parked position as Wu taxied the jet for takeoff. Repeatedly punching, Ford could see in his peripheral vision down the cockpit hatch to see airport pavement going by. Liu was able to get his leg around Ford and throw him off. Ford and Liu were both on their feet again, and Ford went after him by placing his leg behind Liu's, then pushing him over. Liu fell backward in the rear of the cockpit, and Ford took advantage of him being down once again. Ford went over to attempt to throw him down the cockpit hatch opening, but Liu was too fast and scampered out of the way.

Ford took out his pistol and pointed it at Liu, but the wild Devil Dragon taxiing by Wu from the firehouse tarmac to the runway made Ford lose his balance. The fast and hard turn forced Ford into the cockpit bulkhead, and he dropped his P226 handgun on the floor near Liu. *Shit!* Ford thought. Liu immediately picked it up and started firing rounds at Ford.

Because they were taxiing and in motion, firing a handgun

accurately in a closed space was a chore. Ford was lucky as each fired round missed him, and if he'd counted correctly, three rounds came out of the weapon so far. From the front cockpit, Ford could now hear Wu yelling in agony. *Wu must have been hit!* Ford was able to push Liu's firing hand down toward the floor in the chaos and taxiing, and hold his arm with one hand and bang on his forearm with the other. Out came the weapon from Liu's hand onto the floor again. Ford attempted to grab it but accidentally kicked it off to the side with the movement of the aircraft. Ford used his body weight again to get Liu down on the ground. Liu was now on his back, and his head was toward the open hatch, with Ford punching his face continually with his fists. At a minimum, Liu's nose had to be broken, along with dislodged front teeth, and based upon the blood Ford could see, Liu had some pretty good gashes on his face.

Wu was now on the runway, ready for an opposite end takeoff with the wind at his back instead of at his nose. His toes were pushed forward on the rudder pedals, stopping the jet completely.

"Don't stop. Don't stop! Get the fuck out of here! TAKE OFF!" Ford yelled to Wu.

The throttles were pushed forward at that instant because the jet leaped forward like sprinters at a track meet. Ford and Liu rolled together to the back of the cockpit. *This is my only chance,* Ford figured. He quickly stood up faster than Liu could and briskly began stomping on Liu's face and then kicked him in the stomach. Ford knew they were on the takeoff roll and had to be only fifteen or twenty seconds away from being airborne. Ford kicked him in the face again and bent down. Ford took another punch to his face, but he took it in order to roll Liu. *This is it*, Ford figured. Ford was bent down to roll him, and he did. Ford pushed and rolled Liu toward the opening in the cockpit floor, with every intention of shoving him down and dropping him from the Devil Dragon. Liu was nearly completely outside the cockpit hatch, hanging on to the last rung of the cockpit ladder with his left hand. They were scorching down the runway now, and the side-to-side motion nearly stopped, as they had to be nearly close to lifting off.

Ford, looking down at Liu, saw that his flight suit was now caught and hung up on the hatch and was ripped pretty well. Ford moved his eyes from the ripped flight suit and saw that Liu was still clinging on to the ladder with his one hand. Ford, in a final effort to get rid of Liu, stomped on his fingers with all his might, vengeance, and body weight. Liu finally let go and slammed hard onto the runway in his underwear, and the Devil Dragon continued rapidly on its takeoff run. His flight suit had ripped right off as Liu fell, caught on the cockpit ladder, and it remained with the Devil Dragon just flapping in the slipstream. Ford reeled the flight suit inside the aircraft, closed the hinged hatch quickly, and locked it.

"Wu, we're good. Let's go! Let's go!" Ford told him.

Just as Ford started to sit and buckle into the copilot's seat, the runway lights turned on, most likely from the air traffic control tower. It was still hard for them to see a flat-black, fast-moving aircraft, but nevertheless, it was possible.

"Ford...ah, two things," Wu said, struggling to breathe. "Ah...I'm hit in the leg. Liu shot me in the left thigh, up here by the knee, and...I, ehhh, I am bleeding pretty good. Need you to fly. Second, this runway is active now, and an Air China 747–200 is coming straight at us to land..."

"Push those throttles up, Wu. Come on," Ford excitedly said to Wu.

"If we use afterburner, we'll light up this place like a shopping mall."

"Wu, if you don't, we're going to collide. We will *die*. That 747 can't see us, but we can see him. I've got the controls!"

Ford pushed up the throttles past military power and into afterburner, and they could see the glow of the flame on the ground next to them in blue and orange. Immediately, the jet lurched forward with immense power and built up immediate airspeed.

"What's V1 speed, Wu? Takeoff speed? Rotate speed? I need it now!"

"Pull back at 145 knots. One-four-five. You'll have plenty of power now to make that 747. Now! Right over her. Go vertical from...there," Wu said, breathing heavily, wincing in pain. Ford felt terrible for Wu and wanted to help him, but he had to fly in order to save both their lives and the mission.

"NOW! ROTATE!" Wu yelled.

Ford yanked back on the center stick and the Devil Dragon leaped into the air, flying right at and then over the Air China 747 on its landing roll. The pilots of the 747 couldn't have stopped if they'd wanted to, due to their slow speed and size.

"WHHHHOOOO-HOOOOO!" Ford yelled, as they cleared the 747 and went straight up like a volcano.

Down below and out of sight, the 747, landing at over 500,000 pounds, rolled down the runway, making a normal landing. During its landing, the Boeing 747 main gear rolled right over Liu, killing him instantly. No rumble or jolt was felt by the passengers or crew, and the crush of the large Boeing jet nearly cut Liu in two lengthwise and flattened him. His face and his hands would never be recognized. Later during an investigation, the conclusion was that he may have been a stowaway and was hiding inside the wheel well of the landing gear. Since Liu left his helmet inside the Devil Dragon, and they flew sanitized without a wallet, dog tags, or identification, the mystery man would not be identified. For a while, that is. All that would be identified in the short-term was an old pair of standard issue army boots.

Ford brought the jet up to nineteen thousand feet, completing an Immelmann maneuver. The half loop followed by a half roll on top, helped them rapidly reverse the direction of flight. Ford pulled back the throttles out of afterburner for a while, as he did not want to make too much of spectacle. He reached down to remove something he was sitting on and moved his hand around under his butt. Ford pulled out another cell phone. *Must be the copilot's phone* he'd figured and threw it over on to a small shelf on his right.

"Wu, this thing have autopilot?"

"Yes. Yes, rotate that...dial up there to your desired altitude," as Wu pointed to the round black dial on top of the dash. "Flip this lever here to turn it on. Then, ah, set the heading for...wait, where is your aircraft carrier?"

Ford had to think for a moment, as there was a

tremendous amount going on. He looked at Wu's moving map. "We need to go southeast. Way southeast, at least another eleven hundred fifty miles to Naha, Okinawa, then another two hundred fifty miles past there...hope we have the fuel for it. Yes?"

Wu glanced down at the fuel gauges and saw something different he had not seen before. He tapped the window of the glass, but nothing happened.

"Ford. One of those bullets must have hit the fuel tank because we are leaking fuel from tank number four." Wu was struggling. "Let's, ah"—coughing—"let's climb up to about sixty or seventy thousand feet and use altitude to our advantage. Just spin your dial up there, and we'll climb right up," Wu instructed Ford, and Ford did it.

"Wu, if we can go higher, let's do it. We'll be in your Chinese missile range if your Air Force wants to shoot us down. If you can get seventy thousand feet, we'll have the speed and height advantage against your missiles and fighters," Ford said.

"Ford, no one can see us. No one can chase us. There's no flight plan on file with the air traffic controllers. Any fighters that wanted to come up here would flame out. Between our special fuel, the stealth design, and the speeds, we're hidden."

Ford was troubled right away about two things. First was getting shot down, as history was full of countries shooting down surveillance and reconnaissance aircraft. *Gary Francis Powers and his U-2 over the Soviet Union come to mind*, Ford thought. Second, he wasn't sure how bad the fuel leak would be but was a bit apprehensive because if he couldn't get on the ship during the first landing try, called a pass, he wanted the option to go around.

Even a third time was a helpful option, so that he could bring the Devil Dragon on the deck in the best and safest way possible.

Wu looked at the moving-map display and pointed. "Set the waypoint for where you want us to go with this little joystick. Ship is down here, past Okinawa? Yes?" Wu asked.

"Yeah, about two hundred fifty miles southeast of Okinawa," Ford answered. "Here, wrap this bandanna around your leg. It'll help stop the bleeding. How bad are you?"

"Thanks. Um, let's use this, ah...this tampon. Here take the wrapping off, and plug the bullet wound."

"Tampon? For real? Where the hell did you get that?"

Wu laughed. "I was at the—"

WHOOP. WHOOP. WHOOP. PING. PING. PING.

Wu put his right hand up to silence the warnings.

"WARNING. FUEL LOW. WARNING. FUEL LOW." said the female voice again, over their flight helmets. Wu did it a second time, reaching up to the dash and pressing the light with his gloved fingers.

"Shit! Get in those flight checklists there on your right, Ford," Wu said, pointing at Liu's pile of checklists and kneeboard cards. "Fuel leak is...bigger than I thought. Get us a max range airspeed and power setting. I'll take a look at some of the winds and get us the best tailwind we can," Wu directed Ford.

Wonderful...written in Chinese, of course, Ford said to himself. "OK, OK, Wu. Slow down. It'll take me a minute to translate this shit to English."

"Stop complaining," Wu replied back.

Ford had his head in some of the Devil Dragon aircraft

performance charts. To make the most of the range of the Devil Dragon, they needed to get the maximum distance for each pound of fuel burned. It was a basic math formula for fuel flow, or pounds of fuel burned per hour. Align it on paper with some thrust curves mixed in with some multiplication and division, and you got a rich detailed chart that spit out power setting and airspeed to get the jet the farthest distance available.

"We won't be able to fly anywhere close to the Mach numbers you talked about, Wu. According to these charts, and if we really are leaking fuel, we have to slow *way* down. I'm talking *way* down. Then, climb and ride her out. Looks like we can only fly at about two hundred fifty knots or so," Ford said.

Wu closed his eyes. "So sorry, Ford. This jet is capable of so much more. At least we'll have the altitude to keep us safe."

"With these slower speeds, we'll see the sun coming up. At least a daytime landing is better than night. And we'll have about five hours to catch up with each other."

All this way, and out of fuel! Ford thought to himself. *Come on, ole Dragon, keep flying...*

USS *ABRAHAM LINCOLN*, 248 miles SSE of Okinawa, Japan

Mark's phone was still connected on the ship's Wi-Fi network, a benefit the US Navy provided to the ship's crew so they could keep in touch with loved ones back at home. It was up and working most of the time, and today it was giving users full strength.

He felt the vibration in his pocket, pulled it out, and read to himself.

Ford: METS

No shit? he'd thought. *Phenomenal.* Mark was pumped that the mission was going as planned. Certainly, he was not aware of the difficulties Ford and Wu had getting out of town but was genuinely joyful the team could pull it off so far.

"Hey, Emily...Robert, got a sec?" as Mark walked to a corner of the dark CDC. "Just heard from Ford. He texted me METS...he's in the jet now. Gone."

"Bugger!" exclaimed Emily. "Any timeframe?"

"Nothing other than the code word," Mark answered.

Robert nodded, his way of approving the operation, ever so stoic. "Well, time to get the Deputy on the horn. We have two big items to bring to his attention. And one for Muddy."

"We do? What?" Mark asked.

"The way I see it, we should have NSA boys go in and start deleting their phones off the servers at the Chinese telecommunications companies. No trace. Should be easy for them to do remotely," Robert recommended. "Second order, he should get the director more involved, and if not available, go over to the Pentagon and talk with the Secretary of Defense. The SecDef. Like, right away." Mark raised his eyebrows, and Emily nodded in agreement. "The what-if scenarios are tremendous. Like what if they get caught? What if they have an accident? You know how that works. And, although above my pay grade, talking to the National Security Council."

Mark looked at Robert, then at Emily. "Hmm. You're right."

"Yeah. And, finally, this flight deck crew. The colored

shirts. They have never recovered a jet like this. This is a black program, and since we can't limit how many folks are going to see the Devil Dragon, we need to do something to limit the leaks. We'll have to have Muddy call them in, maybe introduce one of us for a talk on what they are about to do."

The SecDef, or Secretary of Defense, was the overall senior leader of the department. Nominated by the President of the United States and confirmed into office by the Senate Armed Services Committee and then by the full Senate. Certainly, the SecDef is the most powerful civilian in the Pentagon, and he is responsible for nearly everything that goes on in DOD, from civilian and military policy, to human resources to intelligence. Good or bad, it's on the SecDef's watch.

"Good points, Robert. We'll need to get Deputy Burns on the phone then and perhaps gin up some talking points for him," Mark admitted. "Let's use the ship's phone system."

The three walked over to Muddy, seeking to explain that the jet was inbound but without a timeline.

"Muddy, you have a moment?" Mark asked.

"Yup. What's on your mind?" Muddy asked.

"A few items, Muddy. First, we just received confirmation via a text message that our pilot, Captain Ford Stevens, reached the Devil Dragon and was taking off. So, they are coming. As we both know, not only will this be difficult on radar, but they won't be able to talk on the frequencies. Perhaps, only a suggestion, but treat this like a lost comms situation. We bring it up because your radar folks, in addition to your flight deck crew, won't know when, or what, type of jet is landing. This mission is of the highest sensitivity on a national security level. And with today's young sailors, the Generation Y and Millennials you have up there, for heaven's sake, no personal cameras or cell phones. Nothing," Mark explained.

"Totally. Understand," Muddy said.

Robert cleared his throat. "Muddy. I'd also like to ask something...offbeat. It's regarding sensitivity and classification. Is it possible, say in fifteen minutes, to gather your flight deck guys—your colored shirts up there—by the island for a talk by us? Team DIA? I'll start out down here with your air traffic control folks, the radar team, and then the electronic warfare guys. I can swear them to nondisclosure statements verbally and legally," Robert explained.

"Yeah, that is pretty nonstandard, but I guess something like this is unheard of. OK, we'll do it," Muddy agreed. "XO, make it happen." He turned to Big XO with the order.

The XO called up the chief petty officer of the ship and explained that he would be announcing soon that all the men and women on the flight deck were to meet at the island in fifteen minutes. A "special meeting," he phrased it, and both men knew for sure that the rumors would be flying around the ship in two minutes or less.

"CDC! May I have your attention please?" the XO said loudly. "Now that I have your attention, everyone step over here to the light table." The CDC, about eighteen to twenty sailors and officers, made their way over. "Sir, floor is yours."

"Thanks, XO. Ladies and gentlemen, I want to introduce to you three members, guests from Washington, of the Defense

Intelligence Agency. The DIA. They are here on a special mission and need our help tonight. Please give them your attention," Muddy announced.

"Thank you, Captain. Hello, everyone. My name is Mark, and these are my teammates Emily and Robert. We are with the DIA. We are here on a historic occasion, and so are you. I appreciate your time tonight. Within a matter of minutes, or hours, depending on how the mission is going, a Chinese stealth bomber is going to land on this ship. The pilots are friendlies. They are not going to attack us, so don't worry. I bring this to your attention because anything can happen as they get closer."

"What do you mean, sir?" asked a young sailor, who looked to be barely nineteen years old.

"Thank you for asking. The jet coming in tonight has tremendous stealth capability, so you may not see him on radar that easily—or at all, frankly. I encourage you to keep your eyes open and report anything that may seem unusual, or nonstandard. They may not talk on the radio, so it will be difficult to communicate. Their avionics may not be compatible with this ship or any other US ships in the area. For landing, they may land the first time, or go around many times. We aren't even sure they have night vision goggles...just be ready for anything, OK?" Mark said, attempting to keep the young and talented crew informed and calm. "We may be here, the three of us, or we may be up on the deck or up on the bridge. Your CO and XO will know how to get ahold of us," Mark let a moment or two go by. "Any questions?" Mark looked back at Muddy. "Oh, last thing. Anything you see or say tonight, you may never repeat. Ever. For your lifetime. Ever. This mission tonight is crucial to our national security. We need your help, folks. Thank you." Mark was finished and hoped to himself they bought in to the idea of how serious this was.

"OK, *Lincoln* Team, back to your stations. Thanks for the support," Muddy announced.

Robert walked over to Emily and gave her a nod while looking at the digital map. "See these ships here? One of them will be a destroyer or cruiser with a powerful radar and at least an aircraft or two up and airborne that can visually ID something for us," Robert said to Emily.

"Hmm. You think coming out of Okinawa, like on a 220-heading outbound?" Emily took her right hand and followed out from the last island in the Japanese island chain.

Robert nodded. "Exactly." He looked down at the radar screens to see if anything was on there, but it was clear. "Muddy. Before we go up and talk to the flight deck team. Can we ask this ship here, what is it here...the, ah, the USS *Gettysburg*, to launch a helicopter flight out to visually search? See if they spot the Devil Dragon?" asked Robert.

"Sure. We have contact with them. They have an AN/SPS-49 air search radar that may help. Want me to call over there?" Muddy offered.

"That'd be terrific...thanks," Robert said.

Muddy walked over to the officer of the deck for the CDC. "Get me *Gettysburg* skipper on the phone."

"Yes, sir," answered a young lieutenant. He picked up the phone, talked in hush tones, and within a minute, had his guy on the phone. "Sir, *Gettysburg* commanding officer on hold."

"Rocko, Muddy Waters here over on *Lincoln*," Muddy said. "Listen, I don't have time to bullshit. Need you to radar sweep an aircraft we are looking for. Not a friendly, but this isn't a warning order, so don't get all freaked out. She's high, coming over Okinawa, and coming our way, and we just want to track her, with no action requested. No, no, stay quiet for a minute and let me finish. OK, she'll be on the two-twenty radial out of Kadena and landing on us. Unknown altitude...a fast mover. Maybe launch a bird or two for a visual...good?" he continued to explain. "Yup, yup, just have your CDC contact ours with anything you got. Thanks, man." Muddy gave the phone back to the lieutenant and turned to Robert. "Done."

The XO led the way from the CDC through a maze of passageways on the ship. Some were gray, others white, and most had an area you had to step over or you would trip. There were hundreds of folks in the halls, all working and walking and keeping busy. They passed one of many gyms, a dining hall, a rec room, and the ship's store. They walked down hallways, made turns, climbed ladders, and went down more hallways. One room was even painted black. Everyone was friendly, and most greeted the CO and XO with "sir" and "good evening."

They arrived on the normally busy flight deck, to a crowd of clean-shaven teenage sailors with baby faces. They were all wearing a variety of colored shirts, as depicted earlier from the chart shown aboard the C-2. They were greasy from cable and aircraft grease, but happy and definitely dedicated.

The XO stopped into a small office surrounded by windows

on the flight deck, full of officers and sailors doing work related to positioning of aircraft on the flight deck. The sign on the door said "Flight Deck Control," FDC, and the sailors were huddled around a large tabletop model of the ship, called a Ouija board. There were also miniature toy models of each aircraft that were replicas of the carrier's flight deck, a scale of one-sixteenth inch to one foot.

"Check this out! A game board!" Emily said, gaining smiles from all the men in the room.

The flat wooden board was about six feet long and two and a half feet wide, and if something could fit on the game board, it could fit on the ship's flight deck. The flight deck was a dangerous place, with massive aircraft in continuous motion, hot jet exhaust, dirty steel cables, rotating helicopters, and steam catapults, all while moving fifteen or twenty knots into the wind at sea. Day and night.

"Chief, come on over here. XO, you, too. I want to launch an E-2, couple of Hornets for tankers, plus two more for combat air patrol. Add an H-60 Seahawk for starboard delta pattern SAR. Get them on the flight schedule and launch as soon as you can. PACOM told us to expect anything, and if there are chasers out of China who are pissed off we stole their child, they are gonna be PO pissed. Questions?" Muddy said, pointing his finger to make a point. "OK, Chief, get the guys around for a talk."

"Flight deck crew. Flight deck crew. Report to the FDC. On the double," was heard over the loudspeakers.

A moment later, the crowd gathered around the base of the island.

"Get over here. Pay attention," the crusty and experienced

chief petty officer of the ship said to the flight deck sailors, standing around and waiting for the meeting to start. "We are going to flight quarters soon. Launching only four Hornets, an E-2, and a SAR SH-60. We are expecting something very unusual to land though. NO CAMERAS. NO CELL PHONES. So pay attention to this gentleman. GOT IT?"

"Yes, Chief," they all said in unison.

"Thanks, Chief. Ladies and gentleman, I'm Mark Savona, and I am from the Defense Intelligence Agency. The DIA. I'm here with two teammates, Emily and Robert." At that moment, the catcalls and whistling started after they started staring at Emily.

"Hello, boys!" Emily yelled, giving them a smile and a wave. They were all paying attention now.

"SHUT IT!" the chief told them.

Mark continued. "We are here on a special mission, and so are you. We need your help. Sometime soon, a unique aircraft will be landing on the *Lincoln*. None of us have seen it before. It's a Chinese aircraft with a friendly crew. Again, the pilots are friendlies. For you tonight, you can expect no tailhook, which is why you helped work the barricade. So, again, no tailhook. Also, expect nonstandard comms, so those men and women working with the...the landing signal team, it will be a bit different. Be ready for anything. Part two of this plan is the welding team. Those guys over there"—Mark nodded—"are DIA welders. After the Chinese jet lands, they are going to cut off the wing with their welding torches as fast as they can. Your role will be to get the wings, and then the fuselage, on the airplane elevator as fast and as safely as you can. Park her in the hangar deck." Mark let a long pause go. "Are there any questions?"

"Is that hot blonde single?" asked a voice from the crowd. Everyone broke out laughing.

"Sorry, fellas. I'm taken," Emily answered.

"Shut it, Henrik," the chief told the sailor.

"We'll have the medical team here, too, as one of the pilots is not feeling well," Mark paused again. "OK, if no other questions, we really do need your help. Thank you."

Mark turned to Emily and Robert and gave a big smile. "Kind of nice out here tonight. Clear, but cold...and peaceful. Well...let's give Washington a call."

14th Street Bridge, Washington, DC

"This is Jason," he said, answering his Blackberry from the backseat of the Chevy Suburban. Jason was traveling with the Deputy, inbound to the Crystal Gateway Marriott Hotel in Crystal City to speak at the Annual Association of the United States Army, one of the countless Washington, DC, lobbying groups for army soldiers and defense contractors in the National Capital Region.

"Jason, this is the watch officer. I have an inbound call from the USS *Abraham Lincoln*, officer of the deck. There is a 'Mark S' who wishes to talk with the Deputy."

"The *Lincoln*? No, no, the Deputy is preparing to give a speech and is unable to talk, so why don't you—"

"Who is that Jason?" the Deputy asked.

Jason hid his Blackberry in his chest. "The USS *Abraham*

Lincoln? Someone named Mark? I told them you were busy and that—"

"No, stop that. Give me the phone," the Deputy said. He cleared his throat. "This is Calvin Burns."

"Sir, this is the watch officer. I'm patching through a call from the USS *Abraham Lincoln*. Go ahead, caller."

"Sir, this is Mark. Are you there, sir?" Mark asked.

"Hello. Go ahead, Mark. I'm here. How are you guys doing?"

"Terrific. Ah, you in the green?" asked Mark.

I don't have a goddamn clue. The Deputy pulled the phone off his ear and looked at the screen but couldn't tell from a glance. "Jason, is this goddamn thing cleared for classified? We green here or what? Let's hurry up," said the Deputy, bothered with the bureaucracy. Jason nodded yes.

Annoyed, Calvin told him, "Oh, for Christ's sake. Yeah, yeah, Mark, go ahead."

"Sir, Ford and Wu took off from Tianjin in the jet. Not sure of their status or takeoff time, but we're expecting them sometime soon. The *Lincoln* is fully prepped and expecting them. Both the admiral and the *Lincoln* aren't too happy about us landing a foreign jet without a tailhook, but they accepted it. We feel that they'll land in the coming hour or hours. Ah, *Lincoln* did a nice job preparing. Welders are here. NDAs signed for ship crew. Just a waiting game now."

"All right, all right. OK. Keeping PACOM informed?" asked Deputy Burns.

"CO of the ship, a Navy captain named Muddy Waters, has

that covered for us. Sir, what we recommend, and soon, is that you back brief the director, then the SecDef."

"*SecDef*? Huh. Well, the director is traveling at the moment with USD (I). Both are inbound to the NATO conference in Brussels."

"Sir, the unclassified, public schedule says SecDef has no public appearances today and is not traveling. He must be at the Pentagon."

"Oh, boy...yeah, you're right. Agree. OK, I'll...I'll cancel my AUSA speech and go over to see him. Keep me in the loop. Deputy out."

The Deputy ended the call and looked down at the floor. He just wanted a moment of white space to think about the events and consider a decision that would keep the SecDef informed. Walking in to see him might or might not work, but working through the military assistant would.

The SecDef had two military assistants, known as mil assists, the junior being a colonel and the senior being a lieutenant general, who assisted the secretary with nearly everything he did. From travel to speeches to DOD policies and correspondence, they handled everything for the largest department in the US government. Army Lieutenant General Gil Hastings was the current senior mil assist, and he worked closely with DIA when he was on a sensitive Special Forces detachment a few years ago. He'd take the call for sure.

"Jason, cancel my speech, and get me Lieutenant General Hastings on the phone at SecDef's office. Hey, Martin, we need lights and sirens. We're canceling the Crystal City Marriott location. Take us to the Pentagon, please."

Martin, the executive driver, knew the DC roads like the back of his hand. It was no issue to reroute while driving from Crystal City to the Pentagon, especially since they were right next to each other. The drive was no longer than ten minutes from their current position on the beginning of the 14th Street Bridge, but the DC traffic was, as usual, horrendous. Martin leaned down and threw on the lights in the grille, and the chirps of the siren moved the DC commuters over with a purpose.

"Watch it! Watch it! Driver pulling out!" yelled Jason.

Martin swayed out of the way to avoid the Tesla S darting out to the right. The heavy black Suburban nearly crushed the $100,000 vehicle. Martin moved in and out of the traffic, weaving to get them to Virginia. The accelerator pushed them into their seats.

"Hello, Gil? Calvin Burns here. Deputy at DIA. I've got a current situation that SecDef needs to know about right away. Tier one level, time sensitive. Yeah, happening live right now. USD (I) is away with the DIA director, and it can't wait." Calvin Burns bobbed his head up and down. "Yup. Yup. OK, I'm inbound now with lights and sirens. Ten minutes? I can make that timeslot." Calvin turned to look at Jason and gave him the thumbs up, and then pointed over at the Pentagon, which was in view from their position on the bridge. "OK. See you in ten."

Martin had them soaring across the Potomac River, driving on the right shoulder of I-395 south, and moving the Deputy with determination. Easily passing now at sixty mph with the regular lanes nearly stopped, Martin's near thirty years of executive driving experience got them there with fortitude.

Approaching Okinawa, Japan

"How's that leg, buddy?" Ford asked, as he listened for the response and scanned the aircraft instruments. "You doing OK?"

"I never...I never thought it would end like this, Ford," Wu said, coughing away from Ford.

Ford looked at his sunken face under his flight helmet and jaundiced skin and eyes, as the pink glow from the sunrise off in the distance started to peek on the horizon. Ford admitted to himself that Wu looked terrible; he felt so badly for him. He also saw that Wu was crying, with his face down toward the floor, wiping the tears from his cheek. Ford extended his hand to Wu's and held it.

"I'm here for you, brother," Ford said, attempting to console his best friend who was fighting for his life.

"Thank you, Ford. I wanted to have a family. I wanted them to meet you, and your parents, and your brother and sister. And bring them to America for rock music like Bruce Springsteen, and eat hot dogs, and see the Chicago Cubs...and the Grand Canyon. And watch *Furious 7* and *Transformers*. I wanted to grow old."

Ford didn't say anything at first. "I know you did, Wu, I know." His voice trailed off softly.

"I had a whole list...a goal sheet of things I wanted to do before I die. You want to...ah, hear a few?" asked Wu, breathing a bit heavier now.

"Sure, yeah. Of course. Like, what, you have a 'kick the bucket list'? What's on there?"

"I had a list with some titles, like Adventure, Learning, Trips, and Mystery. Things under there were like attending a Golden State Warriors game, seeing what happens to Donald Trump...ah, reading the book *The BFG*, driving one of those GMC Acadias, drinking a margarita or mojito, playing Pokémon Go, and, oh, getting a Netflix subscription."

"Wow, Wu, yeah. That's a hell of a list. Those are pretty cool," said Ford, realizing how morbid the conversation was becoming. *So young to have his life taken from him.*

"Oh, it was way more, Ford. It also included more things like...ah, visiting Berkeley, dancing with DJ AM," coughing again. "Visiting Nice, France. Eating at Chipotle Mexican Grill, and, umm, well, taking the Hershey Chocolate Tour. You know, with my wife and kids, if I had them."

"*Hershey Chocolate Tour? What the hell is that?*" Ford asked, laughing his ass off.

"Yup. I like chocolate."

"A tour of a chocolate factory? Wu, come on. Really?" Ford asked again, still laughing.

"Yeah, I like that movie we saw when we were kids. You know, the one where the little people ride a river of chocolate."

"*Willie Wonka and the Chocolate Factory?*" Ford asked, laughing again.

"Yeah, that one," Wu answered. A few seconds went by. "Hey, is Netflix as cool as I read about? Can you really watch anything you want?"

"Yeah, Wu, you can. All sorts of movie and show options. Really, that's a hell of a list," Ford replied, then remained quiet for a few brief seconds, scanning the instruments. "Well, Wu, you could have taken your family white-water rafting, too."

Wu started laughing, then coughing, and was now smiling. "Stop, you're making my gut hurt. From vivid memory and this scar on my head, I've had enough white-water rafting. Wait, wait. My last bucket list item."

"What was that?"

"Getting groceries at Wegmans Food Markets."

The Devil Dragon was on autopilot still, in calm air, and cruising along as calmly as things could be. The thin wings performed flawlessly as two best friends darted across the South Pacific. The sky above was still dark due to their altitude, and the blue sea that surrounded them below started to become clearer as the sun came up.

"Wu. Our dream as teenagers was to fly. We both did that. How many kids can decide at a young age that they want to do something and set a goal, like we did, and do it? Hardly anyone. We did it. We did. And here we are right now, flying together."

Wu didn't say anything at first and thought about what Ford had just said. "Yeah, Ford. You're right. Hey...can you take a selfie of us? Of us flying together? I bet your dad would like it."

Ford got out his smartphone, searched for the camera app, and opened it. "Here we go. Ready? Smile!" He pressed the button to take the shot. Just the right amount of sunlight was coming up now, and it was a fine-looking sunrise.

"Ford. I'm ready."

"Wu, we just took the photo," said Ford, looking at Wu strangely. "We're done."

"No, no. I mean I am ready to go."

"Go where, Wu?"

"You know. I'm ready to go. I don't want to die, but what I mean is that you helped me get ready to die. I feel...better about it. I treasure life and all my experiences, but I am ready to go when God calls me...Ford. I'm lonely and in such great pain, both emotionally and physically. It will be soon," Wu said, opening up his heart to Ford.

"We don't know that, Wu. You could have much more time here with us. Yes?"

Wu looked down at the flight deck floor. "Maybe. But if and when the time comes, Ford, I want you to know that I lived. I mean I really *lived*. With the exception of a wife and kids, no regrets. The opportunities came in life, and I took them. Relationships with girls, test pilot school, travel, flying hard, more travel, college, family with my mom, family with you and the rest of the family," Wu said, wiping his nose with his sleeve and a quiet sniffle.

Ford got out of his seat to give Wu a hug. "You're family, Wu. I cannot imagine us doing anything different than what we are doing right now. Look down below. Beautiful Pacific Ocean all around. Sun already up. Is this a great view of the office or what? Our office!"

"Thanks, Ford. Thank you. I am so grateful you came."

Ford looked at his watch, stretched his back, and double-checked their position on the moving-map display. He sat down to buckle in. "About an hour or so, and we'll be on the deck of the carrier, Wu. Hang tight, brother." Ford had a tear in his eye now, fully understanding Wu's feelings.

USS *Gettysburg*, 102 miles E of Okinawa

The USS *Gettysburg*, hull number CG-64, was on a rare Pacific Ocean tour, usually patrolling the Mediterranean Sea on deployments out of Mayport, Florida. *Gettysburg*, a Ticonderoga-class guided-missile cruiser in the US Navy, is named after the Battle of Gettysburg during the Civil War. Her 567 feet in length carried four General Electric LM 2500 gas turbine engines with eighty thousand-shaft horsepower, controlling two reversible pitch propellers, along with two rudders. Her thirty-three officers, twenty-seven petty officers, and 340-person crew could get *Gettysburg* up to thirty-two-plus knots, helping to launch its two MH-60R Seahawks or other visiting helicopters. She also carried guided missiles and rapid-fire cannons, and was capable of facing and defeating threats in the air, on or under the sea, or ashore.

A US Marine Corps AH-1W Super Cobra attack helicopter, on detachment from the Thirty-First Marine Expeditionary Unit in Okinawa, was assigned to *Gettysburg* for a three-day visit. They had launched forty-three minutes prior for instrument practice, scheduled for a two-hour flight.

"GUNFIGHTER 78, *Gettysburg*," was heard over the UHF frequency on radio number two.

"This is GUNFIGHTER, go ahead."

"GUNFIGHTER, stand by for *Gettysburg* six," said the controller.

Inside the cockpit of the *Cobra*, aircraft commander Padre and copilot Lefty were two of the best *Cobra* attack pilots in the US Marines. They were both experienced instructor pilots on their second overseas deployment, night-systems qualified, and were both approaching two thousand hours of flight time. Flying was what they loved to do. Busting chops on squadron mates was a close second.

"*Gettysburg* six? Who the hell is that? It's not on the smart sheet," Padre asked Lefty over the intercom, searching their kneeboard paperwork. The smart sheet is a condensed sheet of information about a particular mission printed in a way that perfectly fits on a pilot's kneeboard.

"Yeah it is, you dumb ass; look at the bottom of the last page."

"Oh, shit...yeah, there it is...ship CO. What the hell does he want with us? You leave the iron on in your room, Padre?" Lefty said, laughing, always a smart aleck to a fellow gunfighter. "Too much hair gel left near the heater?"

"Shut it. Yeah, I was ironing my flight suit," Padre said, then quickly flipping the switch up to transmit outside the aircraft and reply.

"GUNFIGHTER 78, this is *Gettysburg* six here. Special request."

"Go ahead, sir."

"*Gettysburg* ATC is going to give you some magnetic headings to fly. A few vectors. Need you to keep your eyes open and let us know if you see...eh...any unusual aircraft. You may see her, you may not. Bottom line is that we need your help."

"UFO, Lefty. Aliens are coming," Padre said over the intercom. Then transmitted outside on the UHF freq, "OK, sir. Wilco. We'll look for your traffic," he quickly transmitted back to the ship.

"GUNFIGHER 78, how do you hear?"

"Four by four, GUNFIGHTER 78."

"GUNFIGHTER, turn left to zero-three-zero, climb and maintain angels ten. Report upon arrival."

"Ooohh, Lefty. A female controller. She likes you." Padre said on intercom, then transmitted outside, "Roger, *Gettysburg*, GUNFIGHER in the climb to angels ten."

Padre pulled more collective with his left hand and pulled back the stick. The *Cobra* zoomed from their current altitude of three hundred feet above ground level to ten thousand feet. It took them only five minutes or so, and they reported upon arrival.

"Well, here we are, smoking and joking. I don't see shit up here. But keep your eyes open, Lefty," Padre told Lefty. "No sleeping up in the front. Hey, tell your girlfriend we're here at her altitude."

"*Gettysburg*, GUNFIGHTER, reporting in at altitude."

"Squawk one-two-five-six. Turn right to two-two-zero and fly max endurance airspeed."

"Come on, sweetheart. Really? How many bags of gas does she think we have out here? Max endurance airspeed? I have to look in the charts." He transmitted, "One-two-fix-six and Roger, we'll look it up."

"Smooth, kid. You look it up."

"You look it up, you lazy ass," replied Lefty, who really was a righty.

Padre cut him off. "Hey. Shut your pie hole. Look at that over there...shit. What the hell is that up at eleven o'clock, left to right, passing away from us?" Padre asked.

"Huh. Never seen that aircraft before. Looks like a...what, a black...F-117. But different. Something isn't right about her. Tough to tell size from here, but this one looks bigger. Much wider," Lefty said to Padre.

"*Gettysburg*, GUNFIGHTER 78. Reporting in with your unidentified aircraft."

"Go ahead, GUNFIGHTER."

"From my position, we see a black jet, high altitude, heading two-four-zero magnetic at about three hundred knots. Closely resembles an F-117 stealth fighter from the US Air Force."

"*Gettysburg* six copies. Thanks, GUNFIGHTER. You're cleared to resume training with controller or on own. See you upon landing."

"Roger, sir. GUNFIGHTER 78, request vectors for a PAR..."

Gettysburg CO put down the headset he had up to his ear and turned to the OOD for a connection to *Lincoln*. It took a bit longer than he had hoped because it was a challenge for the *Lincoln* crew to locate their skipper.

"Muddy, hey, Rocko Cooper here. Got your aircraft. Ready to copy? OK, we had a Marine Cobra crew attached to us...got him vectored around for a bit. At 1658Z, the flight crew, from ten thousand feet at our zero-eight-zero radial, reported that they saw a black jet at high altitude, heading two-four-zero magnetic at about three hundred knots. They said it looked like an USAF F-117. A...a stealth fighter. No electromagnetic detection or passive emissions. No radar signature." *Gettysburg* nodded. "Yup. Got it. Will pass to my crew. Thank you. Cooper out."

Gettysburg CO paused, didn't say anything, then called over the OOD.

"What's going on, sir?" asked the OOD.

"Get the ATC controller and bring her over here for a moment," asked the CO.

A tall female sailor came over, not sure why she was coming over in the middle of her shift to talk with the boss. She approached him timidly.

"Yes, sir?" she said quietly.

"Good morning. Just wanted to pass good job on the vectoring. I also wanted to pass, and OOD, this goes for you as well...that was a foreign jet from another country, and the intelligence community is working it. It is a sensitive mission, so we aren't going to talk about it. Forget it ever happened, OK? For the rest of your life, this didn't happen," the CO said, nodding his head yes. "Until death. And OOD, I want to talk to that GUNFIGHTER crew upon landing. They can get their asses in here, too."

River Entrance, Pentagon, Washington, DC

The black Suburban passed the security checkpoint on the west side of the Pentagon, police lights in the grille illuminating the front of the SUV. Martin knew the uniformed Pentagon Force Protection Agency officers well after serving in Washington for so many years and gave them all a wave as they drove through. Martin took the Deputy and Jason over the red, pop-up, antiterrorism physical barriers with ease, and up the twisted cement vehicle ramp to the parking lot on the river entrance side of the Pentagon. Martin then drove through the river parking lot and stopped in front of the staircase so Mr. Burns could exit.

The river parking lot was full of black four-door sedans and Chevy Suburbans, all with tinted windows, some with engines running, and some parked in numbered spots. Some sedans were for military Service Secretaries or Secretaries in the Office of the Secretary of Defense, while others were for the general and flag officers in the Office of the Chairman of the Joint Chiefs of Staff. It seemed like every general or admiral had at least one vehicle, sometimes two, along with a junior officer aide to carry comms gear, weapons, and correspondence. From combatant commanders to four-star senior leaders assigned to distant places like Korea or Europe and visiting the Pentagon, most or all of them traveled with some variety of speechwriters, protective security detail, legislative liaisons, political advisers, and public affairs officers. If a visiting head of state was visiting, a defense minister, prince, prime minister, minister of defense or senior member of the House or Senate, or anything close to those titles, the river lot could be full of competing agency vehicles. It was a sight to see for any visitor to the building, but on this day, Deputy Burns didn't have time to screw around.

Jason got out first and walked around to meet Deputy

Burns on the sidewalk. They both stepped up the wide exterior staircase and passed between the thick five-story-tall marble columns and through the large gold wooden doors. Jason led them through another security checkpoint and up the historic black marble stairs that nearly every President has walked on since January 14, 1943. Deputy Burns always stopped to glance at the framed oath of office—no matter how jammed he was for time—that hung in the corner of the landing. It reminded him and all who passed there what their legal and moral obligation was to their country.

"Sir, I don't know all the details, but do you want me to go in first and talk to the general, or do you just want me to bring you to the Secretary of Defense's office and wait?" Jason asked, as they made it to the top of the staircase.

"Thank you, Jason. I'm good with speaking with both the general and the secretary," the Deputy said, making a left at the top of the staircase in the E Ring.

Like rings on a bull's-eye, the inner ring of the Pentagon was the A Ring. It had a view of the internal tree-lined grassy courtyard and was where the less powerful players of the Defense Department sat at their desks. The most outer ring of the Pentagon, the E Ring, was where the power in Washington sat. The Secretary of Defense, the Deputy Secretary, the Service Secretaries and Undersecretaries, and the generals and admirals of the Joint Staff, all sat in the outer E Ring.

Just then, the Deputy Secretary of Defense walked by with his people, heading down the staircase to another floor. The Deputy usually handled strategic topics of importance internal to the department, ranging from new weapon systems being acquired to readiness of the force to dealing with the service chiefs. Most senior leaders thought of the Deputy Secretary as handling business internal to the building, and the secretary handled things outside the building, such as the President, Capitol Hill, international diplomacy, and shaking hands with the troops.

"Hello, Calvin, nice to see you," said Deputy Secretary of Defense Manny Lorning.

"Hi, Manny, good to see you as well," replied Calvin Burns.

Calvin and Jason continued down the E Ring, past the large hallway of oil paintings of past secretaries of defense. "Lorning. What a jerk," he said, adding in a hushed tone, "Keep that quiet, Jason."

"Hi, Sergeant Brewer. Deputy Calvin Burns, DIA, for the secretary," Jason said, announcing their arrival. "He's expecting us."

"Of course, sir. Please go in. The general is expecting you first, before the secretary," said Sergeant Brewer.

Jason led the way to Lieutenant General Gil Hastings's office, just next to the secretary's office. Jason stepped to the side so the Deputy could greet the general. "Hello, Gil, thanks for fitting me in."

"Hello, sir. You're welcome. Ah...sir, listen, the secretary is already overloaded today. He has the chairman's upcoming retirement, issues with the SASC, and a new policy issue with the administration on number of Navy ships. Plus, he's got next fiscal year's budget dispute bursting at the seams. Whatever you got, I hope it's low key."

"That's all? Regular day around here, Gil," the Deputy said, making them all laugh. "Well, no, it's not low key. We have something developing right now in the Pacific. As we speak. He needs to know."

"OK, sir. PACOM handling it?"

"No, not exactly. Our mission, with PACOM support."

"What are the details?"

"We...acquired a new, previously unknown and undisclosed Chinese Stealth Bomber. An H-18. The Chinese pilot who was test flying her is the best friend of one of our US Air Force Reserve pilots. Together, they just stole it from the east coast of China, and they are currently inbound to the carrier *Lincoln*, a few hundred miles off Okinawa. Depending on what happens in the coming hours, the secretary may or may not want to know. Perhaps even higher to the NSC and POTUS."

"No kidding? That's pretty heavy," Gil said as he stood up. "He'll want to know that. All right, sir, let's go see the boss." Lieutenant General Gil Hastings led them out of the room and into the small carpeted hallway, only making a quick right turn to walk the five steps required to hit the SecDef's doorway.

"Hey, sir! Sir..." Sergeant Brewer said, jogging slowly with a folder in his hand and attempting to get a hold of them before entering the secretary's office. "Sir, excuse me, I have an 'eyes-only' report from the National Military Command Center for Deputy Burns."

"Thank you, Sergeant Brewer," the general replied, as he took the folder from him and handed it directly to the Deputy.

Deputy Burns nodded in agreement as he read it silently.

"Well, things are coming along nicely in the Pacific. Turns out that USS *Gettysburg* had a Marine Corps AH-1W Cobra flight crew attached to them. During the flight, the Cobra pilots had an eyes-on and relayed it back to the ship. Pilots described it as looking like an F-117 US Air Force stealth fighter. Next paragraph is from DIA. They're reporting detecting two cell phones at altitude passing over Okinawa, Japan, and were triangulated to be the same location as our jet. DIA analysis determined the two phones are registered to our guys working the mission; I can see their names here on the report."

Lt. Gen. Gil Hastings, US Army, had close to thirty years of service and was still amazed at the technology and speed with which the US Defense Department could relay info. Here something was happening halfway around the world, live, and we were tracking it. He was impressed.

"Thank you, sir. That's a hell of a mission...let's go in and talk with him," General Hastings said quietly, then turned to knock on the secretary's door. "Excuse me, Mr. Secretary?"

The office had windows that lined the left wall from waist height to the ceiling and had a stunning view of the Potomac River to the right, Washington Monument straight ahead, and to the far right, the top of the Capitol dome. If you looked out the window to the left, you could see the White House, and farther back, the gray steeples of Georgetown University. Inside his office sat two love seats that faced each other, with a coffee table between them, staged so well that it looked like they were placed and set up by an interior decorator. Someone had taste in this area of the Pentagon.

"Yes, Gil. Please come in," said Secretary of Defense Daniel B. Woods. The secretary was seated at his desk, which faced the windows, reading a folder full of papers on military personnel policy. His large handcrafted mahogany desk was surrounded by metal challenge coins from the troops. Books were stacked on his desk, at least eight or ten hardcover ones, ranging from economics and biographies to foreign policy, along with already read copies of the *Japan Times,* the *New York Times,* the *Wall Street Journal,* and the *Los Angeles Times.*

"Pardon, me, sir, but as I mentioned a few minutes ago, the Deputy director of DIA is here, Mr. Calvin Burns. He is here to—"

"I know Calvin. You out there, Cal? Come on in here. Let's sit down on the couch." The secretary came out from behind his desk. "Coffee?"

"Hello, sir. Great to see you again. Yes, coffee, thank you," Calvin Burns said as he walked over to shake hands with the secretary. "Thank you for fitting me in."

"Cal, I'll always make time. I know if you're coming and bypassing folks, it must be hot." The Deputy thought that was a strange comment. *Oh, crap. Did he mean bypass, like he thinks the director and USD (I) don't know this plan?* Either way, the Deputy didn't have to time to worry about things like that.

"Yes, sir. It's time sensitive. So my visit is to let you know DIA has been involved with an operational mission related to China.

"Oh, really? What do you have?"

"Well, sir, a Chinese stealth aircraft. We've acquired,

essentially co-stole, a previously unknown and undisclosed, Chinese stealth *bomber*. It has both conventional and nuclear capability, in addition to a robust intelligence collection package."

"I don't recall being briefed on this technology previously," said the Secretary, taking his glasses off.

"We were only made aware of the existence and capabilities when a Chinese pilot walked in at a consulate in China. The H-18 jet, called Devil Dragon, can fly completely invisible to our systems. Undetected."

"Did you say Devil Dragon?" asked the secretary.

"Yes, sir. Complete stealth capability. Zero radar signature. Also has unbelievable speed, upward of Mach 5, using specially designed engines we don't have. Yet."

"We don't? The boys out at the Areas and Groom Lake don't?"

Oh, boy. An Area 51 Groom Lake referral...this is Air Force's lane, not mine, Burns thought.

"No, sir, and certainly, that's historically CIA's lane, and Air Force's lane, based on history with the A-12 Oxcart and all. To add some drama to the situation, the Chinese pilot only did this walk-in because of his love of America, growing up with the US Air Force pilot's family, but the fact is...he has terminal pancreatic cancer."

"Whoa," said Secretary Woods. "Cancer. Hmm. Well, I'm familiar. *Believe me*, I'm familiar," as he put both hands in the air and motioned a push-away gesture.

Whoa, I didn't know the secretary had cancer, or is recovering from it, Calvin thought.

"Yes, sir. The Chinese pilot, Captain Wu Lee, and our Air Force Reserve pilot, Captain Ford Stevens, are flying it inbound to the USS *Abraham Lincoln*."

The secretary put his glasses back on and then took them off again. He raised his eyebrows and had an unpredictable look of zero expression on his face. Calvin thought it must have been honed after so many years in the Senate. "Really? Let me get this straight. They are going to land a Chinese stealth fighter—or rather bomber—on the flight deck of the *Lincoln*?"

Oh shit. That's not a great tone of voice. "Yes, sir, they are. The jet just flew undetected through Chinese airspace, then South Korean airspace, and now through Japanese airspace and—"

"Wait a sec. We flew through *their* airspace? Did they coordinate? Get diplomatic clearances?"

"No, sir. It flies invisible to all radar. They are still airborne right now and just moments ago passed over Okinawa. We think they will land on *Lincoln* in about an hour."

"Well, shit. There goes the diplomacy card," said the secretary. The Secretary looked down at the coffee table and was no doubt considering his options, and who needed to know what, including the President. This wasn't the first time the military and intelligence community was involved in other countries, but this was the first time meddling with the Chinese like this. The secretary was a student of history, and Calvin knew he'd be thinking of the 1960s shoot down of Black Cat Squadron U-2s by China. Classic smoke and mirrors.

"Who else knows?" asked the secretary, tapping his gold Cross pen on his white pad.

"Very close hold, sir. Not many. Just the folks on the Navy ships, helping with the recovery. A few folks in the operations centers relaying the messages and phone calls might know and may know of the title, OPERATION WHIRLPOOL. And, ah, my team that is facilitating the operation."

"Oh, who are they, and what's this op called again?"

"I have the lead as Mark Savona, an expert in Chinese aircraft. Robert Dooley, ah, working HUMINT. Emily Livingston, MI6, assigned to DIA as liaison from the United Kingdom. Last, the pilot, Captain Ford Stevens, was borrowed from the Air Force Reserve. Ahem, originally without his command or Air Force Reserve knowing."

"Good. Pretty close knit circle of folks. Let's keep it like that," the secretary said. He scratched his cheek. "Air Force Reserve, eh? We can take care of the kid, that's no big deal. And MI6. We'll have to call them as a courtesy when this is over. Well, Gil, what do you think?"

There was a long silence for the requisite thinking going on in the general's head. He let out a breath and tapped his pen on his memo pad, which was nearly blank. "Sir, I'll take care of the Stevens kid, the pilot, and call upstairs to the secretary of the Air Force and make sure Lieutenant General Maria Ruiz at Reserves takes care of him. But, ah, it seems like DIA has caught the big fish. Not sure what the technology is in that jet, but if this thing is completely stealth, it could deliver whatever weapons it wanted without us knowing. Or coalition countries. Or do collection on us, and we'd never know. So, a good catch by DIA," General Hastings answered. "It's a toss-up if you want to talk to the President about it, sir, but I am thinking...no. Maybe I can work with the ASD Public Affairs to gin up some talking points if the story leaks, but with something this big, we usually keep a lid on it."

"Thanks, Gil. Calvin...um, any action for me to take? What do you recommend?" asked the secretary.

"Sir, do nothing for the moment. After we land her, cut off her wings to hide her in the hangar deck and fly her off in pieces a few weeks from now to a secure location. The Chinese won't know where to look. Their satellites will be everywhere and nowhere, all at the same time," answered the Deputy. "Furthermore, the Chinese general officer on this, the father of Chinese stealth, is an Air Force three-star named He Chen. He's been described as a hothead, a drunk, and a micromanager type who will be not only embarrassed but will have some explaining to do to the party. If you relay this to the NSC, VPOTUS, or even POTUS himself, then their aides and their immediate staffs know, and we both know the potential for a leak magnifies," Calvin explained.

The secretary stood up to look at the National Mall. He was biting on the edge of his black rimmed glasses. "Thanks, everyone." The general and Calvin stood immediately. That was the cue the meeting was over, so they shook hands and departed the secretary's office. Gil Hastings shut the door behind them but stuck his head back in. "Sir, do you want me to talk with the chairman?"

"Once the mission is complete. PACOM is monitoring, and I'm sure he'll mention it to the chairman later today or overnight," replied the secretary. "Gil, if we get caught somehow, this is big enough that I'll lose my job. Make sure you and Assistant Secretary Mike Phillips in PA—ah, public affairs, dedicate some time to those talking points."

"Yes, sir. Will do."

"You know the drill, Gil. Red folder for bad. Blue folder for good. Gin me up two sets of talking points."

Xining Caojiabao Airfield, China

Lieutenant General He Chen's Dassault Falcon 8X business jet aircraft just landed at Xining Caojiabao Airfield, located hundreds of miles west of the Gansu Airport. The Xining Caojiabao Airport, serving Xining, capital of Qinghai Province, is located about thirty kilometers east of downtown Xining, complete with a modern 12,497-foot-long runway. Chen's 8X personal pilots taxied off the runway and got onto the taxiways. The jet belonged to the military, but he was lucky enough to use it extensively. The longer cabin had additional windows for Chen to look outside and was divided into three different zones for comfort. At thirty-six thousand pounds, the jet could fly 6,450 nautical miles on a tank of gas with eight passengers, which allowed Chen to follow Devil Dragon to new destinations, or commute from western China to the Spratly Islands with ease.

The sun was ready to rise any minute in this portion of China, but it was still dark outside, and Chen could only see the *Y-9* maintenance jet as he taxied in. He looked around and checked outside quite a few windows of the aircraft, and he did not see the Devil Dragon. "Must be inside the hangar already."

Chen had finished his seventh or eighth baijiu this morning, which the staff would know at first sight; they would avoid him at all costs. Baijiu, a distilled alcoholic beverage with an alcohol content greater than 30 percent, was his favorite drink in the early morning. Many Chinese drank the rice-based drink because it was so similar in color and feel to vodka, that baijiu was sometimes known as "Chinese vodka." Coming out of the jet and walking down the stairs, Chen stumbled on the second to last step, nearly planting his face on the tarmac pavement. If any politicals or four-star generals were watching, they would not be pleased.

Chen walked off and away from the aircraft, unsteady as he moved. He shuffled from side to side and into the office next to the hangar. Upon entering, he saw an office full of his team sitting at computers and standing around talking, versus their normal positions inside the hangar and maintaining the Devil Dragon.

"What are you all doing?" Chen asked, leaning on the counter in the office. "What is going on...you are in here instead of working. What...are you *doing*?" Chen wiped his mouth on his uniform sleeve.

The room full of people stared at him, and no one uttered a word. The silence in the room was deafening, and they were embarrassed for him, and they were scared to tell him what they all knew. The Devil Dragon was overdue.

"CHIEF! COME HERE!" Chen yelled, wiping his brow with a white handkerchief.

"Yes, sir," the chief of maintenance said quietly.

"Why are you not working on the DEVIL DRAGON?" Chen roared.

The chief maintained his silence for a brief few moments, hiding, then spoke up. "General, Devil Dragon is not here," the chief replied.

"She is in the hangar!"

"No, sir. Devil Dragon had not arrived."

"What do you *mean* 'not here'? Why *not*?" Chen slurred loudly.

"They have not landed yet, sir. Not checked in. No calls. Nothing. She has missed her landing time."

Chen took a deep breath and stormed off to his left, past the counter of binders and papers. He angrily put his arm up on the counter and rapidly slid them off to the floor. They slammed down hard with a loud boom, and when the binders hit the metal filing cabinet, it vibrated, sounding like rolling thunder. Lieutenant General He Chen was boiling mad, and he was just getting started.

Chen reeled out of the office and kicked open the door to the hangar with his foot, nearly losing his balance. The metal door swung out all the way through its hinges and lodged in the open permanently. He wanted to see the empty aircraft hangar for himself. He barged through the doorway and was nearly blinded from the bright white lights and shiny white glossy hangar floor. Chen put his hand up to protect his eyes, but only for a moment. The hangar doors were slightly open, enough for people to walk through, in addition to fresh air blowing into the empty hangar. Chen stumbled in and saw for himself, there was no jet. He took some slow steps into the massive empty room and stopped. There were no maintenance crews. No flurry of activity. No mechanics working...no avionics technicians deep inside the engine compartment. No one was working on the most modern jet in Chinese history because she wasn't there. No Devil Dragon.

Sitting alone in the center of the hangar were four, black Husky sixteen-drawer tool chest and cabinet sets, the heavy-duty welded-steel construction ones that had wheels for free maneuverability around work sites. Many of the tools were specially made for the titanium aircraft skin and were intricate in detail and use. Each Husky chest was five feet in height, could hold twelve hundred pounds of aircraft parts and tools, and could be rolled on and off the Y-3 easily for the Devil Dragon mission. Chen slowly stumbled over to the tool chest closest to the hangar doors and leaned on the small tool chest counter. He looked down in one of the open drawers then slammed it shut in fury. The tools sliding around in the drawer, in addition to the drawer hitting the cabinet, echoed loudly in the empty hangar.

He stumbled away from that toolbox and went to the next one, with a single drawer open. "What the hell is going on around here?" Chen slowly walked over, grabbed a heavy-duty ratchet, and turned around to walk toward the open doors, stopping short of the opening leading out to the ramp.

Staring out into the early morning sunrise and pink sky, then down at the floor, he put his arms in the air, putting his head back toward the heavens. It was as quiet as an airport could ever be, with not a single aircraft flying that moment. Just about the entire ground crew was watching him from behind, lined up quietly watching the agony, not daring to make a sound. Chen smashed the ratchet tool down on the tarmac as hard as he could, breaking it instantly, with the silver metal pieces sliding quickly across the hard, flat surface in all directions. The sound was piercing.

"Lee. Lee. LEE. Leeeee! *Leeeeeeeeeeee!*" Chen yelled, his chubby red face filling up in disturbing rage. His deep-pitched scream was so penetrating and intense that it disturbed the birds living in the hangar ceiling, and they flew out of their nests in force. "LEEEEEEEEEEEEEE!"

The bald eagle, living in her nest on top of the light pole in front of the hangar, ate her newly captured rabbit and stared down below at the activity. Her chicks, oblivious to the activity below, began eating from their mother's pale yellow beak. Chen, fully engulfed with complete indignation and wrath, fell onto both his knees, and put his face in his hands.

Approaching the USS *ABRAHAM LINCOLN*, 203 miles SSE of Okinawa, Japan

"Wu, let's get your descent checklists going and get ready to land. Only about forty minutes until landing, or less, and we need to get lower," Ford said.

Wu was breathing heavier now, in great pain between his lower back and stomach, chest and ribs from his lungs, and desperately wanted some pain meds. "Ford," he said slowly, "checklists on the right in book. You...you do it. You can land her, Ford."

"OK, Wu. I'll get it. Take a look outside. Gorgeous sunrise, warm, orange sky, and another beautiful day. Look outside, Wu, it's—"

FUEL LOW. FUEL LOW. FUEL LOW. WHOOP. WHOOP. WHOOP. PING. PING. PING.

Ford muted the warnings and looked in the checklists. He recognized that most of what he saw was the same, no matter what language or aircraft. *More Chinese*, he said. Luckily, Ford could read and speak Mandarin from growing up in China and could translate the checklists again. He also had with him on his phone all the identification and frequencies required to land on the *Lincoln,* so he tuned and ID'd the tactical air navigation (TACAN) on channel 72Y. It provided him the exact distance to the ship, along with a bearing.

"Wu, *Lincoln* is one-seven-one degrees magnetic at one-seven-six miles." *Hope we make this*, Ford thought as he looked at the fuel state. "I'm going to tune in the instrument carrier landing system, the ICLS. It'll help us land on the ship, OK, buddy?" Ford explained.

Wu was laughing. "Ford, you're...talking...Greek. Explain what...what you're talking about," Wu said. His breathing was awful.

"It's just like the ILS, the instrument landing system, at the runway, but it's for the ship. When I flew F-18 Hornets, we had it, and it was a huge help to get on board. Gives us heading and descent guidance."

The ICLS is just like the civilian instrument landing system, or ILS, and gives flight crews an all-weather instrument approach guidance from the carrier to the aircraft. The ICLS uses the AN/SPN-41A, which has separate transmitters for azimuth and elevation. The azimuth transmitter is at the front of the ship, slightly below the centerline of the landing area. The elevation transmitter is above the flight deck, behind the island. The aircraft receiver displays the angular information on a crosshair indicator, which the Devil Dragon has for runway landings. The vertical needle of the display corresponds to azimuth while the horizontal needle corresponds to elevation, or glideslope.

"Wu, can you calculate a landing weight and airspeed for us? Can you do that?" Ford asked.

"Jojo...rising."

Ford had his head down, looking at his notes section in his smartphone. He tuned the radios as he was going to use them, punching in approach and tower, and wanted to monitor them to see who was in the area. He knew VFA-34, an F-18C squadron known as the "Blue Blasters," using the call sign JOKER, was embedded on the ship, but he didn't hear anyone chatting on the frequency. Ford didn't transmit anything either but kept it open for monitoring.

Done with punching freqs into the radios, Ford was ready to manually fly the jet. It had been hours since he did so, and he was excited to wiggle the sticks a bit to land. "Wu, I'm going to dump the autopilot and take her down manually. Expect a rapid penetration descent, right down to the ship. Ready?"

"Born...ready, Ford. Do it." Ford passed over the drinking water bottle he spotted below them in the center console. Wu took a long drink, licking his lips, which looked to be excessively dry.

"Here's my plan. We are exceptionally low on fuel, so we should stay high as long as possible and do the slam-dunk approach. I'm sure these engines are also more efficient at higher altitudes. Normally, ah, we triple the distance, so we're up here at around fifty thousand feet, starting the descent down at one hundred fifty miles would give us a nice three-degree descent angle. Fifty times three is one hundred fifty. The longer we wait, the steeper the descent angle...but still doable and a good way to save gas. We could also take a nice steep descent, gear down, boards out. Out here, we are definitely in a nonradar environment now, so no chance of any kind of radar detection," Ford said.

Ford pulled the jet to idle on the throttles and dumped the nose. The Devil Dragon immediately built up massive airspeed, as Ford secretly wanted to see how fast he could get her. This was game time, though, not air-show time, so he skipped the fast airspeed dream and controlled the airspeed with pitch using the stick. It wasn't time to see what the Devil Dragon was all about. Ford looked out his window to the right, and just a bit surprised, he saw a Hornet on his wing.

Ford waved with his hand and received a wave back. He then moved the center stick from left to right, giving a universal and friendly wave to the Hornet crews, just so there was no misunderstanding by other aircraft behind him that he couldn't see. Ford scrolled through the Devil Dragon's air-to-air radar, completely oblivious to him for at least the last hour, and now saw two Hornets in formation with him.

"Wu, we have a Hornet off our wing, and your radar shows

another at our six o'clock. We should start to slow up and get dirty...so I can feel the jet for landing. Fuel state is sketchy, at best. What do you think?"

Wu was barely conscious but was able to open his eyes to look at the fuel gauge. "Yes, you'll make it, Ford." He coughed. "We'll make it...one pass with these tanks."

Wonderful...one pass? This may be the most difficult landing in aviation history, and I get one pass. Just wonderful. OK, then. We're doing it, Ford thought to himself.

Ford glanced down at the airspeed indicator and looked for the needle to line up in the green, telling him his speed was OK for the landing gear to safely come down. "Gear and flaps, down," Ford announced, putting the gear down himself. Normally the flying pilot would not do it himself, but considering Wu's medical condition, Ford reached his hand up and yanked the handle down. "Flaps, fifty percent," as Ford reached his hand between the seats to move the flaps lever to fifty percent. As soon as he saw the airspeed for 100 percent flaps, he moved the lever all the way. "Flaps at one hundred percent, Wu. I got it."

They were down at three thousand feet now, flying at a smooth 180 knots at six miles for a straight in.

"I'm on short final, Wu. Piece of cake. We got this."

Wu had his eyes open, looking for the ship. "It's so small...so tiny. We're...landing on *that*?"

USS *Abraham Lincoln* Flight Deck

"There he is!" Emily yelled with excitement, jumping up and down twice, pointing at the aft end of the flight deck. The black speck on the horizon grew larger and larger with time, even though the ship was pulling away from them and facing into the wind. "That sound. That sound is unbelievable. They are loud, no? A roar, like a...deep thunder. Bloody fun!"

"You bet that's them. Yes!" Mark yelled, high-fiving Robert, who was standing right next to him.

"Well, no shit. You live long enough, and you get to see everything. Here they come," Muddy said under his breath but just loud enough for the DIA team to hear them. "Air boss, CO here, what do you have?" Muddy said into his walkie-talkie.

"That's your bird, sir. Deck is cleared. All remaining aircraft are hidden behind the island or down tucked in the hangar deck. Min crew on the deck for safety. JOKER 43, flight of two, is with them. Had positive hand waves between flight crews. JOKER reported a wing wave as well. Flight of two F-22s behind them with shoot down capability out of Kadena."

"Right. Thanks, Froggie. Continue."

Two miles from USS *ABRAHAM LINCOLN*, 205 miles SSE of Okinawa, Japan

Ford was massaging the throttles and was impressed with the quick response time of the engines, compared to the afterburning turbofan engines he had always flown with. His engines usually took a few long seconds to provide thrust, while the Devil Dragon's thrust was near immediate.

"Wu, we gotta run some numbers. Get me some speeds and weight."

Wu was markedly weak and could barely look at the charts on his left, but it didn't require much energy to look at the open checklist page. He sighed, slowly looked down, and traced what he thought was the proper airspeed and weight.

"Just land at a hundred forty-five knots, a hundred twenty-five thousand pounds."

"God almighty. We are super heavy. Much heavier than I thought. Are you sure? That's our real weight?"

"No, I'm not sure. Ford...this isn't some little toy fighter you used to fly. This is a big...big boy bomber. Yes...that's our weight," Wu replied. Wu's health had deteriorated rapidly since Ford arrived, and his breathing seemed to get worse with each passing moment.

Ford ran through his B-1 flight characteristics and experience rather than his Hornet background, remembering this jet had mass. With mass came thinking ahead of the jet a bit more, only because the larger size meant a one or two second delay once a control input was entered. Certainly it would require a combination of both jet aircraft skill sets to get on the deck of the ship safely. He would have to land something larger than an F-18 in size, heavier on the weight, with close to no fuel and only a minimal amount of wing clearance on the right wing due to the ship's vertical steel island. *No damn tailhook*, Ford said under his breath. It was just starting to sink in now that in addition to a difficult landing, he had no tailhook. Ford was feeling the brunt of the mission now, and he had his work cut out for him.

"Wu, you haven't said much in a bit. Your breathing, and your bleeding, must be a tremendous burden. Almost there. Not much longer, Wu," Ford reassured him. Wu moved his hand, but there was no reply.

Ford checked the instruments again, then moved his scan outside. He looked out front and had not only a clear view of the entire ship but a straight shot at the meatball and the laser. The flight deck was near empty, a rare sight to see. The long-range laser lineup system on the left side of the flight deck landing area was something new and helpful to all flight crews, especially today. The small size of the landing area required a precise lineup control by all approaching aircraft, and the Devil Dragon was no different. The nature of the angled deck on the *Lincoln* presented a unique challenge to the Devil Dragon, because the landing area was constantly moving from left to right relative to the nose of the aircraft. The long range laser lineup system used color-coded lasers to provide visual lineup information to approaching aircraft. The *Lincoln*'s low intensity lasers were projected aft of the ship and were visible out to ten miles at night and five miles in the day. Ford could see them easily at a mile out, saying the code word "Bull's-eye" under his breath.

"I'm hanging in...there. You just land on that ship. You know how...how I love water," Wu replied. "No swimming today, please."

"OK, Wu, OK. At least your instruments work. Picking up the ship great. Gotta love the Chinese avionics."

Ford scanned inside again to verify his gear was down, the

flaps were down, and he was lined up for the deck. He had nothing to lose at this point by transmitting just a quick phrase on the very high frequency, the VHF frequency, so he quickly made up an aircraft call sign and transmitted "WHIRLPOOL 22, gear down." Ford had no idea if the Chinese radios were compatible with the *Lincoln* and transmitted anyway because VHF was a line-of-sight radio system. There was a slim-to-none chance that anyone would hear that transmission except the ship because there wasn't another soul around.

Five seconds went by, then without skipping a beat, the controller came on the radios with "Altimeter 30.21. Winds 220 at nineteen. WHIRLPOOL 22, you're cleared to land." Ford wasn't sure the voice on the frequency was the air boss, but that's all he wanted to hear. He raised his eyebrows and smirked. *No shit?*

Ford manipulated the throttles with his left hand, moving them ever so slightly to get the rate of descent accurate, and moved the nose of the aircraft with the stick ever so delicately to drive the 145 knots of precise airspeed down to the deck. The white-capped waves in the Pacific were really coming into his peripheral view, and Wu watched in silence from the left seat. Ford chanted the *aim-point-airspeed* phrase the same way he did for every landing. Ford leaned forward in his harness to make sure it was locked and reached over to ensure Wu was locked in his. This was the moment they were all waiting for—weeks of work, stress, and lives at stake. It was cumulating into one landing on this ship at sea, or it was over. All the risk, all the effort, could be for nothing.

"Holy shit. This is it," Ford said excitedly. "Hey, Wu this is it, dude. Almost there. This is it, brother. Shit!"

Ford checked his instruments inside the cockpit, then the fuel one last time, and saw he had almost nothing in the tanks. If he was waved off now by the Landing Signal Officer, or if the deck was fouled, they would be in trouble. At this point, they were committed to no longer flying. Either land, eject, or hit the water.

Just a few more seconds of descent. Some more forward airspeed. *Almost there...almost there.*

WHAAAMMM!

Ford flew the Devil Dragon right down on to the deck of the ship, slamming it into the hard steel around the four wire, while simultaneously catching the nose of the Devil Dragon into the barricade. Sparks flew in all directions when the left main landing gear tire blew and drug down the flight deck sideways. Ford stomped on the Devil Dragon brakes with all of his humanity, so it is no wonder the tire blew. Ford throttled up the two dominant engines to full power upon landing, and because of their vigorous power, he thought they were going to fly right off the ship again. Ford and Wu were thrown forward into their harnesses hard upon impact, but due to the barricade, they were safely on the ship and at a complete stop. There was no going around for a second attempt. They had made it onto the *Lincoln*.

"*Jesus Christ. Jesus Christ!*" Ford said out loud on the intercom.

"WHIRLPOOL 22, safe on deck," was heard inside their helmets.

"Shit almighty. Fucking jojo rising, Wu. Jojo rising!" Ford said with a somewhat cocky smile, looking at him in the seat.

487

"Holy shit. We're here. Whoooo!"

Wu barely smiled, not because he was scared of the landing, but his health was much worse over the course of their flight. "We made it...we...made...it," leaning over to grab Ford's arm. His head was back in the seat, and he had his eyes closed while barely licking his dry lips.

Ford had already pulled the throttles back to idle and then pulled them back all the way and directly up toward the cockpit ceiling, and back farther, to shut down the engines. *How do you shut this shit off?* The engines immediately blew out like candles. The black jet was being sprayed with aqueous film forming foams from some of the twenty-two hose stations on the port and starboard sides of the *Lincoln* deck. The 1.5-inch and 2.5-inch hose lines were plugged into hydrants, now spraying with force. Some of the spray was making it on to the canopy of the Devil Dragon, partially obscuring the view from the cockpit. White suds were seen splashing on the canopy, similar to a car wash.

"Yeah. Yeah, brother...we made it," as Ford unbuckled himself, then Wu.

VVVVRRRRRRWHHHOOSHHHH!

Two US Air Force F-22 Raptors from Kadena followed two US Navy F-18C Hornets and whizzed by on their left side with a loud pass, just as Ford predicted and were there to ensure they would make it to the ship safely. Ford figured the CO launched them for safety, flying alongside to give Ford the confidence that they were in good hands, while the second one was most likely prepared to shoot them down if they were not friendly. JOKER 43, the flight of two Hornets, would divert to Kadena AFB in Okinawa with their Raptor brothers for fuel since the flight deck was going to be busy for a while.

Banging was heard from below the aircraft, and then the cockpit hatch opened upward from below. "FORD! WU! ARE YOU OK?" It was Mark's voice, loud and full of emotion and concern, coming from below, along with the strong scent of kerosene waffling up from the steel, gray and dirty, flight deck.

"MARK! Yeah, we're OK. I need your help. Wu is hurting. He's in bad shape. We need to get him out now! Tell the corpsmen down there that he sustained a gunshot wound. Left leg is bleeding pretty good. Get them up here."

Mark turned to the medical team standing there and relayed the info. They went in ahead of Mark in order to get Wu out of the jet and into the *Lincoln* infirmary. Ford, along with the corpsmen, handed Wu down from the seat and down and out of the cockpit to a nearby flat stretcher, and belted him down quickly. They all heard the word "gunshot" and wondered what the heck happened.

"Did he say *gunshot wound*?" Emily asked.

Emily and Robert were under the jet, too, overlooking Wu getting taken care of. Once Wu was carried off, they took a close look at the impressive titanium and alloy skin exterior of the Devil Dragon, in awe of the Chinese engineering. Even the rivets were unique. Robert stepped on the crew ladder and placed his hand up high on the fuselage so he could feel it then turned to Emily. "Amazing."

"What kind of aircraft material is that up there?" Emily asked.

"This is intense. The Chinese used composite materials just like we did. This iron ferrite material coats the airframe...it absorbs the radar, not reflecting the radar," Robert explained. "Mark will love this once he gets a chance to examine."

Ford climbed down from the ladder and saw Emily. His face was bruised, and the left shoulder of his flight suit was torn and full of dried blood. She placed her hands on his face. They embraced with a hug and then a long kiss. Mark and Robert were there, too, giving him a hug.

"I knew you could do it, Ford. You're my special guy. I love you," Emily said to Ford, giving him a wink.

"You made it, Stevens. Glad you're back, kid. Welcome to the *Lincoln*," Mark said. "Hey. Someone special is here to see you. A visitor."

"Yeah, we did make it. Thanks. Whoo! Yeah, I'm concerned about Wu, but, yeah, we made it. Ah, a visitor? For me? Who is it?" Ford asked, puzzled who would know him way out here in the Pacific Ocean.

Alexandria, Virginia

The Burns family lived on Southdown Road off George Washington Parkway, just north of Mount Vernon, in Alexandria, Virginia. Their two-story white colonial was on the Potomac River and had a stunning view of Maryland to the east. The closeness of such a wealthy community to a large city was attractive to the family, as they were able to absorb the culture of the city, while taking country walks along the Mount Vernon Trail along the river.

The secure work phone started ringing next to Calvin's bedside stand, and he rolled over quickly to answer it. "Hello?"

"Sir, this is the watch officer at the operations center. Sorry to wake you, sir."

Calvin Burns rubbed his eyes and glanced over at his bedside stand and looked at his clock. It read 2:23 a.m. "Good morning. Yes, go ahead."

"Sir, message from USS *Abraham Lincoln* states, and I quote, 'OPERATION WHIRLPOOL complete. Safe on deck. Mark sends.'"

"OK, thank you. Ah, tell Martin, my driver, I'll be driving myself in today. I'll just see him at the office. No need to pick me up today. OK?"

"Yes, sir."

Calvin swung the blankets off of him with a purpose and a smile, happy to have achieved yet another team success. He got up, showered, kissed his wife good-bye, and was out of the house by 3:00 a.m. and on the George Washington Parkway northbound soon after. At this time of morning, from where he lived to the office was not more than twelve minutes.

He parked in his marked spot and walked over to the entry area to badge in, then quickly up to his empty office. Giddy with suspense, he quickly put on a pot of coffee near Jason's desk and scurried back into his office to quickly log on to his computer.

Calvin Burns was astounded at the photos he was seeing from Mark. They were clear, up close, and impressive, and demonstrated how advanced the Devil Dragon really was. He could see the cockpit details, four large engines, rooftop air intakes, vertical fin, flaps, wings, and fuselage skin. The weapons storage section was particularly impressive, and Calvin was curious how many nuclear and conventional weapons could be carried there. "Oh my, look at these photos." The antennas and cameras, located in the nose, were shocking. Not only that the modern technology existed, but that the US military and intelligence community did not detect any of this sooner.

There was no mention of Ford and Wu in the e-mails, but he assumed they were in getting looked at by the doctor. He decided to place a call out to the ship via the DIA operations center downstairs.

"Good morning, Lieutenant McCarthy, Deputy Calvin Burns here. Please connect with me with the USS *Theodore Roosevelt* operations center. Wait, sorry. The USS *Abraham Lincoln,* I mean. The *Lincoln,* the *Lincoln*. I'll hold."

Deputy Burns sat on hold for close to eight minutes while the ship's OOD located Mark Savona to chat. The OOD had to track down the CO first, who was somewhere on ship that was one thousand feet long, with over five thousand people, in hundreds and hundreds of rooms and compartments on multiple decks. The OOD finally tracked down the CO and Mark in the hangar deck, just as the deck sailors were getting the fuselage pushed inside. The wings, cut off earlier by the welding team, were already wheeled inside and at the far end of the hangar on carts.

"Sir, this is Mark. Hello!" Mark answered the phone.

"Hi Mark, Calvin Burns here. Just wanted to wish you and

the rest of the team congratulations. Ah...how are things going?"

"Terrific, sir. They made it on the ship successfully. I'm in the hangar deck now. Wings are off, and the fuselage just got in here. A bit of concern about the tail hitting the overhead ceiling beams, but we were able to raise the gear and get her down on some smaller wheels to move her in." Mark paused. "Sir, this is some jet."

"I'm sure it is. Understand. I appreciate the photos you sent. Looked at them already. High-end technology. Impressive. On another note, and more important, how are our two captains, Stevens and Lee?"

"Well, sir, Wu is a bit worse than expected. Not only is his cancer bad, but he sustained a gunshot graze from Ford's pistol."

"*Ford shot him?*"

"No, not exactly, sir. From what we know so far, the Chinese copilot showed back up at the jet earlier than planned, and Ford was involved in some old-school hand-to-hand. Ford sustained a knife wound to his left shoulder but should be fine. During the melee, Ford was separated from his weapon, and the copilot attempted to shoot Ford. He missed Ford but shot Wu by accident. It ended when Ford wound up throwing the copilot out the cockpit hatch while they were on the takeoff roll. Unknown copilot whereabouts and health status."

"Whoa. That's pretty heavy."

"Hmmm. They also had one of the bullets tear through the left-wing fuel tank, so they were leaking fuel the whole flight over. Rather than fly at some of the insane Mach speeds it's capable of, they had to set a much lower power setting just to get here."

"Ohh, OK, got it. Was wondering what was up on the timing. I'm going to back brief the secretary later today if you think that is a good idea. If you get updates, please call them in and let me know."

"Yes, solid idea. Will do, sir. Oh, two more items. The Herc mission should be complete, with the help of the Bureau...via the embassy. Special thanks to them for the mission air drop. Should be a great smoke-and-mirrors ploy. Last, thanks for arranging for the special guest. I had no idea. Ford hasn't seen him yet, so I'm sure he'll be surprised."

"Glad I could help. He is a terrific man and someone I have known nearly my entire career. Thanks, Mark. Please pass my thanks to the ship captain, as well as the rest of the team. Well done," the Deputy said, ending the call.

USS *ABRAHAM LINCOLN*, 332 miles East of Okinawa, Japan

Wu had a morphine intravenous drip in his left arm and was groggy but conscious enough to talk quietly, even with his oxygen mask on. The bullet that was fired during the scuffle turned out to graze his left leg, which explained why Wu did not have a large hole or an exit wound. It bled pretty heavily, but the wound was not life threatening. Unfortunately, the cancer was. Wu held Ford's hand.

The intravenous drip of $C_{17}H_{19}NO_3$ was set up with a machine to deliver two milligrams of morphine every ten minutes. The flight surgeon was full-up on Wu's cancer situation and set up a lockout dose that insured only a certain amount of morphine could be delivered over a specific time. It's different for every patient and condition, and the doctor knew Wu's time was short. Morphine is a respiratory depressant, and the doctor kept a close watch on Wu's respiratory condition and his breathing. The oxygen mask forced Wu's lungs to stay inflated, helped control breathing, and kept the arteries open for increased blood flow. At this point, the flight surgeon was just keeping Wu comfortable, until it was his time.

"Ford," Wu said slowly and quietly, "No...ventilator. Not even oxygen," as he struggled to pull the mask off.

"OK, Wu. Yes. No mask."

"I can't believe...we...made it. Heck of a flight here."

"Yeah, Wu. I knew we'd fly together someday. To think we both were able to land that thing on a carrier. You bet we made it."

The *Lincoln* infirmary was filling up with a few more folks now, some civilian, but mostly military and quite a few medical team members wearing green scrubs. Robert, Mark, and Emily stepped closer to Wu's bed.

"Captain Lee, I am Robert, and this is Mark. We are with the Defense Intelligence Agency, the DIA, and we work with Ford. We last saw you on the VTC at the US consulate. Congratulations," Robert said to Wu.

"Hello, Captain Lee," Mark greeted Wu. "A pleasure to finally meet you."

Two civilian men wearing black golf shirts and khaki pants came up to Ford and pulled him aside as the others were talking with Wu. They were definitely not with the ship's crew from a quick glance.

"Captain Stevens, do you have a moment?" one of the men said. "Captain Stevens, you may not recognize us from the VTC, but I am Chris Sans of DIA, and this is Vic Damone of the FBI. We are out of the consulate in Chengdu, China, and arranged for Wu's final requests. Essentially, his last will and testament.

"Yeah, nice to meet both of you. Ah...I don't understand. Wu had requests?" Ford asked, somewhat puzzled by the comment.

"Yes. I have in my possession the paperwork to accept People's Liberation Army Air Force Captain Wu Lee, and his H-18 Devil Dragon aircraft, into the hands of the US government, signed by the President of the United States. I also have Captain Lee's two requests," Chris said out loud, so everyone could hear them in the infirmary on the ship.

The sea state of the ship as they sailed eastbound toward Hawaii was really picking up outside, and the movement of the ship, pitching and rolling, was really felt now. The storm that Robert pointed out to Emily was upon them.

"What are Wu's requests? He wanted a payment or something?" Ford asked, surprised that Wu would request anything, including money. It didn't make sense, Ford thought.

Just then, Ford's special visitor whom Mark and Calvin Burns referred to, walked into the infirmary. It was Chad Stevens, Ford's dad, and he walked over to see him.

"Dad? DAD! What? What are you doing here?" Ford exclaimed. He was really confused because this was a military mission, and his civilian father was out at sea with them. Behind Mr. Stevens was Emily. "Wait a minute. I don't understand. Dad, what are you doing way out here?" Ford asked, giving him a hug.

"Hello, Ford." He hugged him warmly. "So happy to see you are mission complete. And to see Wu again."

Ford Stevens was really puzzled by the recent chain of events. All of the stress of getting the jet, seeing Wu in his condition, and now his father was out on the carrier.

"Son, I am a close friend of the Deputy director, Calvin Burns. He personally helped arrange for me to come out to the *Lincoln*," his dad explained.

"Oh, OK." A brief pause. "How…how do you know him? I don't understand. Was Mr. Burns in the oil business at one time?"

"No, not exactly," Mr. Stevens replied, laughing. "Ford, all these years…moving around to different countries, different offices. I was never really employed by the Shell Oil Corporation. My career was, as they say, different. You and your siblings never knew the true background. You never knew the full truth. I was really a DIA officer. An intelligence officer. We moved around the world so I could help collect intelligence…to support national security," Mr. Stevens admitted.

"Wow. I had no idea, Dad. Just…wow. You had one heck of a career," Ford said, surprised and puzzled at the same time. "Wait, does Mom know?"

Mr. Stevens, sporting his snappy white shirt and sport coat, said with a smile, "Of course she knows. She has known for forty-three years, Ford. Best spouse anyone could ever ask for, especially in this business," Mr. Stevens replied. They hugged again. "Believe it or not, I also know Robert. When you introduced us on Hilton Head Island, over at the Boathouse Restaurant, we recognized each other immediately. We worked together on a mission about ten years ago in Europe, but we couldn't say in the restaurant publicly."

Ford smiled and shook his head. "I knew it! I knew you guys knew each other! Dad!" punching his father in the arm. "Have you been on a carrier before?"

"Ford, stop. I have more carrier time than you do! Remember Vietnam? How do you think I got around the Asia theater?"

Everyone standing in the room turned to focus on Chris and Vic, who each had a pile of paperwork in their hands. Vic grabbed a pen, in addition to his smartphone, and they walked over Wu's bedside again.

"Captain Lee, hello again. Can you understand me OK?" Chris asked.

Wu closed his eyes slowly and opened them, nodding his head. But he remained silent.

"Captain Lee, I have your request here to become a citizen of the United States of America. Standing next to me, you know him well, is Mr. Chad Stevens. Per your wish, he is going to administer to you the Oath of Allegiance to the United States of America to become a US citizen," Chris said.

Emily came over to hold his other hand, making every attempt to comfort him. She smiled, and Wu smiled back, but he did not say anything. The flight surgeon monitored the morphine drip, as well as his breathing and heartbeat on the monitors.

"Doc, you're giving him the right amount of drugs to make him feel comfortable, right? Not too much?" Ford asked.

The flight surgeon nodded yes in front of Wu, then stepped aside to talk with Ford and his father. "Yes. There's a medical difference between natural dying and dying from too much morphine. If Wu received too much morphine, we wouldn't be able to wake him. What will happen here is Wu's breathing will become very slow but regular. He may have only one or two breaths in a minute. Wu appears to be calm and comfortable, from my experience."

Medical doctors have said that near the end of the dying process, a patient like Wu will have shallower breathing. The muscles used for breathing will become weaker, just like the rest of the body's muscles. From a glance, it may look like the patient is working hard to breathe, but they may not be short of breath. They may also breathe irregularly, with a few pauses, and the pauses may be followed by a few rapid, deep breaths. Someone like Wu passes when he does not draw a breath after one of the pauses.

"Thanks, Doc. I wish we could all do more for him," Ford replied.

"Yes, I understand. We're doing everything we can for him right now."

The Oath of Allegiance to the United States of America is an oath that must be taken by all immigrants who wish to become US citizens. The oath may be administered either by the US Bureau of Citizenship and Immigration Services or in a federal court. Mr. Stevens moved back to the side of Wu's bed, and everyone looked at Wu now.

"Hello, Wu, it's me, Chad Stevens. So happy to see you again, Wu."

Wu held his hand for a moment.

"Some of the senior leaders I know in the US government gave me special permission in this signed letter to administer the oath to you today," Mr. Stevens shared with Wu, holding up a document. "Please raise your right hand, Wu, and repeat after me..."

Emily helped Wu with his hand and smiled. Mr. Stevens quickly administered the oath to Wu, making him a US citizen, and a round of applause was heard in the infirmary. There was a light round of applause from the team of doctors and nurses standing near the monitoring station.

"Wu, this is Mark. We also have your second request," Mark announced in the room.

Wu turned to look at Ford and requested a sip of water. It was the dry mouth again, and Ford helped him by putting the bottle up to his lips. Ford didn't give him much, but nearly all of it spilled down his neck and on to the bed. A nurse came over and patted him dry.

"Ford. I want to become...a US Air Force officer. An Air Force pilot...like you, on the same...team," Wu said, coughing again.

"Ford, when Wu was at the consulate, Chris and Vic took his final request. Believe it or not, his request was to accept a commission as a US Air Force officer. Because he is now a US citizen, and since he brings a special skill to the United States, we can offer a direct commission to him, right now. Immediately. As a captain," Mark said.

Ford's eyes opened wide, and he raised his eyebrows. "What didn't you think of, Wu?" Ford laughed warmly.

"Ford, I would like you to administer the oath...to me," Wu said, coughing some more and closing his eyes.

The flight surgeon placed his stethoscope to his ears and the disk to Wu's chest. From the look of his face, time was running out. Wu would pass soon. The slight beep on the monitor reinforced this opinion, as his breathing was getting weaker and weaker.

Wu raised his right hand, again with the help of Emily, and Ford administered the oath.

"...so help me God," Wu finished, opening his eyes.

Ford, his dad, Mark, Robert, and Emily were around him now, on either side of his bed. Emily continued to hold his right hand and Ford and his father held the other. He kept his eyes closed.

Quietly, and barely audible, Wu spoke. "Thank you...Mr. Stevens...for...everything in my life."

Mr. Stevens was deeply shaken, but he didn't say anything. Tears were streaming down his face, as they did for many in the room. The usually somewhat loud 1,092-foot-long ship, with a crew of thirty-two hundred and additional aircrews of nearly twenty-five hundred, had become eerily quiet. Even peaceful. No airplanes were launching, no steam was hissing, and no hums of motors were heard.

"Ford," Wu said, licking his lips, "you are the brother...I

never had…I want you to know how much I love you," gripping his hand. "I love…you."

"I love you too, Wu," Ford told him, "and you will always be a member of our family. You're my brother."

Ford had tears falling off his cheek and was lost in emotion at the upcoming loss of his best friend. Ford leaned down to his ear, so he could talk quietly. "Wu, it's OK to go. It's OK to go. It's OK…" Ford reassured him.

Wu no longer moved. He lay silently for a while and no one in the room said anything. They stood looking at Wu, and the *Lincoln* chaplain came in and said a prayer. Ford, his dad, and Emily all said a prayer together.

Another few hours went by, and they looked closely at Wu. His face had a slight smile on it, and then he suddenly raised his hand out of Emily's, very slightly, with his finger pointed. "Mom…Dad…I see…you. I'm…coming…"

After a quick moment, Wu slowly lowered his pointing hand, and it remained quiet on the ship. Again, no one said anything in the room. After a few short seconds, Wu's hand slowly released from holding his family's hands. The pulse oximeter and heart-rate devices that were monitoring Wu went flat on the scope, and the monotone beep that was heard in the infirmary of the carrier no longer pulsed slowly. The flight surgeon placed his stethoscope on Wu for the last time.

At 15:07 Greenwich Mean Time, Captain Wu Lee, US Air Force, died at sea while in the service of his country.

Epilogue

Arlington National Cemetery, Washington, DC

Arlington National Cemetery in Northern Virginia was quiet this time of year, except for the passing airplane taking off or landing over at National Airport to the east. The beautiful Christmas wreaths were already laid down at most of the graves by volunteers, whether by college alumni, the Wounded Warrior Project, or Team Rubicon, and were aligned perfectly out of great respect. The limestone headstones were all lined up in symmetry, and they, too, also looked tight and sharp.

The DIA arranged for a burial for Captain Wu Lee at Arlington, and the funeral service was held for him weeks after returning from the Pacific. He was escorted by the Stevens family, in addition to Mark, Emily, and Robert.

In section 60, the newest part of the southeast section of the cemetery, was where Wu's funeral ceremony was held. A caisson, pulled by four horses supplied by the US Army's elite Third Infantry Regiment, pulled US Air Force Captain Wu Lee. Stopping curbside in section 60 where Wu was going to be laid to rest was where the escorts parked their cars. Mark's red Chevy held the DIA team, and Ford borrowed Emily's BMW to drive his family, including Sam and Charlie.

As they were talking with the priest graveside, two black Chevy Suburbans pulled up curbside in front of their two cars with their blue-and-red police lights flashing in the front grills. A personal protective detail in dark business suits, earpieces, and sunglasses got out and opened the rear doors of the second vehicle.

The Stevens family, along with the Emily, Robert, and Mark, all turned their heads to see who was arriving.

"Were you expecting someone?" Mark asked Ford.

"No, no one. No one else even knows we're here."

From behind the open door and tinted windows, stood a man who could not be recognized from the angle they were at. Everyone exchanged glances at the special guest, until they realized it was Calvin Burns. The Deputy director of DIA was out of his vehicle and began walking across the soft brown-green lawn toward them, suit buttoned, wear a crisp white shirt and sunglasses.

"Good afternoon, Cal," Chad Stevens said to his old friend, giving him a hug with both arms.

"Hi, Bud. I'm sorry to hear of Wu's passing," he said, then turned to hug Marion Stevens. "Hello, Marion."

"Hello, Cal. Thank you for coming out this morning," Marion said to him. "Always great to see you."

Calvin Burns stood among the group that orchestrated one of the biggest grabs in US history. He was also with a group of family and friends who had lost someone they loved dearly, and it didn't matter at this point in time what some piece of hardware hidden in a hangar deck meant. Being the leader that Burns was, he not only wanted to pay his last respects but be the senior leader he was by demonstrating his loyalty to the team.

"Good morning, all. I know that you all knew Captain Wu Lee well and thought of him as an extension of your loving family. We are all so sorry to see him go and thankful he is no longer suffering. But we are also grateful as a nation for the extreme risk he took in delivering us his package. Today, we celebrate his life—and celebrate it by truly living every day," Calvin said.

The sun was bright the air cool, a perfect day to celebrate one's life at Arlington.

"I'm sorry to intrude on your service, but I did want to pay my respects to Wu, to each of you, and personally thank Ford in front of his family for risking his life on this operation," as he shook Ford's hand. "As a result of Wu Lee's performance, I am honored this morning to posthumously award him the National Intelligence Medal for Valor. Second only to the National Intelligence Cross and the Intelligence Star, this medal for Wu this morning acknowledges the exceptional and secret accomplishment, along with a whole host of other members of the intelligence community," the Deputy shared with everyone.

"Thank you, Cal. That is most generous of you," said Mr. Stevens.

"In addition, Captain Ford Stevens, US Air Force Reserve, I am honored to award you with the Distinguished Flying Cross for your brave actions in the face of danger. Not sure how we'll write it up on paper due to the sensitivity of the mission, but please know on behalf of the DIA, we appreciate your service. The Secretary of Defense has already talked to the chief of the Air Force Reserve for you."

"Thank you, sir. It was an honor and a privilege to work with you and your team. And thank you for recognizing Wu for his actions," replied Ford.

The priest finished the service, and the attendees paid

their last respects. Ford was last out of the group, completed his good-bye, and turned his head toward the east when he heard the low and deep grumble of multiple aircraft. Above the trees at the Pentagon was a formation of black aircraft. It wasn't just any formation of aircraft, though.

"This...this was the least we could do," Calvin announced, pointing his thumb up at the sky toward the sound.

Coming overhead was a formation of three *B-2 Spirit* Stealth bombers from the US Air Force Global Strike Command, Missouri, along with two F-117 Nighthawk stealth fighters from Nellis Air Force Base. Flying in the fingertip strong right formation in the shape of a V, the third B-2 jet in the formation peeled away into the afternoon sun, just as they passed over the cemetery. It was a stunning, private, and secret sign of respect for Wu.

Ford looked up in awe at the sight and grinned. He placed his hand up to shield his eyes from the sun, then put it down as he hung his head down for a moment. He looked down at Wu's grave, read what was on the headstone, and then smiled. Awkwardly, Ford started laughing over the roar of the jets.

"Ford. Ford! What on earth are you laughing at?" Emily asked in a stern voice.

"Let me guess, Robert, a final request?" Ford asked, pointing to the name on the headstone.

The white grave marker, already chiseled out, named this grave for:

CAPTAIN WILSON LEONARDO, US AIR FORCE

"Yup. That was the name he requested, since we couldn't use his real name," Robert explained. "He told Chris and Vic back at the consulate that's what he wanted. Said everyone in the Stevens family would get the joke."

"Hey, he was adamant about it, too, Chris told me. Wu was positive that's how he wanted it to read," Mark added.

"Oh, yeah! Yeah, that's his American name...his nickname...when we were kids!" answered Sam Stevens, laughing and pointing. "Remember from the van during white-water rafting?"

Ford got out his smartphone and looked for the app with music. He scrolled down with his thumb and found the song he was searching for. He pressed play on "LA Woman," a tribute to their "Jojo rising" saying, and it belted out on the phone speaker.

Ford continued to smile, looked at Emily, then glanced up and over at the rear of the stealth aircraft formation again as they departed over Rosslyn, Virginia to the west. The roar of the jets was getting softer as they flew off over the horizon. "Jojo rising, Wu. Jojo rising..."

THE END

***

EXCERPT FROM: THE BLACK
SCORPION PILOT

"All warfare is based upon deception."

-Sun Tzu, Chinese military general and strategist, 544–496 BC

Present Day

Defense Intelligence Agency Headquarters, Washington, DC

The deputy director of the Defense Intelligence Agency sat at his desk reviewing the morning *Early Bird News* when his assistant, Jason Cohen, knocked on the door.

Though hesitant to bother the boss first thing in the morning, the young man spoke first. "Morning, Mr. Burns. We got a bit of a problem right outta the gate," he said.

"What is it, Jason?" said Deputy Director Calvin Burns, looking above his cheater glasses on the edge of his nose. "Sorry, I should have said good morning to you. Yes, Jason, good morning."

Jason was still cordial. "A few months ago, you had me bring up to your office a missile analyst from downstairs. Employee named Mike Klubb."

"Hmm."

"Do you remember him?"

"Absolutely. Yup. Why do you ask?"

"Well, Mr. Burns. He's here. Says it's urgent. Something he has to talk to you about, a problem from the past. He won't talk to me about it, says I don't have a need to know. Clearance thing.

Says he'll only talk to you. Said you would understand?"

Calvin sat back in his leather chair, rubbed his chin, and thought of Mike. *Why would he come back here?* the deputy thought. "Here? In the waiting room?" The deputy looked at the wall of red digital clocks that told world time zones lining his office.

"Yes," Jason answered.

"OK, send him in," Burns instructed.

Mike Klubb walked in, more like rolled in, looking like he'd gained another few pounds since the last time the deputy saw him. His disheveled, white, collared shirt was untucked a bit in the rear, his black necktie was a wee bit too short, and his scuffed brown leather shoes had apparently never seen polish. "Hi, hello, Mr. Deputy Burns, sir."

"Hello, Mike. How are you? What brings you back up this way?" asked the deputy, coming around from his desk to greet him.

Mike was a missile analyst at the Defense Intelligence Agency, the DIA, working out of the headquarters on Bolling Air Force Base in Washington. He was a typical government bureaucrat, always keeping an eye on the clock and counting down the time until he could leave for the day. So many of the government employees were very talented, educated, and dedicated to the mission at DIA, but Mike broke the mold. He entered the facility at 6:00 a.m. sharp, walking like a zombie from the parking lot each morning, just staring at the ground, and never looked anyone in the eye. Before leaving each day for home at exactly 2:30 p.m., he always made sure to bring home the black lunch box his wife packed for him. Mike only put in the minimum effort for what was necessary to keep his job, sometimes doing what was asked, but never more. He gave other solid, hardworking government employees a bad name.

His last run-in with the deputy was inside the DIA auditorium when Mike and his team started to look into Chinese missiles a few months ago. The indications were detected by the Space Based Infrared System satellites, the SBIRS, which orbited the earth at some twenty-two thousand miles, watching from afar. SBIRS was used for missile defense and battle space awareness.

During the auditorium brief, analyst Mark Savona showed up uninvited and confronted Mike, leading to a nasty public argument. The deputy was forced to weigh in on the revolting confrontation and eventually told Mike to stop looking into the Chinese missile situation. A short week later, the deputy called Mike up to his office, shared that the Chinese event was highly classified, and gave him a personal gold and blue Deputy Director of DIA Challenge Coin to go away. Mike has it displayed on the fireplace mantle at home.

"Sir, we have more of your missiles over China," Mike explained.

"Missiles? I don't understand."

Talking quickly, Mike continued. "Sir, last time we met in the auditorium, it was because the SBIRS team out of Buckley Air Force Base detected missiles over China—the infrared ones that the Air Force monitors. We...we thought it was maybe another Chinese ICBM test. You brought me up here and told me to stop looking into it. It was going to be compartmented, and I never heard or talked about it again. Until now."

Calvin stood and stared at Klubb in disbelief. Calvin turned his head sideways in thought. "Really? Tell me more."

More nervous, Mike pressed on as asked. "We detected, or rather Buckley detected, eighteen flashes between last Thursday and today. It looks like another large ICBM, but...nobody has figured it out. The signature that is. But I remember this specific signature. The computer doesn't know it, but I do."

Calvin turned his head sideways in thought. Squinted his eyes a bit, and kept staring.

Located at Buckley AFB and housed in a humongous Satellite Operations Center facility, was the US Air Force's 460th Space Wing. The airmen from the wing controlled and watched the country's SBIRS, as well as the older system, the Defense Support Program, known as DSP. The group of hundreds of service members in active, Reserve and Air National Guard units watched the earth, giving decision makers the information as it came in. Their clients could be intelligence community agencies, the Pentagon, Department of Homeland Security, the military Combatant Commanders, and even the National Security Council.

Using the best poker face he could scrounge up, Calvin turned to look at the wall, then back at Mike while biting his bottom lip. "Very interesting, Mike. Thank you. Perhaps, if it's not too much trouble, could you send me what you have? Would that be all right? And, Mike, it doesn't require your team, just you; quietly bring it up here or send it to me on secure email. I'd be interested in seeing what you've got," asked the deputy. *What did this guy see?*

Mike instantly turned into a frenzy of activity, without ever moving from his original standing position. Talking even faster, he answered, "Oh, right away, sir. I've got everything. Everything from last week and from last night. I was having my morning hot chocolate that my wife makes for me every morning and, I..."

"Mike. Mike. Terrific. Take it easy," the deputy told him, moving his palms in a downward motion to keep him calm. "Just bring it on up. Yes? Good?"

"Yes, yes, sir. Will be right back. Thank you, Deputy Burns," Mike answered, as he massaged his hands together into a sweaty ball. Klubb turned around and banged his shin on the glass coffee table, backed up awkwardly, and left the room.

Deputy Burns could not believe what he just heard. He walked over to his couch and sat down, placing his forearms like he was sitting on the toilet. Leaning back, he stared out into the air for a few long seconds. He let out a sigh. *I'm retiring in a month*, he said to himself.

"Jason!"

Jason came hurriedly into the office. "Yes?"

"Get Mark Savona's ass up here ASAP. I don't care where he is on this earth; he needs to get his butt in here. We got issues. ASAP."

Jason took off on his mission to find Mark Savona from the Chinese Aircraft Directorate, while Calvin leaned over on his couch and placed his face into his hands. He rubbed his nose and eyes after taking off his glasses. Calvin stood up and folded his arms to think, reflecting that he thought he had seen everything in his intelligence officer career, from the Cold War to Gulf War I to Iraq and Afghanistan. Now this.

Even stealing the Chinese stealth bomber Devil Dragon from a few months ago was a career highlight. Just this past Tuesday, DIA and the US Navy had just finished the crane operation at Graham Island, Canada, about a thousand miles northwest of Vancouver. Devil Dragon was drained of the few last drops of fuel remaining, sawed and weld cut into specific pieces, packed in large nondescript crates, and loaded onto a commercial ship from the island to the mainland. Devil Dragon was then hauled via tractor trailer to Tonopah, Nevada. This latest news, though, topped everything for him. Burns was nearly speechless, bordering on shock.

Christ almighty...I just can't believe this. A month before retirement. The goddamn Chinese had two stealth bombers built. We stole one...and now they're test flying the other.

ABOUT THE AUTHOR

Veteran military pilot Lawrence A. Colby is the #1 Amazon Bestselling Author of the Ford Stevens Military-Aviation Thriller Series.

A graduate of both the US Navy and US Air Force Flight Training Programs, Colby is part of a select group of pilots qualified to fly jets, prop planes, and helicopters. He held numerous squadron, air group, and wing positions, flying multiple operational missions in Iraq, Afghanistan, and other global locations. He flew under the callsign "Cheese."

Five years at the Pentagon as a military assistant provided Colby with an extensive understanding of government policies and power—knowledge he uses to add political as well as military realism to his fast-paced military adventure thrillers. Colby lives in the Washington, DC, area with his family.

He can be found online at ColbyAviationThrillers.com and through his **Instagram** and **Twitter** handle **@ColbyThrillers**.

www.ColbyAviationThrillers.com

ACKNOWLEDGEMENTS

A warm and sincere thank you to the following individuals for their expertise, encouragement, and research. Thank you!

Jodi, for your love and patience.
Gavin and Brennan, for the positive attitude and story idea. Sean M., for the edits and technical aspects.
Jerry T., for the love of the characters and story development.
Neal B., for the historical accuracy and review.
Mom and Dad, for everything.

Thank you.

PERSONAL NOTE

Wu Lee's health condition was based off my great friend, John, a retired C-130 Air National Guard pilot. While flying with a major airline, he was misdiagnosed multiple times, both in Europe and in the United States. He later passed away after fighting stage four pancreatic cancer after only six short months.

I appreciate the tremendous outpouring of support from readers who have related to Wu's condition. From kids sharing stories about their parents to co-workers sharing stories about their friends, I am happy to have helped bring a smile on your face and aid in celebrating their lives.

If you enjoyed this book, it would mean a tremendous amount to me to leave a positive review on Amazon.com.

Thank you.

All the best,
Cheese Colby

Made in United States
Orlando, FL
06 September 2022

22087210R00318